LETTERS FROM THE PAST

An English Family in the 19th & 20th century

Michael Pantlin

First edition published in 2022 by
Strawberry Tree Publishing,
Betsy Perkstraat 49,
2135 HM Hoofddorp,
Netherlands
Chamber of Commerce Amsterdam number 34328361

ISBN: 9789083222905

Some of the material in this book was previously published in *How I survived the Great War* which is a collection of John 'Jack' Handley's war memories, edited by Michael Pantlin.

Cover photograph: Jack Handley and his daughter 'Bunty', Christmas 1931

Cover design by Martijn Pantlin — www.orgonemedia.nl

Letters from the Past - An English Family in the 19th & 20th century tells a compelling story of four generations of the Handley family. The characters experience the hardships faced by many of our ancestors: single parenting, constraints of pious religious beliefs, gruelling terror of war, and poverty. This fast-paced novel will carry you along with creative dialogue and descriptive images. At the end, you'll fill your cup of appreciation for the courage and strength of those who came before us.
Cynthia Young, Author, *Leaving was just the Beginning*

In this novel, Michael takes heirloom letters written by his ancestors, and skilfully interweaves these into this novel to create a compelling story of their lives down the generations. He takes the reader through a century of his ancestors' lives, bringing their thoughts, beliefs, feelings and suffering together in a clear and captivating way.
Trevor Newton, Writer

Michael Pantlin has truly honoured his ancestors in this multi-generational saga. Each chapter seamlessly unfolds from one generation to the next. Placed in their respective historical events, the relatable characters show lifelong effects of relationships, navigating horrific circumstances, and overcoming grief and loss.
Brenda Litolff Barber

A simply exquisite journey spanning a century through the eyes of the Handley family. Follow their lives as their children blossom and the family extends branches of care and love throughout their history. Peek through the letters written by Gladys as she navigates early life, the loss of her mother, and support from her grandmother to compensate for a distant father.
J. L. January Asbill, MBA, MSHiED

Letters from the Past shares the story of four generations of the Handley family, a working-class English family, striving to survive through good and bad times. This is a chance to journey around England using the eyes of the Handleys to guide you as their culture changes from an agrarian society to an industrial / commercial one. Religious and political beliefs are also explored. Joys and sorrows abound with a touch of humour popping in now and again. I am amazed how they persevered despite the pitfalls they often endured.
Ann Ward, B.Sc.N., Author, *In the Shadow of Brilliance*

In his *Letters From The Past - An English Family in the 19th & 20th century,* author Michael Pantlin takes us on a well-researched and delightfully readable family history, beginning with the young Ann Handley in 1851.

What could have been a recitation of dry facts, this story instead shows us relatable yet flawed characters. Their believable motivations give them dimension, and the interjected wit keeps us entertained.

The author does not shy away from difficult subjects, from rape to tyranny to absentee parenthood to a spoiled daughter. We witness important events of the times and a meticulous rendering of places, bringing history and geography alive.

I am not particularly taken with military history, relating better to the pacifist members of this family. Yet, Jack's wartime experiences during The Great War are riveting, as were civilian descriptions of wartime England in both World Wars. And the interweaving of religion — which should not be ignored in most family histories — is done without judgment, existing primarily to convey what can influence both the admirable and the despicable aspects of human nature.

Though not related to this family, I devoured this book. For researchers of English social history from 1850-1950, there are many details to draw upon. For writers and readers alike, there is much to admire.
Elizabeth DuBois, JD, Author, *The Louisa Saga*

Letters from the Past is a portrayal of how a common English family coped with the challenges of daily life in good and bad times — in poverty, war, and illness. Each generation, in its own way, tried to pursue prosperity and happiness for their loved ones. Although it's history, this story contains themes that still make it worth reading today.
Anne Marie Stoof, RN

Dedicated to my ancestors
who look upon me to retell their stories for future generations.

"It's the past that tells us who we are.
Without it we lose our identity."

Stephen Hawking

PREFACE

Discovery

After living most of my life in the Netherlands, where I have no roots, I grew an interest in my British ancestors. What part of the country were they from? How did they earn an income? What were they like as a person — their personalities, talents, and short-comings?

Fortunately, my mother fed this budding passion by giving me bits of information, old letters and postcards, and telling me family stories. At the time, I just dumped things in a box for later. When later came, I sorted out the box and a rather fragmented picture of my ancestors evolved, so I felt the need to do research and fit the pieces together.

In doing so, I was humbled by the sacrifices my forefathers and foremothers had to make. They survived war, depression, hunger, illnesses, and poverty — things that I have never had to endure. They did their best to ensure their children would be better off than they themselves, and they definitely achieved it.

Exploring my family was a journey on which I reunited with relatives and found new cousins in the extended family.

Fiction or non-fiction?

I based this book on stories passed down by my ancestors and genealogical research. To let my forebears come to life, I've used my imagination to fill in the gaps, creating a mixture of facts, interpretations, stories, and fiction. All rolled together, the stories have become my truth. Anyone else writing this saga would have written a different story when given the same 'facts'.

Except for a few minor characters, their names are authentic, as are events with specific dates and locations. All dialogue is fictitious.

I don't know the actual feelings my ancestors had in their important moments, but I've imagined their circumstances and dilemmas, and, while writing, I became part of their lives and felt their emotions.

The book has seven parts covering four generations of the Handley family, my maternal ancestors, each part focussing on a character and how he/she viewed the world.

The addendum includes a simple family tree of the main characters, pictures, and a list of references. You can find more information and additional photographs on website www.pantlin.eu.

PART ONE

Ann Handley

CHAPTER ONE
FATHER KNOWS BEST

1851

Ann left school as usual, mid-afternoon, and crossed the lane to the footpath leading through the fields. It was a fine spring day with a bouquet of flowers amongst the hedgerows, but she felt down-hearted. Today was her last day of schooling, and she knew she would miss it as an escape from home. She wasn't in a hurry, because she had a tense relationship with her parents; they were strict and demanding and being outside gave her a feeling of freedom and independence.

Because of her father's attitude, Ann only attended the practical lessons of weaving, knitting and sewing. Father had been clear, "You'll be a housewife and learn all you need to know from Mother. There's no use wasting time at school learning to read and write."

Hints Farm, where her father worked as a labourer, provided them with a thatched cottage - a simple abode with three rooms, a brick floor, and one fireplace. The water from the nearby well needed boiling before drinking.

Upon her return home, she entered the kitchen and saw her mother pouring tea.

"Ah, you're back. Here —" Mother said, handing a steaming cup.

Ann reached out to take it but the mug fell to the floor and broke; liquid splashed everywhere.

"You stupid girl! Look what you've done. Clean it all up immediately," Mother bellowed, pointing to the mess on the floor.

"You let go before I had hold of it," Ann whined, her shoulders slumped.

"Don't blame me for your carelessness."

After clearing up, Ann poured herself another cup.

The incident confirmed her frustration about her parents. Mother often complained about Ann being slow with her jobs, or hanging about instead of doing something useful. Ann did, though, enjoy helping with meal preparation, and Mother praised her for her bread. As they had no oven, she took her dough to the village bake house and waited until it was ready. Their principal foods were milk, cheese, and eggs. Fresh fruit and vegetables were available in the garden and pickled or made into jam for winter. Twice a week they cooked a meal with smoked meats or bacon. Fancier dishes, like black pudding, were only for special occasions; they were treats the family could rarely afford.

One Sunday morning, the Handley family went to St Peter's, the local parish church in Coreley, a farming village in Shropshire. Ann wore her simple blouse. Her brown hair and dark eyebrows framed her face of light complexion, and blue eyes. At fourteen she no longer ran around in the boisterous way her young siblings did, climbing on walls and balancing on top.

During the lengthy sermon, Ann's mind wandered. Eyeing other girls in church with their ornate dresses made her envious. She yearned to wear skirts with flowery patterns, but her father objected to modern dress, saying it was boastful. He insisted she wore a simple long skirt and a grey head-scarf. The aggravation caused her to scratch the back of her hand until it bled. Mother noticed and gave her arm a swipe; Ann's cheeks blushed with embarrassment. She longed to be outside, with the other girls, chatting about boys.

After dinner, Father always read from the bible, for ages it seemed. She didn't protest because she knew there was nothing to gain by complaining.

"Today I'm going to read about obeying rules. It's from Deuteronomy," he said, opening the worn-down bible.

"If a man has a stubborn and unruly son who will not obey the voice of his father or mother, then his father and mother shall take him to the elders. They say, 'Our son is stubborn and rebellious; he won't obey us; he is a glutton and a drunkard.' Then all the men of the city shall stone him to death with stones. So you will purge the evil from your midst, and all Israel shall hear, and fear."

Ann and her siblings remained silent. She thought how terrifying it must be, to be stoned to death in front of your parents, the ones you'd hoped loved you.

Father explained. "God gave us rules for living. On the road we have the rule that carriages keep left. Without rules, there would be more accidents. We trust that the on-comer will stick to the left because he knows the rules too. If we all do what the bible says, we'll have the same rules and all know what to expect from each other. Rules also apply in families. You children need rules so that you feel safe and know what's expected of you. God, our Creator, expects us to follow his rules as His children. Rules give us order and have been turned into laws so that judges can pronounce punishment on those not obeying the rules."

Mother told a story about a cousin who didn't observe the law.

"A relative called William Handley went out shooting with his brother and a friend. One night they crept into Shoulder of Mutton woods to place traps," she said.

"Where's that?" Ann's brother, George, asked.

"Over near Bayton," Mother replied. "Anyway, the day after, someone overheard them talking about going back for the game and alerted the gamekeeper. That night he heard a gunshot and walked carefully to the fence, so's not to disturb the poachers. Sticks cracked as if there was a person nearby. He ducked behind the fence. When he peered over the fence, he glimpsed a figure who raised his gun and shot."

"Have you made this up? It sounds like a tale," George said, in disbelief.

"It's a true story. It happened about twenty years ago. Anyway, the gamekeeper staggered home. He'd been hit in the right eye, blinding him. They caught and arrested the men. When questioned, the friend said William fired the shot. He was tried, sentenced to death, and executed."

Father added, "So, you need to watch yourselves!"

"I'd do nothing like that," George said. "They should have been cleverer at poaching."

Ann could see a serious look on the younger children's faces as the message sunk in that their father would punish them if they did anything unlawful.

After the evening meal, Father ordered, as usual, "Ann, get moving, clear the table and help your mother with the washing-up. George and Thom, I want you outside straightaway. We've got work to do." The boys stood up and scrambled to the door.

Being the eldest daughter, Ann was painfully aware she had to help her mother. She asked to keep going to school, but Father objected. Mother didn't contradict him as Ann's extra hands would lighten the workload in a household of five children, and a dog. The young ones, William aged ten, and Fanny, aged seven, needed regular attention. Ann's older brothers, George and Thom, had left to work on farms further away, where they boarded. But when they came home, they brought dirty clothes and joined in the meals.

Ann reluctantly accepted working at home where she had to endure constant criticism. She did her part to help with the washing, cooking, changing beds, and looking after the little ones. Weekly chicken coop cleaning was the worst job, when she wore a scruffy old apron and a frayed scarf. Droppings covered the perches and boxes, and revolting crusts had to be scraped off. An ammoniac smell irritated her nose when she scooped up dirty bedding from the floor, making her eyes water. After she laid down new straw, the coop was clean and the air sweet.

Her mother complained if she didn't clear up immediately after making a pie, or muttered about her being slow to hang the washing on the line. When her father came home, things were worse. He could be furious about the smallest annoyance, such as slippers not in the correct place, or a lack of firewood next to the fire. He expected things done his way and in the proper order. Ann didn't dare defy him, she kept calm, and took satisfaction from having a hearty meal ready when he came home.

Ann always looked forward to the annual village fair, a weekend each summer when everyone in the village enjoyed themselves. Prizes were awarded for the best cow, sheep and horse. But also for the finest cakes and jewellery. Each year, Ann did her utmost to make a prizing-winning cake and often won an award. There was a raffle with prizes of local produce and craft work. Games included skittles, hoopla, and quoits. On Saturday evenings, the band played and Ann joined the country-dancing. That weekend, her father and mother were usually more relaxed about the rules.

After enjoying the fair and returning to the daily chores and criticism, Ann felt even more depressed and longed for a change in her life.

CHAPTER TWO

Ups and Downs

1858

Ann, now twenty-one, had learned how to run a household, and especially how to cook. They still lived on Hints Farm, where her father fed the pigs, milked the cows, repaired fences, cut wood, cleared ditches, and more. In the peak season, he helped at Hemm Farm since young John Starie inherited it.

In Ann's presence, Father spoke to her younger sister, Fanny. It was a familiar story to Ann.

"Now you're fourteen, it's time you stayed at home to help your Mother."

"But I want to go to school! I'll miss my friends," Fanny said, arms crossed and a frown on her face.

"Your duty is to be a housewife and you won't learn that in those lessons."

"But other girls aren't leaving. Why should I? I'll start new subjects."

"They'll be no use. You'll learn all you need from your mother," Father said, with a raised voice and fists sunk into his sides.

"But Ann's here, so why do *I* have to help?" Fanny said, defiantly.

Ann realised it was her chance to escape her retched situation.

Mother interjected, "Fanny, Ann is an excellent cook, and can earn some money. You must take her place." Turning to Ann, she said, "It's time you started to work."

"I'd like to. Perhaps I can prepare meals for someone else?"

To Ann's delight, Father said, "I'll talk to Starie. I think he needs a cook."

Fanny huffed, stamped out of the house, slamming the door behind her.

"She'll cool down later," Mother declared.

"I remember John," Ann said to her father. "He wasn't in my class, but he seemed a likeable person." She hummed, as she set about peeling potatoes.

It took Ann thirty minutes to walk to The Hemm. Her route took her past the school, across a brook and along footpaths through the fields. She enjoyed the early morning air, larks singing high in the sky, and red campions in the hedgerows. John Starie welcomed her and showed her the kitchen and scullery. From the kitchen window, she had a view to the orchard and vegetable plot. She looked forward to picking fruit to make pies and jam; to pickling vegetables; to drying herbs for winter. The oven delighted her - she could bake her own bread and cakes.

It didn't take her long to acquaint herself with the kitchen and John's preferences. He gave her a free rein, making her feel trusted and confident: a feeling she did not have at home. She looked forward to when he came in for his nineses, elevenses, dinner and fourses. She made sure she had his favourite food and a pint of beer ready. He expressed his delight with the meals, glad she worked for him. His praise was a relief from the criticism at home.

But something about his attention caused her to be uneasy.

1859

In April, Ann arrived home after a day's work and found her mother wailing over her father's motionless body sprawled on the floor. Fanny stood in a corner, transfixed, clutching little Elizabeth with tremoring arms.

"Bring water!" Mother shouted.

Grabbing a mug, Ann rushed to the pump. Mother splashed his face and shook him. He was colourless, lifeless, his eyes closed. She laid his head down and looked up at Ann. "He's left us, gone to his fore-fathers," she sobbed, her face wrinkled in despair.

They both wept, clutching at each other. It was all so sudden. Thoughts rushed through Ann's mind. He was *never* ill. And he'd been fine when she departed earlier that morning.

Losing a parent was an enormous shock to Ann. Because her father had been such a dominant figure all her life, she couldn't fathom life without him. A strong and healthy man, only in his fifties. She loved him, despite his unrelenting strictness. She appreciated his commitment to the bible and his insistence on doing things as written in the scriptures. Others spoke of his stubbornness, but she admired him for standing up for his beliefs. She wondered whether God had called him to his day of judgement. Surely he would be judged favourably because he'd sternly adhered to His word.

Ann was crying when she vaguely heard her Mother's voice. "Calm ……, Ann, ….. help". She looked up and tried to concentrate. "Ann, listen to me," Mother said. "I want you to fetch the doctor. And the parson. You know where they live."

Still wearing her coat, Ann pulled her scarf tighter to keep out the rain before making her way up the winding lane. Before long, she was returning with the men and a church elder.

The doctor confirmed the death, then they lifted Father's body from the floor and laid him on the bed. Mother straightened his clothes and ran her fingers through his hair, and then sat down beside him. The elder asked Ann to find a cloth to cover the mirror so the reflective glass wouldn't trap her father's spirit. They also drew the curtains, and stopped the clock from ticking and chiming.

Ann saw that Fanny was at a loss and got her busy brewing tea. From the kitchen, they could overhear the reverend. "Dear Lord, we pray to you for Joseph Handley, to grant him eternal rest through the mercy of God, and let perpetual light shine upon him. Guide his soul to the holiest place. Reward Joseph for his dedication to God's word, and look after him in Heaven. Rest in peace. Amen. Lord, please help Maria Handley and her family to overcome their sorrows. May they come to you to share their sufferings. Amen."

The next morning, Ann woke from a dreadful night's sleep, eyes gummy, and lacking energy. On arriving at the farm, she found John busy in the yard. He looked up when he noticed her.

"You're wearing black. Has something happened?"

"John, ……," she burst into tears before she could say a word.

He put an arm around her shoulder, saying, "Tell me. What's the matter?"

"It's my father…." Before she could explain, a torrent streamed down her cheeks.

"I'm so sorry to hear," he said, embracing her. He cocked his head to one side, "My poor Ann, how did it happen?"

"I came home, and …, and …, he was lying on the floor. Mother was next to him and said he'd passed away." Her shoulders shook with each sob.

"That's terrible. I liked your father, he was such a great help. Too young to leave this world." He squeezed her tighter, laid his chin on her head.

She withdrew from his arms, sensing an intimacy between them that didn't feel right. His warmth had calmed her; a man had never shown her sympathy like that, but her instinct was to withdraw. "Thank you. I should get on," she said, wiping her eyes she squared her shoulders and moved away from him. It relieved her to be on her own and find comfort in preparing the midday meal.

Ann could see her mother was so distressed she couldn't concentrate on what needed to be done, so it was a godsend that Aunty Marianne, came to help.

"A coffin needs to be made," Marianne said.

Mother nodded.

Looking at Ann, Marianne asked, "Can we ask your Uncle John to talk to the carpenter?"

"He's coming tomorrow, so I'll ask him then."

Marianne turned to Mother. "We'll prepare the body in the morning. Has the parson come to see you?"

"He came first thing. He knows, … knew, Joseph well," Mother said, clearing her throat. "Said he knows enough for the sermon."

"Did he say anything else?"

Ann answered: "We have to dig the grave. I'll ask George and Thom to do that."

"It'll take three of us to prepare the body," Marianne said. "We'll need all our strength to wash and dress him. Can you help?"

Ann turned her head away and closed her eyes. At first, she couldn't speak. Then a shrill voice came from her throat, "I can't bear to look at his dead body!"

"Well, we'll ask one of his sisters," Marianne said.

After preparing Father, they laid him in the coffin, which rested across two chairs. Family members took turns watching over him day and night. To Ann, he didn't quite look like his real self. The strong, dominant father she knew was now like a figure of candle wax.

Joseph Handley was so well-known for his piousness that the church was bulging with parishioners for the funeral. On giving their condolences, many said how surprised they were by his sudden death at only fifty-three. John Starie came to show his sympathy and shook hands with Ann, holding her hand longer than need be, while wishing her strength.

The service began, and the reverend's words echoed through the church.

"As we lay away Joseph Handley to rest, his body returns to earth in the natural way, by an act of God. For He said, 'Out of the ground wast thou taken, for dust thou art, and unto dust shalt thou return'. God is our refuge and strength, an ever-present help in trouble. Therefore, we must not fear. He is within us and will help us at the break of day. The Lord Almighty will save us. Amen."

His prayers didn't resonate with Ann, as her mind kept switching from sadness about her father to thoughts about John Starie.

CHAPTER THREE

The Hemm

1859

Ann appreciated John's attention in the weeks following her father's funeral. He often took time to comfort her when they sat down for the midday meal. One rainy day, she was laying the table when she heard his footsteps on the wooden floor.

He stood beside her, placed a hand on her shoulder and cocked his head towards her. "How are you faring today?"

A ray of sunlight shone through the window, reflecting off the cutlery. "I'm alright," she said, placing another knife.

"How is your mother coping?"

"She's managing. My brothers are helping her out. William does any heavy work around the cottage. George and Thom come home more often and make sure Mother has enough money." The room darkened as the sun disappeared. "Let me serve the soup."

They sat down, and tears filled her eyes. John reached forward and took her hand. She didn't pull away. "What's upsetting you?"

"I don't know," she sobbed. "It's difficult for my mother. She's got no savings and has to leave the cottage."

"Why does she need to move?"

"The farmer needs it for a new farmhand."

She dabbed her eyes with her apron and did her best to stop crying. John squeezed her hand and then let it go. They started their soup in silence.

After a while, John said, "There's a cottage down the road, near Bache Farm. The people there are leaving soon."

"I don't know the place."

"I used to live on that farm. After I was born, my mother fell seriously ill, so they sent me to Mr & Mrs Jones, at the Bache. She's my father's

Aunty Sarah. They didn't have children, and treated me like a son. He taught me everything I know about farming."

"How dreadful not to have lived with your own family!"

"I never knew differently. I enjoyed being on the farm."

"Where were you born?"

"In London. My parents are still there. Father had no interest in this place. He runs a bookshop. The Staries have owned the farm for generations, so I'm proud to keep up the tradition."

"Do you go to London often?"

"As little as possible. When I do, I'm always glad to be back here. I don't like the busy, dirty place."

A few weeks later, Ann was clearing the table and John followed her into the kitchen. He complimented her on the meal and her prettiness. Standing behind her, he took hold of her shoulders, but she quickly stepped away and turned to face him. "What are you doing?"

"You've been here a while and we're getting to know each other. Let's get to know each other even better," he said, and stepped towards her.

"Well, why would I want to allow that?" Ann said, scratching the back of her hand.

He laughed, tilted his head, and looked her in the eye. "Why wouldn't you?"

He reached for his pipe, filled it with tobacco, and moistened his lips before putting it between his teeth.

"You're my employer. My father warned me."

"Warned you about what?"

"He said I shouldn't befriend an employer." She folded her arms across her chest.

"You can't disagree that we're both young and single. What harm is there in being closer?" He struck a match and lit the tobacco. Smoke wafted through the air, the aroma reminding Ann of her father.

"Right now, I think it's the *barn* you need to be closer to," she said, turning away. "I've pastry to get on with."

But as time passed, Ann found it increasingly difficult to resist John's advances. Absent of a conscious decision, their relationship became more intimate; their touches lingered longer, their playfulness increasingly sensual.

One afternoon, when she was working in the kitchen, John came up behind her and grabbed her hips. She felt his warm breath on the nape of her neck and then a kiss. She turned to face him and he put his hands on her waist. Their eyes met.

"You look lovely," John whispered.

Ann smiled, but was unsure what would follow. She turned her eyes away from him, but his hands moved slowly up towards her breasts. When she looked back at him, she saw a determined expression on his face. He looked different, somehow.

"No John, it's not right!" she said.

But still his hands roamed across her body.

"Stop it!"

He pinned her against the kitchen sink.

"No! John, get away!" she said, louder now, struggling to free herself from his grasp. He was so strong and forceful that she couldn't break loose, however she tried. She begged him to let her go, but her words got lost in her tears. John didn't seem to notice those tears, or he simply didn't care. Either way, he didn't stop. He was only determined to get what he wanted. When he'd finished, Ann felt sickened. Tears trickled down her face. Sobbing, she fled to the scullery to wash herself.

In his presence, she no longer felt safe, kept her distance, avoided physical contact and communicated as little as possible. She did as he asked if it related to her work, fending off his other suggestions. She was afraid of antagonising him, and spent each day on edge, wondering whether the same thing might happen again. She was also grieving for the loss of what she'd had before – a job she enjoyed, and a little happiness for the first time in her life.

She didn't dare tell anyone when she found herself pregnant. She feared her mother's reaction and was unsure about John's response. Months later, after church, she drummed up the courage to tell Mother.

"I'm ashamed of you, Ann. It's shocking!" Mother's bottom lip quivered in anger. "Who's the father?"

Ann lost control of herself, the tension erupting after keeping the secret for so long. She cried, sorry she had to disappoint her mother while she was in mourning.

"Was it John Starie?"

Ann sobbed so much she couldn't speak, but nodded.

"How could you let yourself go? And so soon after your father's death? He warned you so many times to keep a distance - just to do your job. You're a disgrace to this family and the church."

"It all happened so quickly."

"You'll have to marry him."

"I can't!"

"You must, otherwise people will scorn you. No other man will want to marry you, and you'll end up in poverty."

"But he forced himself on me. I didn't know what was happening. I was busy in the kitchen when he came in."

"You should have pushed him away."

"I tried! He was too strong." She held her palms up, hoping her mother would sympathise.

"Have you told him about your situation?"

"Not yet," Ann said, in between sobs.

"Well, you tell him tomorrow. He must ask you to be his wife. He's the father."

"But I can't be near him like that!"

"You have no other choice, girl. You'll have to marry and move in with him, because you can't stay here."

Ann was at a complete loss, ashamed and guilty. Had she brought it upon herself? She cursed herself for playing along with his flirtations, giving him any inkling that she wanted more.

The next morning, she walked to work as usual. John attempted to be friendly, but she pushed past him.

"What's the matter?" he said, in an irritated tone.

"I'm with child," Ann blurted, looking down at the floor.

"What! Who's the father?"

"Well, who do you think?"

"It can't be me!"

"There's no other, so it must be you." She crossed her arms, defiantly.

"That cannot be," he said, his eyes cold.

"There's been *no other*!" Ann said, her face glowing with anger.

"Don't expect me to marry you." He turned his back on her, pressed his fingers to his forehead.

"But it's your duty!" Ann said, punching her fists into her waist. "It's your duty to marry me! It says so in the bible. How can you deny it?"

"I'm not marrying an illiterate labourer's daughter employed as a cook. What will my family think?"

She couldn't believe what she was hearing. It was the last straw. She picked up her bag, ready to leave.

"Where are you going?"

"I'm leaving. I've no interest in a man who declines to accept the truth."

"Then it's the end of your employment here. I'll find someone else."

Ann left, kicking a bucket on her way out. She ran back to her mother's, completely distraught by the rejection, not only of herself but also of her unborn baby. Had her own day of reckoning come? She had lost her father, disobeyed him by not keeping her distance from her employer, and now she had run away.

She told Mother and broke down in tears.

"What am I to do? If I can't live with my child's father, where will I go?"

CHAPTER FOUR
Single Mother

1859

Ann's mother rented a small cottage on Brick Kiln Floor farmstead, so the family prepared to move. Her older brother, George, now twenty-nine, still lived with them, and made countless cart rides with their belongings. Given her advanced condition, Ann could only do light work, so she helped by keeping little Elizabeth out of everybody's way.

They settled in and soon reverted to their normal routine. Mother had an interest in medicinal herbs and earned some money by giving advice to people with ailments, selling them herbal preparations. It enabled her to stay at home to look after Elizabeth. George worked as a servant and handed a sizeable chunk of his earnings to Mother to cover the cost of food and lodging. Ann did temporary work as a maid until her expanding size would give away her condition. She wore loose, wide garments, and stayed inside when she could. She directed her attention to knitting baby clothes, although her mother also gave her items she no longer needed.

Since her father's death, and John Starie's gall in leaving her stranded, there were no dominant men in Ann's life anymore. The question of finding a husband haunted her, but she quickly dismissed it whenever it came to mind. She wasn't sure she wanted a man at all.

She often had nightmares, in which faceless men attacked her from behind, forcing her to do things against her will. She pushed them away with all her strength and fled to find consolation amongst women who kept her safe. But they became ghostlike and slowly disappeared, leaving her lonely and vulnerable.

The worry of managing as a single mother gnawed on her, day and night, until she realised she needed help and would need to reach out.

"Mother, I've been thinking about what to do. After giving birth. I'd like to stay in Coreley, but I'm afraid people will look down on me. It's better for me to leave. "

"It'll be good for you to have a fresh start elsewhere, but who's going to mind the baby?"

"I don't know. Family, I hope," Ann said, cautiously.

"What family? I've had enough of minding babies. Elizabeth will soon go to school, so I'll be glad of more time on my hands. I'd like to be a midwife."

"You'll be excellent at that, I'm sure."

"There's a single-mother home in Ludlow. Why not try there? You could ask teacher to write a letter asking whether they'll take you. He's someone you can trust not a gossip."

Ann looked vaguely at the washing flapping on the line. A fear of being on her own flooded through her. She was losing the bond with her mother, just when she needed it most. But she said nothing, only scratched the back of her hand. She knew it was her own fault; she'd brought this on herself; she sorely regretted being flirtatious with Starie from the start.

Three weeks later, a letter for Ann arrived. She took it to the teacher, who read it out loud.

Dear Mrs Handley,
Your request to find accommodation has reached us in good order. It is
with pleasure that we can inform you that a room will soon be available
in a house in Rock Lane, Stanton Lacy, just outside Ludlow. There is a
charge of four shillings a week. The private home is owned by Mr
Monday. Mrs Tantram is the housekeeper, and she is looking forward to
making your acquaintance.

"Oh, that's delightful news," Ann said, with a smile. "Thanks for reading it."

"Do you wish me to write a reply?"

"Yes, please. Let them know I'll visit in the next few weeks."

She walked home with a divided heart; the thought of a new life excited her, but she worried about how to pay the weekly amount.

"Mother, the letter says I'm welcome in Ludlow, but they charge four shillings a week. How am I going to pay that?" She bit her lower lip.

"You can apply for a benefit, but it means appearing before officials and swearing you truly know the father's name."

"I'm not doing that, ever!" Ann cried. "He'd only deny it."

George heard her raised voice and came to ask what had upset her. When he understood, he offered her a pound from his savings, sufficient for five weeks of rent.

"Oh, thank you George, you're wonderful. When I find work, I'll soon pay you back," she said and wrapped her arms around him tightly. "Mother, I'm determined to earn a living, enough to care for my child, so I don't have to marry."

1860

In January, there was a cold spell with snow on the ground for several days. On the evening of the eleventh, a pain shot through Ann. It was an unfamiliar pain, not like her monthly pain. Mother told her it was the beginning of contractions. They would be increasingly frequent and harsher, so they'd better try to get some sleep. Knowing delivery might happen in the night, Mother didn't change into her nightgown.

Before sunrise on the twelfth, snow fell heavily. All was quiet outside, but in the cottage Ann shouted, "Mother! Mother! … Come quick! … Mother! I think the baby's coming!"

Mother was up in a jiffy, rushing to Ann's bedside.

"Take deep breaths, dear. The spasms will come and go. Try to relax in between. Slow your breathing down. That's right. I'm just going to wake George so he's ready to fetch the doctor in case we need help."

She returned with a cup of camomile tea and peered between the curtains. "The snow is deep. I won't ask the midwife to come. We'll manage without her," Mother said.

Between panting breaths, Ann asked whether she'd be all right.

"Don't worry. Do as I say and it'll soon be over."

Ann's cramps came more swiftly. She felt her mother's warm hands on her stomach and heard her comforting voice.

"The baby's in the right position. It won't be long now. Are you comfortable?"

"I'm trying to get comfy, but I can't relax. *Oohh.* My back aches so much. *Oohh!*"

Mother massaged her back and wiped her clammy forehead with a cool, damp cloth.

"Now, lean backwards, take deep breaths and let them out slowly."

Her mother sounded so calm, so confident, and Ann felt herself relaxing, despite the pain.

Two clean sheets were already at hand. One went on the bed between Ann's legs, the other across her tummy, ready to wrap the baby in.

"I can see the baby's head," said Mother. "Keep pushing."

"I can't …. *Oohh*!"

"Push again!"

"*Oohh*!"

"It's coming. Don't push hard anymore, just pant," Mother said, reassuringly, putting her hands around the baby's head. "The head's out now. Well done. The worst is over."

Ann contracted a few more times before the baby fully appeared.

Mother held the newborn up for her to see, "Look, it's a boy."

He started crying and coughed up some fluid.

"That's a good boy, get rid of it all," his grandmother said, tipping his head down. "He's a lovely baby. Well done!"

Ann reached out, took the baby, and held him against her breast while her mother knotted and cut the umbilical cord. She beamed with happiness. His skin was yellowish, but he looked healthy and sweet. She adored him immediately. His nostrils were tiny dots, his little hands clenched before his chest, his eyes closed. The sound of his cries filled her heart with joy and a love she'd never known before.

Ann soon recovered. Her breasts produced enough milk for her eager son, and his yellowish complexion turned pink. He slept in a cozy wooden box she'd lined with woollen material to keep him warm. After feeding and washing him, she cooed while putting him in the cot, and placed it on a chest so it wasn't on the cold floor.

George took her to the registrar's office to record the birth. She named him Joseph Starie, out of respect for her father, and as a sign of who the baby's father had been. When the registrar asked how to spell Starie, she said she didn't know. So he recorded: 'Joseph Stary Handley'.

He turned towards George. "Are you the father?"

"He's my brother," Ann replied quickly. "He brought me here."

"Who is the child's father?"

"I don't know."

The registrar left the father's name blank and asked her to sign.

"I haven't learned to write," she said.

"That's alright. Just put a cross here."

Spring was in the air, and daffodils were flowering among the trees when Ann asked George to take her to Stanton Lacy with Joseph. She packed all they needed for living there permanently. As he loaded the cart, she said goodbye to her mother and Elizabeth.

"Let me hold Joseph before he leaves me," Mother said.

Ann gladly passed him to her.

"My dear boy, I'm going to miss you. I hope I'll see you again soon," Mother cooed. Looking at Ann, she added, "Make sure you find work as quickly as you can."

"Don't worry Mother, I really want to earn my keep," Ann said, and touched Elizabeth's cheek. "I'll miss you both."

"You'll be alright. It's only for the time-being, till you get a job. Then you may have to go elsewhere," Mother said.

"Yes, I'll let you know where I end up. We'll be back to see you, when we can."

She took hold of Joseph, kissed Elizabeth and Mother, and climbed on the cart.

George shouted, "Giddy up," and off they went.

Birdsong and baby noises filled the air. Trees and bushes had early shoots of green. Ann marvelled at the parallels between her budding Joseph and the budding of spring.

CHAPTER FIVE

Cook

1860

George stopped the horse outside a house on Rock Lane, where the road sloped up out of Ludlow. In Ann's eyes, it was a large residence with white plastered walls and windows symmetrically positioned on each side of the porch.

George leaped from the cart. "This looks a pleasant place. Plenty of rooms, I'd say."

Ann climbed down, holding Joseph. "I'm so excited. Will you come in with me? We can bring the luggage later."

With Joseph in her arms, she approached the door and rang the bell. A woman with a broad smile welcomed them, introducing herself as Mrs Tantram. She showed them to the front room. "You must be tired after such a journey. Take a seat and I'll make some tea."

Ann glanced at George, who said, "I'll just stay for a cuppa and then be on my way."

After his departure, Mrs Tantram suggested showing Ann around the house.

"Do you mind if I first feed the baby, Mrs Tantram?" She shifted Joseph on her lap.

"Of course, by all means, and please call me Mary. I'll leave you to it and come back later."

They walked through the house, downstairs rooms first.

Upstairs, Mary opened the first door on the landing, "This is your room."

Ann moved to the centre of the room. "Thank you, it's all I need."

"There's a delightful view of the garden from this room. Over there is the common with the woods beyond," Mary said, pointing towards the horizon. They moved further along the corridor. "Mr Monday is the owner. He's quite elderly, so needs some looking after. He's out at the moment; you'll see him later. My two sons, Herbert and Fredrick, have this room. Herbert's an errand boy and out all day. Fredrick's at school. The room at the end is Mrs Holloway's. She's another Mary, which can be a trifle confusing. She's a widow and lives here with her son."

Ann guessed Mary was a widow too, probably in her early fifties.

Ann initially found it difficult to settle. She'd never slept away from home and was now in a strange place with new people, without family or friends for conversation and to share her joy of young Joseph. She missed her mother, although there were moments when she wondered whether Mother had been glad to see the back of her.

Mary soon took a liking to Ann and asked her to assist with the meals, giving her the opportunity to practise her cooking skills.

"Ann, how do you like living here? Have you settled in?" Mary asked, lifting a cast iron frying-pan on to the stove.

"I have, thank you. I miss my family, though. They seem so far away."

Ann filled the kettle and placed it on the stove to heat, while Mary took cups and saucers from the cupboard.

"I'm lucky to have relatives in town, but for you it's a day's journey back home."

Mary laid the saucers on a tray.

"At church I've met a few friendly women my age, but I haven't got to know anyone properly yet."

Steam wafted from the kettle, so Ann spooned tea in the pot and poured in the boiling water. Mary opened the larder for milk and filled a jug.

"You're free to bring someone to visit, if you wish."

"Thank you. Perhaps I'll do that," Ann said. "Maybe I should first look for work. I want to earn enough money to save for Joseph's education when the time comes."

"There are several big houses around here. Surely there's one in need of a maid."

"I'd love to be a cook."

"Cooks are better paid, too. When do you think you plan to start?"

"In a couple of weeks, when I've weaned Joseph off breast-feeding. I don't know what I'll do with him. Someone needs to look after him."

Once Joseph was on baby food, Ann went to houses asking about vacancies for a cook. But to no avail. They all had cooks, and none were planning to leave. At one place they showed her a newspaper advertisement for a house in Chesterton, beyond Bridgnorth, quite a long way from Ludlow or Coreley, so she dismissed it.

Back at the home, she mentioned the vacancy to Mary. "Well love, go there to see what it's like. You're a wonderful cook and I'll write a note recommending you."

The carriage ride to Chesterton, near Worfield, took two-and-a-half hours. As the lush Shropshire countryside passed by, Ann thought about how to bring up the subject of a child. Would they turn her down when she mentioned having a baby and no husband?

She found Chesterton House in the middle of the village: a red brick building with the entrance right on the road, covered by a wooden porch. A pretty maid with dark wavy hair opened the door and gave her a warm welcome. Her vivid eyes struck Ann.

"Please come in. You must be Mrs Handley, coming for the position of cook. Follow me, please."

As Ann walked behind her, the swing of the maid's walk distracted her. Her nose caught whiffs of soap and baked bread on the way to the kitchen. A staunch cook came into view and Ann's mouth suddenly felt dry.

"Good afternoon, Mrs Handley. I'm Mrs King, the cook. Have you had a pleasant journey? Let me take your coat." While hanging Ann's cloak on a peg behind the door, she nodded towards the maid. "This is Miss Emma Roberts, our parlourmaid."

Emma offered Ann a cup of tea, and the three women chatted about the weather and Ann's journey, which eased Ann's anxiety.

"Let me take you to meet Mrs Marindin, the mistress." Mrs King stood up and led the way out of the kitchen and down the hall. She knocked on a door at the front of the house. A firm voice said, "Come in". As they entered the room, a stout lady stood up. Ann's pulse raced as she came towards her, holding out a hand.

"I'm glad you've taken the trouble to come, Mrs Handley. We'll need a new cook soon."

"Thank you, Madam." Ann cleared her throat. "Here's a letter from my previous mistress."

Mrs Marindin took it and skimmed through the praising words. "Well, you sound just the right person," she said, turning to the cook. "Will you show Ann around the house, please, Mrs King? Thank you."

The rooms were cosy, neat and tidy. Sunlight shone into the lounge through doors opening onto the terrace and garden. They ascended the servant's stairs to the staff bedrooms in the attic. Ann's room was small but light, facing the early morning sun. She peered out of the window and saw a kitchen-garden surrounded by a red-bricked wall, fruit trees trained along its length, and a host of different vegetables. Flowers brought vivid colours to the beds surrounding a lawn. At the side, she noticed stables and a cobblestone exit to the street.

During their tour, Mrs King introduced her to two younger servants, the housemaid and the stable boy. Back in the kitchen, Emma asked what Ludlow was like. By the way she spoke, Ann could tell she was her own age, about twenty-four, and thought they would get on well together.

Looking around her workplace, she noted a decent set of pans hanging on a white-tiled wall, a coal-burning cooking range and a softwood table for cutting and chopping. In the corner was a large cupboard for utensils and cutlery. At the window, a table and two chairs looked enticing and, as if Mrs King could read her thoughts, she suggested they sit down. After pouring tea, she explained the family's eating habits and asked Ann a few questions about her experience cooking for a family.

"You seem to have the experience required here. You'll be a worthy successor, I'm sure," Mrs King said, shifting her chair to stretch her legs. "Let me tell you about the mistress. She's long been a widow and lives here with her three daughters, son and his wife. He's an assistant master at Eton, so not around much. There's another married son, but he hardly ever visits."

"When do you expect to leave, Mrs King?"

"I'd like to stop next month. My family's in Bath, so I want to go down there."

The warm welcome at Chesterton House made Ann eager to take the position. She asked Mrs King about a home for single mothers in the village.

She frowned. "No dear, there's no such place in Chesterton. Mrs Marindin expects all domestic staff to live on the premises. How are you going to manage?"

Ann mirrored the frown. "My son is only a baby," she said, scratching the back of her hand. "I'll ask my mother to look after him."

"Well, I need to tell you that the mistress is very strict when it comes to working hours. She won't be happy with a cook who needs to be away frequently."

"Thank you for warning me. I'll miss little Joseph but won't let that get in the way of my duties."

"Shall we go back to Mrs Marindin?"

They went to the study, taking tea and biscuits for the mistress.

"Well Mrs Handley, what do you think of our abode? Would you consider joining us as a cook?" Mrs Marindin asked.

"Yes Madam, I'd love to take the position. Everyone is so friendly. But I first need to find a home for my son."

"I understand. You need time to sort things out. Can we agree you'll send me a letter when you decide? Will you do that by the end of next week? You can start here as soon as you're able."

Ann was relieved she hadn't been questioned about a spouse. She thanked Mrs Marindin and made her way back to Stanton Lacy.

Ann had no choice. If she wanted to be independent, she had to work, and to do that she'd need to leave her son in someone else's care. She chatted to Mary, who often had wonderful suggestions.

"I'm sure I'm going to like Chesterton," Ann said.

"What makes you so certain?"

"I liked the mistress and the staff. The parlourmaid is about my age; I think I'll get on nicely with her. It's a pity I can't take Joseph." Ann looked down at the floor.

"Well, he can't stay here, so what'll you do?" Mary asked.

"I need to persuade my mother to look after him."

"Why don't you go to her with Joseph? Let her hold him, play with him. It'll make her realise she'll miss her grandson. Perhaps that'll make her change her mind. Will it help if you say you'd like him to grow up in Coreley, amongst family?"

"I want to raise him myself, but I can't see how. I need to work," Ann said, as if convincing herself. "It's better for Joseph to be with my mother than with someone else."

"What's holding her back? Is it to do with her daughter having a child out of wedlock?"

"I don't know. It's *my* fault, so why would people hold it against my mother?"

"They might blame her for not bringing you up according to the bible, and think it's her fault you've wandered."

Ann and Joseph arrived at Mother's in Coreley on a summer's day.

"Hello dears, come in. Let me just hang this on the line."

She carried the basket of wet clothing out to the garden, pegged everything on the washing-line. Coming back in, she gave them both a kiss. "What a big boy you are, Joseph."

They sat down at the kitchen table. Mother took Joseph on her lap, stroked his blond hair to one side. Bobbing her knees up and down, she sang:

> Ride a cock-horse to Banbury Cross,
> To see a fine lady upon a white horse;

Rings on her fingers and bells on her toes,
And she shall have music wherever she goes.

"You're such a lovely little boy," Mother chuckled, rubbing noses with him.

Ann was aware of the clock ticking and the fire shifting. She brushed her hands in a circular motion on the tabletop.

"I had a day out to Chesterton yesterday," she said.

"Where's that? I've never heard of it."

"It's a village beyond Bridgnorth," said Ann, waving her hand in a northerly direction.

"What's going on there then?"

"They're advertising for a cook."

"That's a long way off. Why there?"

"I can't find a job in Ludlow. The people at Chesterton are friendly. It's not a vast place, but there's a big kitchen-garden. The cook's leaving."

"Are they interested in you?"

"The mistress has offered me the position and a room in the attic," Ann said, scratching her left hand.

"Can Joseph be there with you?"

"They want all staff to live on the premises. I told her about Joseph and she didn't ask about a husband. But the cook warned me that the mistress wouldn't want me distracted by Joseph. There's no single mothers' home in Chesterton, so that's not an option. She's given me a week to work things out."

"Who's going to look after him?" Mother said, pursing her lips, Joseph still on her lap.

"I don't know. I'd like him to be in Coreley, to grow up amongst his kin." Ann bit her lip and scratched her hand again. She walked to the scullery for a cup of water, waiting for a reaction. Mother put Joseph down and watched him crawl and push himself forward with his knees.

She turned towards Ann, not looking at her but at her own hands. "Some people in the village ignore me now, you know. How would they react, if I took Joseph under my wing? It could even affect my work as a midwife."

Joseph tried to open a cupboard door, so Ann went to pick him up. She jostled him in her arms, kissed him, and looked at her mother, avoiding eye-contact, not saying anything.

"You know I've had enough of toddlers." Mother folded her hands across her chest.

"I don't want to depend on a man's income," Ann said. "The only way is to work. I have no other choice, Mother. For Joseph's future, I need to be sure to have an income of *my* own, for his education."

"Ann, the same goes for me. How can I manage if I don't work? I've got Elizabeth here. Having Joseph would mean more expenses."

"I'll pay for his upkeep."

"It's not only the money. I don't want to feel tied down."

"I know it's difficult to be a midwife and look after a baby," Ann said, handing Joseph to her mother again.

"Coo, coo, you're such a sweet boy," Mother said, with a playful face.

"He'd be happier here than boarding out with strange parents."

"But it doesn't seem right that you have to pay your own mother."

"I know, but I'd have to pay foster parents, anyway."

"I admit, being available at all hours is exhausting me."

Ann picked up the wooden rattle and shook it to draw the baby's attention.

Mother continued, "I was thinking of doing less tiring work."

"If you stop being a midwife, you'll have more time to help people with herbal medicine. You've always liked doing that," Ann suggested.

"That's true," Mother said, tickling Joseph's toes. "We'll manage. ... My neighbour sometimes looks after Elizabeth so I'm sure she won't mind having Joseph now and again." She took the rattle from Ann and gave it a shake. "And if I don't have to rely on my midwifery work, I can care less what people think."

"It would be *so lovely* for him to be here."

Mother looked at Ann and smiled, nodding her head.

"And it will be lovely for me to have him around. It'll be fine, Ann."

"Oh, thank you, Mother. I'm so glad you'll look after him. He'll be happy here."

Back in Stanton Lacy, Ann asked Mary to write a letter to Mrs Marindin to confirm a starting date. It meant she would hardly see her son, but at least she could provide for him and support her mother's household.

At Chesterton, Ann soon felt settled. It was an all-female household; the son was rarely home and the stable boy only in his teens. The lack of dominant men was a relief for Ann. She worked every day from early morning till eight at night, preparing all the meals, scrubbing the kitchen floor and cleaning pots and pans. As there was just herself and two maids to run the house, they worked together, sharing duties. Ann helped to lay fires, and Emma aided in the kitchen. They enjoyed chatting and gossiping about the Marindin family and their visitors.

Each evening, Ann and Emma retired to the attic to be together, mostly in Ann's room, which was slightly larger. One day, at dusk, they stood at the open window to watch the peaceful sunset. The garden's colours were warmed by the reddish light, the shadows were long and the sky was all shades of blue, pink and red. Their shoulders touched, and Ann reached an arm around Emma, saying how lucky they were to have met each other.

In Emma, Ann found a friend with whom she could confide, telling her about her son and her experience with his father. She told Emma how she missed Joseph, how she missed seeing him grow up, missed giving him her affection. But she also admitted she wasn't keen to raise a family. "I'm not particularly good with children, and certainly not interested in a man in my life."

Emma spoke about how she had longed to leave home. Being the youngest daughter with younger brothers, she had felt squeezed in the middle and ignored. Ann had been a middle child too and shared similar emotions of disregard. Their common experience and sympathetic understanding was a source of comfort, a foundation for a special relationship.

CHAPTER SIX

Chesterton

1866

Twice a year, Mrs Marindin allowed Ann to have an entire week off, excluding Christmas, when all the Marindin family came to Chesterton. Ann took a break every January for Joseph's birthday, and another week in July when Mrs Marindin was usually away. This July, she arrived in Coreley in excellent spirits, looking forward to being with Joseph.

Her mother greeted her. "Good morning Ann. Come in. I'm sorry to say, Joseph is poorly."

"Oh dear, what's the matter with him?"

"He's been in bed for a couple of days. I've given him cod liver oil and kept him on a bland diet."

"Is he eating well?"

"He's eating well enough and doesn't have a high temperature. I think it's influenza."

Ann went to her son, and was relieved to find that he didn't seem very ill.

That evening, she and her mother sat down to catch up.

Mother picked up a plate. "Would you like some apple pie?"

"It looks delicious!"

Ann noticed the clock chime eight, as her mother cut them each a slice. "Do you remember Mr Stinton?"

"Vaguely. Doesn't he live down at Cornbrook?"

"That's him; he's a widower. Your father knew him. They often worked on the same farm together. We've been conversing of late, about the past, and how people in Coreley have always stood together."

"Have you had contact with him in the past?"

"Not really, just the odd chat after church." Mother's cheeks flushed. "I've taken quite a liking to him."

Ann's eyes widened. "You're not going to marry him, are you?"

Mother handed her a saucer with a slice of pie. "I might. He's twenty years older than me, but I don't mind. I'll be better off than staying on my own," she said, biting her bottom lip. "It'll be a marriage like brother and sister."

Ann worried about her Joseph. She thought the change would upset him if it meant moving house and having less attention from his grandmother. She shook her head. "I never expected you to marry again. You're independent now, just as you've wanted to be."

"Don't forget, I'm fifty-six. I can't earn enough selling herbs."

"But he'll expect you to care for him in his old age!"

"Mr Stinton can still care for himself. Besides, God expects us to look after others. He's asked me to move to Cornbrook."

"Joseph's so happy here with you and Elizabeth!"

"Cornbrook is closer to school. It's not far – it's still part of Coreley. I'll be at home more often. Any rate, it's better for Joseph to have a man around."

"How long have you been talking to Mr Stinton?"

"A few months now. It started after church when we had a lengthy chat. He said as we're both alone, perhaps we should talk about getting together." Mother touched Ann's arm. "Don't worry. If I decide to live with him, I'll give Joseph all the attention he needs."

1867

In January, Ann went home for Joseph's birthday - his seventh. When she arrived, she marvelled at how he'd grown and how happy he was. Her mother was bringing him up with good Christian manners, not that she expected otherwise. Ann's primary aim was to make sure he would learn to read and write, and when she saw his progress, she didn't understand why she hadn't had those lessons herself. There was no point in complaining now. It had been her father's doing, anyway.

She joined Mother at the kitchen table. "Isn't Joseph back from school?"

"He'll be here in a minute. He said he'd bring friends to share the birthday cake."

"How's he doing?"

"His teacher said he's good with words and likes woodwork lessons."

"I'm relieved." Ann placed her hand on her heart and leaned back in the chair..

"I need to tell you …there's less positive news." Mother winced. "Boys have been calling Joseph a bastard. He came home crying last week."

"Oh!" Ann clasped a hand over her mouth. "How terrible for him!"

"I told him that sometimes children don't have a mother or a father. It's the way God works and we can't always understand."

"Children can be really nasty! Thanks for being vague. When he's older, I'll let him know more. How has he taken it?"

But just then, Joseph came in, followed by a group of friends. Holding out something to his mother, he said, "Look what I've got!"

Ann smiled. "What's that, Joseph?"

"It's a spinning top. And a whip." He bounced on his toes.

"Show me what you can do with it."

Joseph wound the string around the top, put it on the floor, and pulled the whip.

Ann leaned down in interest. "Wow, that's spinning well. Where did you get it?"

"The man next door helped me make it out of wood," Joseph said, whipping the top to keep it whirling fast.

"Happy birthday, Joseph! Are you coming to me for a birthday kiss?"

He left his top to spin and jumped into her arms. She hugged him tighter than ever after hearing they'd bullied him. After a moment, he tugged himself loose and ran into the garden, following his friends.

Ann turned to her mother. "Let's cut the birthday cake."

Mother cleared her throat. "Before they come back, let me tell you about my plans. You know I was considering marrying Mr Stinton ...?"

Ann nodded.

"Well, we've both decided to go ahead."

Ann moved closer. "I understand your reasons and I'm happy for you."

Mother took her hand. "Don't worry about Joseph. He gets on well with Mr Stinton. He taught Joseph how to fish. I'll look after him, as I've always done."

"Thank you, Mother. I have no doubts. When will the wedding be?"

"In May, on the sixteenth, Mr Stinton's birthday. Can you come?"

"I hope Mrs Marindin will let me. I'm sure she'll understand."

"We're not making a big do of it, just immediate family, privately after the church service."

"What about bridesmaids?" Ann asked.

"I don't think so. We want to keep it simple."

When the wedding day arrived, Ann walked up the lane to St Peter's with Joseph and Elizabeth for the Sunday service. She pointed out red campions and foxgloves along the roadside, bringing back memories. She took a fresh look at the small, familiar church with its wooden shingle spire. How tranquil it looked, bathing in the sun. A group had formed around the entrance. Getting closer, she saw her siblings and their families: now, quite a large crowd. There was another one on its way, as Fanny would soon give birth. Half a dozen young children ran around and needed calming down before going inside. After the service, they waited for the others to leave and for the parson to prepare. He then gathered them together before the altar and performed a short and sweet wedding ceremony.

The new Mrs Stinton moved to Cornbrook Cottage with Elizabeth and Joseph. The next time Ann visited, she was pleased to observe there was a vegetable plot, fruit trees, and a chicken coop. A recently hoed patch of herbs signalled Mother had put in her medicinal plants. A mixture of flowers grew where they thrived best. At the bottom of the property, there was a brook where Joseph caught fish, frogs, and newts. He said he loved building dams to hold back the water until they overflowed and washed away. Mr Stinton had a small workshop where he taught Joseph to make a fishing-rod out of cane and helped him carve a fishing-stool with twirly legs. When Ann saw them together, relief and gratitude filled her heart.

1870

Ann received a letter from Mother saying Mr Stinton had turned poorly. A week later, a telegram arrived.

"Oh, Emma, a telegram is a sign of bad news," said Ann, opening it. "Mr Stinton has passed away."

Emma put an arm around her shoulder. "I'm so sorry to hear. It must be quite a shock for your mother, so soon."

"It will be more of a shock for Joseph. I need to go to take care of things. Will you be able to prepare the meals in my absence?"

"Yes, of course."

Ann tilted her head to Emma's shoulder. "There's nothing special on this week. I'll give you instructions tomorrow morning."

Mrs Marindin gave Ann a week off, and she travelled straight to Cornbrook. She found Joseph distraught. Taking him in her arms, she said, "I'm so sad for you, Joseph. You had good times together. He loved you."

Joseph's chin trembled. "Why has God taken him from us?"

"God has decided Pa's time has come. We can't know all of God's ways and have to accept He's right." Ann wiped Joseph's tears away with a handkerchief. To distract him, she took his marbles out of the draw and asked him to play.

Once Joseph was playing on his own, she set about aiding her mother to prepare for the funeral, knowing what to do because of her father's death. She had fewer worries about preparing the body, as she was less attached to Mr Stinton.

"Mother," said Joseph. "Pa was not my proper father, was he? Why don't I have a real father like other boys?"

His watery eyes saddened her. His questions didn't surprise her; he was ten now, and bound to wonder. "Joseph, Pa has been good to you. You were like a son to him. Remember him as your father."

"But who is my true father?" Joseph demanded, with a raised voice.

"That's not important today, Joseph. He's not around, is all you need to know. God wants us to think of Pa now. Let's pray he may go to heaven to be with the angels."

Mr Stinton had been well-liked in the village, so a large group gathered for the funeral. The men wore dark suits, black gloves, and black bands around their hats. Ann and her mother were in black, their dresses covered with black crepe. Joseph and Elizabeth wore their normal Sunday clothes. After the service, the congregation followed the coffin up the aisle and out to the graveyard. As Ann was leaving the church, she caught sight of John Starie in the rear pews. She avoided eye contact and hoped she could keep her distance in the cemetery. Luckily, he didn't approach her.

1874

Joseph and his grandmother were outside clearing away snow when Ann arrived for her January visit. She wished Joseph a happy birthday and opened her bag. He peeped in and saw a cake, with a large 14 on the white icing. "Thank you, Mother. I have friends coming this afternoon. We're going to fish in the brook."

"Well, we'll all share it and enjoy a piece with tea when you come in to warm up."

The next day, when Joseph arrived home, Ann asked him to sit down. He drew back a kitchen chair and sat down in a rigid posture, as if waiting for bad news.

"Now you're fourteen, we need to talk about you going to work."

He didn't react, but looked slightly dazed. "I don't want to work on a farm."

"Don't look down on farm work. It requires a lot of skill for ploughing, mowing and sowing. The duties call for judgment and dedication."

Joseph slumped. "What else is there to do in Coreley?"

"Yes, I'm not saying you *should* do farm work. At school, you were very good at wood-work..?"

"I like carving. Mr Palmer taught me how to make furniture."

"Mr Palmer lives along the lane," Ann's mother explained. "He's a carpenter. Perhaps he knows where Joseph can find a carpentry job?"

Ann had always wanted Joseph to have other opportunities, other than farm-labourer like her father and brothers. "Would you like that, Joseph? A carpentry job?"

He shrugged his shoulders, "I'd like to learn how to do more with wood."

She sensed he was anxious about changes in his life and wasn't ready to step out into the world without some support. Knowing she would have to leave it to her mother, Ann said, "Mother, will you ask Mr Palmer next time you see him?"

"Shall we go to him tomorrow, Joseph?" Mother asked. "Then we can tell your mother what he says before she leaves."

Joseph sounded excited when they came back from Mr Palmer. "He knows a carpenter in Shrewsbury who needs an extra pair of hands. He'll speak to him and let me know. Perhaps it'll be an apprenticeship."

Mother added, "He said Joseph's a good lad and has the right touch with wood, so hopefully he'll recommend him."

When Ann returned to Chesterton, she observed a low-spirited Emma peeling potatoes in the dim winter sunlight.

"Mrs Marindin asked me to send you to her as soon as you came back," Emma said, avoiding eye contact.

"What's wrong?"

"She's angry."

"Angry about what?"

"About the meals."

"What do you mean, 'about the meals'?"

"She said I'd let her down."

"What happened, then?"

"I did my best. It wasn't my fault."

Ann felt her throat tighten. She looked around for clues. "Tell me what went wrong!"

"They didn't deliver things we ordered," Emma stuttered. "We didn't have …"

"Why weren't they delivered?" Ann shouted.

"I don't know. They just didn't come."

"Didn't you go to the grocer to demand delivery immediately?"

"There wasn't time, so I made alternatives."

Ann rolled her eyes and left the kitchen.

In Mrs Marindin's study, she was confronted with an icy welcome.

"Mrs Handley, we've had two poor meals during your absence. Mrs Roberts told me the grocer had received no orders so she couldn't do anything about it. How can you explain it?"

"I'm sorry to hear that, madam. I don't understand. She had a list of what to order," Ann said, feeling a knot in her stomach.

"Well, I hold *you* responsible. You're the cook, not Mrs Roberts. It's not acceptable. I can't give you extra days off if this sort of thing happens, especially when we entertain guests."

Ann scratched the back of her hand. "I'm sorry, I'm not trying to blame Mrs Roberts. I'll find out what went wrong and make sure it doesn't happen again."

In the kitchen, Ann said, "Emma, the mistress has complained about the meals you prepared. She said the order hadn't been placed. You told me they didn't deliver!"

"I thought you'd placed the orders," Emma replied.

"But I gave *you* the list of things to order!"

"I thought it was just so's I'd know what to expect!"

"You didn't listen properly. I asked you to *place* the order," Ann barked. "It's your fault. You need to listen better. I've told you that before."

"You thrust it in my hand, said it was the order, and then rushed out. How was I to know I was to place the order? It's your fault!"

"I clearly told you to order the items on the list," Ann said, with flinty eyes. She had scratched her hand so hard that it was bleeding. "From now on, I'll do the ordering myself. I can't trust you."

They glared at one another for a moment.

"Since Mrs Marindin's son died, I haven't been myself," said Emma, eventually. "Things are different with his wife being here."

"That's no excuse. Now get back to work. I need to make sure we put on a proper meal this evening," Ann said, waving Emma away.

She purposely distanced herself from Emma to show she was the senior, exercising her authority. She'd been close to Emma, but that would need to stop.

A couple of weeks later, word reached Ann that the carpenter wanted to meet Joseph and watch him do some work. She needed to ask for another day off to go to Shrewsbury with Joseph. She knew Mrs Marindin would need to be convinced that the meals for the day would be up to standard.

She ordered from the grocer herself and gave Emma detailed instructions. "I should be back at the end of the afternoon, but don't count on me."

She was given leave and met Joseph at Shrewsbury station from where they walked to the carpenter's workshop. They found him standing in a pile of wood-shavings, bent over a piece of wood in a vice, busy repairing a cartwheel. At first his face wasn't visible, covered by his hat, long beard and a pipe in his mouth. After they exchanged greetings, Joseph asked how a cartwheel was made.

The carpenter pointed to a large log. "That elm is what we use for the nave. The spokes are oak and fit into these slots in the nave. For the outer ring, we use ash or beech. I buy standing trees, and after they arrive here as logs, we saw them to the sizes we need."

Joseph was keen to show his interest and asked how he made the iron tyre.

"The blacksmith makes it. I heat it so it expands enough to fit the wooden wheel inside. The ring cools down and then sits tight."

"That's clever," Joseph said.

"Yes, it sits really tight. It would be dangerous if it didn't. We don't want people losing their tyres, do we, mate?" the carpenter said. "Now, I'd like you to show me what you can do. Can you make a spoke identical to this one?"

Joseph did his best to produce a perfect match. When he'd finished, only a trained eye could see the difference.

"You've done a good job of that, mate. It'll do nicely in a wheel." Smiling at Joseph, "Would you like to start here as an apprentice?"

"Aye, I would," Joseph replied. "How does that work?"

"To achieve qualifications, you'll need to practise here for seven years. I'll teach you the trade, and when you can work on your own, I'll pay you a small sum."

"Is food and lodging included?"

"Don't you live in Shrewsbury, mate?"

"Nay, I live in Coreley, but I'd like to work here."

"Well, that's too far away. You'll need to live here somewhere."

Joseph looked at his mother, who said, "We'll find lodgings for you."

The carpenter continued. "Your duty will be to avoid damage and waste. You're not to do unlawful work or another job. If you stick to your duties and can work on your own, there's a weekly pay of six shillings. Every year the pay will increase by a shilling up to ten shillings a week. Is that clear?"

"That's clear. When can I start?"

"As soon as you like."

After leaving the workshop, Ann asked Joseph how he liked the man.

"He was friendly," Joseph said.

"Do you really want to work for him?"

"Yes, I think so."

"Seven years is a long time," Ann said. But before Joseph could reply, she carried on. "I've got a plan for lodgings. I want to change jobs, so if I come to Shrewsbury we can live together."

"I'd like that, but why change jobs?" Joseph asked.

"It's not so pleasant in Chesterton any more. The mistress's favourite son died in an accident, so everyone's grieving. The death has devastated his wife, and she's moved in. She's trying to change the way we do things, making it difficult for us to do our work as we used to," Ann said. "Everyone's depressed and irritable. I can't concentrate on organising the meals and cooking. I've decided to leave."

A few weeks later, Ann travelled to Shrewsbury for a job interview and met Joseph at the station. They walked to the marketplace where the hustle and bustle of activity overwhelmed him. He didn't know where to look first. Old buildings were being replaced and new ones constructed. He could tell the town was flourishing.

They asked a passerby to point them towards Abbey Foregate. The man said he was going that way, so they walked together, chatting about the labour market. The trains brought prosperity as they connected north-south and east-west. At the bridge over the River Severn, he directed them towards the Abbey on the opposite side, and said Abbey Foregate was right there. Striding over the bridge, Ann and Joseph could see the top of the Abbey above the surrounding buildings. They went inside to have a look. She commented on the impressive nave with its high ceiling, never before had she seen such a large building. Joseph pointed at the fine woodwork in the pews, and the intricate carving of the choir stalls.

Joseph waited in the abbey while his mother went to the interview. He was looking towards the door when she returned, her arms swinging and a big smile on her face.

"I've secured the position of cook, Joseph!"

"Congratulations, Mother!"

"And, there are lodgings for us both."

"That's marvellous!"

"The mistress, Mrs Juson, is very likeable. She said I had all the experience she needed. There's a spare room, and you can have it as long as you behave well and eat meals with me and the other servants."

"What's the place like?"

"It's a fine, three-storey red-brick building. Mrs Juson is a Scottish widow who lives with a cook and three maids. We can move in when you start the apprenticeship."

And so, a new chapter dawned for Ann and Joseph.

PART TWO
Joseph Handley

CHAPTER SEVEN

Carpenter

1881

"My job's boring," Joseph told his mother, staring off into nothingness. "I'm just making the same things over and over again. It's always hubs, spokes and wheel rims."

"Sounds like you need a change."

He looked at her and yawned. He wasn't really tired, but lacked energy.

"It's time you started thinking about your future," she said. "You could be a carpenter in your own right, and start a family. You can't stay here forever."

Joseph fidgeted. "But I don't want to leave my friends."

His mother talked about her own experience; how she'd hated leaving Coreley, but she never regretted it once she'd settled down in Chesterton. She easily made new acquaintances at work and in church.

"I'll keep an eye out for a job elsewhere, then," he said, looking away.

His master had been proud of him and had complimented him on his meticulousness, his sense of duty, and willingness to put in extra hours when needed to finish an urgent repair. He preferred working on his own, uninterested in small-talk. He was happy in his own thoughts, thoughts that sprang from the books he was reading, those of Robert Louis Stevenson and Arthur Conan Doyle.

Soon after that conversation, he and his mother visited his Grandma, and he told her about wanting more challenging work.

"Perhaps Mr Palmer can help again," Grandma said.

"I'll talk to him and tell him I've got my certificate."

He strolled down the lane until he arrived at a cottage with piles of wood outside. The carpenter was in his workshop. After Joseph explained he was ready for something new, Mr Palmer showed him an advertisement in the paper: 'WHEELWRIGHT - wanted, competent young man, to live in house. Must be a good hand. Apply Mr J. Davis, Wergs Hall, Tettenhall.'

"But that's what I do now. I'm hoping to find something more varied," Joseph said.

"At Wergs they're building a pleasure ground, a park with grand attractions. They probably need wheelwrights to maintain the carts on the premises."

Joseph's eyes widened. "It may be an interesting place if there's a lot going on. Perhaps I'll be able to do other jobs too."

"It's always worth a try."

Dear Mr Davis,
In the newspaper, I have seen your advertisement for a wheelwright. I
have completed an apprenticeship with a wheelwright in Shrewsbury and
have obtained my carpenter certificate. I am a trustworthy person
seeking a carpentry job and would appreciate the opportunity to talk to
you about employment at Wergs Hall.
Looking forward to your reply, I remain yours sincerely, Joseph Handley.

Joseph's letter was in neat handwriting with clear open letters, comparable to a schoolteacher's style. It showed his ability to work tidily and precisely. A response soon came, asking him to come for an interview.

He embarked on the journey to Wergs wearing his best waistcoat and jacket, a handkerchief in his breast pocket. He had groomed his fingernails and checked that his moustache was immaculate. On arrival, he walked up the drive towards the cream-coloured two-storey building with pillars at the main entrance. He'd been instructed to go round to a side door.

"Hello Mr Handley, thanks for coming. I'm Mr Davis, the head wheelwright and blacksmith."

"Good afternoon, Mr Davis."

"Let me show you around. I'm sure you'd like to see our workshop. There's more work than we can handle, so I'd be glad of another hand."

As they walked through the grounds, Joseph saw construction going on all around him.

"What sort of work would you expect me to do, sir?"

"You'll be a wheelwright. There are lots of carts and carriages here, and there's always some needing repair."

Joseph's shoulders dropped, and he looked away.

"You look disappointed, Mr Handley."

"I was hoping to do all sorts of carpentry …" Joseph waved his arms, "… like furniture, doors, gates, perhaps even carving."

"But I don't have a position for a carpenter. The advertisement clearly said wheelwright."

"I'm sorry I've wasted your time, Mr Davis. I'll be going then." He turned to walk away.

"Wait a minute, don't go. Tell me more about yourself."

Joseph spoke about his training as an apprentice wheelwright, his wish to do more elaborate work in the future, and that he sought a job that would cover a range of carpentry skills.

"Well, perhaps I can offer you more in due course. My younger brother is learning to be a wheelwright, so he's doing more of that work. We've got plenty of other woodwork, like making benches for visitors, constructing gates, repairing doors," Mr Davis said.

"That's more the sort of job I'm looking for."

"Well, come and work for me, then. We can find you some varied tasks."

Before Joseph could respond, Mr Davis continued. "Mr Perry lives in Wergs Hall with his two unmarried sisters and a young cousin. They employ over a hundred people on the estate. All sorts — gamekeepers, farmers, gardeners, housemaids, butlers, cooks, clerks. Most of them live in cottages in the village, like we do. Wergs is a lively place. If you wish, you can be a paying-guest in our cottage. I live there with my mother and brother."

The liveliness and range of activities convinced Joseph to take the job and move in to Mr Davis's cottage.

1882

Joseph settled in to the job and was glad it offered him a broader spectrum of carpentry. After the day's work, Joseph and the Davis brothers walked to the cottage where their mother had a meal ready. Not wishing to be with them all day and night, Joseph made a point of going to his own room to read in the evenings.

Crossing Wergs estate one day, he caught up with a maid, who looked about his own age, walking in the same direction. She had a purposeful gait as she strode along in her black dress with a white apron and cap. He liked the way she moved, a determined yet supple movement. She carried a bucket of washing, and he could see she was struggling with the weight.

"Excuse me Miss," he said, and saw her jolt, obviously not expecting a man's voice from behind. "Can I give you a hand?"

She turned, looked him up and down, "Good morning, that's nice of you. I'm on my way to the hall. I haven't seen you around here before."

"Mr Handley," he said, slightly bowing, then straightening his jacket and stroking his hair. "I work for Mr Davis at the smithy, and I'm on my way to the farm to repair a cart with a broken wheel. Please, allow me to carry your bucket."

She put it down. "I'm Miss Done. The twins employ me."

"Who are the twins?" he asked, looking into her eyes, resisting the urge of his gaze to drift to her breasts.

"Mr Perry's sisters are twins. I'm their housemaid."

He picked up the pail, trying to impress her by making it look light. They walked to a door at the side of the hall. He searched for words, and, not able to think of anything better, said, "I'm glad I came here. There are so many friendly people to meet."

"I like it here too. The Perrys are demanding, but they're good to all of us. Where do you come from?"

"Coreley, in Shropshire."

"I've never been to Shropshire. We never go far from here."

At the scullery door, Joseph handed her the bucket, and their hands touched, accidentally. He moved back, tipped his cap, "Good day."

"Thanks for helping me, Mr Handley," she said, with a tone which meant goodbye. Joseph went on his way with a spring in his step. He pictured Miss Done in his mind's eye, her round face, light brown eyes, wavy hair and a fine complexion. He would find an excuse to cross the grounds, taking a detour to meet her again.

Their encounters were fleeting, as he felt awkward and needed to get on with his work. When out of other people's view, he offered Miss Done his hand when they greeted or said goodbye. The texture of her soft skin sent tingles throughout his body, like ink spreading on blotting-paper, a sensation he'd never experienced before. He longed to hold her, to feel her warmth, to be close enough to let her fragrance make him light-headed, to kiss her.

On one of their furtive encounters some weeks later, Miss Done spoke about her family in Wednesfield, near Wolverhampton. "My father started as a wheelwright like you, and now he's a joiner and a bailiff."

"What sort of joinery work does he do?" Joseph asked.

"He makes furniture, mostly for farmers."

"Have you got brothers?"

"Yes, five. One is a wheelwright. Two others run a bakery, and the other two make animal traps and padlocks. All, except one, are married with children."

Joseph envisioned he would fit in well with the men in her family, as they were all craftsmen.

She looked at him in expectance. "Aren't you going to ask me about my sisters?"

He smiled. "Have you got female siblings?"

She smiled. "Three older ones. Susannah, who lives in Leamington with her husband Robert and two children. Louisa is still unmarried. Elizabeth has two children. My younger sister, Mathilda, is courting."

"It sounds like a busy family."

Miss Done flinched. "My mother died six years ago. She was so busy she hardly had time for us younger children. The older ones drew all the attention and always got their way. I should have stood up for myself more, but it was easier just to go along with things." She looked down, a frown on her face. "I don't want a life like my mother's, slaving away at home for a husband and offspring."

"But surely you want a family?" Joseph asked.

"Yes, but not so many children. I'd like to do more than look after the household."

"Like what?"

"I don't know. I just know I want to have a choice."

Her straight-forwardness put him at ease, making it less painful for him to mention his family. He briefly said he had grown up with his grandmother and that his mother was a cook in Shrewsbury. Rather than talking about family, he wanted to talk about his thoughts for her, but his shyness overwhelmed him. His heart ticked faster when he was with her. These feelings were foreign to him - a mixture of fear and trepidation. In bed he often fantasised about her, the curves of her body, the way she walked, her smile. In her presence, he was both relaxed and excited, longing to spend more time with her, to learn more about her. His mind was full of thoughts about how to be closer with her. How could they see each other in private on this estate? Would they be sent away if seen together?

CHAPTER EIGHT
Miss Done

1882

One day, Mr Davis entered the workshop and inspected a wheel Joseph was repairing. "That new spoke you've made looks rather thin. Much thinner than the others. What have you been doing?"

Joseph felt dazed. His mind had been wandering off. Never had Mr Davis disapproved of his work. "Ah, yes, that's not right. I'll make another."

"You need to be more careful, Joseph. Wood of this quality is expensive," Mr Davis said, his eyes searching the workshop for something else. "Where's the tailboard I asked you to collect?"

Joseph blushed, and a cold sweat prickled his back when he realised he'd forgotten it.

"I'll pick it up when I return this wheel, Mr Davis."

"I wanted to work on it now. How could you forget to bring it in? That's not like you." Mr Davis raised his voice. "Fetch it. I'll finish this wheel."

That evening, at the dining table, Joseph had little interest in the general conversation. Miss Done preoccupied his thoughts and he found himself adding salt to his dish a second time. Mr Davis said, "You're quiet, Joseph. Are you alright?"

"I'm fine. Just thinking about how I could've forgotten that tailboard today. I'm sorry," he said, avoiding any talk about Miss Done.

Joseph visited his mother in Shrewsbury on his next day off. The stable boy took him to the station where he paid eight shillings for a third class return ticket. He'd not travelled by train before and the thought of its high speed unnerved him. Pacing up and down the platform, he saw the train come around the corner, chugging as if struggling up the incline, black smoke billowing from its funnel. At the station, the smoke ceased, the brakes squealed, and the engine let out a cloud of steam, as if relaxing after arrival.

He and a few others boarded, and off they puffed. The clattering of metal wheels on the rails produced a rhythm, which gradually increased in pace until at top speed. The wagons shook and shuddered. Smoke came in through the glassless windows and irritated his eyes. He removed a handkerchief from his breast pocket to dab his watering eyes. After stopping at a few other stations, the train arrived in Shrewsbury.

No longer having a key, he went to the back and entered the kitchen. The parlourmaid, Mary Wells, was startled by the door opening unexpectedly. His mother, Ann, was cutting vegetables on a rectangular softwood table. It crossed his mind that she looked plumper than when he'd last seen her. She quickly wiped her hands on her apron, stepped around the table and threw her arms around him.

"How are you faring, Mother?"

"I feel well. Did you have a good journey?"

"It wasn't very comfortable, but it was quick." Joseph turned and greeted Miss Wells.

"Yesterday, Mary and I had time off together, so we went into town. We got on very well, didn't we?" Mother said, looking towards Mary.

"We had a great time together," Mary said.

"How are you getting on at Wergs?" his mother asked.

"I'm doing well. On sunny days, the pleasure gardens are bustling with visitors from Wolverhampton, strolling through the park, boating on the lake. My work has changed more to maintenance, which is less challenging. But … that leaves time for fun in town."

"And who goes with you?" Mother asked, motioning Joseph to sit at the table.

"Lads from Wergs, depending on who wants to go. The more the merrier."

"No girls?"

"No, not yet."

"What do you mean, 'not yet'?"

"There's this maid I like. I see her every day walking from building to building. We walk around the grounds together when we can. But she hasn't been to town with me."

"Where's she from?"

"She's from Wednesfield, the other side of Wolverhampton. Her name's Miss Done. Her family has a bakery and other businesses. When she has time off, she goes back home. It's then I realise I miss her."

"Well, well," his mother said, a sparkle in her eye.

A few weeks later in spring, Joseph set out across the estate to repair a gate. A pattern had emerged between himself and Miss Done. He knew her daily routine and geared his activities on the estate so that he'd encounter her. Approaching the hall, he saw her in the garden, cutting flowers. "Good morning, Miss Done. Are you enjoying the sun?"

She looked up, and with a slight tremble in her voice, said, "My mind is on other matters this morning."

He noticed her troubled face. "What's worrying you?"

"Someone has stolen things...."

"What things?"

They moved to the garden gate so they could stand closer together.

"A silver plate and jewellery belonging to the Misses are missing. They were away, and when they returned, they couldn't find them. The police have questioned us all. We feel we're being treated like thieves. It's horrible. I would never steal anything." Her bottom lip quivered.

"Then you've nothing to fear. They're questioning everyone because they have to."

"But it makes me look at the others as if they've done wrong," she said, wrinkling her brow. "I keep trying to remember when I last saw the silver plate, and what could have happened since. The police say only the staff would know where things are kept. But the door from the garden is never locked during the daytime. Any artful dodger could have sneaked in and gone up to the boudoir."

"You haven't done it, so you've nothing to fear. It's best to just do your work as usual," Joseph said, trying to calm her.

"But I see the Misses every day," she said, with a tremor in her voice. "I've told them how distressed I am that this has happened in their absence. I should've been more on the lookout to catch the thief." She fiddled with her bonnet. "They talk about it all the time, so I can't ignore it. I ... I think the butler, J ... James, may have something to do with it. While the Misses were gone, he ... he suddenly departed. Should I tell the p ... police he went without telling anyone he was leaving?"

"Has he not returned?"

"No, we ... we haven't seen him back yet."

"It's best to inform the Misses about his departure. Then it'll be off your mind."

"Thank you, Mr Handley."

"We've known each other a while, so it's time you call me Joseph."

"Joseph, please call me Mary Ann."

"Mary Ann, what a lovely name," he said. He found small-talk and flirting rather difficult. The more serious subject of the missing jewellery was easier for him to handle. "Don't worry about the theft. I'll try to see you tomorrow to hear if there's any news."

It was later than he thought when he arrived back at the workshop. Mr Davis looked down his nose at Joseph. "Have you been chatting again?"

"I'm sorry, I didn't realise it was so late."

"Who do you spend time with?"

"I've met a girl at the hall. We often see each other in passing."

"Rather like her, do you?"

"Yes, Mr Davis, she's my type."

"That's all very well, but I've noticed your work's been shoddy of late. That must change, Joseph. During working hours, you must concentrate on your job. You can speak to your girl afterwards."

Relieved he'd got off with a warning, he promised it wouldn't happen again, knowing he had the discipline to adhere to the rules.

The next day, he met Mary Ann again and asked how she was.

"Oh," she said, letting out a huge breath. "I feel so much better, thanks. I went straight to the Misses after we'd spoken and told them I had something to report about the theft. They looked at me as if I was going to own up. I felt awful, couldn't say a word, and cried. I managed to say 'James', and they told me to sit down and gave me some tea. Then I informed them about his disappearance. They said it was right of me to speak up. The police came later, and I told them the same. They're now searching for James. The jewellery had been in the safe, worth fifteen hundred pounds. Whoever stole it must've had keys."

"It makes me happy to see you with a smile on your face again,' Joseph said, clutching his hands. "But I'm less at ease today. Mr Davis gave me a warning. He claimed I was back late and that I shouldn't spend time chatting. He asked who it was."

"Did you tell him?"

"No, no! I said I'd make sure it doesn't happen again."

"I need to watch out, too. I don't want people to start talking."

"Have you got time this evening?"

"I can get away at about nine. I'll be in the kitchen garden," she said, with a playful smile.

Promptly at nine, Joseph leant against a tree opposite the garden gate. He kept himself behind the trunk, not wanting to be seen from the house. In his mind, he'd pictured her smile all through the afternoon, which had heightened his longing to see her. He envisioned a happy future for himself - a loving wife, a well-paid job, a family. Mother and Grandma would be proud of him. Perhaps word would reach his father, making him proud too, and making him want to seek contact; he wouldn't mind that.

Ten minutes passed, and no one emerged. The trees caused long shadows across the kitchen garden as the sun was setting. He waited another five, and then a figure appeared, moving towards the gate. His heart missed a beat; it was Mary Ann. He moved from behind the tree, still cautious not to be seen by anyone else, and raised his hand to beckon her. Almost running, she came towards him with a radiant look on her face. He grabbed her hand, taking her into the shadows. Branches brushed against them, leaves tickled their faces. It was like fleeing, a mixture of exhilaration drenched with a fear of being caught.

Once out of sight, they slowed their pace. His hands trembled. "Let's walk along the lake. I know somewhere we'll be out of view."

He kept his distance, although in his mind he was close to her. "We should do this more often. It's grand to be on our own, just to talk," he said.

Mary Ann pointed to the water. "Look at the ducks chasing each other."

"That drake is very determined. Oh, now she's flown away from him. Perhaps she's not ready to accept him," he said.

Watching the ducks, he thought he was in a similar situation. He wanted to touch Mary Ann, to hold her in his arms, but he couldn't have her, not yet. His strong Christian beliefs forbade close physical contact before marriage, but surely a hug could do no harm. Halfway round the lake, he tugged her from the path and behind a rhododendron bush and took hold of her hands.

"We shouldn't be doing this, you know. It's not right for me to be with you alone. People will gossip," she said.

Despite his religious beliefs, Joseph could not hold himself back. "Who cares if they talk?" he replied, with a soft voice. "Hmm, ... it's lovely to hold your hands and catch a whiff of your delicate scent." Their eyes locked, drawing them closer. Neither was in full control of themselves and their lips met briefly, and with uncertainty.

Pulling away, Mary Ann said, "This doesn't feel right. We shouldn't be doing this. Let's go back."

"But nobody can see us here! God has brought us together and surely he will approve!"

She raised her hand to his cheek, looked him in the eye with a smile, "I don't feel comfortable being here ... Someone will notice us. Let's make our way back."

Joseph dropped his hands to his sides and they went back out to the footpath, where he took a moment to scour both directions to ensure they were not about to be seen.

Strolling respectably towards the hall, Mary Ann told him about her afternoon. "The Misses assembled all the staff together. A letter had arrived saying a bag had been left at Wolverhampton station, addressed 'To be called for'. The police collected it. It was full of the stolen things. James hasn't returned, and they're still trying to find him. I'm so glad it's all over with," she said, holding her hands to her face and shaking her head.

But Joseph wasn't really listening. His mind was preoccupied with finding a way to spend more time with her. That evening, he wrote a letter.

Shrewsbury
Dear Grandma,
I hope this letter finds you well.
In my last letter, I said I would write more about Miss Done. Her name is Mary Ann. She is a fair young lady with a soft complexion and dark eyebrows. Her light blue eyes have a deep blue rim, which makes them special. When she smiles, her eyes seem to look into my soul and I feel at ease.
She's talkative and I like the way she speaks about her large family. She tells me little secrets about what's happening in Wergs Hall, about rows between the Perry sisters and their brother.
Mary Ann shows an interest in me, asks about my life in Coreley, and I tell her how indebted I am to you. We meet each other in church and in passing on the grounds. When I see her, I'm delighted. As she gets closer, her gentle smile fills my heart. A sensation I have never had before. I'd like to spend more time with her, but she's afraid of us being seen together. I hope to share my future with her, but perhaps I'm day-dreaming.
Love and affection, Joseph XX

Coreley
My Dearest Joseph,
Thanks for your letter. All is well here. I was pleased to read more about Mary Ann. You seem very excited about her. It sounds as if you're in love and I am so happy for you.
I can understand that it's difficult for you both to meet and be close in public. Perhaps a way out is to walk back to Wergs together after church

every Sunday. That would be permissible. It will give you time together. I
hope your dreams will come true.
Love and affection, Grandma xx

CHAPTER NINE
Bible lessons

1883

On Sunday mornings, most of those at Wergs attended the Parish Church in Tettenhall. During the service, Mary Ann and Joseph sat with their own groups, but afterwards he approached her without being too obvious. More often than not, they walked back together. The shortest way to the hall was the footpath past Danes Court and the cricket ground - a forty-minute walk. The sermons gave them something to talk about. They discovered that they both wished to be true to the scriptures, interpret them precisely, and be disciplined in applying the Christian ways. Joseph was serious about his beliefs and fully convicted. Not being comfortable at small-talk or flirting, the seriousness appealed to him, and he felt Mary Ann was happy with that too.

As an excuse to see each other, they attended bible lessons in the vestry each Wednesday evening. The Perry twins gave Mary Ann permission to have those evenings off, given the righteous purpose.

They were the only ones to walk back to the hall after bible class, so they dilly dallied in the evening light. They dared to hold hands while in the more secluded spots along the path, and kiss briefly as dusk settled.

One bible lesson, the theme was 'the importance of family — the God-ordained purpose in life'. The parson asked all present to talk about their families, and Mary Ann spoke about growing up in a large family with ten siblings, making her a firm believer in close relatives. Her father lived with her brother's family since her mother passed away seven years ago. She said next of kin was important because they would always care for each other. Her dream was to have a family and a home of her own.

Joseph spoke to the group about being raised by his grandmother, seeing his mother only twice a year, and lacking a father. He told the group that watching others with their families made him realise he'd missed the belonging and closeness of a family, including brothers and sisters. He was determined to have a proper family, a wife and children of his own. Not only because that is the way it should be, but also to attain eternal life through Jesus Christ.

That bible lesson triggered him to think about the father he never had. "I used to see other boys with their fathers, doing things together and being taught to use tools. But I've missed that," he told Mary Ann. "My step-grandfather, Mr Stinton, was too old; it wasn't the same."

Mary Ann moved closer and touched his shoulder. "I can't imagine not having a father and hardly ever seeing my mother. A father is so important for a son."

"I often wonder who he was, and whether I resemble him? What sort of father would he have been?"

"Why don't you find out? Your Mother surely knows."

"She has always been vague," he said, his eyes darting away. "How can I get her to tell me more?" he added, lost in thought. After a short silence, he looked up. "I've got an idea. My full name is Joseph Starie Handley. Where did the name Starie come from? Why did she give me that name? I intend to ask her to explain and I'll insist on a straightforward answer."

Soon after, he visited his mother. They had tea together and enjoyed small-talk before Joseph directed the conversation towards his goal.

"I was thinking the other day, why did you give me the name Starie?"

"I liked the name because it was unusual," his mother replied, adjusting her apron.

He sensed there was more. "Has it something to do with my actual father?"

"Joseph, I'm sorry I haven't told you about him earlier. I was his cook. He was very nice to me just after my father died. But something nasty occurred between us." She wrung her hands together. "And I found myself with child, expecting you." Her eyes focussed on his. "I was afraid I couldn't raise you if I was unmarried. So I went to tell him I was with child. He was furious and refused to wed me. We've had no contact since. I wanted you to know later in life who your father was, that's why I gave you his name."

"Is it Starie, then?"

"Yes, John Starie. He's on Hemm Farm in Coreley."

Joseph's mouth fell open. "All the time I lived with Grandma, my father was just the other side of Coreley!" He was dumbstruck and turned away, covered his eyes. He stood up, knocking his teacup to the floor.

"Oh Joseph, I *am* sorry!"

"I can't believe it," he said, turning to look at his mother as if to check she was really telling him the truth. "He must know who I am and have seen me going to church. He knows about me and I know *nothing* about him!"

"I didn't want you to contact him because I was afraid he'd reject you. That would have been painful for us both."

"If he denied being my father, how can you be sure?"

His mother shook her head in frustration. "I know for certain! I had *no* union with other men."

Joseph regretted not pursuing his father's identity earlier. "What sort of man is he?"

"He's a quiet person. Doesn't mix much with other people, stays on his farm. He married, but they have no children."

An empty sensation grew in the pit of his stomach and his throat became dry. He hadn't prepared himself for the news that his father may reject him.

He travelled back to Wergs, determined to find out more about his father. The first chance he met Mary Ann, he told her everything his mother had said. "I want to meet him, to know what he's like," Joseph said, squinting his eyes as if to imagine John Starie.

"I can understand you're curious, Joseph. But have you thought about his reaction? If he refuses to accept he's your father, what will you gain from meeting him?"

"He could be glad to see me. Perhaps he'll be happy to get to know his son, especially as he's without children."

"If he had wanted to have contact, surely he would have approached you himself?"

"Maybe, but my mother didn't want any contact. When I said I'd like to meet him, she said 'I can't stop you from doing that. Just don't involve me'. If I don't contact him, I'll never know who he was."

"What are you hoping to gain?"

"A father, and more importantly, a grandfather for my children."

"Are you hoping to inherit the farm?"

The question irritated Joseph. "No, why are you saying that? You know I'm not interested in farming."

"You could sell off some of the farmland and set up a workshop," Mary Ann suggested.

Joseph shook his head and looked away.

"What will you say when you meet him?"

"I'll pretend I'm looking for work," he said, still avoiding her eyes.

"At what point will you make yourself known to him, Joseph?"

Joseph swallowed and cleared his throat. "I don't know, maybe I won't, maybe I will."

The next opportunity Joseph had, he travelled to Coreley to find his father. The trap dropped him at St Peter's Church where he asked the warden the way to Hemm Farm. "Just follow the path from the back of the graveyard, keep going without taking any side paths, and it'll take you there."

Joe followed his directions. The closer he got, the more unsure he became. He pressed his fingertips against his brow in an attempt to alleviate a sudden headache. He wondered what to say and how the conversation would develop. Would he be welcome? Recognised? Sent away?

He arrived at the farm, strode to the farmhouse door, and knocked. A woman opened.

"Good afternoon. Can I speak to Mr Starie please, missus?"

"I know you, you're Ann Handley's son. You'll find Mr Starie over there in the cowshed."

Being immediately acknowledged took Joseph aback. He retreated a few steps, uncertain what to say or do. He hadn't expected to be recognised at first sight. Lumbering across the yard to the shed, doubtfulness flitted across his mind. He peered through the door. In the dim light, he could make out a man piling up straw with a hayfork. The farmer looked up and turned towards him.

"Hello young man. How can I help you?"

"I'm looking for work, sir," Joseph said, standing in the doorway, clasping his hands.

The farmer stood his fork against the wall, and came forward into the light, his back bent.

"Oh, now I see who you are. You're Joseph Handley. Looking for a job, are you?"

Joseph hesitated, not sure what to make of the situation, shifting his weight from one foot to the other. He took control of himself, triggered by an unconscious feeling that the man's reaction ignored their relationship.

"Well, as you know my name, may I ask whether you know my second name?"

"Has your mother told you about me?"

"Yes, she has. I asked her about my Starie name, and she told me you're my father."

"Whether or not I'm your father, you are welcome to view me as such, Joseph."

Joseph observed a likeness in the man's build and movements, leaving him in no doubt the man truly was his father. "Thank you, Mr Starie. It seems queer to call you 'father' as we've never met. You're a stranger to me. Why haven't you ever contacted me?"

"Your mother decided to go her own way and wanted no further contact," Mr Starie said, scratching his beard and keeping his distance.

"But didn't you feel the need to see me?" Joseph said, in a higher tone of voice, his body trembling with nerves.

The man that was his father just stared at the floor and scratched his beard again.

"Do you want work, or not?" Mr Starie said, in an agitated tone, steadying himself against the doorpost.

Joseph felt no warmth, but a void opening up inside him, filling him with the emptiness of being neglected.

"You should have given me more than work. You should have been a father. Why didn't you care?" Joseph said, with a furrowed brow, stepping backwards.

Mr Starie stared at the floor again. Joseph waved his arms out of hopelessness, anger swelling up within him.

"You show no interest in me, so I will have nothing more to do with you," he said, striding out, expecting to never return.

The next Wednesday evening, as Joseph and Mary Ann walked back to Wergs, he told her about the confrontation with his father. She said he had done well to speak to him, that he would have regretted it later if he hadn't. She was sorry he hadn't received a warm welcome and hoped that, when the time was right, they would meet in a more congenial setting.

"Do you know what dawned on me this evening?"

"Tell me, Joseph."

"The bible is clear. God provides man and wife with a child, expecting them to look after the child. Mr Starie hasn't heeded God's word. My mother is a believer, and this man is truly not. They were too different to bring me up in God's name, so He put my mother on another path, perhaps for my best will."

CHAPTER TEN

Proposal

1883

It was a fine evening when Joseph and Mary Ann returned from bible class. Shadows cast behind them as they strolled past the fishpond on Wergs Hall grounds. Although it was called a pond, its size was more like a small lake. At the far end, they came to a copse. He coaxed her to duck under the branches and disappear amongst the trees. Looking back, and concluding that no one could see them, she followed with only the slightest hesitation. He took hold of her smooth hands and felt their warmth.

At first, they just stood that way, focussing on each other's eyes, slowly gravitating towards each other. A leafy branch sprung between their faces. They laughed, trying to push it away. Joseph searched her face, looking for the slightest indication as to whether she would let him go further. He gave her a quick kiss; she slightly tilted her head back. A longer kiss followed, and it felt right. His body throbbed from head to toe. He pined for more, but knew to take it slowly. He didn't want to lose her.

"I love you," Joseph professed, as they stood there holding each other, "and I believe you're not indifferent to me."

"I certainly like you a great deal," was Mary Ann's cautious reply.

After a pause, he proclaimed, "We must get married. I'm longing to be with you for the rest of my life."

"I'm very fond of you ... But, you haven't proposed to me yet."

"Well . . . may I propose to you now?"

"I think it would be the right moment... And to spare you any discontent, I think it fair to say I'm willing to accept you, should you ask me."

"Mary Ann!"

"Yes, what are you about to say to me?"

Joseph played along. "You know what I'm about to say to you."

Her cheeks blushed. "Well, I'm curious to hear it."

He went on his knees, pushing some branches to one side. He took her right hand and kissed it, "Mary Ann, will you marry me?"

"I'd love to marry you, Joseph."

He stood up. She gave him a kiss on each cheek. They embraced and kissed each other's lips. He checked himself and slowly pulled back, not wanting to go too far, not wanting to run the risk of being pushed back by her. But she moved towards him, and they kissed again, longer this time.

"I must return to my evening jobs before the Misses retire." She removed herself from him. "Be careful no one sees us on the way back."

Joseph held on to her hand. "Let's get engaged at the earliest opportunity, then we can be seen together."

They ducked under the branches and left the copse. As they walked along the lake's edge, dusk was falling and Mary Ann said, "We'll go to Wednesfield soon. I'd like you to meet my family."

They planned a day off to visit her father at brother Henry's house. The tram took them from Tettenhall to Wolverhampton market, where they waited for a carriage to Wednesfield. On arrival, Mary Ann's sister-in-law, Mary, welcomed them. Mr Done sat in a chair near the window where he had a view to the cross-roads in front of the house. His grey head turned towards Joseph, and with a smile he said, "Good morning, Mr Handley."

Joseph observed a man who appeared tired in his old age but had clear eyes. He wore a white shirt, black waistcoat and jacket, and grey trousers. Mr Done pointed to the opposite chair, and Joseph understood he may sit down. Mary and Mary Ann withdrew to the kitchen to allow the two men to talk in private.

"Tell me about yourself, Joseph," Mr Done said, lighting his pipe with a match, and sucking on the mouthpiece.

Joseph spoke about his love for woodwork and the jobs he did at Wergs. He spoke briefly about his schooling and upbringing in Coreley, without mentioning his parents or living with his grandmother. A carpenter himself, Mr Done asked about Joseph's work, particularly what he would like to do in the future.

"I enjoy carving wood in intricate patterns. To do that, I need to find a job elsewhere. At Wergs we're mostly repairing carts, gates, fences — heavy-duty outdoor stuff."

Mr Done exhaled smoke. "There's more money in carving. Your future will be bright if you can get into that business." He drew on his pipe again. "What does your father do?"

"He's a farmer." Joseph thought it best to tell the truth. "My parents never married, and I grew up with my grandmother."

"Have you no contact with your father?"

"Very little."

"I'm sorry to hear that."

A silence fell, Joseph not knowing what to say next.

Mary came in with tea and biscuits, followed by Mary Ann who sat down next to her father, and asked how he was. "Old soldiers never die, they simply fade away," he replied.

Mary Ann turned to Joseph. "Father never complains. He says he's lucky to be with Henry and Mary, and doesn't want to be a nuisance." She went on to chat about their journey, the weather, and Mary's family. Later Henry arrived and joined the conversation, saying he had been to a farm to make rabbit traps. The rabbits had been nibbling too many crops, so the farmer wanted to catch some to sell to the butcher. Mary called out to their four-year-old son, asking him to come in. He ran in and jumped on his grandfather's lap. The loving atmosphere struck Joseph; he was instantly at ease with Mary Ann's folk. As a boy, he'd not had the warmth of a family like this.

After church a few weeks later, Joseph and Mary Ann were walking back to Wergs Hall, when he said, "I must talk to your father about us engaging and ask his permission to marry you."

"I'm sure he'll agree. I think he likes you."

"I want his blessing as soon as possible. We can then get engaged, and be together in public. I'm thrilled about the prospect of having more time with you."

"But I've not yet met your mother. Before we engage, I should make her acquaintance."

"You're right," he said. "Let's meet her in Coreley, then you can see Grandma, and the places where I lived as a boy."

The first part of their journey to Coreley was the train to Ludlow. While they were watching the countryside pass by, Joseph extracted a piece of paper from his jacket pocket. "Let me read you a poem that I found the other day. It's by John Holland, and called *Hopes of Matrimony.*"

> "How fair is home, in fancy's pictured theme,
> In wedded life, in love's romantic dream!
> Thence springs each hope, there every spring returns,
> Pure as the flame that upward heavenward burns;
> There sits the wife, whose radiant smile is given -

The daily sun of the domestic heaven;
And when calm evening sheds a secret power,
Her looks of love imparadise the hour;
While children round, a beauteous train, appear,
Attendant stars, revolving in her sphere."

Mary Ann took his hand. "That's lovely, Joseph. You paint a wonderful picture of the life we'll have together."

He wanted to kiss her but felt inhibited with other passengers looking. Instead, he pointed out the lush countryside, dotted with farms. She spoke about how different it was to the smokey industrial area around Wolverhampton, with its coal mines and factories. From Ludlow the trap took them along lanes with high hedgerows, up and down low hills, until they arrived at the tiny village. They passed his old school, the church, and the brook where he used to catch minnows and newts.

At Grandma's, they found Mother accompanying her at the kitchen table. Joseph introduced Mary Ann, and pleasantries were exchanged.

"It's good to see you two," Grandma said. "I've heard a lot about you, Mary Ann. How do you like your tea?"

"With sugar please, Mrs Stinton."

Mother took the sugar pot from the cupboard and poured tea. "How was your journey?"

"It was lovely to pass through the countryside around here. The light is so bright."

"Joseph told me you're from Wednesfield."

Mary Ann sat up straight. "That's right. Before my mother passed away, we lived on the High Street, opposite the church. I liked it there, we knew everyone. It's changed now though, busier since they built the chocolate factory and ironworks on the canal. Strangers have come to the village."

"How sad you've lost your mother. Was it long ago?"

"God called Mother to Him about seven years ago. She was only fifty-seven. She'd been ill for some time, but it was still a great shock, especially for my father. He's since moved in with my brother. I admire them for it."

"What's it like working at Wergs Hall?" Mother asked.

"I'm a housemaid for the Perry sisters. They're friendly, but quite demanding. I'm the youngest one, so I do things like looking after their clothes and tidying their rooms. I live in the hall and get called on at all hours of the day and night."

Joseph spoke about how they met at bible lessons, and that they'd discovered they both had the same beliefs, taking the scriptures seriously.

Grandma passed the sugar to Mary Ann. "I'm glad to hear that. It's so important to have a full understanding of the bible."

"The wise words of the scriptures are a guide for our lives," Joseph said.

"Are you thinking of any wise words in particular?" Mother asked.

Joseph looked at Mary Ann with a sparkle in his eye, and responded, "Marriages are made in heaven." The others laughed. "We've been seeing each other for quite a while now, and, ... the glorious news is ..... we want to be engaged!"

The faces of the two older women lit up with broad smiles. They both stood up and hugged the young couple.

"You'll make a fine match," Grandma said, joyfully.

Mother warmed to Mary Ann. "And I'll have a daughter!"

Joseph reached out to touch Mary Ann's arm. "We're so happy. We believe God has brought us together and we want to fulfil his wish to start a family. Soon, I'll ask Mr Done to give his permission, and we'll make plans."

"Once we're married, we can't stay at Wergs, so we must find somewhere else to live and work," Mary Ann added.

"Perhaps Shrewsbury would be a good place to come to," Mother suggested. "It's a thriving town now that the railways are here."

Joseph turned to Mary Ann. "I'd thought of that too. There must be job opportunities for me there. We should go to look around."

Mary Ann turned to Mother. "I've never been there before. I'd like to see where you work, Mrs Handley."

"Oh, please call me Mother."

Joseph's grandmother, rubbing her hands together, added, "Please call me Grandma."

On the journey back to Wergs, Joseph and Mary Ann reflected on the day.

"Your grandmother is very supportive — I like her," said Mary Ann.

"She's always encouraged me — just like a proper mother§."

"Your mother suggested we move to Shrewsbury. What's it like there?" Mary Ann asked.

"It's smaller than Wolverhampton and less industrial. I'm partial to it. There's a railway works, a prison, a barracks, lots of shops. Mother lives in a house near the abbey. River Severn splits the town in two."

She took Joseph's hand. "You must take me there to explore."

CHAPTER ELEVEN
A Party

1883

Joseph and Mary Ann went to Wednesfield, to Henry's house, so that he could ask Mr Done for permission to marry his daughter. Her father was in his usual chair, reading the newspaper. He bade them good morning and signalled Joseph to take a seat. Mary Ann gave her father a kiss before retreating to the kitchen with sister-in-law, Mary.

Mr Done put his newspaper down. "There's been an outbreak of swine fever. Farmers in infected areas can't move their beasts. It's a troublesome time for them."

Joseph made himself comfortable in the chair. "I've heard that they must slaughter affected swine. I'm glad I'm not a farmer, I'd hate to see my animals die."

Mr Done continued commenting on the news, repeating himself. Joseph kept silent, avoiding further conversation on that topic.

"Mr Done," Joseph said, eventually, waiting for Mr Done's full attention. "Mary Ann and I have been acquainted for a while now."

"Yes, so she told me. She seems fond of you."

"We're very suited to each other. I've saved some money, and my prospects as a carpenter look good. I'm convinced I'm a man worthy of Mary Ann, so I would like to ask for her hand in marriage." Joseph shifted in his chair.

Mr Done looked him straight in the eyes. "Have you proposed to her yet?"

Joseph sat up straight. "Yes, I have, and she's accepted, pending your approval, sir."

"Where do you plan to live together?"

"We can't stay in Wergs. We'll give up our jobs there, and I'll find other work and a suitable home. Once we can say we're engaged, it'll be easier for us to meet and make plans. May our marriage receive your permission, sir?"

"Well, as a carpenter, you'll be sure of work. You seem to be a sensible young man. Yes, you have my blessing. Look after my daughter and may God bless you both with a family."

Back at Wergs, Joseph and Mary Ann told their master and mistresses about their wedding engagement. Mr Davis was not at all surprised. Mary Ann had often mentioned to Misses Perry that there was a man in her life, and spoken about marriage. They expressed their congratulations when she revealed his name, but a sigh followed as they admitted it was a pity to lose her as a housemaid. The news soon spread and workmates wished them well.

Grandma had reminded Joseph to find a suitable ring, and so he took the horse-drawn tram into Wolverhampton. He didn't know what to choose; diamonds were too expensive, and he was saving for their new home. Anyway, he thought Mary Ann would consider them an unjustifiable expense. After visiting two shops, his choice was a silver ring with a pink gemstone. He didn't buy it straightaway, but wrote to Grandma, describing the ring and asking her advice. She replied that pink was a romantic colour, so he purchased it and had their initials and the engagement date engraved inside.

They planned the engagement party for a summer Sunday, but when the day arrived, it was overcast. Mr Done wanted his entire family to have dinner together, but Mary had talked him out of it as it wasn't practical with so many children and grandchildren. It would have meant having nearly fifty people. Instead, they agreed to have a picnic on the common ground opposite their house, with everyone bringing some food.

Henry rigged up a stall and table, sheltered by some canvassing. Mary laid a colourful tablecloth and set out food and drink. Henry brought chairs over for the celebrating couple and the older guests. They had everything ready, but then had to stay under the canvas when a rain shower came down.

Joseph and Mary Ann walked to Heath Town station to greet his mother, Grandma and Aunty Fanny, his mother's sister. Grandma had said she wouldn't miss the engagement for anything. At seventy-three, she depended on Aunty Fanny's assistance on the journey from Coreley. Umbrellas up, they walked the short distance to the house where Joseph introduced them to Mr Done. He received them with a warm welcome, and when the rain stopped they all crossed the road for their picnic.

Joseph was well-dressed, as usual, sporting a black suit, white shirt, and black bow tie. Mary Ann had chosen a billowy white dress with a lace bodice, her white bonnet adorned with light blue ribbons.

As guests arrived, they presented flowers and gifts to Mary Ann and added food to the table. Blankets were laid down on the damp grass. When everyone was present, Henry tapped a glass.

"May I have your attention, please? Will you all gather round?" he said, at the top of his voice. "Thank you for coming this afternoon." He placed his arm on Joseph's shoulder. "Let me introduce you to this fine gentleman, Mr Joseph Handley. Mary Ann met Joseph at Wergs, and I think I can state they've been seeing quite a lot of each other recently. They say, 'a carpenter is known for his chips'. Have you had a good look at Joseph's chips, Mary Ann?"

Mary Ann bowed her head to hide her reddening face, as the guests laughed, clapped and whistled.

"Let's also welcome the bridegroom's mother, Mrs Handley, his grandmother, Mrs Stinton, and his Aunty Fanny." The women tilted their heads and mouthed 'thank you'. Glasses were raised in a convivial gesture.

"Now, my father would like to say a few words."

Mr Done rose from his chair, keeping one hand on the back to steady himself.

"Good afternoon, my dears. This will be a day to remember, for it is a beginning. The beginning of a new chapter for Mary Ann and Joseph. They believe in each other and in the possibility of love. This afternoon is the announcement to the world for the feelings they have long held. They've decided to engage in marriage, and I fully support them."

He raised his glass, "May the Lord bless them."

Applause and laughter rose from the crowd, and Mr Done sat down.

Henry turned to Joseph, who took a step forward and spoke with confidence. "Thank you for being here on this very special day for Mary Ann and me. Thanks especially to Henry and Mary for organising this lovely picnic. My sincere gratitude goes to you, Mr Done, sir, for allowing me to be betrothed to your daughter. I must have done something right to have the privilege." He took an item from his pocket and turned to his bride-to-be. "Mary Ann, we feel we know each other well. Our bible studies have brought us closer together and we trust that the Lord gives us his blessing. It's in his glorification that I offer you this ring as a symbol of our love and devotedness." He lifted her left hand and slid the pink ring over her finger. They kissed, and applause and laughter filled his ears.

Henry asked everyone to join in prayer. "Dear Lord. We come to you with thanksgiving as we celebrate the engagement of Joseph and Mary Ann. We praise you for the time they shared together, to show the love they have for each other, and we call on you to help it grow. As they plan for this new direction in their lives, provide them the ability to communicate and to enjoy. Give them the grace to value each other's dreams. Enable them to form a strong, righteous bond and bless them with Your loving presence. Amen."

He then raised a toast to Mary Ann and Joseph, before inviting everyone to take something to eat and drink.

Joseph mingled amongst the Done men who cracked light-hearted jokes about him giving up his freedom and being encapsulated by their family. He easily engaged in conversations as if he'd been a member of this family his entire life. He took the opportunity to ask Mary Ann's brothers about job opportunities. James ran a grocers' shop and helped his brother Benjamin in his bakery. Not being familiar with the carpentry business, they were of little assistance to Joseph. Henry and Thomas were equally of little benefit. They spoke about how they bashed metal to assemble traps to kill vermin, catch animals for their fur, or discourage poachers. It surprised Joseph to learn that trap-making was a distinctive industry in Wednesfield, products even being exported. Frederic was a maker of padlocks and worked in the ironworks. Joseph finally had a chat with John, a wheelwright. They had a lengthy talk about carpentry jobs, but Joseph concluded most of the work was in factories, which didn't appeal to him. At Wergs he frequently worked outside, and he felt that he would hate the confinement of a factory.

Mary Ann and Joseph were quizzed about their plans. "Where are you going to marry? Where will you go to live? Have you settled a date for the wedding? Have you found a home?"

"We still have to make plans," Mary Ann answered. "We're not in a hurry. I'm sure we'll stay in the Wolverhampton area, so that we're near you all."

Children were running around, playing games, and getting muddy, but nobody worried. It was an enjoyable occasion.

When the time came to leave, Joseph shook hands with everyone. He felt accepted by the Dones and looked forward to being part of a large family. He took Mary Ann's hand, and they walked to the station with Mother, Grandma, and Aunty Fanny. Mother spoke a few parting words just before boarding the train. "It's been a lovely afternoon, Mary Ann. My son is fortunate to find such a delightful lady. You come from a close-knit, loving family - you're lucky. Bye for now."

The couple boarded the carriage back to Tettenhall, entwining hands, exchanging stories about the day. Mary Ann looked at her hand in his. "I love the ring. It has such a warm shine. I'm proud of it. Thank you." She gave him a kiss.

In bed that evening, Joseph reflected on his conversations with the brothers. Fully aware that Mary Ann preferred to live close to her family, he wanted to find a decent job near Wednesfield, but now he had doubts about finding a suitable one. It looked as if he would either have to work in a factory, or move away to a job that suited him more. The dilemma kept him awake.

CHAPTER TWELVE
Dilemmas

1883

Joseph forged ahead with his work on Wergs Hall estate. He was thankful Mr Davis gave him a wide range of jobs, mainly to do with the pleasure gardens, meaning he was outside plenty. He saw Mary Ann as often as they could allow themselves to be seen in public. But they kept their distance, not holding hands or kissing. The other workers noticed how regularly they were together and made jokes about love-birds.

After their bible lessons on Wednesday evenings, when sure to be out of sight, they flirted. Joseph let go of some of his inhibitions. He took hold of her, pulling her against him with his hands on her buttocks, rocking her as they kissed. He slipped his right hand under her blouse, searching for her round curves. His heart raced, causing a light-headedness.

Other Wednesday evenings, they spent more time talking, often about where to settle after their marriage. Joseph reminded her of what her brother had said — in Wolverhampton there was little work for carpenters other than in the factories. He declared he didn't like the prospect of working in a noisy, dirty place. Mary Ann understood and suggested going to explore Shrewsbury, combining a visit to Mother.

They took the train, walked to the house on Abbey Foregate, and were shown through to the kitchen.

"You look well, Mother. How are you?" Joseph said.

"I'm fine, thank you. Sit yourselves down and I'll first make some tea. I've got some news to tell you."

Joseph and Mary Ann looked at each other with raised eyebrows.

Mother sat down and put tea leaves in the teapot. "I've been thinking about my future, that I'm forty-six and still work for a mistress. I enjoy cooking, you know I do, and the company of the maids, but it's time I had a home of my own. I'd prefer to live in the countryside again, be closer to Coreley, closer to Grandma."

"She'd love you to be near," Joseph said.

Mother fidgeted with her apron. "Perhaps you remember Grandma going to the grocer's shop in Doddington? It's next to the church. A few months ago, she asked me to accompany her to carry the shopping, and we got chatting with the grocer, Mr Dolphin. He's been lonely since his wife passed away a year ago. He looks after the store on his own, but I could tell it's getting too much for him."

She paused. Joseph scratched his head, glanced at Mary Ann, but remained silent.

Mother continued, "Mr Dolphin's a pleasant man, very friendly. He has the shop in good order but could do with some help."

Joseph shifted in his chair. "Are you thinking of marrying him?"

"Yes, I am. He's only three years older than me. We're both healthy, so we can manage the shop together. … I'd like that."

Joseph saw his mother hesitate, and he glanced at Mary Ann, who remained quiet.

"It'll be a tremendous change for me to live with someone for the first time in my life. We'll both have to adjust," his mother added.

"You'll be leaving Shrewsbury then?"

"It's a possibility. I don't want you to decide to move here to be near me, and then find I'm moving to Doddington."

Joseph tilted his chin down and frowned. "One reason for us to come to Shrewsbury was because you're here."

Mary Ann quickly said, "Mrs Handley, I understand you want to start a life of your own. I'm happy for you. I know what it's like to look forward to your own home. It's an exciting time."

Joseph had had enough of this conversation. He wasn't sure what to say because the news upset him. He loathed the thought of having a fatherly newcomer in his life.

Impatient to get on with what he had intended, he said, "We've come to Shrewsbury to see whether we'd like to live here."

"There's a new housing estate across the railway line: Cherry Orchard. Perhaps it's worth having a look," Mother said. "Otherwise, try the area near the barracks. The rent will be lower there."

After some further talk about opportunities in town, Joseph and Mary Ann took their leave to walk around.

Travelling back to Wergs, they weighed up their thoughts about living in Shrewsbury.

Mary Ann said, "I like Shrewsbury. It's much cleaner than Wolverhampton, and the new homes they're building are spacious."

"It's a good place to settle, and I liked it when I was an apprentice," Joseph agreed. "With the railways growing fast, I can surely find a job at the railway works. There's a lot of woodwork in the carriages. ... I'd expected you would prefer to live near your clan."

"That's what I always thought, too. But I see Shrewsbury is a better place to raise a family. I think we should consider it."

"Rent may be higher. We need to save more money for a good start wherever that may be. Money makes the mare go, you know."

"I like the way you always have a fitting expression. Who did you learn them from?"

"Some from Grandma, most from the carpenter."

A couple of months later, a letter arrived for Joseph. The postmark was Shrewsbury, hence from his mother, someone writing on her behalf. He opened it.

Shrewsbury
Dear Joseph,
I hope this note finds you well. Thanks for last week's letter and your thoughts about where you want to set up home. As you know, I have been seeing Mr Dolphin. He's been here a couple of times. We get along very well together and have decided to marry. I'm looking forward to a change in life.

Joseph noticed Mr Davis enter the hall, but didn't look up, not wanting to be disturbed.

"Good evening, Joseph. What's up?"

Joseph's shoulders slumped. "My mother's getting married to a grocer."

"Are you not happy for her?"

"I suppose I should be, but I don't know the man. Mother will leave Shrewsbury. I wanted to move there, partly because she was there too. I'd have liked her to stay close, so that she could be a grandma for our children."

"Why not meet the bridegroom-to-be? Perhaps you'll get on easily and he can be a grandpa for your family."

Joseph pushed up his sleeves, thinking about what Mr Davis had said. "He's a complication, but I suppose I'll have to deal with him for Mother's sake."

Mr Davis carried on to the kitchen, and Joseph continued reading the letter.

As you've not met Mr Dolphin, I would be delighted if you can come to make his acquaintance in Shrewsbury a week on Sunday. I think you should meet before we marry in May. Please bring Mary Ann with you, if it is agreeable.

Love, Your affectionate Mother

The next day was a Wednesday, and Joseph met Mary Ann at the bible lesson. Afterwards, they walked back to Wergs and he let her read the letter.

"Well, we knew this would happen. Let's make it a happy time for your mother," Mary Ann said.

"Pfff … I have little interest in getting acquainted with this Mr Dolphin." It was as if he couldn't help reacting to Mary Ann's positivity. "I thought we were going to settle in Shrewsbury, but now I feel at a loss."

"Well, let's live in Wolverhampton then. At least my family will be close. Perhaps they can assist you to find other work."

"I'd hate to depend on your family. I can manage on my own, with God's help." An inner voice said: Show them you're good enough to lead your wife. It's your responsibility as a husband to provide a home and an income. Don't come across as weak by asking for help. Trust in God and follow his path.

"I'm not saying we should depend upon my family," said Mary Ann. "I'm only saying let's explore opportunities in Wolverhampton a little more."

Joseph inhaled deeply. "You agreed Shrewsbury would be much better for bringing up a family."

"We hadn't decided that at all!" she scowled.

He raised his voice, almost shouting, "You said you liked Shrewsbury!"

"That's not the same as d … deciding," she stuttered. "You're just doing what *you* want. How could you?"

"I'm doing what's best for *both* of us," Joseph said, looking away. "If I have decent work and pay, we'll have a better house. Isn't that what you'd like?"

"I want to have a *say* in what you decide, don't you understand?"

"But you *did* have a say!" he said, moving away, kicking a stone. He heard her whimpering and blowing her nose, but he was determined not to concede. He needed her to accept his authority and the decisions he made.

"I want a say!" she repeated.

He calmed himself, doing his best to keep his temper.

Mary Ann lowered her voice. "Let's go to Shrewsbury, as Mother asks. Perhaps you'll change your mind."

"Alright," said Joseph, shrugging.

They went to Shrewsbury on the next Sunday. On their way from the station to his mother's, they stopped in the red-brick abbey. A service had started, so they stayed. The sermon was about opening up, letting others into your life to expand your circle, accepting them as who they are. He prayed to the Lord to grant him the strength and courage to be his own man.

After the service, they walked to 159 Abbey Foregate and went to the back door. Mother welcomed them with hugs and kisses. Mr Dolphin stood up and shook hands, greeting them with a soft voice. Joseph perceived him to be a modest man, not a person who would obstruct him. They had tea and exchanged pleasantries, but Joseph was impatient.

He had an urge to be on his own. "Mary Ann, I'm going to the carriage works, to learn if it's a place where I'd like to work."

"I'll stay here. See you when you come back."

The railway works was around the corner. A big nameplate spanned the entrance: Midland Railway Carriage and Wagon Co. The main gate was closed as it was a Sunday. A guard spotted him peering through, and came over to speak to him. Joseph explained he was looking for work.

The man introduced himself. "I'm the foreman, Mr Briggs."

"Good morning, Joseph Handley. I'm a carpenter. I'm interested to know whether there's work for me here."

"There certainly could be," Mr Briggs replied. "You're lucky I happen to be on site, as it's a Sunday. Let me show you round."

Joseph followed Mr Briggs into a large workshop. The foreman pointed. "That's a two-horse tramcar for Glasgow Corporation."

Joseph observed they mostly made it of metal, except for the wooden seats.

"Over here is a railway carriage that's nearly complete," the foreman said, with a proud expression on his face. "Would you like to look inside?"

Joseph climbed up and saw it was a First Class Dining Car. His heart warmed to the luxurious fittings and decorations, the intricate woodwork in the arms of the seats. He let his finger follow the lines in the carving. He thanked the foreman, saying he would return when he had definite plans to move to Shrewsbury.

Back at his mother's, he spoke enthusiastically about his visit to the carriage works, explaining the detail of the carving in the partition walls.

"It sounds just the place for you," Mother said, encouragingly. "You've always wanted to carve."

"I told them I'm definitely interested in working for them, and will get back to them soon."

"It's a splendid company to work for," Mr Dolphin said. "They employ a lot of men throughout the Midlands. Railways are a growing business, so you'll be sure of employment."

Joseph smiled. "That's what I think. The town seems to thrive because of the railway."

Mary Ann was silent.

Mother turned to her. "How are your bible lessons going?"

"We're always keen to go, aren't we?" she said, looking towards Joseph. "We never miss a lesson. The stories in the bible give us a better understanding of how God expects us to live our lives."

"Mr Dolphin is an evangelist and preaches regularly," Mother revealed. "When I'm in Doddington, I listen to you, don't I?" she added, turning towards him.

"I believe in being true to the bible, just like you two," Mr Dolphin said, seizing the opportunity. "We believe that salvation can only be attained through faith in Jesus. Come to Doddington soon and join us in church."

Joseph didn't want to start a discussion about how to interpret the bible. "I'd love to see Doddington and Coreley again. It's been a while since I was there. The countryside is beautiful." Looking at Mary Ann, he said, "We need to go soon - to be sure to have time to look around town."

They had a bite to eat and then departed.

Mary Ann told Joseph what she'd heard while he was out, "They'll marry here in Shrewsbury."

"Why here? There's no family here."

"She wants her mistress and workmates to attend. Mr Dolphin doesn't mind. It'll be in the church, opposite the abbey."

"That's the Holy Cross Parish Church. I'll point it out when we pass it."

Before crossing the bridge over the River Severn, they saw the stone church with red brick around the windows. "This isn't a bad area to live. It's not in the centre of town so the rent will be lower. It's almost next to the railway works too. I'm sure we'll find a place to live here," he said, confidently.

Mary Ann took hold of his hand. "When are we going to get married?"

"It won't be long now before I've saved enough," Joseph said, wanting to avoid further discussion. He sensed that Mary Ann wanted more physical contact, but he felt shy and inhibited. The scriptures were clear about not physically interacting before marriage. He blamed his shyness on the fact that he'd grown up without a father and had no role model. In his deepest thoughts he longed to be closer and to feel her soft skin.

CHAPTER THIRTEEN

A Wedding and a Funeral

1885

Birds were singing on a morning in May when Joseph and Mary Ann made their way to Shrewsbury to attend his mother's wedding. Arriving at the church, they looked for Grandma, but she couldn't be found.

"There's nobody here I recognise. They're all strangers. It's as if we're in the wrong congregation," he whispered. "Oh, now I see someone who works with Mother."

Mother and Mr Dolphin walked down the aisle. It was a brief service with four witnesses, his mother's mistress Mrs Juson, the parlourmaid Miss Wells, the housemaid Miss Juckes, and Mr Reynolds, Mr Dolphin's neighbour.

After the ceremony, Joseph went to his mother with outstretched arms and gave her a generous hug. "You look wonderful, Mother. You look so happy."

Turning slowly to Mr Dolphin, Joseph shook his hand. "Congratulations. I'm sure you're going to make a good pair working in the shop together. Mother is looking forward to the change."

He looked back to Mother. "I'd expected Grandma to be here too."

"She was too poorly to travel."

"I didn't know she was ill."

"It's only recently she's been under the weather. She couldn't make the effort." She rubbed Joseph's coat sleeve.

Miss Wells approached Joseph's mother with a present, gave her a hug, and said: "Mary Ann, I'll miss you terribly. You've been such a wonderful friend, and I've enjoyed our time together. As a token of my friendship, please accept this bible. Take care and be happy."

On their journey back to Wergs, Joseph remarked on the ceremony. "It was odd to be there with people we weren't acquainted with."

"Don't forget they're in a different place in their lives because Mr Dolphin was married before," Mary Ann said. "I think they've married out of convenience, more than out of love. I can understand your mother not wanting a big ceremony. Besides, who would they invite?"

"I was sad that Grandma wasn't able to come."

"Why not?"

"Mother said she's poorly. I didn't know. I haven't visited her for a long time ... We must go to her soon."

"On our way to Coreley, we could pop in to Doddington to see your mother."

"We'll see," he said.

1886

The new year brought the death of Mary Ann's father, Mr Done. Joseph accompanied her to the funeral and did his best to comfort her. In the weeks that followed, she seemed preoccupied, not her usual self. She skipped bible lessons, and when he tried to cheer her up or talk about their wedding, she brushed him off. He put it down to her grieving the loss of her father, but it also made him uncertain about their relationship.

Later in the year, Joseph encountered Mr Davis at the cottage door with a letter in his hand, addressed to Joseph. The envelope had a Coreley postmark, but Joseph didn't recognise the handwriting. Opening the letter, he saw it was from the vicar, and his shoulders slumped. He read it in silence, dreading the content.

Dear Joseph,

On your Uncle George's behalf, I am writing to you to inform you about the state of your grandma's condition. It saddens me to mention that she is not well. Most of the time, sleep takes hold of her, relieving her from the pain. Although she has not requested your presence, I think it would be wise for you to visit her before she weakens further.

Yours faithfully, The Vicar

Joseph stared at the wall in silence.

"What's the matter?" Mr Davis said.

"The vicar says my grandma is seriously ill and very weak." His voice broke. "I must go to her as soon as I can."

"I'm sorry to hear that. Stay a few days if you need to."

Thoughts rushed through Joseph's mind. He loathed himself for neglecting Grandma. He'd not been to her since she moved in with her eldest son George, his wife and son, at Hill Side, Hints.

That evening, he showed the letter to Mary Ann.

"Oh dear," Mary Ann sighed, and she let her hand with the letter drop to her side. "You must go to her, Joseph. You've always been so close to each other. I'll accompany you."

During the journey, Joseph spoke about Grandma. "She's always been like a mother to me. She took care of me, encouraged me to do well, and wanted me to have good schooling." He remembered her as a solid woman who had overcome the loss of two husbands. The bible had given her great consolation. He had her to thank for bringing him up to appreciate the value of God's word.

On arrival, Joseph was shocked when he saw Grandma. Her cheeks were hollow, and she looked frail. She showed no sign of noticing their presence. He looked at Mary Ann and then back to Grandma, and was at a loss for words. Mary Ann motioned to Joseph to sit on the edge of the bed. After doing so, he took Grandma's hand, and she turned her head towards him. He knew she perceived his closeness. Mary Ann went to the other side of the bed and took the other hand.

With a weak, croaky voice, Grandma said she was glad to see 'her Joseph' and thanked him for coming. He didn't know what to say, his emotions taking hold of him. He just looked down at her hand and stroked it. Mary Ann filled the gap by saying they were sad she was so ill and would pray for her. Joseph then found the words to talk about what a good childhood she had given him. He was grateful she'd encouraged him to persevere at school and become a carpenter. Otherwise, he would have been a farm labourer, like most other boys in Coreley.

A poetry book on the night-table caught Joseph's eye - *Sacred Poems and Prose* by Frederick Whitfield. He picked it up and flicked through the pages. "Let me read you some prose, dear Grandma. It's called '*The Love of Jesus*'."

> "We love Him, because He first loved us. The sense of Christ's love is the mightiest of all constraining motives; it embraces our whole spiritual nature, touches it in all its springs, moves it in all its affections, stirs it in all its energies. Hope will make men strive, and fear will make men tremble, but love alone will waken love.
>
> Wheresoever the love of Christ pours itself like a flood of light into the soul, it draws all things after it by its irresistible attraction. It drew Peter, James, and John, from their boats and

kindred; Nathaniel from his shade and solitude; Matthew from his custom and commerce; Mary Magdalene from her sins; and Saul of Tarsus from his deeds of blood. It recalled Peter from his denials; drew sinners to wash His feet with tears, and the Elders to cast their crowns at His feet. Other motives rise and fall in their power to constrain; they come and go; they are fainter and stronger, as if fitful and capricious; but the love of Christ never fails."

Grandma smiled. "That's lovely, Joseph, thank you. God be with you both." Her words were just about audible, and she attempted to squeeze their hands.

Joseph's chin trembled. Tears were in his eyes when they bade Grandma goodbye. They departed, knowing they would probably not see her alive again, but feeling grateful to have spent these precious hours with her.

CHAPTER FOURTEEN
Decisions

1886

One Sunday after church, Mary Ann asked Joseph to sit down to talk.

"My family keeps asking me when we'll marry. They're saying that, at my age, they had husbands and chil …"

Joseph interrupted. "I want to save more money before we marry."

She frowned. "We've been engaged for over two years. It's time we married and started a family." Her tone was sharper. "We can find a place in Wednesfield. Rents are lower there."

"I want nothing more than to marry you, Mary Ann," said Joseph, turning away from her. "We'll raise children. That's God's will and He'll trust us to do that."

"As you say, the Lord relies on us to start a family. That means He expects us to marry and start a loving home," Mary Ann said, trying to look Joseph in the eyes.

Joseph put his hands in his pockets. "I need to find work. It's not easy. It's best we start married life after I've secured a job. I don't want us to start with only small savings."

Since the Black Friday Panic in 1873, the economy was in the throws of the Long Depression. The coal and iron industries were hard hit, and Wolverhampton was no exception.

"It'll be easier to find a job in Wednesfield … my family knows so many people."

Joseph looked at her with tight eyes and raised his voice. "Your family is pushing you to live near them."

"No, they're not!" she countered. "It's easier to find a house and a job for you in Wednesfield. We don't know anybody in Shrewsbury."

"Give me a chance to find work, *damn you!*" he retorted, hands in fists. "What with these funerals, I haven't had time."

"How long are we going to wait?"

He loosened his fists. "I need to ask for time off work."

He felt responsible for finding a home and a job. The words of the scriptures were in his mind — 'God is the head of Christ, Christ is the head of every man, and the man is the head of a woman.' For Joseph, that meant his role was to lead his wife and family. He was determined to quickly find a home and a job to show his worthiness.

As soon as he could take a day off work, Joseph travelled to Shrewsbury. His first port-of-call was the railway carriage workshop where he'd seen the fine woodwork in the dining car. He was shown to the railway carriage manager, who said he could offer him a job as a joiner. A letter of recommendation from his current employer would be required. The first month would be a trial period, ten hours per day, six days a week. Depending on his performance, they would give him the normal pay of twenty-five shillings a week. Joseph said he would take the job and give notice about when he could start. The manager asked where he intended to live.

"I will marry soon and haven't found a home yet," Joseph answered.

"If you're interested, I know a place near here. Someone I know will vacate it soon. It's small, but big enough for a young family," the manager said.

"That sounds just right. What's the address, I'll go there straightaway," Joseph said, relieved that his search might be easy.

"It's 11 Argyll Street," the manager said, and gave him directions.

Argyll Street was a row of compact houses. He knocked on the door of number eleven. The current tenant opened the door and showed him a living room and small kitchen downstairs. Two cramped rooms upstairs were bedrooms. Good enough, Joseph thought. The tenant planned to move in February and the rent was five shillings a week. He gave Joseph the name and address of the landlord. Joseph made a beeline for him, and was told the rent remained the same. He said he'd take it.

In the train on his way back, he totted up a weekly budget. Besides the rent of 5s, they would need 10s 6d for food, 2s for coal, 2s for washing and other household matters, and 6d for tobacco. That totalled twenty shillings a week, leaving five shillings to save. He felt confident and self-satisfied. Mary Ann would be delighted and could set a date for the wedding.

He was excited about telling her the news.

"I've been to Shrewsbury and found a house. The landlord said it will be available in February."

She crossed her arms and dropped her gaze to the floor.

Joseph continued with a wide grin, "I spoke to the manager at the railway works. He says I can start any time. They'll pay twenty-five shillings a week. I confirmed I'd take the position."

"It sounds like you've already decided. Why didn't you take me to see the house before deciding?" Mary Ann said.

"You complained of my slackness, and now I've found a home and a job, you complain you want to approve it first," he moaned.

"The house is where I'll live and where we'll raise our children. I'd have liked to have been with you when you chose it."

"It's my duty to find a home and secure earnings. You've previously said you like Shrewsbury and that it would be a fitting place to start a family," Joseph said. "I did consult you."

"And who will furnish our home?"

"You will, of course, that's your duty. A woman's place is in the home."

"How can I think of furnishing a home I've never seen?"

Joseph adopted a conciliatory tone. "I'll take you there whenever you like. I'm sure they'll let us look around."

"Next time there's a major decision to take, I want to be consulted beforehand. Do you understand?"

"I do, but *you* must understand I thought we'd agreed on going to Shrewsbury."

"We'd spoken about it, but that's not the same as agreeing. Besides, choosing a home is different because I'll be the one living in it all day."

"I'm confident it's best for us to live there. There are plenty of opportunities, not only for me but also for our children."

"What's the house like?"

"It's a terraced house within walking distance from my work and the town centre. There's a room and kitchen downstairs and two rooms upstairs. It's small, but fine to start with. There's a garden at the back."

She didn't respond, so he understood the matter was closed.

"Let's prepare for our wedding," she said. "Shall we speak to the parish clerk about what to do?"

"Which parish do you mean?" he asked, as they'd not yet spoken about where to marry.

"I'd like to have it in our local church, here in Tettenhall."

"I'm surprised. I expected Wednesfield. Why here?"

"Because we know everyone here. We attend Sunday service together. Our bible lessons are here, and mates from work can easily attend. I like the parson here too. He'll make it a wonderful occasion."

"Whatever you prefer. I want it to be a memorable day, for us both, for you in particular."

CHAPTER FIFTEEN

Union

1887

Joseph and Mary Ann spent time with the parson after a bible class. It delighted him to hear they planned to marry in his church. "Indeed, the congregation knows you both well, and that will make it even more satisfying. When would you like to hold the wedding, Mary Ann?"

"Monday, the thirtieth of May, was what I had in mind," she replied, smiling.

The Parson consulted his diary. "That would be a fine date. I'll note it down right away."

"Is there anything to prepare beforehand?" Joseph asked.

"Let me run you through the normal process. On Sunday, three weeks prior to your wedding, during service, I'll announce your wish to marry. That allows anyone the opportunity to contest your marriage. About a month before the date, please speak to the parish clerk. He'll record your names and ask you to pay two shillings for registering and thirteen for the wedding itself."

Joseph thought it expensive - more than half a week's wage.

"What'll happen on the day itself, Reverend?" Mary Ann enquired.

"We'll talk about that in more detail nearer the date. Normally the father brings the bride down the aisle to where Joseph and I will be standing."

"My father has passed away."

The parson lowered his voice. "I'm sorry to hear that. In that case, I suggest a brother accompanies you. As I know you both well, I'll prepare a fitting introduction to the formal marriage ceremony. When we speak again, tell me whether you have any special wishes."

Joseph received a letter from the landlord in Shrewsbury informing him the house on Argyll Street wouldn't be available till 1st June. This upset his plans as he wanted their home ready before the wedding. After a short honeymoon, they could then move in. He'd promised Mary Ann to visit the house, but that hadn't happened yet. In his mind, he worked through the tactics. If he could find another place on time, then she wouldn't have to know. But that was a risky plan; perhaps it was better to tell her and delay the wedding by a month.

As they walked to Wergs after church the next Sunday morning, he told Mary Ann about the situation.

"What are we going to do?" she asked.

"We'll postpone the wedding by a month. That'll give us time to furnish before we move in."

"But we've settled the date and told our families."

"They'll understand when we tell them why," Joseph said, convincingly.

Mary Ann sighed and swallowed hard. "Let's sit on that tree trunk and talk." They sat side-saddle on the log, facing each other. "We can stick to the date and then decorate together before moving in."

"I want it ready before the wedding, so we don't have to worry about it. Then we can enjoy the party and have a short honeymoon, and then settle into our home," he said, pushing his shoulders back and raising his head.

Mary Ann straightened her back. "Why can't we move in after our honeymoon and do it up while we're in it. That would save the cost of temporary lodgings. Let's do it together. As soon as we've done the basics, you can start work."

"I want to avoid living in the house while doing it up. It's easier to paint when we're not there."

She reached for his hand. "We'll manage. Let's first see the place; then we'll decide what we need to do."

Joseph agreed because it would save him searching for somewhere else.

They took the train to Shrewsbury and had a thorough look around the house. It was in a row of terraced houses; small, but sufficient to start with. The kitchen was fitted with a cast iron cooking range, and a water tap and basin on the back wall. Upstairs were two bedrooms with no further facilities. An outdoor toilet was in the modest backyard. The place was in reasonable condition, although wallpaper needed replacing throughout.

"How do you like it?" Joseph asked.

"I'm looking forward to this being our home. When we've furnished it our way, it'll be lovely. We need to plan what to do."

"Some of Grandma's things are in Coreley, in Uncle George's barn. There's a table and chairs, a cupboard, kitchen utensils, pots and pans, and more. Mother may have taken a few items, but Mr Dolphin already had a house full of stuff."

"My family has furniture too, things that came from our parents' home. All in all, we'll have a splendid start," Mary Ann said, happily. "Let's move in just after our honeymoon and do it up ourselves."

"We'll have enough furniture, I'm sure. Well begun is half done," said Joseph, feeling satisfied. "We can keep our jobs at Wergs until the wedding day. It'll give us more cash for anything we need."

Their wedding day, May 30th, was arriving fast. Joseph had stopped work at Wergs and went to Coreley to stay with his Uncle George. It gave him time to inspect furniture and household items stored in the barn and organise its transport to Shrewsbury. Mary Ann ceased work a week before the date. Family and friends brought her presents; useful items for her new home, like plates, cutlery, ornaments, and vases. Some offered her jewellery and books. She spread the gifts out in a spare room in the servants' quarters of the Hall, where she also exhibited her wedding dress.

In the meantime, Joseph had purchased the ring. He'd asked the other housemaid to secretly get one of Mary Ann's rings for the jeweller to measure. He chose a gold ring with engraved swirls; the date of their marriage engraved on the inside.

On their wedding day, it was bright and sunny. Joseph wore a black suit and waistcoat, white shirt, bowtie, and white gloves. His mother had arrived the day before and accompanied him to the church. The best man, Mary Ann's brother Henry, met them at the lychgate. He sought Joseph to check the ring was in his left-hand waistcoat-pocket. Luckily, it was. They entered the vestry and spoke to the Parson, who asked Joseph to follow him and stand to the left of him in front of the altar.

As the pews filled with family and friends, Joseph became breathless but quickly composed himself. He recognised most of them — Mr Davis, Mary Ann's colleagues, and others from Wergs. The Misses Perry walked in and took their reserved seats to the side of the front row. Through the door-opening, he could make out flowers being strewn on the path.

He was elated when his bride emerged from the hue of sunlight. Her eldest brother, James, took her arm, and they slowly glided down the aisle. Mary Ann wore a white wedding dress; her head adorned with a wreath of flowers and a shimmering veil. In her gloved hands, she held a bouquet of white roses and pink peonies. Bridesmaids followed — her eldest sister Susannah and nieces. They wore pink and light blue dresses and white veils. The sight of her coming towards him heightened

Joseph's senses; he was suddenly aware of the smell of the old church and the animated sounds of the congregation.

Joseph clasped the bride's right hand after she took her place on his left. The ceremony began. At the formal part, the Parson spoke about their responsibilities as man and wife.

"When God commands us to love Him, He means we shall obey Him. As Christ is to the church, so is man to the wife. Obedience on the part of the wife is the best instance of her love, for it proclaims her submission, her humility, her opinion of his wisdom, his pre-eminence in the family, the right of his privilege, and the injunction imposed by God upon her sex. The man's authority is love, the woman's love is obedience."

Those words struck true for Joseph, confirming his right to decide where they live and that it's God's wish that he use his authority to show his love and care.

"Do you, Joseph Starie Handley, take Mary Ann Done to be your wedded wife, to have and to hold from this day forward, for better, for worse, for richer, for poorer, in sickness and in health, to love and to cherish, till death you do part, according to God's holy law?"

Joseph beamed, "In the presence of God I make this vow."

After Mary Ann had made her vow, Joseph put his hand in his left waistcoat pocket. She gasped when she saw the ring sparkle. He smiled, took her hand, and looked her in the eyes. "I grant you this ring as a token of our marriage." He gently slipped the ring on her finger. "With my body I honour you, all that I am I give to you, and all that I have I share with you, within the love of God, Father, Son and Holy Spirit." The next thing he heard was, "You may kiss the bride."

After the ceremony, the couple entered the vestry, and the family followed. Joseph's mother was the first to hug and congratulate her son. Mr Dolphin had not accompanied her, as he needed to stay in the shop in Doddington. The Parson asked the newlyweds to sign the registry. Joseph signed first, that being the custom. He checked that the registrar had put his father's name down as John Starie, as he had instructed. Mary Ann wrote her maiden name for the last time. Then the witnesses added their signatures — her eldest brother, James, and her youngest sister, Ann Mathilda. Sister Susannah opened the box of favours — sweets for the bridesmaids and corsages. The flower ornaments were a perfect complement to Mary Ann's bouquet. Susannah pinned them on each bridesmaid, the best man, and Joseph's mother.

Joseph was glad his father had not turned up. He'd sent him a cordial card without an invitation to the wedding breakfast. It would've been awkward if he'd been present.

Miss Perry had offered Mary Ann the use of the conservatory. Colleagues had decorated it with flowers and set up tables and chairs to accommodate the guests. A wedding cake, baked by the cook, stood glistening on a side table. The newlyweds took their places, and, once all were seated, Henry asked the couple to cut the cake. Mary Ann picked up the knife and Joseph put his hand over hers. They cut one piece out of the three-tiered cake, then fed each other, symbolising their commitment to look after each other. Two bridesmaids came forward to serve the cake. Henry raised a toast to the bridal pair.

In response, Joseph stood up and placed his hand on his wife's shoulder. "When I asked Mr Done for permission to marry his daughter, he asked me if I would be able to support a family. I said, 'No! I'm only able to support your daughter. The rest of your family will have to look after themselves'."

After the laughs had trailed off, Joseph addressed Mary Ann. "Mary Ann, dear wife, you look absolutely *wonderful* today! I feel privileged to have been at your side before God and that we are now united in matrimony." He turned to face all those present. "We've waited a long time for this day, a marvellous day, thanks to all of you. Our special praises are for Henry and Susannah for making things go in an orderly fashion, and, to Misses Perry for the use of this lovely conservatory. I won't hold you up any longer. Please, eat your cake before it gets cold," he said, smiling. There was more food, more speeches, jokes and some prayer. Everyone had an delightful time.

At one point, Susannah and Mary Ann left the conservatory so that she could change out of her wedding dress. Joseph and Henry soon followed; then the couple were ready to start their honeymoon. As they left the building, the guests formed two rows and threw confetti over them. After hugs and kisses, they departed in a carriage as the family threw old slippers behind them as a token of good luck.

CHAPTER SIXTEEN
Shrewsbury

1887

For their honeymoon, Joseph and Mary Ann went to Leamington Spa to stay with her eldest sister, Susannah, and her husband, Robert.

On their first night together, Joseph loosened up. As he undressed Mary Ann, he said, "Are you familiar with the expression 'there goes more to marriage than four bare legs in bed'?"

"No, but I think I know what you have in mind!"

"Aha, yes. I'm thinking more about the four bare legs than anything else right now!" He felt the spread of her shoulders and let his hands move down her arms, then up again and down her sides, searching her expressions for clues before cupping her breasts. At night, they explored each other's bodies, happy to express their mutual love. During the day, they paid several visits to the Royal Pump Rooms & Baths to relax in the hot, salty waters.

In their new home in Shrewsbury, they spent the first week in the house - cleaning, wall-papering, and arranging furniture they had brought with them. Then Joseph started work at Midland Railway Carriage and Wagon Company.

When Joseph was an apprentice, he and his mother always went to church in the Abbey. Mary Ann preferred to attend a smaller place of worship, so they visited different churches before deciding. At the Abbey, they came across Miss Wells, the parlourmaid at Mrs Juson's, where Mother had worked.

"Are you planning to find a job?" she asked Mary Ann.

"Yes. I'd like to be a maid, but only during daytime, so that I can be home when Joseph comes in."

"I know a lady who needs a new housemaid. Perhaps it's worth going there to offer your services."

The conversation continued about life in Shrewsbury. Miss Wells said she was a regular churchgoer and familiar with several churches.

"I was in the market square the other day and listened to a Plymouth Brethren man," Joseph said. "He had a pure way of interpreting the bible. That's our approach too."

Miss Wells turned sullen. "I'm Church of England and not familiar with the Plymouth Brethren. I only know they expect their members to sever ties with their families."

Mary Ann frowned. "I've heard that too. I can't imagine doing that. I'd hate to not see my family ever again."

She sought the job Miss Wells had proposed and was pleasantly surprised that she could clean during weekdays, just as she desired.

The next Sunday, Joseph suggested visiting the Plymouth Brethren Gospel Hall in John Street.

Mary Ann's eyes narrowed. "Why there? They're very strict and don't allow contact with family."

"Let's see what it's like. We'll trust in God and keep our powder dry," Joseph said. "We shouldn't believe stories we've heard without finding out for ourselves. The way they profess their belief in God is similar to ours."

"But why go if we're not considering joining?"

"Let's first talk to them, and find out what joining would mean. You never know till you ask. Believe nothing you hear and only half of what you see."

The gospel hall was close to where they lived — a nondescript red-brick building with a small cross on the roof. Joseph led Mary Ann to the door where a Brother gave them a warm welcome. He handed Mary Ann a grey scarf and instructed her that women and girls were expected to wear headscarves whenever out of their home. Other Brothers and Sisters came towards them, asking where they were from and saying how pleased they were to see them. In the hall, chairs were arranged in circles around a table covered by a white cloth with freshly baked bread and a cup of wine.

Joseph smiled and listened intently when others spoke, trying to grasp their names. The Brother showed them to seats at the front of the assembly. Joseph beamed; he felt an important guest. He was keen to follow the proceedings, to learn more about this new group.

The meeting began in silence. Next, a man stood up, talked about Christ, and read a passage from the bible. An elder came forward to give thanks for the bread and tore it into pieces which were passed round for people to eat. As Joseph ate his piece, a oneness overwhelmed him;

oneness with God and this new community. Another elder thanked Him for the wine and circulated a cup.

Joseph pulled his shoulders back to fill his lungs with air when the assembly sang in one powerful voice. The meeting ended with prayers. Joseph relished in the rituals. He understood only men were permitted to speak. Women remained silent except for singing with the rest of the fellowship. A Brother explained that the Brethren had no priests because they believed all men were equal; there was no hierarchy. The Gospel Hall was plain, no altar or pulpit, and no windows to stop the evil outside world from looking in.

At home, Joseph expressed his delight about how they were welcomed. "I felt as if I'd joined a new family. They were so easy to get along with."

Mary Ann smiled. "I liked the Sisters. Everyone seemed friendly and showed an interest in us. The service appealed to me too; they're very dedicated."

"I'm impressed by the way the bible is at the heart of their belief," Joseph said. "And that they welcome folk from all dominions."

Mary Ann nodded. "I agree."

In his mind, Joseph had decided they should join. "We know nobody in Shrewsbury. The Brethren can become our friends; they're our type of people."

Mary Ann wrinkled her brow. "I still worry about us having to cease contact with our families."

"They said we don't have to decide just yet. Let's attend Assembly every day, follow bible lessons, and then decide later whether we commit ourselves."

Joseph purchased two copies of the Plymouth Brethren Bible, a special version translated by the founder, John Darby. They joined bible class, and learned the Brethren's beliefs and rules - that they should support the weak, even those who were non-Brethren, that they should not smoke or gamble. Children were not to play with non-Brethren children. They were against war, believing that no man should hurt or kill another man.

At one point, their teacher tested them.

"Joseph, can you name two principles that we must adhere to in daily life?"

"The instructions in the Holy Scriptures preserve the purity of doctrine, so in our daily life, the scriptures must be our sole guide," Joseph replied. "The oneness of God can only be amongst those who are in His Assembly, so we need to avoid those that do not believe in His word."

"What about you, Mary Ann?" the teacher asked.

"To know union with God, we must separate ourselves from evil in the world. At Assembly we celebrate the Lord's Supper by breaking the bread and drinking his blood, to bond our fellowship and unite with God."

"Joseph, what can you tell us about the principles of separation?"

"That we must draw away from the world in a moral sense and show commitment to our fellow Brothers and Sisters by eating and drinking together."

"Does that mean we must completely withdraw from society, Mary Ann?"

"No, we seek to do good to all, so our separation permits contact with non-Brethren."

"Is that all?" the teacher asked.

"We abstain from socialising with others, but join them in education and business," Mary Ann added.

"That's correct. In separating ourselves, we remain good neighbours to others and deal with them as we would deal with each other — honestly and fairly."

"How does that affect our relationships with our families who are not Brothers and Sisters?" Mary Ann asked.

"All contact with non-Brethrens, including members of your family, needs to meet this principle of separation. That means that any contact with family must be limited to helping those in need, just as you would do with any other non-Brethren. You may no longer celebrate with your family. Celebration will only take place amongst the Assembly. You need to talk to each other about how to make this work in practice."

On hearing this, Joseph looked at Mary Ann and saw the shocked look on her face. He knew she would find this difficult and that she needed time to adjust.

"Are you ready to fully commit yourselves to the Brethren?" the teacher asked.

"We'll give you an answer later," Joseph said. "We need to talk about how we inform our families."

As soon as they left the lesson, Mary Ann said, "How can they expect me to tell my family that I don't want to see them? They'll think I no longer love them! They're not evil people, even if they don't attend church! They'll think I'm stupid!"

"No one is asking you to never see them again," Joseph replied.

She tapped her fist against her cheek. "That's what it means. Don't you understand? It's all very well for you, you hardly have any family, and those you have, you never bother to see!"

"That's a horrible thing to say. You know I care for Mother and that she doesn't live nearby."

"We've moved away from Wednesfield, which is bad enough for me."

"You see your family less than before, but I've never heard you complain about not seeing them as often as you used to," Joseph said, trying to keep calm.

"I've not complained because when we see them, we celebrate and have fun. The Brethren despise that!"

"We can visit as long as we restrict celebration." Joseph ran his hands through his hair. "Just think of how lucky we are here. The Brethren will be like a family. They'll help us and we'll help them. It's more important to have close friends here than families further away."

"If only they would allow us contact with my family," Mary Ann sighed.

"If we can limit it to formal events like births and marriages, it'll be alright. We just need to exclude ourselves from effusive celebration parties. We don't attend them anyway."

"How am I going to tell them?"

"You don't need to. When the time comes, we'll think of a reason to leave or not even to go. Imagine the advantages of being with the Brethren. They'll come to me for any carpentry that needs doing. In return, we'll do business with them. It's - you scratch my back, I'll scratch yours."

Mary Ann breathed easier. "As long as I don't have to tell my family that I'm cutting myself off from them."

1888

The job at Midland's disappointed Joseph. He'd expected to do the fine carving he saw in the First Class Dining Car when initially visiting the works. In practice, they produced few First Class coaches. Most of the work was for simpler Second and Third Class coaches. There was no intricate woodwork in those. It was straightforward joinery that had to be done efficiently. He asked to do more challenging carpentry, but the manager said there were others who were waiting longer than him to do the prized jobs.

Before long, the routine bored Joseph, and the pressure was too tiring. To make matters worse, Mary Ann complained of him coming home exhausted all the time. So eventually, he left Midland's to become a travelling joiner. The Plymouth Brethren Brothers used word of mouth to help him find customers in Shrewsbury and the surrounding villages. It went well until he had to do his own acquisition; knocking on doors and asking whether people needed repairs didn't suit his character at all. He was hopeless at promoting himself, not the type to easily start a conversation with strangers.

"I'm not earning enough to keep us going," he told Mary Ann, one day. "I'm glad to be independent but I hate begging for jobs."

Mary Ann prodded his side. "Perhaps we should start a shop."

Joseph flinched. "What sort of shop?"

"Let's set up a chandler's shop. There isn't one in this part of town. We'll attract local customers."

His shoulders drooped. "How will we find the money to invest in stock?" Running a shop was not something that appealed to Joseph.

"Perhaps we can borrow and pay it back later," Mary Ann proposed.

"He that goes a-borrowing, goes a-sorrowing."

"I can run the shop while you carry out joinery. When you're without work, you can make wooden candlesticks to sell."

"It'll mean you have to give up your cleaning job because you'll be in the shop all day."

"I've done enough cleaning for other people, anyhow a shop will earn more."

Joseph frowned. "Who'll lend us the money?" He was objecting, but only half-heartedly. He sensed the idea would take the pressure off.

"Perhaps one of the Brethren?" suggested Mary Ann.

Joseph clenched his teeth. "I don't want them to know we're in need."

"We'll ask my brother, James. He earns plenty of money with both his bakery and the grocery shop. Surely he'll see the potential of a chandler's shop and help us invest. That way, nobody in Shrewsbury will know."

"Normally, I wouldn't ask anyone for help, but I'll put it to James as a business proposal."

Joseph intended to approach James himself because, as a man, he should do the business talk.

The next time he met James, he asked whether he was interested in investing in the shop. James said he was happy to cooperate.

Along Abbey Foregate, a shop was available for a reasonable rent. They took it because it was close to other shops and not out of people's way. Joseph built a counter, work-surfaces and shelves. At the back, he screwed hooks into the ceiling so that candles could hang to dry. Mary Ann painted the walls and purchased materials. She intended to produce candles with beeswax, which was more expensive but sold at a higher price. She expanded the range of articles with readymade candles for a cheaper price. Those were made of paraffin wax, mixed with stearin for strength. Soaps supplemented the collection.

The shop opened six days a week, and business soon picked up as most people in the area had no gas or electricity for light. Their Brethren friends came for their candles too. Joseph carved candlesticks out of unique sorts of wood and helped with the production of candles when stocks were low. Besides that, he did joinery whenever he was asked.

He noticed how wonderful Mary Ann was at chatting with customers, the regular ones lingering longer all the while; she remembered their names and knew what was going on in their lives. He wasn't as sociable with the patrons, but he helped behind the scenes.

In his mind, they lived as he had envisaged. He thought: God's in his heaven; all's right with the world. When He deems wise, we will start a family.

CHAPTER SEVENTEEN

It is well

1888

The Brothers came to know that Joseph enjoyed reading and had a resonating voice, so they asked him to undertake preaching in public. They suggested beginning in the surrounding villages, where spreading the word was less demanding. Joseph said he preferred to stay in town, to speak in the market square.

"Ladies and Gentlemen, Earnest Christians,

In this time, between light and darkness, we seek truth in the Holy Bible. It guides us in how to do good and avoid evil. The word of God looks at man from two perspectives. In Romans, it is written that man is ungodly, strengthless and unrighteous. In Ephesians, man is portrayed as guilty, a sinner, not guilty to man, but guilty to God.

The bible offers three ways to regain approval in the eyes of God. We can be praised by Him for our moral conduct. We can gain his respect by being true to what is laid down in the Bible. Thirdly, our honest behaviour can lead to God perceiving us as adhering to His words.

Only the precious blood of Christ, God's own son, can justify a sinner. Christ is God's anointed man, and His blood can cleanse us of all of our sins. Christ paid penance and met God's requirements in relation to sin. Righteousness and mercy came together in Him.

There is a moral distinction between what is right and what is wrong. Between what is righteous and what is unrighteous. We urge true Christians, as believers of the Lord Jesus Christ, to refuse the evil and to choose the good. The precious truths of the bible need to be admitted into more hearts and evidenced in more lives. But be cautious about what you view as true. Investigate it and compare it with other scriptures before considering it the truth. Prove all, cling to the good and persevere in its purity."

Joseph concluded his speeches by asking the attendees to donate coins for the widows and orphans of those killed in the South African and the Crimean Wars. Sometimes, an individual asked him for more information about the Brethren and he gladly spent time to explain the importance of being true to the Bible.

He had always been shy in groups, but speaking in public helped him overcome any hesitations. Jospeh earned recognition from the Brothers, feeding his conviction that he was at home amongst them. Preaching was his primary contribution to the community and to the word of Jesus.

His intention was to keep his future family on the righteous path so that Lord Jesus Christ would save them. To achieve that, he believed he must read the bible, pray and enforce self-restraint. He and Mary Ann never missed Assembly where all Brothers and Sisters gathered in the name of the Lord for the breaking of bread. After Assembly, they attended bible class, and, on Wednesday evenings, they joined in prayers and bible study.

He inherited Grandma's book of poems by Frederick Whitfield and made a habit of reading to Mary Ann each Sunday evening. "This is a poem called *It is well*."

"It is well when God's voice awakes us
From the fatal sleep of sin;
Well, when His Holy Spirit makes us
Feel nothing but guilt within.

It is well to be washed in the blood
That once was shed on the tree;
To know Christ now, my Saviour and God,
That He gave His life for me.

It is well to be led by His hand,
Through the desert's dreary waste!
And to taste the rich fruits of that land,
So sweet to the pilgrim's taste.

It is well to pass under the cloud,
Though gloomy and dark it be;

To stand where all the chosen ones stood
That have crossed life's narrow sea.

It is well to lie low at the cross,
Forgetting the things behind;
And esteeming all else but as dross,
Press on with the prize in mind.

It is well to look up to the sky,
When Jesus summons us home;
To dwell where love never more can die,
To know as now I am known.

It is well - it is well to be there!
Lord hasten the glorious day,
When Jesus shall all His glory share,
All His wondrous love display!"

"It is well to be devoted and adhere to God's word," Mary Ann said. "But we also need some flexibility. Sometimes, I think you're too strict about not having any contact outside the Brethren. I know you're doing it out of loyalty to the principles, and I respect you for that, but …"

Joseph interrupted, "With what are you in disagreement?"

"My parents were well-known in Wednesfield, especially when my father was a bailiff. They had a wide circle of people from all walks of life and they flourished. But we're confining ourselves to a small circle of like-thinking people who object to us having contact with others."

"There's no problem with that. Why do we need others when we have enough support from our Brothers and Sisters?"

She inhaled deeply. "I feel restricted. Non-Brethren think we're peculiar and look down on us. They've heard you preaching and know you're a non-conformist, and they don't want to be associated with people like us."

Joseph tilted his head back. "We're doing fine! We're selling enough in the shop."

Ann crossed her arms. "It's not true. There are less customers in the shop, fewer conformists. Some ask about our religion, and I sense they disapprove."

"The Brethren will support us, don't worry."

Mary Ann raised her voice. "You've always said you didn't want to depend on others! The Brethren …"

"Don't whine, woman," he barked.

Mary Ann slammed a cupboard door shut. "I'm not whining."

"Stop fretting. God will look after us!" Joseph snapped, and walked out.

CHAPTER EIGHTEEN
Family

1889

On 5th March a healthy, sizeable daughter was born: Annie, named after Mary Ann and Joseph's mother, Ann. They choose Louisa as a second name, after Mary Ann's elder sister.

Joseph rocked the baby in his arms. "She's a gift from God, a perfect baby, a child completely unspoilt by the evil in the world, a manifestation of purity."

He felt the responsibility to protect this defenceless soul and rear her to know and respect God: it was his duty. Above all, he was thankful that mother and baby were in fine shape, and he expressed that in his prayers.

He minded the shop until Mary Ann recovered from the birth. Several weeks later, she returned to the shop with baby Annie strapped to her back. Joseph resumed candle-making, and served customers when Mary Ann needed to feed the baby.

With less money coming in from joinery work, and the shop's business slowing, Joseph found it increasingly difficult to make ends meet. Each week he prayed they could manage to pay the rent. His pride and commitment didn't allow for borrowing again. Anyway, they couldn't ask family because they had practically severed bonds. The financial situation was a millstone round his neck. Looking for advice, he mentioned the rent to a Brother who said he owned a house which would soon become available, on a new housing estate, Cherry Orchard. The rent was lower for members of the Assembly. Joseph knew he shouldn't decide without consulting Mary Ann, so they walked to Byron Terrace and stopped at number five.

"Joseph, I like the big windows," said Mary Ann.

They surveyed the inside and Joseph asked what Mary Ann thought of it.

"The light shines in every room, especially the kitchen. Everything looks very modern."

"If it pleases you, we can move in next month."

After moving, Joseph heard the life insurance business was flourishing. He told Mary Ann insurance agents earned good money, and it required no investment. She didn't object to him setting up a small office in the shop, as long as his business wouldn't interfere with her customers. An insurance company in Telford gave Joseph instructions and training, and then he launched his business at an Assembly.

1891

Two years later, Joseph and Mary Ann had no complaints. The shop, the agency and a bit of joinery work provided a decent income, leaving enough to repay the loan to James. Joseph even found time to enjoy swimming in the River Severn, which was within walking distance. For one shilling, he acquired a license to fish in the river for trout and char, with a rod and line.

Annie was a healthy toddler, and soon a sibling would join her; Joseph stroked Mary Ann's bulging abdomen.

"Can you feel the baby moving?" she asked.

"Yes, it's amazing to think there's a little person inside, preparing to come out into the world."

"We need to decide on a name."

Joseph kissed her belly as if to kiss the baby. "I hope it'll be a boy this time."

"If it is, what shall we call him?"

"I'd like to continue the naming tradition," Joseph replied.

"You mean Joseph?"

"No, John, after my father."

"Are you sure? He's never really been a father to you."

"I know, but I'm certain. In our bible lessons we discussed forgiveness. I'm ready to forgive my father for not being a father to me. He respected my mother's request for no contact, and I can appreciate him for doing that," he said. "I should have been a Starie, and I'd like that name to live on in my son. Let's call him John Starie Handley."

"And if it's a girl?"

Joseph looked out of the window. "Grandma was Maria and my mother Ann, so perhaps Mary Ann, after you too."

"That's a delightful idea. I'd choose Elizabeth, after my mother. We'll see."

Joseph turned to look back at Mary Ann. "We could do with a larger house now that our family is growing. One of the Brothers has offered me a place around the corner, 33 Cleveland Street. It's like this but the rooms are wider."

"Are those the houses with a bay window and a front garden?"

"That's right."

"Seems fine to me. Can we see what it's like inside?"

"I'll ask when I meet him at Assembly. I'm so thankful we're part of the Brethren. I feel that at last I'm part of a family, with everyone helping each other."

"I can tell, and you fit in very well."

"I appreciate the orderly way they do things, the rites. The men have an eye for good workmanship, too."

Mary Ann shifted in her chair and laid her arms on her bulging belly. "I enjoy the Sisters companionship and the strong sense of community. They're always a listening ear or ready to help." She hesitated. "On the other hand, I still feel constrained. We're seen as part of a secretive group who thinks they're better than others, more true to the bible."

"We *are* more true to the scriptures. As it should be. It's wrong to allow evil to enter our lives like so many other people do."

"Why can't we remain true to the bible *and* have contact with anyone we choose?"

Joseph cocked his head and shook it. "Because if we have contact with others, they'll contaminate us with their evil ways. Especially our children. We're doing the right thing for them."

On 17th December, Mary Ann gave birth to a son. Joseph insisted his name must respect the paternal line, so the baby was named John Starie Handley, Jack for short. With two young ones, she had to leave the shop completely to Joseph. It meant he had to stop his joinery work, which he regretted, but the candles and insurance kept him busy.

"Customers ask how you and the baby are doing," he remarked to Mary Ann. "I tell them you're fine, but you won't be coming back to the shop in the foreseeable future because you're too busy with the little ones."

"I'm glad to hear they're asking after me. How are sales going?"

"Soap is selling as well as it was, but there's less demand for candles. Many people are changing to gas or electrical lighting. The beeswax ones are doing well, but of course we don't sell many of those. The grocers now offer Price's candles for less than we're charging." His voice trailed off.

"Can we still manage?"

"I think we can." He tilted his head back. "I'll make more ornamental candlesticks because they're profitable."

He didn't tell her that the life insurance business was sluggish. He concluded it was partly because of the way he addressed potential clients. He wished he was better at small-talk, and more humorous. It had always been Mary Ann that was good at making customers feel comfortable.

He tried to be more attentive by greeting regular clients by their names and asking them how they were. But, more often than not, he couldn't remember names. That made him uncertain and had a counterproductive effect. All the same, he brought in enough to support his family.

CHAPTER NINETEEN
Tensions

1894

Sales in the shop slowly declined, and the insurance business didn't compensate for the loss. Joseph struggled to make ends meet, but was thankful to God for furnishing him with children in a prosperous town amongst supportive people who valued the word of the scriptures. He was, however, also acutely aware that animosity towards the Brethren was growing in the town.

Joseph unfolded the newspaper and slapped it with the back of his hand. "Mary Ann, the conventional churches are trying to convince their parishioners that we're evil. Listen to this piece." He pointed to an article. "The Plymouth Brethren is as bad as all the established Churches and other denominations put together. They are drawing people away from our churches and are critical of our ways. They agree with us to a great deal, but they create a schism amongst our parishioners. Of all sects, they are the most sectarian; of all Christians, the most unchristian in their spirit; of all separatists, they are the most separated from others; and yet of all men, they are the best of men. I am on terms of personal intimacy with many among the Plymouth Brethren, and I respect them as men; but whenever they enter our churches, they cause divisions, for their spirit is division. These friends have a perfect right to secede from us and to hold their own views and principles. But in leaving us, they produce heartburn and bitterness. I can but look upon them as a hindrance to the spread of the Gospel."

Mary Ann shook her head. "What a horrid thing to say!"

"I'm sure we're right in separating from those who condone evil ways. Not that I wish to be separate, but because we must show the righteous way." He threw the paper on the floor. "It makes me wish to speak out even more. What worries me, though, is that they'll think of us as a sect, and that people will avoid us and our shop."

"Perhaps it's better to stop speaking in public - to be less visible? It would also mean you'd have more time for the children."

"What do you mean by that?" he said, raising his voice.

"I just mean you don't always pay that much attention to them," she replied.

Joseph stood up, walked to the window to stare out of it, distancing himself from Mary Ann. He could feel her eyes piercing his back.

She continued, "I'm sure you love them, but you need to show it. You don't pick them up or play with them. They'll only learn to know you as a father who hits them when they're naughty."

"How dare you say that!" Joseph swung round and faced her. "I show my love by providing for them. They'll love me through my authority, and respect me for bringing them up in the eyes of God."

"I'm not criticising you in that sense, not at all. You haven't had a father yourself, but haven't you seen how other fathers bond with their children?"

"Of course I have, but Jack is too young to go fishing and Annie is a girl."

"She's four, and old enough to be taken to the river to feed the ducks."

He looked back out through the window and muttered, "I don't have time to do things like that."

Mary Ann went to the oven, took out the bread, and put it on the table to cool. "The Brothers' influence doesn't help."

"What do they have to do with it?"

"They believe children should be left to their mother's care."

"Rightly so. That's natural. Women are best at that. Men take responsibility for their children's learning and show the way by reading from the bible. We prepare boys for work by teaching them how to use tools. Men don't play with children."

"I'm not expecting you to play with them, but to pay more attention to them. I feel I'm the only one bringing them up."

"That's what you're for!" he snapped, and walked out of the room.

He strode down to the river and along the towpath. At first, he couldn't understand why Mary Ann had complained about his lack of interest in Annie and Jack. But the more he thought about it, the more he realised it was his personality, his introversion; the same trait that made it difficult for him to chat with customers. Mary Ann was the opposite. She could talk a lot - sometimes too much, making him feel embarrassed.

On 20th November, a second daughter was born: Mabel Evelyn. Joseph vowed to himself that he'd give this child the attention she deserved.

Joseph was losing confidence in his insurance business. He didn't like the paperwork, preferring to work with his hands. Struggling to keep his family out of poverty, he was frustrated about his inability to be the 'man' in God's eyes. Shrewsbury tired him too; it had become over-crowded and dirty.

"Let's talk," he said to Mary Ann, after the children were sound asleep.

"What's on your mind, Joseph?"

"We're only scraping through." He sagged back in his chair. "I need more profitable work."

"Why not go back to the railway workshop?" she asked.

"No," he sighed, elbow on the table and head in his hand.

"At least you'll have regular pay."

"The money isn't that good, and it's boring work."

"Perhaps we should move to another town where you might have better prospects. You've tried different things here and they haven't worked out."

"I don't see any point in moving elsewhere," he said, getting to his feet, a hot frustration rushing through his body. "I suppose you're wanting to go to Wolverhampton? I can tell you right now, I'm not working in those dirty factories. Forget it!"

"There are other places," she said, calmly.

"Like where?" he scowled.

"Everyone's talking about Liverpool."

Joseph sighed. "We can't go there!"

"It's booming. They say the harbour is busy with ships from all over the world. There's plenty of jobs."

"Don't be ridiculous," Joseph said. "God will look after us here until the tide turns. We must be patient and pray for his mercy."

Mary Ann leaned back with her hands behind her head. "Liverpool is enormous, second only to London, so surely has more opportunities than here."

"How can you *think* of going there? We've never even been. We know nobody." He clenched his hands, feeling attacked for not being able to support his family. "There are lots of poor Irish immigrants. They're Catholics with permissive beliefs. How will we stand before God in such a place?"

"I think we should leave Shrewsbury. I'm fed up with the looks we get from people on the street." Mary Ann leaned in, her hands on the table. "We should leave. Go somewhere we're not known and start a fresh life."

"What do you mean 'a fresh start'?" he shouted, throwing his arms up.

"Being with the Brethren has kept us in a close circle and limited our business. You're so visible in public that we're seen as outsiders and against the common church," she retaliated.

"Are you saying I should stop preaching?" he yelled. "It's a sin not to follow God's word to do good … Damn you, woman!" He lashed out at her. She held up her arms to protect herself, but he hit her hard on the shoulder.

"Stop!" she yelled, jumping up from the chair. "You're a sinner to strike me. You preach no man should hurt another man. Or does that not include a woman?"

He stamped out of the house, slamming the door behind him.

Grinding his teeth, Joseph strode to the Gospel Hall on John Street and found a Brother doing a maintenance job, a man he trusted. After speaking about repairs to the hall, the Brother asked, "What's brought you here at this time of day, Joseph?"

"I needed a walk. The wife and I had a row. My business isn't going as well as I'd hoped, so I need to find another job. She says we should move to Liverpool because there's work there. It's difficult here in Shrewsbury," he confessed.

"It seems to me she's doing her best to think of a way to improve your situation. Don't take it as criticism, but as a sign from God. Perhaps this is God's manner of showing you a path forward. Listen to his message and consider Moses' trek from Egypt to the Holy Land. He had a sign and followed it."

"Thank you. I hadn't thought of it as a sign."

Walking back home, he regretted having struck Mary Ann. He shouldn't have taken her words as a personal attack. She was merely trying to help.

When he arrived, he could tell from Mary Ann's red and swollen eyes that she'd been crying.

"Forgive me for losing my temper." He touched her shoulder. "I'm frustrated about not being able to earn enough."

She raised her hand to his arm. "I understand." They hugged briefly before he pulled away.

"There's something else I need to tell you. … When I preach in the square these days, there's fewer people gathering round. It's as if they don't want to be seen listening to a Brother. It's because of all that talk in the paper."

"That's another reason for us to move."

"That talk is all over the country, so moving won't help."

"Perhaps we should consider leaving the Brethren."

Her comment shocked Joseph, but he remained silent. A myriad of thoughts crossed his mind. Was she right that they were too confined? *Should* they consider leaving? It felt unthinkable - to be completely on their own.

"I don't want to leave the Brethren," he said. "But I'll talk to the Brothers about moving elsewhere. They may have connections in Liverpool who can help us find lodgings and work."

"I miss my family, Joseph. If we go to them, I'm sure we'd be better off."

"I don't want to go to them. I don't want to go begging for help!" Joseph furrowed his brow. "Besides, that would mean leaving the Brethren."

She threw up her hands. "They'll be only too happy to support us!"

"I'll not hear of it. There's no point wasting time talking about it." Joseph shook his head, and looked at the floor.

"But *I* want to talk about it!"

"I'm going to bed," he said, and went upstairs.

CHAPTER TWENTY
Liverpool

1895

After Mary Ann's suggestion to move to Liverpool, Joseph spoke to the Brothers about it. Their reactions surprised him. They encouraged him to leave, to spread the word of the bible in a city where there was a great need. When he heard them say God gave him the mission to convert the Catholics to the righteous way and a better life, Joseph felt a deep sense of commitment and enthusiasm. An elder offered to contact the Brethren in Liverpool so that Joseph and his family would be looked after on arrival. He told Mary Ann he'd changed his mind and was prepared to move.

In spring, they embarked on the journey to Liverpool. By then, they were too poor to travel by train and had to take a carriage. To pay for the passage, they sold most of their belongings, only taking what they could carry. Their last Plymouth Brethren meeting had been emotional, like saying farewell to a family. They savoured the friendships, and were saddened they were unlikely to meet again. The community wished them well and offered last-minute advice about the journey.

Joseph and his fledgling family started off by walking to the market square. Mary Ann carried one-and-a-half year old Mabel on her back, and tightly held three year old Jack's hand. Annie had just turned six and carried a little bag of her own. Joseph lugged their belongings. He paid the driver to take them to Whitchurch, where they stayed the night in a cheap and dreary inn. The next morning they took a coach to Birkenhead, where they'd board the ferry to Liverpool. They passed arable countryside bursting with fields of crops. Later, the landscape changed to wildflower meadows and grazing cows. The coach stopped in Chester, and all passengers were told to disembark. The coachman announced he wasn't going further and gave Joseph a rebate for the rest of the journey.

Joseph found another carriage, but was short of money, having only enough to go as far as Eastham.

At Eastham, they got off and Joseph asked how far it was to the ferry.

"About seven miles. Just follow this road and it'll take you to Birkenhead."

Joseph turned to Mary Ann. "We'll have to walk the rest of the way."

"That's too far for the children. Is there no alternative? It'll be late before we arrive in Liverpool." Her voice faltered and she bit her lip.

"I'll try to stop a cart and ask for a ride," he said, optimistically. "Let's get going. I'll carry Jack on my shoulders. If you take Mabel on your back, we'll manage."

The road was sandy and lined with hedgerows. Annie kept wanting to pick flowers. "Come on, Annie, don't dawdle. We haven't got time," he shouted many times, his tone increasingly irritated.

When carts passed in their direction, he waved, but none stopped to give them a ride. "Why doesn't anyone stop?"

"I don't know. Perhaps they're so used to people on their way to Liverpool that they've given up stopping," Mary Ann replied.

When Mabel cried, they rested, and sat on a log or stone by the side of the track. Mary Ann gave them all a sip of water and a piece of stale bread.

After a couple of hours, Annie was dragging her feet, too tired to continue.

Joseph tried to encourage her. "Look over there. See the river? It won't be far to the ferry now."

Annie halted, as if glued to the ground. "My feet are sore. I'm hungry."

"Here's some bread," Mary Ann said, passing her a small portion of what was left.

After walking for five hours, they arrived in Birkenhead. Joseph noticed several shipyards where modern steamers were being built. Judging by the number of people, it seemed there was plenty of work.

It was late in the day when they boarded the ferry and sat down on an outside bench. Dockhands took the lines off the bollards and threw them into the water. Black smoke puffed out of the funnel, and they left their moorings. Liverpool's skyline was visible across the river — buildings higher than they'd ever seen before. Lots of boats criss-crossed the estuary, avoiding the ferryboat as it rolled and pitched its course. At Liverpool Pierhead they disembarked, and Joseph was relieved they had almost finished their journey.

The flurry of activity at the docks overwhelmed them. People were bustling around everywhere. Carts carried goods in all directions. He saw sailing-ship masts and steamer funnels as far as the eye could see. A noisy, overhead electric railway transferred passengers from one dock to the other.

At the horse-drawn tram terminal, Joseph made enquiries for directions to their lodgings. He was grateful when he heard tram line four went straight to where they were going.

They were all thirsty, hungry, and exhausted when they arrived at their host's doorstep. The Sister opened the door, ushered them to the living-room and offered them tea, water and biscuits. Her husband carried the luggage up to the attic room. Joseph took Annie and Jack to the bathroom to rinse off the dust and dirt before washing himself. The water over his parched skin helped him relax.

It was well past eight o'clock when they started a hearty meal of battered cod accompanied by bread with dripping. They were all exhausted, and Annie had difficulty keeping awake.

Sister showed them to the attic room where they could board, free-of-charge, until Joseph attained a job and a dwelling.

The next Sunday, their hosts took them to Assembly where the Brothers and Sisters embraced them. One of the Sisters accompanied Mary Ann and the children to a back room where they joined other children listening to bible stories. Joseph mingled with the Brothers. One of them suggested a job at the harbour, loading and unloading cargo. Another said there was work carting barrels and crates to the warehouses.

The next morning, Joseph caught the tram to the docks and spent the day looking around and talking to people. He was appalled by what he discovered. Most work entailed hard labour, with long hours and low pay. He questioned why the pay was poor, and was told the influx of low-skilled Irishmen had spoiled the market. He told himself that, anyway, heavy physical work was not what he was prepared to do — at least, not yet.

The following week at Assembly, he met a joiner who worked for Cunard Line. The man said they were hiring men to help with woodwork on the new ocean liners. Joseph went with him to the shipyard and spoke to the foreman, who explained Cunard built exclusive ships, requiring the very best wooden furnishings. He asked Joseph about his experience and then took him to the manager, who offered to take him for a week, with minimal pay, to see how well he worked. Joseph was confident his perfection would meet the challenge, so he took the offer. They assigned him the job of making the frame for a settee for a ship's lounge.

At the end of the week, the foreman asked Joseph to report to the manager's office where he was told that his work could have been better but would suffice. He knew he'd done better than that, but he was in no position to protest. They offered him a meagre daily payment which Joseph accepted, knowing it was preferable to hard manual labour, and would help them rent a house of their own.

"I'm glad you've taken that job. I desperately want to move. I'm fed up with being in this attic room with the children all day and every day," Mary Ann said. "Today I had lots of washing and that woman complained I was hijacking her kitchen. How does she expect me to wash?"

"Don't worry. I've found a home in Ashbridge Street, in Toxteth. Recently built, in a new area. A two-up two-down, with a bathroom. It's a mile from the southern docks."

"How does it compare to our place in Shrewsbury?"

"About the same size. There's a small garden at the back, nothing at the front. It's in the middle of a row of terraced houses," he explained.

Mary Ann pursed her lips. "I'd like to see it."

"But there's no alternative. The rent is seven and six a week. We can't afford anything larger." Joseph swallowed hard. "It'll have to do till we've the money for a larger place."

"Why have you chosen a house without consulting me? That happened in Shrewsbury, and now you've done it again."

"I know best what we can afford. Bless God that He has given us a dwelling of our own, and we can leave this place. That we don't have to live amongst the Irish in the slums." Feeling his heartbeat quicken, he squeezed his fist to control his temper.

"That's not my point. I want to be involved."

"I'm involving you now, woman. What more can I do?"

"Quieten down. The others don't need to hear us fighting."

Joseph lowered his tone. "I'm not fighting, I'm only explaining. Nothing is ever good enough for you."

"I want to be involved *before* you take a decision," Mary Ann repeated. "It's my home just as much as yours."

"It is my duty to take decisions. Why can't you accept that! I'm fed up with you constantly criticising!"

"You can take the final decision, as long as you involve me. Can't you understand that?"

He ignored her plea, unwilling to give in. "I'm the head of the family and I decide what's best. Wives are to be submissive, it's in the scriptures. Husbands should be considerate and respectful, and that I am."

"I want more involvement. I'm happy to let you have the final say, but take me into account," she said. "Don't just confront me with one option."

"But I need to choose what's best."

"That's fine once we've discussed it." Mary Ann nodded. "Let's leave it at that for now. I must get on with the meal before that woman demands her kitchen back."

1896

Joseph and Mary Ann had settled into their new home. The neighbours were mostly young families like themselves. Annie was six and attended school, but Mary Ann didn't have time to take her there. She asked a neighbourly Sister to walk Annie to and from school with her own daughter, so that she wouldn't have contact with any non-believer children.

One evening, Mary Ann went into the garden to take the washing off the line. Joseph saw her go out and then heard, "'Iya Mary Ann. Got some nice clobber you 'as."

He saw Mary Ann turn towards the neighbour, squinting against the light, or perhaps straining to understand.

"I's seen ya clobber on ya line in mornin'," the woman said.

"Aye, it's a good day for drying the washing," Mary Ann said. She moved closer to the fence, out of Joseph's earshot.

Moments later, Mary Ann came back inside. "It's hard to get what these people are saying. Their speech is so different, I feel like a stranger in my own country."

"I know," Joseph said. "They're amiable, but their dialect gives me the feeling I don't belong here. The Brothers speak scouse too. I don't feel I'm one of them like I did in Shrewsbury."

"The Sisters are the same. They do their best, but it's difficult to understand them when they talk amongst themselves. I can't grasp their humour."

"When I preach to the Irish in the harbour, it's even worse and difficult to make contact. I sometimes wonder what I'm doing there."

Joseph's job at Cunard's suited him, but there was a downside. Labourers were laid off when ships left the docks to pass out to sea. Joseph then needed to find other jobs to fill the gaps, like doing joinery work for Brothers.

The way he had been treated at Midland Railway and again at Cunard's, brought home to him how inequitable society was. Those with money and power used the rest of society for their own gains, hardly paying people enough to live on. Large groups were kept in poverty. Joseph joined the Amalgamated Society of Carpenters & Joiners because he knew employees could only improve their conditions by forming a force against employers.

He became more aware of political injustices. He read Karl Marx, and others, which formed his view of socialism, and he included those beliefs in the words he preached. "God has created all men equal. There should be neither rich nor poor, neither master nor master's man, neither idle nor overworked, neither brain-sick brain workers, nor heart-sick hand workers. All men should live in equality of condition, manage their affairs prudently, and fully conscious that harm to one would mean harm to all."

A fourth child, Mary, was born in October.

1898

"Brothers have criticised me for not having the children baptised," Joseph told Mary Ann. "They say it must be done soon after birth, so that the devil has no chance to steal their souls."

"Well, let's have them all baptised together," Mary Ann said, folding the washing she'd just brought in from the line.

Joseph rubbed his hand over his face. "I don't believe in baptising young children. It should only happen when they're old enough to know whether they want to make the pledge and to decide themselves. That's more meaningful."

"But here they make their pledge later, at confirmation."

"You've always agreed with me. Have you changed your mind?"

"No, but the practice in Shrewsbury was different. We need to accept they have other ways here," she said, carrying a pile of clothes to the cupboard.

"But I don't agree with baptising young children. There's no point. It's just a ritual." He bent down to re-do his laces. "The bible is clear about the need to understand before committing."

"They do that at confirmation!"

"I know, but I want to be true to the scriptures." Watching her pick up another pile of clothing, he said, "I'll speak to the Brothers about it."

"Why can't you just accept the final pledge is at confirmation? What does it matter?" She closed the cupboard and took a seat. "Just accept it. What will the Brothers think of you? It'll look like you're casting doubt on their traditions."

"They need to be told it's not true to the scriptures. Surely we must stand for what we believe? Why aren't you prepared to support me?"

"Because it's a waste of energy, that's why."

"I'm going to talk to the Brothers, anyway."

He spoke to them and they left him no other option than to adhere to their two-step process of baptism and confirmation. He heeded Mary Ann's advice and agreed to have all four children baptised together.

Picking up Annie from Sunday school, Joseph took her teacher aside and inquired about her progress.

"She's doing quite well, but is still playful considering she's nine."

"Do you believe she's ready to commit to our faith?"

"From that point of view, I'd say she is not fully there. She finds it difficult to grasp the meaning. If you want her to fully understand before committing to God, you need to wait," the teacher said.

Joseph relayed the teacher's opinion to Mary Ann. "Annie's teacher says she's not ready to take the pledge, so I don't want her to be baptised with the others. I'll tell the Brothers that she'll go straight to confirmation as soon as she's ready."

"That's alright with me, if they agree," Mary Ann said.

The Elders gave permission and in August, Jack, Mabel and Mary were baptised together. Each was immersed in water to symbolise the pledge of a clear conscience toward God. Annie looked on.

CHAPTER TWENTY-ONE

A Row

1900

Joseph did well at Cunard. His manager promoted him to foreman, which gave him the task of mentoring the younger joiners and dividing the work. The rise in pay was welcomed — their Ashbridge Street home was getting crowded. Mary Ann gave birth to her fifth child in February, a son. She wanted him to have her maiden name, so they registered him as Joseph Done Handley, Joe for short.

Annie was now ready for her baptism, so she and little Joe were baptised together in July.

After the ceremony, Mary Ann spoke to Joseph about their living quarters.

"Annie will soon be a youthful woman, so we need to separate the girls from the boys."

"Yes, I'm with you. And, at some point, little Joe will have to move out of our room. We need a third bedroom. I'll talk to the Brothers about a larger house. Now I've more pay, we can afford it."

"Very well, but this time I want to see the new house before you decide on it," she reminded him.

A Brother showed Joseph a house with three bedrooms on a new estate in Wavertree, a mile from their current home. He agreed to take it, unwilling to admit he first had to consult his wife.

He told Mary Ann he had a new place to show her, so they took the children on a walk to Tabley Road. Arriving at number thirty-three, Joseph was delighted when Mary Ann's face lit up.

She commented on the nice bay window and a small front garden. "That's much better than a front door that opens straight onto the street." After looking around inside, she remarked on the three decent bedrooms.

Joseph pointed towards the back garden. "It's a better size than our plot. There'll be more room for fruit bushes." He took a deep breath of relief when she confirmed she liked both house and garden.

1903

After three years in his job as foreman, Joseph wanted to get back to using his hands rather than instructing the other carpenters. He also preferred a job with less pressure on production. He heard the Morrison Building Company was constructing a cathedral for the Liverpool Diocese and needed all sorts of workmen, including carpenters. The notion of working on God's house appealed to Joseph, for it would allow him to prove his faith in Jesus Christ. He applied for the job, and they put him to work on the pulpit for Wavertree Church. Impressed with his fine work, they transferred him to the cathedral.

Coming home from work one day, Joseph caught sight of Annie mixing with non-believer girls from her class. He marched straight over to her and demanded she come with him immediately. She refused. He grabbed her by the arm and pulled her all the way home. Once inside, he gave her a good hiding, beating the backs of her legs until his hands stung.

"That will teach you not to mix with those girls again. And not to disobey me," he roared. "Go to your room. Get out of my sight."

Annie didn't budge and looked at her mother.

"Don't treat her so harshly," Mary Ann barked. "She's fourteen and old enough to talk about the situation."

"As long as she's in this house, she will obey!"

He was shocked and appalled at Mary Ann's outburst in front of the children, and determined to maintain respect and discipline in his own home. He growled at Mary Ann. "Why is my dinner not ready? It's not the first time I come home and find you tinkering about, but there's nothing ready to eat. You're useless."

Annie inched towards the door, while Mary and little Joe huddled together in a corner, whimpering.

"There's more to do here than prepare meals. I'm fed up with you acting as if you're the only one here," Mary Ann yelled. "If you think you can do better, then do it yourself." With that, she rushed upstairs, and Joseph could hear the banging of cupboard doors. He sat, seething, thinking through her disrespect and how he should deal with it. All the time the children were silent, the younger two huddling close together. Mary Ann stomped down the stairs with two bags. "I can't stand it here any longer. I'm leaving," she roared, striding towards the door.

He felt the shock rise in his throat, and tried to block her way, but she pushed him back, brushed past Annie, and left the house with her bundles.

Joseph sat on a chair with his head in his hands, at a loss to understand why she'd abandoned them. He was exhausted, and frustrated by his powerlessness and inadequacies.

When he looked up, he trained his eyes on Annie. "What are you gaping at? Stop standing by that door," he shouted. "Come over here. You are the eldest daughter, so now you'll look after the house. You're to do all your mother did. No more school for you. Pull your socks up, and get busy. I want this place clean and tidy, and meals on time. Get on with it."

Annie started preparing tea without a word.

During the week that followed, she looked after her siblings, cooked and did the washing. Joseph tried to reduce tension by complimenting her, but Annie remained quiet and just got on with the job.

A week later, Mary Ann returned unexpectedly. She didn't speak to Joseph, entered the kitchen, gave Annie a kiss, and took over. Joseph held his tongue, deeply relieved to see her again.

After a while, Mary Ann asked the children to go to their rooms. She then addressed Joseph, taking a fearless stance. "I'm back because I love my children, but I'm only staying on two conditions."

He interrupted, "You have pledged before God to be with me and obey me. There can be no conditions."

She pointed a finger at him. "Let me finish. I'm leaving for good unless you take more account of me, consult me, and respect my opinions as if they were your own. God created both men and women in his own likeness, and you must value me as no less." Mary Ann placed her hands on her hips. "Secondly, I want us to leave the Brethren. Their rules and ways are too oppressive for me. We should be free to meet other people. The children need to learn about the world, a changing world. They'll have to adapt to it in their own way," she said, thrusting her chin forward. "We can remain true to the Holy Bible and God without the restrictions of the Brethren."

Joseph's impulse was to punish Mary Ann, to strike out, but he restrained himself, knowing punishment would come from elsewhere. "God will chastise you for listening to those who side with the devil."

He needed to be alone, took his coat, and left the house. In the middle of the night, he returned to sleep downstairs, departing the next morning before anyone woke up.

He kept that up for a few days before Mary Ann came down in the night.

"Where have you been all these nights?" she asked.

"It's none of your business."

"How long is this going to carry on?"

"Until you adhere to the rules laid down in the bible, and behave as an obedient wife."

"I have a different view of what obedience means. It doesn't mean I have to be submissive to everything you desire. I want you to consult me and respect me as an equal, then I will stick to whatever we agree."

His nostrils flared with anger. "You're pushing me to give up my position as head of the family. Forget it!"

"Being head of the family means you take account of your family, not rule over them," she implored. "Take Jesus as an example."

He waved her away. "Don't tell me what to do, woman."

"Well, if you won't listen to me, I'm going back up to bed. What's the point in trying to talk to you!"

The next Sunday, the entire family attended Assembly together. After the Lord's Supper, an Elder asked to speak to Joseph, outside, where they could converse in private.

"Joseph, how is your public preaching going?"

"I speak down at the harbour every week."

"As Elders, we've heard you only attract a small gathering, just three or four people. Is that so?"

"That's not untrue, but I can give them more attention and answer their questions."

"Why do you think the gatherings are not larger?"

"I don't know. I sometimes think it's because of my dialect — they're not used to it."

"As Elders, we think it could help if your tone of voice was softer. You tend to come across in a very coercive way. Catholics are not used to that. It puts them off."

"Well, if that's how you regard me, I might as well stop preaching. I can only do it my way. That's the way I am. I've never had complaints before," Joseph said, throwing his hands up.

"We're not complaining. We only want you to be more effective," the Elder said. After a pause, he continued. "Now we're talking, there's something else. Amongst the Brethren, it is known that you're easily inflamed and administer corporal punishment to your children. I must remind you that no man is to hurt any other man, woman, or child. We cannot have our Brothers using corporal punishment. Retribution is not the way. We must talk to our children and teach them how to be better disciples. Jesus never displayed wrath, nor did he punish others. He used soft words, and convinced those who had strayed to follow his path."

Joseph boiled. "Are you trying to destroy me!"

"I'm pointing out how you can be a better Brother and be true to the scriptures," the Elder said.

"I've had enough of this. I'm going home," Joseph said, and turned on his heels.

"Wait, Joseph!" the Elder shouted, but Joseph had already gone back in to the hall to collect his family.

As they walked back home, Joseph was quiet. He had nothing to say to Mary Ann. The whole affair with the Elder had disheartened him. He trudged along silently and, back home, he remained withdrawn.

That evening, Joseph went to the Gospel Hall to pray. Two Brothers were there, and he told them about Mary Ann threatening to leave him. They reminded him that if any member left, no one could have contact with them ever again. So, if she abandoned the Brethren, she would never see her children again. If she took them with her, it would be difficult for her to maintain her family. She would receive no help from the Brethren. That meant she would be unlikely to leave, so he shouldn't worry about it.

He sat on his own, glad of the calm in the hall. A simple cross hung on the wall in front of him as he spoke to God. "Dear God, I have been true to you and Jesus Christ, and been guided by the Holy Bible. Now, I need your personal guidance. My wife is no longer obedient as laid down in the scriptures. Her behaviour threatens to tear my family apart. Please give me your wisdom, direction, and strength."

Expressing his powerlessness to God flooded him with emotion. Looking down at his hands, he remembered the days he first met Mary Ann and how in love he was. What had gone wrong since then? How had he become such a frustrated, angry man? He'd adhered to the bible but should he have paid more attention to Mary Ann? She'd forsaken her family for him, but what had he given her in return?

Not seeing a way out, he placed his hands over his face. Recurring thoughts of hopelessness burdened his mind. *That's it*, he kept thinking. She's leaving, I'll be alone, but I can't manage without her. His head pounding, he looked back up to the cross, waiting for a sign. Then God's answer became apparent. The family is the foundation of life. Man and woman are to procreate children and to care for them in God's name, forever giving them love and enlightenment.

Joseph reflected on God's message. The marriage of husband and wife is more than bringing up children, it's about working together, in union, in agreement. It was now clear in his mind: he needed to change, to listen to Mary Ann and show it. Had he been putting the Brethren community before Mary Ann? The two Brothers he'd just met hadn't given him any support. In fact, he'd seldom felt the support of the Liverpool Brethren. The Elders were no help and had criticised both his preaching and the way he brought up his children. He needed to put Mary Ann and his family first. Perhaps she was right — they might be better off leaving the Brethren.

Returning home, he found her waiting for him. "I was in the Hall," he mumbled, and sat down. She remained standing, crossing and uncrossing her arms, making impatient, fidgety movements. He held his hand out to a chair and waited for her to sit. "I spoke to God. His wisdom has given me guidance. We must stay together for the sake of the children. It's God's wish that we bring them up with love and care so that they grow to be adults in His likeness." His tone was conciliatory. "That is a burden we must bear side by side, and in that light, I'll see you as my equal, respecting your opinions." He waited briefly for a reaction, and when it didn't come, he continued. "Mary Ann, I've been putting the Brethren before you and our family. That was a mistake. You should come first."

Mary Ann said nothing but moved towards him, and hugged him for the first time in many months.

Joseph eased from her hug, but kept hold of her. "Let's talk about the Brethren. It's no longer the same for me. I believe in their ways but don't feel part of the Assembly, not like in Shrewsbury. We should leave. They'll cut us off from all contact and we'll have to move out of this house, but I think we can manage. We'll remain true to the Holy Bible and to God. He will take care of us."

Joseph and Mary Ann prepared to leave the Plymouth Brethren. As their house belonged to a Brother, they needed to find somewhere else to live. On a new housing estate on the outskirts of Liverpool, a house on Barrington Road would soon be available. It was similar to the one they had, but larger, and only a fifteen-minute walk away, in a pleasant area near Wavertree Park.

They ensured they had no personal commitments to any of the Brethren. The break had to be clean and quick. There would be no goodbyes, leaving no time for Brothers and Sisters to upset them. It felt like severing bonds with a family. They, and the children, would miss the community feeling and particularly some individuals, but they were confident they'd find new friends. Mary Ann was motivated by the prospect of seeing her own family again.

Joseph confirmed with the landlord of 65 Barrington Road that the house was ready for them to move in. Then he ran through the plan with

Mary Ann. "We'll move next Wednesday. We won't tell the children till Tuesday evening, so there's no chance of them telling anyone. After we've moved, I'll go to the Gospel Hall and inform the Elders."

"Can we manage all that in one day?"

"Yes, as long as we've packed all by Tuesday evening. A chap will come with a horse and cart early Wednesday morning. While I help him load, you can help the children gather things together and walk over to Barrington Road," he explained.

"It feels like fleeing," she said, half laughing.

"That's what we're doing. Not only fleeing from this house, but from the clutches of the Brethren."

As planned, on the Tuesday evening, Joseph quenched his dry throat with a glass of water before speaking to his family. He was aware of the impact of abruptly leaving the close-knit community and moving to a new home. After telling his children, he saw them look at their mother and each other. They were surprised and anxious. Annie asked why they needed to move. Mary Ann explained they would remain true to God, and that He would bless them and look after them. They were not turning their back on Him but those in the Brethren who were unnecessarily strict.

Joseph reassured the younger ones they would stay at the same school. None of them mentioned losing contact with Brethren children. Jack said he looked forward to making contact with other boys in his class.

They moved on the Wednesday, and Joseph severed contact with the Brethren that same evening.

PART THREE
Jack Handley

CHAPTER TWENTY-TWO
Beliefs

1906

Jack, at fourteen, found life difficult in the Handley household. In fact, he despised the constraints his father inflicted. He seized every opportunity to be outdoors and free of the unbearable rules at home. After school he dilly dallied, fooling around with father-approved classmates. Other boys had more fun, spending time together with less pressure to go home. They played football, climbed trees, and messed with whatever they came across.

On Sundays, the family walked to the local parish church at 9 a.m. and again in the afternoon. In between, they visited other parishioner's families. Sometimes Jack had fun with the boys but was often bored because, as he wore his Sunday clothes, he couldn't go outside.

Prior to every meal, Father said prayers, 'thank the Lord for our daily bread,' and then they sat down to eat. Another ritual took place after every evening meal when Father read a poem. Like his father, Jack appreciated poetry and paid attention when his father recited.

"This evening I'm reading a poem by F. J. Elwood. It's appropriate because it's called *Evening*."

> Rest thee! All His care review;
> Muse upon the love that threw
> Its fair banner o'er thy head,
> ....

Jack's mind drifted off, wondering why he should rest. Was he tired? No, but weary. Weary of this restricted way of life, preventing him from following his own path.

He caught the last few lines.

When the armour laid aside,
When the glory naught shall hide,
Run the race, and fought the fight,
Thou shalt dwell with Him in light.

Jack puzzled why his father chose this poem about fighting. Perhaps Father interpreted it as fighting for the true Christian belief. Jack didn't ask because he knew his father would only preach. He respected him for speaking about his beliefs in public and sticking to his principles but, in Jack's mind, contradictory beliefs were forming that clashed with his father's.

He understood the importance of avoiding people with loose morals, but he didn't believe it was sinful to smoke, visit cinemas, play sport or go to parties.

One day, at tea, Jack announced he and Annie were going to the cinema with friends.

His father flexed his fingers and formed fists. "You know I will not approve of you going to the pictures."

Jack's nostrils flared. "We're only accompanying schoolmates we see every day. What's the matter with that?"

"As long as you're in this house you'll obey me."

Jack planted his legs wide. "We're going to 'Dr Jekyll and Mr Hyde'."

Father slammed his fist on the table. "How dare you ask my permission to see that evil film? I can't think of anything worse. Go to your rooms and only come down after you've prayed to the Lord for forgiveness."

Jack noticed that his father tried to use the fear of God to impose his rules and no longer struck him. In his bedroom, Jack didn't pray because in his mind he'd done nothing wrong and saw no reason to ask God for forgiveness. Surely God would want him to enjoy himself and be happy. He vowed that next time he wouldn't say where he was going or with whom.

In the spring, Father told Jack it was time to think about his further education. "The building trade is prosperous, Jack. You'll do well to follow in my footsteps and learn solid skills that'll be useful the rest of your life."

Unsure what other course to take, Jack enrolled at Wavertree Technical School, where they taught carpentry, plumbing, construction, and technical drawing. The latter appealed to him most.

During his time at school, Jack swam in the recently opened baths on Queens Drive. As a boy, his father had taught him to swim in a local lake. The breast crawl was his favourite. On his weekly visit to the baths, he met other young men, and they chatted at the side of the pool. Finally, he could mix with men from all walks of life.

1910

Jack finished technical school and was eager for employment, the building trade being the obvious choice. A contractor's advertisement for a travelling salesman caught his eye, and he went for an interview. The manager told Jack that he came across as a pleasant, outgoing type who enjoyed meeting people and he offered Jack the job.

Jack loved visiting prospective customers and always arrived with a genuine smile on his face. After taking a seat, he would put his hand in his breast pocket for a packet of cigarettes, offer a smoke and crack a joke. That always broke the ice nicely, and built trust.

The job provided him with the freedom he desperately sought, especially when business trips took him to towns in other parts of Lancashire, requiring overnight stays. But the contrast with his restrained life at home made him realise he needed to live elsewhere soon.

A day in early September, his father asked, "What have you been up to today, Jack?"

It felt like another interrogation to Jack and that whatever answer he gave, criticism would follow. He clenched his teeth. "It was a normal day at the office, recording the sales."

His father smirked. "Helping those capitalist owners cook the books, were you?"

Jack shifted his weight to his left leg. "Nothing of the sort. I wouldn't cheat. I'm honest and just record my own sales. We're a reputable company," Jack replied calmly, brushing off his father's socialist comments.

"Well, tell them to pay people better. There's so much poverty while the big bosses live an extravagant life." His father pointed to a page in the paper. "There were riots again yesterday. Catholic children attacked Protestant pupils at St. Polycarp's. Then an Orangeman shouted scurrilous words to a Catholic Father and tried to pull off his collar. Fighting broke out in the streets, people threw stones at the police, windows were smashed."

"That's the fault of religion, which does more harm than good," Jack retaliated, stepping back in case his father lashed out.

"The genuine cause is that employers, like your bosses, pay the Catholics far less than they deserve." Father clenched his fists and pressed them to his sides. "In the scriptures, it's written that men performing the same work should be rewarded similarly. The churches observing the Holy Bible are not at fault. It's those not adhering to the Bible that are at fault."

Father turned to the *Liverpool Echo* again and cleared his throat. "Look here, a Catholic woman hit a Protestant woman in the back with a hammer, injuring her seriously. Another case. An elderly Catholic woman, who kept a shop on Orange Street, was so badly harassed and threatened that she died. What sort of people do this sort of thing? Why can't they follow the word of God, that no man should hurt another man."

"Now you seem to agree with me that churches are the problem," Jack retorted, the pitch of his voice rising.

"Those churches are losing sight of the genuine word of God. They should help the poor and not side with employers, but pay workers a fair amount. That is the enlightened way."

Jack took the opportunity to stand up for his beliefs. "Pay should be fair, whatever church people attend. People fight because they've been led to believe those from other churches are wicked." He moved his weight to his right leg. "Churches are too divisive and too restrictive. I want to live the Christian way without being part of a religious group. Every man should be free to make his own choices, and mine is to be independent." He paused for a moment. "Independent, but caring for one another, working hard, keeping high standards, but also enjoying life."

"How can you live without guidance from the scriptures? You'll have nothing to refer to when you're in trouble."

Jack's confidence swelled. He often thought about where the world was heading and concluded the church should play a less dominant role. "I have my own inner guidance. The scriptures are from a time long past. They don't address today's problems. We must use good principles and fair judgement."

"Well son, your principles are those I've brought you up to follow. But you must pray and use the Bible. It will be a blessing all your life and you'll stand well in God's view."

"I can believe in God and His principles without being part of a church," Jack said, before retiring to his bedroom. Reflecting on standing up to his father, he recognised it was a first step towards more freedom, but that other decisions would trigger his father's disdain before long.

CHAPTER TWENTY-THREE
Manhood

1910

Jack was an avid reader of the *Liverpool Echo*. The daily news provided topics for small-talk with clients, enabling him to demonstrate he was well-informed about construction work in the city. An article that caught his eye was about the art school expanding to a building on Hope Street because of increased interest, especially from young ladies. The article claimed the suffragette movement had made women keen to develop talents other than for the household, and art school was a way of meeting and being creative.

In Jack's day-to-day life, he didn't often meet those of the opposite sex. There had only been boys at technical school and his job was in a man's world. His parents discouraged social activity outside the family and church. Attending the art school offered him the opportunity to meet young ladies. The courses were free-of-charge for ratepayers.

"Father, I've decided to take drawing lessons at Liverpool School of Art."

"What will you be drawing, son?"

"All sorts of things I imagine. I liked technical drawing at school and know I can do more. I've always wanted to paint."

"You're wasting your time. You need to concentrate on your work, read about business, and study the bible more often. Painting is a woman's hobby!"

Jack's facial muscles tightened. "But I don't want to be busy with work all the time. I want to meet people from different walks of life. The art school is a reputable, well-respected institution. There's nothing wrong with going there."

His father sighed. "Can't you see art is an expression of hedonism? The bible teaches us to express ourselves to God because only He can understand our inner feelings and guide us. Drawings and paintings are a distraction from what is truly important. Only illustrations made in God's glory are of use."

"Well, I intend to register anyway," Jack declared.

The swish of Mother's ankle length skirt singled her entrance into the room.

Jack faced her. "Mother, what do you think of me attending art classes? I liked technical drawing and want to explore forms of drawing and painting while meeting other people."

Mother frowned. "How can you attend lessons while working?"

"There are evening classes I can join after work. It's free-of-charge, with an evening studentship."

She cocked her head. "You'll have to buy painting tools."

"I've already got some brushes, although I might have to procure more. I'll need money for materials, drawing paper and such," he added.

Father twisted his head towards Mother. "He'll be asking you for more pocket money next."

"I earn my own keep," Jack barked. "All my wages go to Mother, but I should have some for my own development."

"Let me talk it over with your father," Mother said, with a slight smile.

Jack left the room, knowing his mother would sort it out, meaning he could avoid any further confrontation with his father.

The school year started on Monday, 26th September. Hope Street was just over two miles from home, so he walked. About thirty students attended the introductory session. Most were young ladies of his own age, chattering in groups. He noticed one who was particularly attractive. She had a straight posture, a soft complexion, and she seemed to listen more than just chat away. He wished to make her acquaintance. When the lesson commenced, he made sure he sat close to her, near enough to establish contact.

After class, he exchanged pleasantries with her. He travelled home on the electric tram, feeling light-headed and happy. The next week, he arrived at the art school expecting to meet her. To his dismay, they had split the class in to two foundation courses, and she was in the other group. On asking, the teacher said he could switch groups the next week.

The following week, he made sure he was at Hope Street early, to watch her arrive. While waiting outside, he drew his cigarette-rolling tin out of his breast pocket, opened it, and took out the little packet of cigarette papers. Using his right thumb and forefinger, he removed some tobacco and put it between the rollers in the tin lid. After pushing the tobacco down, he stroked the glue edge of a cigarette paper with the tip of his tongue, and carefully placed it along a roller. When he closed the tin, a complete cigarette popped out, and he planted it between his lips. He'd just lit it with a match when he saw the young lady in question walking towards the school.

He dropped the cigarette and extinguished it with a twist of his shoe, followed her into the classroom, and chose the chair next to her. They exchanged polite greetings but before he could continue the conversation, the teacher called for attention and began explaining how to draw perspectives. That was a godsend for Jack as he'd learnt to draw perspectives at technical school. He could now whisper tips into his neighbour's ear, showing off his knowledge.

Each week students took more or less the same positions in the studio, enabling Jack to frequently sit next to her to make her acquaintance. He learned she was Miss Grime, and lived on Rocky Lane, above her mother's tobacco shop. Over time, they exchanged views on art and freedom of expression, and he grew to know her as an independently thinking person, like himself. But he seldom had the chance to further engage because her best friend, Miss Lamont, was in class and they always departed together.

At home, his sisters were increasingly vocal about equal rights for women. With horror, they had heard repeated stories of Suffragettes being imprisoned because of publicly demonstrating for women's voting rights. In prison, they went on hunger strike and were often force fed via a nostril or stomach tube. Annie, Mabel and Mary thought that was dreadful - it seemed like torture.

Their father was of the opinion it was the demonstrators' own fault for being militant. He stated that although his belief in the bible held him back from supporting their cause, he could accept their right to demonstrate, but only if it was peaceful. He forbade his daughters from going near the protests.

At art school, Jack heard stories from students who were part of the suffragette movement. He relayed one story to his sisters. "A man who supports the suffragettes lashed out at Winston Churchill with a dog's whip. An escorting policeman grabbed the fellow before harm was done. It goes to show that men are asking for more rights for their wives."

Annie put her hands on her hips. "Well Jack, what do you think? Do you agree?"

Jack paused, wanting to choose his words carefully.

"I see no reason why women should have less voting rights than men. Why shouldn't they be allowed to express their views and influence the course of politics?"

"Will you come with us to the suffragette meeting next week? You can be our chaperon."

Their father warned, "You'll lose your jobs if you're seen anywhere near those suffragettes. None of you should be seen there."

1911

Since leaving the Plymouth Brethren, the family occasionally went to Doddington to visit Grandma Handley and her husband, Mr Dolphin. In their grocer's shop, Grandma was always behind the counter, serving customers. Mr Dolphin dealt with the suppliers and delivered groceries to those who couldn't get to the shop. Jack enjoyed accompanying him while his sisters helped serve in the shop.

Jack loved going to Doddington. The rolling landscape was such a change from the stench of smoky, dirty Liverpool. His favourite walk was up to the top of Clee Hill. To the east, the view was spectacular — a green sea of rambling countryside on the midland plains. To the west — the dark mass of the Welsh mountains visible on the horizon.

Jack and the family were at home when a telegram arrived on 26th February. Father opened it, read it in silence, and took a deep breath. Jack was aware of the clock ticking.

With a strained voice, Mother said, "What does it say?"

"It says: Mr Handley, Ma very ill. Pls come. Dolphin," he read, with a trembling voice, staring at the paper in his hands.

Jack immediately understood that Grandma was close to passing away, and his chest tightened. He thought how sad those few words on a piece of paper mark the ending of her life. Never will her voice and laughter be heard again.

"If Mr Dolphin sends a telegram like that, it must be truly serious. You should go," Mother said.

"I should have gone to see her more often, and now it's too late."

Mother pursed her lips. "All the more important to go now, Joseph. It might be the last time you see her. You'll regret it later if you don't go."

Father nodded. "I know. I'll leave first thing in the morning. I don't know how long I'll be away, it'll depend on her condition."

Jack's father embarked on the journey to Doddington amidst snowstorms and a wind whipping up snow drifts. He returned the day after, and, as he came through the door, Jack regarded the tired, sad figure, weighed down by his bag.

His father slumped on to a chair. "I was too late. The train was delayed because of the weather, and when I arrived Mr Dolphin said she had fallen asleep for eternity just before my arrival." His shoulders sagged.

Mother hugged him and Annie put her arms around them both. Jack and the other children joined them.

"Were you able to take leave of her?" Mother asked.

"I was too late to speak to her. She was in the bedroom. I knelt down next to her and prayed for her soul. I told her I was sorry I hadn't been earlier," he said, sniffing and wiping his nose.

Jack had never seen his father in such a state.

His father continued. "She looked peaceful. I touched her hand, and it was still warm. I told her how valuable she'd been to me, how hard she'd worked to give me good schooling and a better future." He wiped his nose. "Mr Dolphin said she loved serving customers in the shop and did it right up to last week."

Jack had rarely seen his grandmother. Liverpool was just too far away for regular visits. He remembered her as a hard-working, warm-hearted person, and could well imagine her wanting to keep going till the end.

"Do you know when the funeral will be?" Mother asked.

"Not yet, but we've spoken about what to put on the gravestone. Something like 'the Lord gave, and the Lord hath taken away'. They'll bury her in the graveyard next to the shop. I said we'd come back for the funeral."

The journey took them the best part of the day; the train from Lime Street Station to Crewe, another train to Ludlow, passing Shrewsbury on the way. A horse and carriage delivered them to Doddington, where Mr Dolphin showed them to a friend's house for the night.

That evening, Jack's father recalled memories of his mother. "She came from a farming family and knew what hard work that was, both for men and women. She wanted me to have a better life, so she worked to pay for a decent school for me. I grew up with Great Grandma Stinton while Grandma worked as a cook. I only saw her twice a year, but when she came to see me, she was loving and I knew she wished the best for me. We lived together in Shrewsbury when I did my apprenticeship there. That's when I got to know her better. She was a wonderful cook, friendly, but not easy on people when it came to working standards. She hadn't married my father because she didn't like him, and she wanted to be self-reliant. Both she and her mother sacrificed a lot for me, and I'm thankful to them both. I feel guilty about not seeing much of her since she went to Doddington."

Annie shared her thoughts. "I always thought of Grandma as a determined person. She didn't beat around the bush."

Jack recalled, "I liked the way Grandma showed an interest in what we were doing."

"She did well to reach seventy-two," Father said with a sigh. "Let's pray to God for her soul."

When summer came, the school year ended giving Jack and his siblings time for other pastimes. Jack did more reading. In the Sunday Chronicle, he pored over the 'Awake England' articles which warned about the military threat coming from Germany. Wanting to know more, he plunged into Van Bern-Hardi's *Der Tag* which set out Germany's vision of the future. Another book was Erskine Childer's *Riddle of the Sands,* about Germany building troop-ships capable of crossing the North Sea to attack England on the Norfolk coast where they would not be expected. He became convinced of a build-up to war, and that the youth of Britain should 'Be Prepared'.

Annie, a teacher at junior school, used her summer holiday to finish her teacher correspondence course. But she had enough time for her boyfriend, George Davies, who, after serving in the Royal Horse Artillery in India, was a telegraphist in the post office. Mabel continued working through the summer as a clerk for a merchant supplying ships' provisions. Mary spent her time reading and sewing new clothes. Joe enjoyed taking things apart to see how they worked.

CHAPTER TWENTY-FOUR
Breaking free

1911

Jack's preoccupation with Germany's military strength led to heated debates with his father. Jack maintained the view that Britain should prepare for war and build a North Sea navy. His father believed that if Britain built up its navy, then Germany would only build their navy further. He was convinced diplomacy was the best solution to avoid war. Being a pacifist, he declared he could never agree to one of his sons enlisting.

Another issue that caused tension between Jack and his father was the subject of money. The household principle dictated that anyone who worked surrendered all their pay to Mother. She then gave them pocket money.

Jack broached the subject at supper, just after they'd finished their rice pudding. "Mother, I'd like to discuss the pocket money we receive. We receive the same amount, but I don't eat here every evening, and have to pay for my lunches."

"Your father and I have spoken about our household expenses. They're increasing because you're all big eaters."

"What does that mean?" Jack asked.

"That means we want you to pay for your upkeep," Father frowned.

"I'm not objecting to paying my share. But my pocket money should be higher because I eat here less and have to pay for meals elsewhere."

Father looked away from Jack. "It's fair that you each have the same pocket money out of your earnings."

Jack raised his voice. "It's not fair, though, that's what I'm saying. I'm often away for the night. Besides, we don't all earn the same."

"Yes, but you eat more when you are here," his father said. "You earn more than Annie, so it's fair enough."

Mother took back control of the conversation. "I'll work it out with each of you. At the end of each week we'll see how often you've had tea here."

Jack said no more, knowing his mother would find a way out.

Annie seemed quiet; Jack knew that she and her sisters were frustrated by the disciplined life they had to live. They knew they could do little but accept it, but they felt for their mother and, like Jack, tried to avoid causing scenes and tension.

Through his work, Jack was experiencing more of the world and realised there were approaches to life other than his father's confining view. His interest in politics had grown since the general transport strike in August. A crowd of 100,000 men had gathered on Lime Street and the police charged on them, injuring 350 people. The event appalled Jack as workers were only asking for better rights. The situation escalated after Home Secretary Winston Churchill sent troops who opened fire, killing two men, both Catholics.

At home, Jack and his father spoke about the developments at tea each day. Father said he'd joined the joiners' trade union. Jack agreed workers have the right to unionise, but disagreed with his father about how the unions should achieve their goals. Jack supported the protest, but his father didn't approve of violence. He warned the children to stay at home, "It's dangerous to go out now. Protesters are all over town. Stay away from the crowds."

Jack was in favour of action. "They're striking for a just cause; better working conditions and more rights. They're tired of being treated like scum. I think they deserve our support. I'm going to join them."

"If your boss finds out, he'll fire you. And don't come to me looking for help. Their cause may be right, but their means are not. The devil has got into them," his father said.

The argument about losing his job rang true to Jack. His employer would view him as a traitor. He didn't join the mob, but the protest spurred him to learn more about the world at large. To quench his thirst for knowledge and opinions beyond what he had learnt at home, he took up reading philosophical books and following the political news.

1912

One day in autumn, Jack spoke to his boss, Mr Hutchinson, about the threat of Germany invading England. "I've read about boats full of soldiers in Northern Germany. They can easily land on the flat Norfolk beaches overnight. We have no defences there, and no decent naval force on the North Sea. They assume the Germans will cross to Dover."

Mr Hutchinson tucked his clipboard under his arm. "I don't know much about the navy, but I can tell you what the army is doing."

He was an ex-army officer, and now a voluntary colonel commanding the Territorial Force Artillery Unit in Harrowby Road, Birkenhead. "As Territorials, we're assigned to home defence, but we give our chaps a proper military training. We're a voluntary army to support the regular forces, without resorting to conscription."

"Where do your men serve?" Jack asked.

"They assign soldiers to anywhere in Britain. Overseas service is voluntary. There's a normal wage for the hours spent training and in camps. Do you want to help Britain be prepared, Jack?"

The army appealed to Jack as a path to become self-reliant and learn new skills. The downside was that Territorial Force soldiers based in Liverpool lived at home until posted elsewhere. How long would that be? Jack's aim was to leave home and his father's restrictive rules as soon as possible. In the long term, the army was attractive if a period overseas would pay towards his own abode. And he liked the notion of travelling the world.

Jack loathed the Germans. Not only because of the books he'd read, but because of his dislike for the only German he'd had contact with — a company partner called Herr Hirsch at Kleine Fireproof Flooring. Jack's employers, Builders' Merchants Hutchinson & Weston, were agents for Kleine. Visitors normally tendered their cards at the enquiry desk and waited to be ushered into the principal's office. But not Herr Hirsch. He was a stiff soldier-figure with a kaiser-like moustache; he was arrogant, ruthless, and mannerless. He would crash into the office, lift the counter-flap and walk straight into the principal's office. Jack, in the outer office, heard his staccato thunderous broken English, as if he were laying down the law. Jack detested this German and determined to take revenge.

Further news of Germany's aggressive behaviour convinced Jack to join the Territorial Force. It was a means to better his position. Joining appealed to his need to serve his country and protect it from invasion. Being still twenty, he had to wait a few months until he was 'of age'.

It was a dark evening on Tuesday 13th February when Jack walked to the temporary army centre at Princes Park, close to home. The captain welcomed him and asked whether he wanted to join.

Jack stood straight, his chest forward. "I've spoken to Colonel Hutchinson about the threat of war, and I want to be ready to serve my country when the time comes."

"You've taken the right decision, lad," the Captain said. "How old are you?"

"Just turned twenty-one, sir."

"Good, then I'll take your details for the Attestation Form." After filling in the form, the Captain went to call a witness. He came back with a mate and addressed Jack. "I'll read the oath to you and then you need to sign right here."

He pointed to 'Signature of Recruit' and read out loud. "I, John Handley, swear by Almighty God, that I will be faithful and bear true Allegiance to His Majesty King George the Fifth, and that I will, as in duty bound, honestly and faithfully defend His Majesty, His Heirs and Successors, against all enemies, and will observe and obey all orders of His Majesty, and of the Generals and Officers set over me. So help me God."

Jack nodded, picked up the pen, and dipped the nib in the ink pot. His heart skipped a beat at the weight of the moment as he carefully signed his name.

The Captain stretched his hand out to congratulate Jack. "Welcome to the Territorial Force, Mr Handley. You're assigned to the Liverpool Rifles, 'H' Company, in the rank of Private." His right hand went to his temple. Jack pulled his shoulders back and returned the salute, proud to be in the Liverpool Rifles. They issued him a uniform. "You're only to wear this to training. At no other time."

A sense of fear came over Jack as he walked home. His father would obviously protest and his mother would worry about his safety. He'd given them no fore-warning.

As he opened the front door, his father happened to be in the hall. Jack had hoped to see his mother first.

Father peered at what Jack was carrying. "What are you doing with that uniform?"

Jack rolled his shoulders. "I've signed up for the Liverpool Rifles."

Father bared his teeth. "What? You fool, wars only serve the needs of capitalists."

Jack tried to step past him. But his father moved forward, pushing Jack back to the door. "You're going to get yourself killed. Take that back to where it came from!"

Hearing the kerfuffle, Mother and Mabel came from the kitchen. On seeing the uniform, Mother tried to calm her husband down. "Let's hear Jack out before we get upset."

Father gestured towards the uniform. "It's clear what he's done. There's no need to hear him out. No son of mine will ever serve in the army!"

Mother put a hand on her husband's shoulder while addressing Jack. "What have you committed to, Jack?"

Jack took a deep breath. "I've sworn to defend our King and country. Don't worry Mother, I'll only be training two evenings a week."

Mother shook her head. "You'll be deployed if war breaks out, you know that, don't you?"

Mary and Joe came down from their rooms, but remained on the stairs.

Father repeated: "No son of mine will serve in the army to keep those evil capitalists safe!"

Jack stepped back and bumped against the door. "*I* will. *I* will serve my country to keep us *all* safe. I've signed, so there's no point in shouting at me."

"Get out of my house!" Father shouted, pointing at the door. "I don't want to see you again until you leave the army."

Jack tried to push past his father. "I'm not going anywhere except to my room!"

Looking at Father, Mother threw her hands up. "You can't force him out like that!"

"Yes, I can!" Father retorted. "Go and get what you need and then leave. I want you out of this house this evening."

Jack's chin quivered. He'd expected his father's objection but not to be turned out of the family home. A heavy feeling formed in his stomach as he regretted not warning his mother. He went up to the bedroom he shared with Joe, took clothes from the cupboard, and his camera from a drawer.

Joe picked up the uniform out of interest. "What are you going to do now?"

"I'll go to a friend for tonight."

Joe had tears in his eyes. "I'm proud of you for wanting to be a soldier, but I'll miss you."

"Don't worry, Joe. I won't be leaving Liverpool. I'll be at work as usual. All that will change is that I must attend training two evenings a week. We'll still see each other."

Mary came to say how scared she was that he might have to fight. He tried to soothe her by saying that the country wasn't at war. "Anyway, the main role of the Territorials is to remain in England for home defence."

He carried two bags downstairs and bade Mabel and his mother goodbye.

Mother looked at her son with tears in her eyes, embraced him, and said, "Look after yourself, Jack. Come and see us whenever you can."

Jack left the house without saying anything to his father. He felt a mixture of loss and relief. Now he was free, but he would miss his family.

Walking down Barrington Road in the dark, Jack contemplated where to go for the night. His intuition was to proceed to his friend George Pickles. George had joined the army a year earlier and was in the 6th Liverpool Rifles, First Line Battalion. Jack knocked on the door. George opened it, smiled at Jack, saw the baggage at his feet, and raised his eyebrows.

"What's up, Jack?"

"My father sent me packing."

"I think I know why. You'd better come in."

"He only gave me time to gather my things, so I haven't found lodgings yet."

"I'm sure my mother will approve of you staying here for the night."

The next morning, George took Jack to his aunt's house on Smithdown Road, just two streets from Jack's home on Barrington Road. The aunt showed him a spare room. As he was George's friend, she only asked for a nominal rent, which included an evening meal. No visitors allowed. He settled in to his digs and, looking out of the window, he let out a sigh of relief. At last he had his own space, and was liberated from his father.

Jack continued with his job and attended army training in the evenings. As art classes clashed with army training, he dropped them, regretful he'd not see his classmates anymore, especially Miss Grime.

'H' Company trained mainly in Princes Park, where their barracks were located. It was half an hour's walk from Smithdown Road, and Jack considered that part of his physical exercise. The new recruits regularly had weekend camps in the countryside, where they picketed and trained in a more realistic setting.

The march to camp was always a grand and memorable activity for Jack. He ensured his boots and uniform were clean and smart, and that he had packed his rucksack carefully. Walking into Princes Park, the impressive number of men mustering overwhelmed him. Eventually, the Colonel gave the final moving order, "Advance in fours to right of companies", and they marched off. The rattle of the kettle-drums and the shrill clarion of the bugles thrilled him. They paraded through the streets of Liverpool, being sure to march correctly before the populace.

New men had basic training, to enhance physical fitness and confidence, and to instil discipline and obedience. The day at camp began at 5.30 a.m. with reveille, a bugle call to awaken the recruits. After dressing, cleaning their quarters and having a cup of tea at 6.30 a.m., they paraded to train their general condition. Breakfast was at 8 a.m. and the morning was spent learning to march. After lunch, they drilled till the end of the afternoon when they polished boots and other gear. The unlucky ones were given jobs around the camp, while the others were off duty.

By summer, after settling into his new life, Jack was ready to go back to evening art classes. He enrolled for the 1912-13 school year, choosing evenings that wouldn't clash with his army training. When lessons started, he was glad to see the other students again, including Miss Grime. He noticed she was cordially close to Frank Redmond, so he didn't approach her for fear of being rejected.

CHAPTER TWENTY-FIVE

Baptism

1914

There was great excitement among the troops with the possibility of England going to war. Rumours abounded that other companies had already moved towards the coast, ready to cross the Channel.

On 4th August, Jack and his Company were loaded into open lorries for an unknown destination. In the early morning hours, they rumbled through the streets of Liverpool. People appeared at their doors and windows, waving and cheering, as if the soldiers were bound for the front. At the railway station, again crowds applauded and wished them well. Jack and his comrades boarded the train, which took them to Cross Battery, not far from Liverpool, where they picketed. It was a clear, starry night but there was a cold northerly wind. They slept in the sand-hills without blankets, and with empty stomachs. With only snatches of sleep the men had to get up regularly to stamp about for a little warmth.

At daybreak the Company rose early and marched for parade. Jack observed his lieutenant dash to a grocery shop. He came out armed with all the chocolate he could buy and shared it among his soldiers so that they weren't famished.

The aim of the parade was to discover who would volunteer for foreign service. Some companies offered to join outright. Not falling victim to the enthusiastic patriotism, Jack's Company remained passive. Not one of his group stepped forward to enlist for the regular army.

The next morning Jack and his mates spoke about volunteering. Peter Conroy expressed his intention to join, triggering Jack to take the same step. They informed the lieutenant, and he praised their decision to serve their country and gave them both the £5 mobilisation bounty.

That evening, he wrote a letter to Hutchinson & Weston informing them he wished to resign in order to do his duty. A second letter was written to his mother.

6th August 1914
My Dear Mother,
It is with great regret that I am writing with news which I would have
preferred to tell you in person. We've been informed that Great Britain
declared war on Germany last night. Germany has not respected
Belgium's neutrality and has entered the country, presumably intending
to move in to France and even cross to Britain. This is what I have been
expecting for some time, and for what we as a country have prepared. We
will stop those Huns in their tracks.
I feel I have to fulfil my duty to serve and have volunteered for foreign
service. We're now commencing further training near Liverpool which
will give me the chance to see you all before we are moved towards the
Channel.
Love to you and the others,
Jack XX

The volunteers marched all the way back to Liverpool, where people cheered as they filed down Bold Street and Church Street. Annie and Joe met Jack, and Annie released him of the letters and £5 cheque, which he told her to take to Mother.

The days passed quickly, training every morning and afternoon. Jack's pleasantest hours were in the evenings, especially just before going to sleep. He and his mates skirted the room and told many a yarn, frequently bursting into loud laughter. Jack thought it was almost perfect joy and was at ease with the world. When they were exceptionally noisy, the Corporal of the Guard came in and threatened to 'clink' them all.

To record his enjoyment, Jack took numerous photos of soldier life. His brother Joe made many a trip back and forth, supplying Jack with film and prints of the pictures he'd taken. He shared them with his comrades as a memento of their days training together and the good times they enjoyed.

'H' Company boarded a train that took them down to the south where they pitched in Heighton, Sussex. Jack made the village his 'home frae home'. He was head of his 'family', comprising Fox, Smith, Weatherley, O'Connor, and Parker. To his regret, he hadn't been able to include his favourite mate, Peter Conroy, who was promoted to Aide-de-Camp to Sergeant Playfer.

Willer's general shop was a focal point in the evenings; the place where their dinner was cooked and devoured. The Willers were very easy-going people and allowed Jack and his mates to have the run of the house. Every day, after supper, they filled the house with songs. Miss Willer, a shy girl of about eighteen, pretty but pasty-faced with coral lips, was often favoured with O'Connor's attention. This caused him much teasing, sometimes to the edge of fierceness.

The team's primary responsibility was to ensure food supplies for the Company. Every two days a replenishing supply arrived on the 10.05 am train at Newhaven station. Jack's party carried the goods to their tent. On the shoulders of two men, plodding along as slow as a snail down Heighton Road, was a sack bulging with meat, potatoes, carrots, and bread. Two more mates bore an oil sheet with the sundries, such as bacon, butter, condensed milk, and apricots.

Jack considered the food exceedingly appetising. The spuds, vegetables, and an enormous block of frozen beef, twice as much as they could eat, were straightaway taken to Mrs Willer to prepare for dinner. The remainder was stowed in their larder: a hole dug in the ground just outside the tent. They fitted a box and covered it with a lid of wood, and spread an oil sheet on top. It made a grand storage place, cool and moist.

This pantry resisted rain, heat and dirt, but the wasps kept entering. Wasps were in the milk and jam, on the cake and butter; wasps were everywhere. However well they covered the larder, on bringing out the jam for the next meal, they found the infernal wasps an inch down into the preserve, necessitating them to spread the jam out on their bread to make sure they didn't eat wasp jam.

Jack was Patrol Commander and organised his team into two-hour guard shifts, day and night. They watched for any strange activity near camp, especially any German spies coming up the valley from the beach.

He savoured walks or marches through the countryside with its beautiful scenery. Stretching his legs with O'Connor one day, he reminisced, "The landscape reminds me of when I was a boy and our visits to my grandmother in Doddington. We walked over Clee Hill, one of my favourite spots with panoramic views on all sides."

"Where's that?" O'Connor asked, cupping a lit match to the cigarette dangling from his lips.

Jack's eyes widened and he smiled. "In Shropshire, not far from Shrewsbury, where I lived before moving to Liverpool. At the end of our road we had a lovely open space with grass fields, trees and a weir on the River Severn." He spread his arms wide apart. "I went there to escape my parents' attention, loved strolling along the green tunnels of overhanging branches. The light played through the branches, giving me a sense of freedom. My mother warned me not to go near the water, but I went anyway, just to be on my own. She was always in her chandler's shop, so she wasn't home when Annie and I came back from school. We were supposed to go to the neighbours where the missus gave us tea, but I often wandered off to the river. I missed that in Liverpool."

When his thoughts turned back to the present, patrolling to make sure no German scouts were entering the country, he realised that soon he would miss the pleasures of Sussex when the Company moved into action.

Jack wrote home as often as he could, as he knew his mother and siblings worried about him.

My Dears,

Thanks for yours that arrived yesterday, it took five days to get here. I hope this letter finds you all well. We're in a little village in Sussex. There's nothing much to do here, so we fill our time with a routine inkeeping with army customs.

My daytime pattern is to rise at 7 a.m., prepare breakfast, and rouse the men at seven-thirty. By ten o'clock, we've cleared the meal, beds and equipment are out of the tent, flaps rolled up and our abode given a good airing. Between one and three o'clock I'm occupied with dinner and going in relief vehicles to the shop. Two orderlies prepare tea for five-thirty. While it is light, two men are allowed away from the post, but as soon as dusk falls all must be in. Then we can be seen letter-writing by candlelight, reading and smoking or perhaps having a little sing-song. Time never hangs heavily. Meals take such a long time and our persons receive so much attention that the time remaining is not very much. Fox is always writing letters. Weatherley lies at ease, full length on the grass reading the Spectator sent from the Liverpool YMCA.

We patrol at night, along the railway line. The monotony of it makes it arduous, and in wet and windy weather, very fatiguing. When wet, the sleepers are terribly slippy, entailing careful walking to get a sure grip with the feet which soon tires one. The great anxiety is to keep an eye open for the oncoming trains. One has to look where to step and invariably, on looking up, one would step on the edge of a sleeper and slip off. The trains come so silently! You can hear them from a considerable distance and then lose the sound of them until they are right on you. A train windward will, we have tested it, come to within a dozen yards in absolute silence.

I can't write about the details of what we do and why. We're all bound to secrecy for fear information leaks out to the Germans.

The countryside around here is beautiful with its rolling hills and views. I love the hours that I can get away for walks. On my way back, I pop in to the local shop to stock up with tobacco. The shop-owner, Mrs Willer, is very favourably inclined and cooks our dinner with the food we bring to her. We have nothing to wish for on that score.

My love to all of you at home, Jack XX

He slid the letter into a special army envelope. Not wanting to make the home front worry, he omitted the dangerous nightly patrols. It was a wonder so few men were killed on the job. But there were also humorous events.

He recalled an incident involving O'Connor, the team's most sincere guard. As he was patrolling at night, he heard a sound in a bush a few yards away. He halted, and without a word, silently fixed his sword on the bayonet. His comrade, Fox, was alarmed to see him making for the hedge, which he charged in grand style. The only outcome of this was that his bayonet got stuck fast in the bush's trunk and could only be extricated with some difficulty.

Fox was the victim of another delusion. One moonlit night he saw a man was standing up against the plate-layers' hut and so howled out "Halt – advance four paces". There was no reply, and the man made no attempt to move. It turned out to be the shadow thrown by the chimneystack which ran up the side of the hut.

Any incident was passed along from post to post and even the most outlying sentry post was fully up-to-date with all rumours and stories. A tale that went all the way up the line related how a patrol grew uneasy about a noise in a bush. He called his sergeant. This worthy got jumpy and excitedly let off a few rounds into the bush. The noise ceased, and further along the hedge, something crept away. He fired at it. In the morning, the place was examined and spots of blood were noticed. The sergeant promptly concluded he'd hit the supposed German spy who had escaped. At first, the men felt a shred of admiration for their worthy sergeant, for his prompt action and his accurate shooting; for his skill in distinguishing the noise made by a spy from all the weird, wonderful and witchlike noises heard at night. The punchline came a day or two after: a sheep was reported in a butcher's shop — with a bullet in it.

Some days, Jack had time to walk alone over the Wolds of Sussex. Their charming curves delighted him, with mists in the angles and their sombre browns, yellows and greens. The scene vividly reminded him of a picture of the Wolds by Copley Fielding. He thought the painting was most simple, and yet he knew if he tried to paint the same landscape, he would fail at it completely. His mind went back to Liverpool, and he realised he missed the art lessons and seeing Miss Grime.

From the Wolds he had a view towards the English Channel, a streak of light azure blue on the horizon. In vivid contrast to this dream of peace, he saw twelve British warships sweeping along, silent and grim, on their mission of war, death and destruction. They were visibly connected by the smoke and invisibly connected by signals and wireless telegraphy. He knew it wouldn't be long before he was part of that ghastly world.

CHAPTER TWENTY-SIX
Ypres

1915

Jack and his Company were ferried across the English Channel to France on 24th February, the same day they formally joined the regimental army as part of the 6th King's Liverpool Regiment, with Jack in the role of Company Range Finder. A train took them to Bailleul, not in first or even third class, but in cattle trucks: forty men per truck. Covered, but with no seating accommodation, they lay partially on top of one another on the floor. They billeted in a nunnery, where the sisters still occupied a sealed off portion. When Jack woke in the morning, crystal patterns were on the windows and he had his first experience of breaking the ice in the tub to wash and shave. Amongst the men there was a suppressed excitement, mixed with a peculiar restlessness close to fear. They had now entered the theatre of war.

After a minimal breakfast, Jack was ordered in to the Sergeant Major's quarters. On entering, he saluted, "You called for me, Sir."

"Yes, come in and take a seat. We've had reports of your good conduct, especially the way you motivate and look after your men. We're making you Corporal and you're being transferred to 'D' Company. Any questions?"

"No questions, Sir. Thank you, Sir." Jack saluted and turned on his heels. He was pleased with the promotion in rank, but sorry to change company, leaving his mates behind.

Jack and other men were handed over, and their Commanding Officer wrote a note saying, "They have invariably done their duty in a thoroughly soldier-like fashion, and I feel confident that, wherever they go, they will maintain the good reputation which they have quickly earned in the field and during their Territorial training in England."

'D' Company went straight up into the famous Ypres salient. The town was a ruin after being hit by deluges of German shells. As a Corporal,

Jack commanded three sections of eight men, and a signaller. They billeted in cellars of unoccupied houses in the narrow streets. Their first task was to reconnoitre around town to find their way about, and organise food.

The German artillery battered them with frequent salvos of 'whiz-bangs', fifteen pounders and 'Big Berthas', which sailed over them like distant express trains, dropping into Ypres. The only reply from their guns was a single salvo of fifteen pounders at dusk each evening. This paltry response made Jack and his men feel naked, and the disparity seemed ominous.

To Jack's surprise, a letter from home arrived.

Dearest Jack,

Many thanks for your letter which we received two weeks after you posted it. You have given us a descriptive account of your journey to France. We're happy knowing you are in fine health, well fed and enjoy views of the countryside as you march. You must be seasoned with your training by now.

Our news is that Annie and George married in St Bridget's on 3rd April. It was a lovely day. Annie shone in her wedding-dress with white roses in the bouquet and across the front of her veil. The vicar gave a divine sermon and asked us to pray for the safety of those fighting for our country, and, of course, I prayed for you. It was a pity you could not be here.

We are all well. Joe is excelling at school and thinks he wants to be a motor mechanic. That's certainly the job of the future. Mabel and Mary are busier than ever at work because so many men have been called up, and they feel they're doing their best for the country by stepping up to what's needed. Your father goes to his work at the cathedral and that's a useful distraction from his anger about the war, as you can imagine. Please look after yourself. We've heard that the last of the French Reserves have been dispatched to the front and young, raw recruits called up. They will be glad of help from the British troops.

All of us send our love and affections, Mother XX

Reading the letter, an inner warmth rose in Jack's chest — a significant contrast to the grim conditions surrounding him.

To break 'D' Company in to the conditions of war, the 1st Battalion fathered over them. The colonel ordered them to perform nightly forays carrying rations, sandbags, and ammunition up to the frontline trenches.

It was tough going. They trudged across country, in the pitch dark, battling the worst weather winter could provide — sleet, snow, hale, and gales. Besides their load, they lugged their standard gear: their backpack, a goatskin coat, and rifle. They slipped and slithered in the mud, passing dead animals and men, chiefly Frenchmen, that stunk to high heaven. "Dead cow on the left" or "Dead horse on the right" were messages passed down in the stygian darkness for the holding of noses or breath. They ran the gauntlet of whiz-bang shells, rifle and machine-gun fire. Ricochets sang and whined as they flew by, or until they plopped into the mire.

This continued for two weeks. Their initiation over, they moved up into the front line. Under threat of an enemy attack, they occupied trenches on the Yser canal, on the right of Hill 60. They spent nights making a show of strength by firing over the trench parapet, ten rounds of rapid fire at certain intervals, bringing German retaliation of artillery and machine gun fire.

Those first nights in the trenches were engrained in Jack's memory. Expecting a German attack, the men had an ominous feeling of impending tragedy, compounded by the knowledge of their force's weakness. The adrenaline coursed through their bodies during the periods of rapid fire and their first experience of direct enemy attack. All the time, the cold was almost unbearable. Jack and his men's 'baptism' was an unforgettable and haunting encounter.

At one point, Jack's pal was hit. The lieutenant instructed him to help his comrade to the dressing station in Bleauport Farm. The command distressed Jack, as the day before he'd observed that Bleauport Farm was under continuous heavy German shellfire of salvos at regular intervals of about one a minute. He helped his mate slowly down the little valley, through the wood, and across a ploughed field to the farm gate with the barrages still falling. Approaching as near as he dared, they waited for a salvo and then made a dash for it - as quick as a wounded man was able.

On reaching the farmhouse, they turned in at the first doorless entrance, and saw a shambles of a bare room open to the skies above except for one far corner, where a small remnant of ceiling provided a little cover. There, seated at a table, was a signaller, calmly working his radio set. He directed Jack to the dressing station in the cellar, down the steps of which they dived just as the next salvo arrived.

Jack handed over his charge, and was about to leave when someone from the Medical Corps called him. "Wait a minute. I think we've got one of your chaps here. Perhaps you can recognise him." He led Jack down a damp, dark narrow cellar, where on the floor lay a row of figures covered with blankets. He raised the blanket from the head of the last one, saying, "Know him?" Jack identified the man, their first casualty: Captain Montgomery, a much-liked officer. Stunned, Jack staggered away, blinking in hard disbelief, catching his breath from the despairing truth that this might be his fate.

CHAPTER TWENTY-SEVEN
Hill 60

1915

Wild flowers dotted the hedgerows and meadows as the days became warmer and drier. The mud was less evident, and the chilling wind no longer pierced the body.

On the completion of their 'seasoning', 'D' Company was entrusted with the sole occupation of a frontline trench. On a dark and stormy night in April they relieved the Dorsets and occupied sap No. 38, which ran out from the main line to just below the summit of Hill 60. Jack and his men were only fifteen yards from the German line, on the very crest of the hill, near enough to lob hand grenades into each other's trench. The Huns had a visual command from their higher position, hence the British troops couldn't move in daylight without soliciting enemy fire.

Hill 60, being sixty metres high, was a strategically important location. The force holding it could dominate the area down to Ypres, visible on the horizon. From the end of Jack's trench, British mining engineers were tunnelling under the hill in order to take it. He and his pals facilitated by pumping in fresh air and carrying away heavy bags of earth that had been removed, all in the darkest of nights. Everything was done in silence to avoid alerting the Germans on top of the hill.

The next day, 17th April, at noon, the British blew up Hill 60 with a thunderous explosion. Jack instinctively ducked and when he looked up, he saw the erupting earth rise in the sky over the treetops. Then the action started. In response, the Huns retaliated with a barrage of heavy artillery on British trenches, including Jack's. His company incurred many casualties, the first death being that of their Machine Gun Sergeant.

Near Jack, in the middle of the trench, a young rifleman went berserk from shell-shock, foaming at the mouth, moaning and groaning. He tried to burrow into the earth with his hands; a pitiable sight. Shell-shocked soldiers were treated with rum to sedate them enough to sleep. The wounded, the exhausted, and those with the flu were also doctored with rum. Extra doses were handed out to men prior to major battles or in freezing conditions.

The Germans seemed to have unlimited supplies of ammunition, as their use of it was continuous. The battle on Hill 60 continued for nights filled with endless explosions that lit the dark skies.

Jack and his men inched up the hill and eventually entered a German communication trench. To Jack's surprise, it was unoccupied, so they crept further until 'D' Company took command of the very crest of the hill. A sense of victory mixed with anxiousness overcame them as they knew the Hun would retaliate.

Still manning the trench on the 23rd April, Jack heard a heavy bombardment on his left from beyond Hill 60. He smelt a strange odour in the air, like a mix of pineapple and pepper. The news filtered along the trench that the Germans had gassed the Canadians and Algerians off Pilkem Ridge. The Huns poured through the gas-made gap and advanced to within a thousand yards of Ypres, where they were kept at bay by British support reinforcements of officers' servants, cooks, stores-men, engineers, and signallers.

'D' Company's position was precarious in the extreme, for if the enemy reached Ypres, they would be cut off with only a narrow escape area to the south of the town, which could easily be closed.

The order came to dump valises, and, in light marching order only, keep alert for the word 'Every man for himself', the signal to get out as well as they individually could. Several tense days and nights were spent in this nerve-racking state until Jack heard that major support from further afield had arrived and driven the Hun back.

Night after night, rumours circulated about being relieved for a well-earned rest. Jack reasoned it was wishful thinking. After nineteen days of severe tension in the muddy trench, strained by a shortage of food and ammunition, Jack and his men were at last replaced with other troops.

They moved back across the fields, navigating in a cold and wet night. At about 5 a.m., they reached the outskirts of Ypres and halted in a small wood shattered by bombardment. All the shelters were destroyed, so the men remade cover from the rain in the hope of rest. Jack had just completed a rough hideout from scraps of corrugated iron that were lying about, when at 6 a.m., the command "Orderly Corporals" rang out. Jack, the orderly for his platoon, was instructed to form a ration party. They collected breakfast, bacon and bread — a feast after three weeks on bully beef and dog biscuits. Jack shared out the food, after first putting his own to one side. He was about to eat it after serving everyone when two late arrivals turned up. Jack willingly sacrificed his portion for them and was left with an empty stomach.

Exhausted and almost starved, Jack and his men arrived back at their billets in Ypres. They now had occasion to read and write letters to their families, grateful to have survived the battle on Hill 60. Jack penned his words carefully and neatly on the military paper provided.

My Dears,

Thanks for your letters and the news. I'm glad you are all well, despite the turmoil. I can understand why people are ransacking German shops, although I don't agree with it. The threat of limited food supplies must have been part of the reason it happened.

It's gorgeous sunny weather here in Ypres and they have given us a few days off to recuperate from three weeks at the front. That explains why I haven't been able to put pen to paper earlier. I hope you've not worried about me because of the lack of word. Worry not, I'm well and so are my men.

We hear little about the progress of the war in general, you probably know more than I. We're fully occupied with our daily duties and only notice what's happening in our vicinity. You may have heard that the Hun has used a mysterious gas against us. Fortunately, we only smelt a whiff of it and have no casualties. Next time we'll know what to do if we smell it again.

Thank you for the package you sent a few weeks ago. I truly appreciated the tobacco because the Belgian stuff is filthy. Please send some more when you have the opportunity.

Love to you all, Jack XX

The poisonous gas was Jack's greatest dread because he and his men were defenceless, ignorant and unprepared. He instructed his men how to recognise it by its smell and pale green colour. They were told to urinate on their handkerchief and hold it over mouth and nose, and to hasten away from the gas cloud which moved with the wind.

After a three-day break, Jack and his company marched back to Hill 60 to bury the dead. Only the darkness of the night provided any cover as they carried out the macabre duty. At all times, they were in danger of sporadic shell fire and bullets. Their constant confrontation with death spurred a callous attitude and their humour reflected it.

Two brothers, probably twins, named Smith, were given the job of burying a dead Hun. He was an enormous fellow, swollen up with internal gas and had, on being dragged by the feet to a shell-hole for internment, got impaled on a stump. He lay with arms outstretched behind him on his back. They asked for Jack's help and, putting his hand under the body, he found the jacket hem caught on the stump. Jack got hold of a wrist, took a firm stance and commanded, "One on each leg. When I lift him, pull." He gave a mighty pull, and the man sat up all too quickly and unexpectedly. The remaining outstretched arm fell over with a thwack. A light shot into the air, revealing a blanched face. His head fell forward, and he gave a husky groan caused by escaping internal gas. The Smiths dropped his legs, scattered in alarm, and refused to return to the body. Jack had to find two other men to finish the job.

On 5th May, 'D' Company was withdrawn from the front. The survivors mourned the loss of many pals and officers killed or wounded. HQ promoted surviving officers who had shown outstanding performance, resulting in rapid promotion for those in lower ranks. So it came about that Jack rose to Machine Gun Sergeant and was sent to Bailleul for machine gun training. Returning from training, he shared a lean-to shelter behind the trench with the Company Sergeant Major, a rather elderly man — elderly for war service, at about forty years of age.

'D' Company occupied a trench subjected to heavy 'minenwerfer' bombardment. Enormous bombs exploded, making cavities in the sodden soil, big enough to engulf a bus. During one concentrated attack, the Company Sergeant Major suggested to Jack that they play chess to divert their mortal anxiety. He taught Jack the game with the earth trembling, the light dimmed with smoke, and amongst showers of exploding earth. It helped to keep them sane, but near misses often shattered their concentration. For Jack it felt like chess on the edge of eternity.

The fighting on the Ypres Salient settled down to trench warfare of a more static kind, for a few months. Later, what remained of 'D' Company was withdrawn. Jack and his men were now regarded as experienced troops and moved south to the Somme in France, where they were merged into the 55th West Lancashire Territorial Division.

CHAPTER TWENTY-EIGHT
The Somme

1916

Our Dearest Jack,
We're awfully glad to know that you're doing well and have moved away from that terrible Belgian front. The news we hear is that there have been many losses and we can only be thankful to God that you are safe.
Our glorious news is that we now have a grandson! Annie has given birth to a healthy boy, Reggie. We're so pleased that mother and child are doing well.
Mary and Mabel are working overtime to help the war effort. Mabel's company now provides supplies for the warships that come to Liverpool to stock up. She goes to the ammunition factory at weekends, much to your father's displeasure, but she wants to do her bit too.
Commercial ships are being converted to ships-of-war, so Father was asked to help with the carpentry work. He has declined, of course, and says that he will only do work for God's grace and that the cathedral and churches are a place for solace for those men coming back from the front. Joe has started his motor mechanic apprenticeship and his garage helps repair military vehicles and other machines. So we're all doing our best on the home front too.
Take care, Your loving Mother, XX

Dear Loved Ones,
My sincere congratulations to Annie & George on the birth of Reggie. Annie, you must be overjoyed. I wish you both the very best of good health. Pleased to hear that everyone is putting in an extra effort to help us all win this war. Here at the front we feel your support, both in mind and heart.

For a change of scene, we have taken over the French trenches along the River Somme, and were amazed at what we found. Entering the last village nearest the front, we encountered the streets teeming with 'poilus'. Guides directed us to the trenches, which, to our amazement, were empty. The Frenchmen had evacuated them before our arrival, leaving a gap for the enemy to walk into had they known. We British always remain in position until our relief has occupied the trench and not till then do we move out.

At dawn we found ourselves on a slight hill overlooking a French village surrounded by trees, through which we could observe a German sentry on guard outside a house and others moving about. Nobody bothered. Everything was very pastoral and peaceful. It seems here that trench warfare is a kind of truce, to be played as happily as possible.

I hope to come home on leave before long. I'm dying to see you all and little Reggie.

All my Love, Jack XX

In June, Jack and his men moved to the rear of the firing line to prepare for the Battle of Guillemont. Each day, after a very early breakfast, they marched to the training zone, where they partook in manoeuvres designed specifically for this battle. After a snack, they filed back to camp.

The route was along the valley of the River Somme, which was visible across the fields. In the dry, hot, sultry weather, Jack marched in clouds of dust and sweltered in the heat.

Marching past the streaming water, he longed for a dip. "Captain, may I suggest we stop for a swim in the river?"

"Yes, Handley. Collect volunteers who have a similar inclination. The rest of the company will move on. You make sure the swimmers all come back to camp."

Jack and the swimmers scampered across the fields to the river. The first man to dive in was Sergeant McMaster, a noted Merseyside long-distance swimmer. He immediately stood still in the water.

"What's it like Mac?" Jack shouted. McMaster didn't answer. Jack dived in, but on surfacing, stood as still as McMaster. The river ran fast in the shade of rows of trees and the water was icy. In Jack's heated state, the shock took his breath away, and his legs felt as if gripped in a contracting iceberg. He understood why Mac had not answered. When adjusted to the temperature they enjoyed the cool cleanliness of the plunge.

On their way back to camp, the swimmers passed fields where farmers were undertaking their usual work, and, on seeing a field of carrots, they pulled some out and marched along munching. A young boy ran to Jack and marched alongside him, holding a stick as if it was a rifle.

The next day, at noon, the Company was ordered to advance and hold the captured position for two days, when new troops would relieve them. In need of more rations, they first formed parties to go to the store during the night.

Jack and his party departed at 2 a.m.. They had not gone far down the communication trench with the Germans shelling it heavily, when they caught up with another group who were waiting for clearance of a blockage. News came that the HQ party was hit by a shell and all killed or wounded and the trench blown to pieces. Time was short to get to that store, which was sited near a spot that Jack could see by the flashes from shells falling on the fields. In that instant, he decided to lead his party in a bee-line across country, anticipating they would strike the Longueval-Flers road near the ration store.

"Over the top, boys," Jack shouted, motioning them forward. One or two demurred, but all followed, leaving the cover of the trench. They stumbled in the darkness, with the shells plummeting about them. The venture paid off, as they arrived only a few yards from the store.

On loading up with their sacks of rations, Jack realised that, with the first faint glimmer of dawn visible in the east, the other parties would not make it. So he seized an extra jar of rum. His party returned the same way successfully and were the only party to 'deliver the goods'. Jack's triumph called for celebrating. He opened that jar of rum, and found — lime juice! Observation, resource, and daring were disappointingly rewarded.

At noon, the battle launched, and all hell let loose. So terrific was the din that Jack couldn't hear himself shout. He pointed forwards, heaved himself over the top of the parapet, and his men followed. They ran into a devastating fire and men in front began to disappear. He noticed that five or six had bunched up together, which they should not have done. Out of the sky, a black speck dropped amongst them; the earth spouted up, and when he reached the spot, not a man remained alive.

By this time, there was no sign of men in front and Jack decided their stand was too hot. On his right he saw an ex-German communication trench, and dropped into it. Others followed feet first, pressing themselves against the trench wall and guns readied as they caught their breath. In the leading position, Jack advanced cautiously up the trench towards the enemy, with what remained of his company close behind. Just as they were about to reach a sunken road, an order was passed up: "Halt, and make way for the Battalion Bombers." Jack was angered and disgusted, but obeyed the command, saying to a mate, "Well, let them get on with it and take the main risk".

Jack had been careful to peep round each block, making sure the next traverse was clear of the enemy before entering it. The Bombers, armed with hand-grenades, pushed forward and walked straight into the next traverse. Two were shot by a wounded Hun who was trapped in an earthfall. On learning the German had shot the officer and sergeant, both loved and respected characters, Jack was tempted to shoot him. But he couldn't kill a defenceless, trapped man, so instead put a rifleman on guard over him commanding, "If he makes a move, take no chances, shoot him first."

Another night, Jack led his team over the top. He was the first to plunge into the dark brown mud of no-man's-land, with his best mate, Tom, to his left. A few bare and blackened branches were all there was to be seen in the wasteland. Distant Hun gunfire added to the chaos. Then a sharp whistle pierced the air. Jack glimpsed Tom scrambling through the sludge a few yards ahead, then BANG! The mud exploded, covering Jack all over. A crater had opened up in front of him. He jumped into it – safe from the line of fire.

He drew breath, raised his head and glanced around. And there it was, a body flat on its face. Blindly, Jack scrambled out of the crater and grabbed Tom's leg. He was compelled to get him back to safety, to the trench. He started dragging him, his grip hindered by his muddy hands. The attack had been called off. Other comrades were returning. Two passed him and disappeared into the trench without aiding Jack. He was nearly there, still dragging Tom desperately.

A third soldier came by and was shouting, "Drop him! For God's sake! He's dead. Drop him!"

It took Jack a moment to make out what he was saying. He persevered and reached the trench, confused and disappointed that no one had helped. His captain took up the shout, "Handley, drop him and get down here. He's a goner!" Someone grabbed Jack's ankle and then his arm, and hauled him down into the trench, forcing him to let go of Tom's leg. Jack hunched down against the wall, shivering. One of the men covered him with an army blanket. Jack pulled it around him to conceal his inadequacy. After a few minutes, he realised Tom would not have wanted him to sulk, so he stood up and followed the Captain's orders, his face expressionless.

The division had lost so many men that it was now a mixture of experienced soldiers and newcomers. While making an inspection of his men, just prior to going over the top again, Jack found a newcomer leaning against the back of the trench instead of taking protection close to the front wall. Jack ordered him to move forward, and he did so sullenly and reluctantly. On Jack's return, he found the newcomer back again in danger of shrapnel bullets, but this time he was slumped over, bleeding helplessly from a bullet through his neck artery. He had committed suicide by his action, in his despondency and fear of meeting the enemy for his first time. Without a shred of hope, the newcomer had courted the very fate he feared.

Another most unfortunate case was that of Jack's dearest friend, whom he met at the Liverpool School of Art, a sculptor from Norton-on-Tees, Jimmy Armstrong. Jack had persuaded him to join the Terriers and they had remained together ever since. Jimmy, a sniper, went over with the first wave that was decimated going up the valley and was wounded in a foot. For two nights and days, he lay out there, surrounded by lifeless comrades. Gangrene set in and his foot had to be amputated. If Jack had only known, he would willingly have risked everything to recover Jimmy and his foot might have been saved.

At last, Jack and his men were relieved. The few survivors marched out and back behind the battle zone, ending their share in the Great Somme Offensive. In August, the Company was replenished with new soldiers and they promoted Jack to Assistant Company Sergeant Major, commanding fifty men.

CHAPTER TWENTY-NINE
First Leave

1916

In November, Jack was allowed ten days of leave, his first since arriving in France in February 1914. After being away for so long, he was glad to escape the destruction, and, on seeing the cliffs of Dover, white as snow in the bright sun, tears came to his eyes. The journey to Liverpool took all day, and he was so exhausted that he slept most of the way. Another passenger woke him when the train stopped at Lime Street Station. He didn't look out for anyone waiting to meet him, for he hadn't been able to write in time to let his mother know he was coming. In front of the station, Jack jumped on the electric tram to Barrington Road. He watched the city pass by, noticing how it had changed. Most people on the streets were women and children; the men were elderly or wore military uniforms. It was clearly a city involved with the war. As he approached the outskirts, he wondered what sort of reception he'd receive at home. How would his father react? Would he be allowed in?

Jack was just about to get off when he remembered they'd moved to Langdale Road in his absence, which was the next stop. It was a long straight street lined by red-brick terraced houses with bay windows; number eighty-two was at the far end. He didn't have a key, so gave the door-knocker a couple of good whacks.

Mother opened the door with a baby in her arms. Her mouth fell open. "Jack! It's you! Come in, come in. You look terribly exhausted."

He kissed Mother on each cheek. "You must be little Reggie," Jack said, touching the baby's chest.

Tears came to Mother's eyes. "My dear boy, I'm so glad to see you. We've been so worried. Come along in. You look tired and in need of a good meal. I'll get you some tea and biscuits. The others will be home soon. Would you like a wash and a change of clothes? You've got bits of mud all over you."

"I've come straight from the front and could do with a wash," he said. He noticed his mother was jumpy and pale. "How are you Mother?"

She put little Reggie in the playpen that George had constructed. "Fine. I'm so happy you're back after such a long time."

Jack assumed she didn't want to talk about what troubled her yet. There would be time later. He went to wash and thought how wonderful it was to be at home, to feel his mother's warmth, to feel safe. The horrors of the front seemed far away from Liverpool, although they were very much still on his mind. The refreshing water and clean civilian clothes helped him relax.

He had just sat down for a cup of tea when a young fellow came in, looking preoccupied.

"Hiya, Joe!" Jack said.

The lad raised his head and then grabbed his brother's shoulder. "Jack, I can't believe you're here! What a wonderful surprise to see you."

Jack stood up, and they hugged. "You've changed a lot. You're a real man now, Joe. It's been nearly three years since I last saw you."

"It seems like ages. So much has happened since you left," Joe said.

Jack sat down again. "Such as?"

"I've done such a lot at the garage. There are so many different vehicles coming in for repair; there's something new every day. What sort of motors have you seen at the front?" Joe asked.

"We still depend on horses. They pull the guns, ambulances, munition carts, rations, everything. Occasionally a motor car passes with a high-ranking person and his driver."

"You probably saw a Vauxhall D-Type. It has a 4-cylinder, 4 litre engine, and can take five passengers to sixty miles an hour. An amazing machine. We had one in the garage the other week," Joe explained passionately.

Jack heard a key in the door and a noisy entrance, so he knew it was his father. His breathing accelerated.

"Well, well, our war hero is back home!" Father said. "God has answered our prayers and kept you safe, we must be truly thankful." Jack took it sarcastically, but didn't show it, for he saw a smile on his father's face.

Standing up, Jack said, "I've been fortunate. Many others less so. Even though we're well-trained and use our wits, luck plays a big part. It's easy to be in the wrong spot at a disastrous moment."

"I'm glad to see you all in one piece. How long can you stay with us?" Father asked, and Jack relaxed.

"They expect me back at Dover in five days. That will give me time to rest, speak to you all and some friends."

Annie, Mabel, Mary and George all arrived home from work, the girls in tears when they saw Jack. He was keen to hear their stories. When asked about what it was like at the front, he kept talk light by telling them amusing tales.

"We rested in a quiet, old world French village in lovely wooded countryside. Snow was on the ground. It was extremely cold, but we enjoyed several boar hunts. Villagers had complained of their potato plots being raided."

"That surely wasn't a job for the army?"

"No, it was unofficial, but we used our service rifles. We wanted to keep friends with the locals because they provided us with a change of food and drink," Jack said. "Boars come out at night, and, in the dark, we saw something moving and fired several shots. But it turned out to be a hare!"

They laughed. "Did you eat it?" Joe asked.

"Of course, our labour was to be rewarded, so, the next day, we took it to Madame Gonet who cooked it for our supper."

Annie solicited more detail. "How did you spend your days when you had a rest period?"

"They didn't let us rest! We still had to train during the day. But we were free to drink in the evenings, which, of course, we did. The local beerhouse was too small for all the troops, so I walked my men to another village, which was four kilometres away. Being the sergeant, I had to make sure they all got back safely. What a job that was! I was the only sober man, and had to coax the others home, pulling them out of ditches, all blind drunk." Jack expected his father to start talking about evil and was relieved when he remained silent.

"Did the villagers give you food?" Mother asked.

"We brought a catch which Madame cooked for us," Jack said. "One morning I found a dead hen in the snow. Nobody claimed it, so I took it to the estaminet and asked her to boil it for me. She objected, but not understanding her, I insisted on boiling. For the next evening, I arranged a little party, saying there would be a special treat. We sat down with our mouths watering and started to cut the delicious-looking meat. But it was like rubber, impossible to cut, never mind eat." They all laughed.

Mother grinned. "It must have been a very old hen that had died of old age."

"That's probably why Madame had not wanted to boil it. She could see we were very disappointed and suggested we were to leave it to her and come back in two days. Our highest expectations were met. She'd garnished it with herbs and cooked it for hours. It was delicious, literally as tender as a chicken."

"Where did you sleep?" Mary asked.

"I slept in a stable, in the hay bin, with a horse in the stall. I couldn't fully stretch out, but it was comfortable enough. The only thing was that the animal rubbed his haunches on my bed, waking me up. He made rude noises in the night, and when I woke in the morning, I was half asphyxiated."

Mother said it was time they all went to bed and let Jack get a good night's rest. Jack hung around, wanting to speak to his mother privately. When they were alone, he asked her, "Tell me, Mother, how are you?"

"I'm managing, but the war has taken its toll on us all. The girls are working long hours, which makes them irritable. There are so many of us here that there's a lot to do in the house and big meals to cook. Then there's Reggie to take care of."

Jack leaned in. "How are you doing for food?"

Tears came to Mother's eyes. Jack took her hand and lightly squeezed it. "It's a struggle." She withdrew her hand to dry her eyes. "The days are long and there seems to be no end to this horrible war."

"I know," Jack said, softly. "We're doing our best to stop the Hun but they're so strong, it's taking all our effort."

Mother sniffed. "I'm so glad you're safe, Jack." She pulled him towards her and hugged him tight. "Do take care!"

The first night, Jack couldn't sleep. After so long in spartan sleeping quarters, the soft bed felt strange. In the morning, Mother brought him a cup of tea and found him asleep on the floor.

He was happy to be back from the trenches, but it wasn't like two years ago. There was hardly anyone on the streets of Liverpool. In the pubs there were only old men: men the army didn't need. There were a few younger men who had refused to enlist, but Jack had no inclination to join their company. None of his mates were around. He went to the office to say hello, but saw few faces he remembered — the new ones were women.

Jack visited the art school to see if it was still open. To his surprise, it was functioning. He went upstairs to look at his old classroom and bumped into Miss Grime.

"Miss Grime, how wonderful to see you. How are you?"

"Hello Jack. I'm well. Are you here to start lessons again?" she asked.

"Ah, no, I'm home on leave for a few days, so can't come to class. Are you still taking evening classes?"

"No, evening classes have stopped because of a lack of funding for lighting. Anyway, most of us prefer to stay at home after dark. The blackouts make it unpleasant to travel to school."

"Which courses are you taking now?" Jack asked, to keep the conversation going.

"I do four lessons a week. Design for Manufacturing, Embroidery, Jewellery and Cloisonné. I wanted to do Life Drawing, but there's a shortage of coke for heating the classrooms. Nude models were freezing so their classes were cancelled," she giggled, and Jack laughed. "They stopped some other lessons because male teachers were conscripted. I must go to my class now. Will you be back later?"

"No, I'm due back to the barracks tomorrow. See you next time," Jack said, and departed, thinking that perhaps she attended art school as a way to ignore the war and avoid pressure to work in the ammunition factory.

The evening before leaving, Jack had a talk with his father before retiring to bed.

"You've been promoted several times, I recall," Father said.

Jack put his hand through his hair. "I did my best and took on extra duties. They said they appreciated the way I plan ahead and organise my men."

"How did you get on with your mates?"

"I've always been fair and not taken the easy way out when things were difficult. My duty is to my men as well as to the army. We're comrades."

To Jack's relief, his father said: "You've done us proud, Jack," and gave him a hug.

After a good rest, Jack returned to Folkestone. As the train departed from Lime Street Station and rumbled into the tunnel, he realised Liverpool wasn't the same any more. There were no friends around and his family all had their own lives. So he didn't regret going back to the life he'd chosen, but dreaded the thought of what waited for him in France.

CHAPTER THIRTY
Railway Wood

1917

'D' Company was ordered north to Ypres again and given further training as new recruits replaced experienced men who had died. In February, Jack partook of the Infantry Course in Poperinghe, which covered new techniques, such as assault tactics for an offensive approach. 'Pops' as the British soldiers called it, was a gateway to the battlefields of the northern Ypres Salient. An important rail centre, it played a pivotal role for the distribution of supplies, for billeting and training troops, and housed casualty clearing stations.

Those early 1917 months were the worst winter could conjure up. Snow lay on the ground for weeks and the bottom fell out of the thermometer. Movement in the slippery conditions was exhausting, with falls and sprained ankles adding to the casualties. Trench feet and frost-bite were common and one man froze to death at his post. Handling the cold metal of the rifle was like touching red-hot iron. The morning rum ration sent a tingling infusion right down to Jack's feet.

Returning to Pops for a rest, with the snow on the ground and a bitter north wind blowing, the company occupied a camp of wooden huts. There was no coal for heating as all coal went to the cookers. Anyone stealing it would be court-martialled, so the men had to hunt for faggots.

In the store, Jack found writing material and, fingers almost frozen, he wrote a letter.

My Dearest Folks at Home,
It was wonderful to receive your letter. It's a great consolation to know
that you are all well and managing as best you can. My news is that
we've arrived back in Belgium. It surprised us to see mine dugouts in the
trenches here. I had thought that impossible in Belgium with its high
water table. They're shallow shafts mined just below the surface,

*providing good shelter and accommodation. We need not be in the mud
all the time!*

*I still have to tell you what happened as we were leaving France. On
being relieved, we had to hand over things to those coming in our place. I
had given various handing-over duties to the sergeants. I ordered
Sergeant Owen to handover fifty gumboots and ask for a receipt. The next
day, the Colonel called for me to explain the absence of the receipt. I
called in Sergeant Owen and he denied my order of handing them over
and getting the receipt. The Colonel said, "Both of you go back and get
that receipt, or I will charge you with neglect of duty."*

*After breakfast the next day, we hitch-hiked to where we had left the
gumboots. We walked out to the support trench, where we were pinned
down by a heavy German bombardment. By the time we got to the store,
it was dark and raining and, going into the store, we saw not one
gumboot remained. The hard-headed Sergeant Major refused to give a
receipt without proof. The only solution was to count those boots on the
feet of the men, as they did their various duties. We toured the entire
length of the trench; entered no-man's-land to wiring parties and their
advance guards; sought working and carrying parties, until wet to the
skin, cold and hungry, tired with mud-slogging. At the end of our hunt, we
could only muster forty-six pairs. The Sergeant Major would still not sign
for fifty, though we assured him there were many more. What a job we
had scrounging those last four pairs! We dug them out of the mud; we
searched in holes and corners, finding a single boot here and there.
Dawn was breaking when we achieved the fifty and got the receipt.
Hitch-hiking back, I handed the receipt to the Quartermaster, and all was
well. The joke was on us, for the entire battalion had spent that day at
ease, on rest and recuperation. Such is army life!*

*We are seated around a wood fire to keep out the cold, most of us writing
home.*

*I do hope you are surviving the winter weather and enjoying some snow.
Love, Jack XX*

By the time Jack and his mates were ordered to the front, heavy
shelling had driven the Germans back, and their trenches were empty.
However, Second Lieutenant Colley was reported missing. Jack formed a
party to search for him in the dark and under serious fire. After a quick
search, Jack didn't want to put his men to further risk and returned the

party to camp. When German shelling paused, they made three more attempts, but, much to Jack's regret, they needed to give up. Colley was later found dead. The loss of him meant more promotions. Jack was raised to the rank Company Sergeant Major, commanding 200 men.

By July, the troops had prepared for the Battle of Passchendaele. Jack and his men found themselves assigned to a hill called Railway Wood. To Jack's surprise, a train took them in the dark to just behind the trenches. It had a specially adapted engine, with the footplate blacked-out and a shielding plate over the funnel so that sparks weren't visible. Jack gave orders not to smoke and to remain silent, so close were they to the enemy. When they arrived, there was no trace of a wood, for it had been bombed away.

On the 31st July, the opening phase of the battle started - to finish the war, as they were told. The attack was to begin at the first light of dawn, but under a nimbus cloud, with the rain pouring down, it was as black as ink. The tense, ominous hours spent during the night waiting for zero hour, caused some men to pray, others to curse, and some to think and talk of home and loved ones. But Jack had a splitting headache, which, with the fear, put him to sleep.

Awakened for the final stand-to, the deathly silence, that he knew proceeded a battle, oppressed him: the calm before the storm. Even the enemy seemed to save its ammunition for the imminent cataclysm. Each and every one of his men waited, tense, resigned to meet his end or whatever pain and anguish fate held in store for him.

One gun broke the heavy silence and a second later there came an ear-splitting thunder, as thousands of British guns fired simultaneously. Jack's battalion went forward in four waves, but first they had to get through their own barbed wire. During the night, parties had cut lanes through the coils, laying white tapes for the men to follow. The first wave ran forward on zero. Wave two went half a minute after, and over the parapet Jack climbed, leading the Company HQ. The other waves followed at half-minute intervals. As he followed the white tape, it horrified him to find himself tangled up in their own barbed wire. Knowing from experience the enemy would rain a deluge of blasting shells on the front line within three minutes, he frantically tore himself through the obstructing wire, hurrying ahead out of the most dangerous area. When clear, he looked around, but in the darkness could see no one. There was no sign of those who should have followed.

As far as Jack could make out, he was alone, but continued forward, until he fell, tripped up by the German wire. He plunged into the mud and rifle shots flashed and cracked from the enemy trench just in front.

The bullets whizzed past his head. His rifle was useless, choked with mud. Pulling out a hand grenade, he released the lever and lobbed it as near as he could to the source of the shots. He bobbed up to see the explosion and saw several heads silhouetted against the flash. At that moment, one of the company's Lewis machine gun teams arrived and Jack led them into the German trench, where, in the half light of dawn, they found only one badly wounded Hun.

Jack had been ordered to find Jasper Farm and set up company HQ. It was a case of plodding through shell-holes and around small earth mounds. Skirting a mound, Jasper Farm came into full view. It was an enormous cube of concrete with gun slits, a pill-box. Stark and bare, it looked grotesque, the bombardments having blown away the earth which had concealed it. It surprised him to see six Germans lined up in front of it. They immediately put up their hands in surrender. Pointing his useless rifle at them, he waved them forward towards the British lines. On reaching the old German front line, he handed them over to one of his sergeants for escorting to captivity.

On returning to Jasper Farm, Jack waited for the other members of Company HQ to appear, but only one or two reported. They too had been caught on the wire and by the German shells. Ultimately, it transpired that Company HQ was virtually wiped out. Jack had escaped and wondered whether it was by premonition or experience.

As no officer could be found, Jack set about locating the troops of his company and setting them to work. This done, he prepared the reports for battalion HQ, reporting known killed and wounded, the number of active men, amount of weapons, and that they had occupied their target. He was about to sign it when a young second lieutenant arrived in a demented state. "Look what I've got!" he said, showing Jack a collection of German helmets. Jack thought the man had gone crackers. Given the man's rank, it was his job to sign the report. If Jack signed, the honours would be his, but then the second lieutenant would have to explain his absence with serious consequences. Jack took the more honourable, unselfish action, "Never mind those, sign this report for HQ." The officer signed, without reading and knowing what he authorised.

The day wore on with the enemy raining explosive shells on Jack and his men under a leaden sky and in a steady downpour. The mud was appalling, the shell-holes and trenches filled with water, adding discomfort to continuous danger. Fortunately, Jack could enjoy the comparative comfort of the concrete pill-box, but whenever an alarm of enemy counter-attack was signalled, he had to dash out and man a newly dug support trench, which was nearly waist deep in water. It was like jumping into a bath - a freezing bath, in which they had to stand for hours.

After two days and nights, 'D' Company was withdrawn from battle. On marching back to behind Ypres, Brigadier Duncan, a hard, stern soldier whom they feared, stood by the roadside taking the salute. "March to attention", rang out the order. Then, "Eyes right", and as they turned their heads, they saw the brigadier standing erect, his right arm raised in salute and tears streaming down his face. It was a sorry brigade he saluted that day for barely a quarter of his troops returned.

There was rest and recuperation for a few days, then training started again for the next attack. New drafts of men arrived to reinforce the company. During this period, Jackie Shaw, a school friend of Mabel's, turned up. He had been a very good-looking, jovial person, but had changed character completely — from happy and carefree to sad and morose. He made no secret of his premonition: he was doomed to die in the coming battle.

CHAPTER THIRTY-ONE
Silver Cigarette Case

1918

When 'D' Company was built up to strength once again, Jack found himself amongst unfamiliar men as Companies had been merged into 'D' Company, and new recruits added. They were ordered to France to prepare for another major offensive and further training. Jack, being one of the most experienced, helped train the machine gunners. In the evenings, he caught up with correspondence.

Dear Jack,
Every day we look out for your letters, and when they come, we're deeply relieved to read all is well. It's now three years since you first crossed to France and so many dreadful things have happened around you. You've lost pals, too. We constantly hear of friends and neighbours losing their young men, it's so saddening. There seems to be no end to this war, although we keep hearing that the final battle is coming.
Let's hope the Americans will help put an end to it. They are disembarking here in Liverpool in massive numbers. Ships arrive at the docks full of troops who march to camps at Knotty Ash. We see them going down Queens Drive and we're surprised by the number of motorised lorries of all sorts and sizes. It's all very impressive in scale and modernity. The vehicles fascinate Joe. Have you seen Americans where you are?
The Government has now introduced further rationing. Not only for sugar but also for meat, cheese, butter and margarine. Per person, per week we're allowed 4oz butter, 4oz margarine, 8oz meat, and 1½oz tea. Milk first goes to nursing mothers, invalids and children, so Annie has applied for extra milk for Reggie. He's doing well. He runs around all

over the place. We have to watch him, otherwise he'll run off before we notice and then we have to search for him. He loves playing games, especially hide and seek.

We're careful not to throw away food. They prosecuted a restaurant owner for wasting bread by having the crusts cut off toast and throwing them in the bin. Some people just don't think. They brought a woman before the courts for hoarding 64lb of sugar.

We all keep saying it's time we saw you again. You must need another break.

Take care and God bless you, Mother XX

Dear Loved Ones,
Thanks for your letter. I'm glad to read about how well little Reggie is doing. He certainly seems to be full of life as he explores his surroundings. I hope to come home before long so that I can play with him, and see you all.
We're now in France again, on a canal, across which we have a view of the still pit-heads and slag heaps of the coal mines.
The other morning, when I was shaving, the Captain suddenly appeared, ordering me to go at once with him to reconnoitre battle positions just behind the front line. "No time to finish shaving," he said, so I quickly wiped my face, one half clean, the other bristly, dressed fully and stepped into the farmyard where we billeted in the barns. He stood by two horses. Indicating the bigger one, he said, "This is yours." On seeing the massive brute, I blinked twice. "But I can't ride!" He replied, "You will this morning. I'll give you a leg up."
We walked down the road, I in front, over the bridge, turned right down the towpath at a trot, to which I managed to adjust myself, becoming quite happy and confident. Shortly, we crossed a level plank over an entrance to a small dock. The planks moved and creaked; the horse took fright, and away we went at the gallop. I could not rein him in, but so easy was his action that I actually enjoyed the rocking chair movement, my only concern being that he might run me into the German lines.
He later broke into a jog-trot, a more difficult problem for me, as the four corners of the beast seemed to bob up and down unevenly, to which I could not adjust myself and slipped over on the canal side. Every frantic effort to regain balance was useless. I slid further and further. Just as I was about to fall off and possibly tumble down the canal bank into the

barbed wire infested water, the Captain rode alongside and righted me.
We reached the support trench, tethered the horses, and walked to a small
wood where we mapped out possible reserve battle positions. The ride
back was uneventful, and I succeeded in keeping my seat, though the
entire event was a memorable experience and interlude from war.
My dears, as you see, life here has its pleasant sides, which are dearly
cherished as this war drags on while we live through another winter in
an unsightly black country.
You may have heard that troops in France are suffering from 'la grippe'.
Doctors call it the 3-day fever because it only lasts three days. It's highly
infectious but I haven't had it. I do my best to eat well, sleep well and
keep fit.
Hope to see you all soon,
Love and affections, Jack XX

There was an air of tension and expectancy in those early days of March 1918. There were rumours the British were making underground tunnels leading to the front line. A German attack was feared, foretold by their massive artillery bombardments. After the heavy fighting that Jack had survived in the Somme and twice in Ypres, he wasn't looking forward to being in a fourth, so-called 'final battle'. He felt war weary, his nerves so depleted that he needed a break.

A request was made asking officers to volunteer men for promotion to the rank of officer, for a commission, as it was called. Most pre-war officers came from families with military connections, the gentry or the peerage, and a public school education was almost essential. Other men could only become officers by being commissioned because of their outstanding performance. The commissioned person went back home for further training. That vision appealed to Jack as he was worn out and needed to get away from the front for a while, so when he heard about the request, he asked his captain to submit his name.

At first, the captain voiced agreement, but then said, "You and I have run this company for quite a long time now. Why not let us see it through, you and I together?"

This appeal to comradeship, and the challenge it evoked, brought Jack's approval.

Soon after, he was called to his billet and to his surprise all the company officers were there, and the Captain presented Jack with a token of their esteem. A gilt-lined solid silver cigarette case inscribed 'In appreciation for excellent work to Company Sergeant Major J. S.

Handley from the officers of 'D' Company, 6th Kings Regiment Liverpool, Territorial Army 1915-18 '. That recognition, and the possibility of a commission later, gave him renewed vigour and confidence to concentrate on his job.

About a month afterwards, the captain came to Jack in high glee, saying he was being posted back to England for six months' rest.

A heavy sensation hit Jack's stomach. "What about our private compact?"

"Oh! I can't let a good thing like this go begging."

Jack stood firm. "Very well then, you can put me in for that commission."

Two weeks later, the order came through for Jack to proceed to 'Blighty'. He had to return to Battalion HQ, with the next ration party to pick up the papers for the journey. He was in the front-line trench under heavy German artillery bombardment. The shells were the biggest he had ever encountered, blasting enormous craters in the earth with thunderous explosions, soil flying high. Those remaining few hours seemed like years, as he stood by to catch the ration carts, with sudden death expected every moment. His chin trembled as he watched and waited. He feared being baulked at the last minute and, feeling uncontrollably jittery, his war-weary state almost gave way. A direct hit landed on his trench, just to his left, on the next shelter. His luck held. There was chaos a few yards away, and a gaping crater. Everything was blown to atoms, including the unfortunate occupants of that shelter. He had nerve-racking thoughts — having got the range precise, would the Germans blast the whole trench off the face of the earth?

Dithering on the brink of eternity, he waited, but no more of those shells fell and his time for departure came. He said his goodbyes and left that hell to meet the ration carts. While waiting for them to arrive, he took out his cigarette case. It surprised him to see it had a dent. When he looked at the damage in his tunic, he realised it must have saved his life from a stray bullet.

The train journey to the port of Boulogne was a joyride with its promise of England, home and loved ones. Tents were packed with hundreds of men of all ranks going home on leave or on duty. The next morning, the order, "Every man on parade", rang out. As Jack dressed, the rumour spread of a massive German attack and break-through. The rolls were called, after which the commandant ordered: "All men proceeding home on duty fall out and reform on the right." Jack complied, along with a few others. The majority were then informed that all leave was cancelled and they would be returned to their units. Jack observed a pitiable sight. They had presents for loved ones on top of their baggage; dolls, perfumes, and other trinkets. Some men broke down in tears.

Jack boarded the ship to Folkestone and had a drink with a group who had come from France. They told him that, back at Givenchy, the Germans had made a mighty effort. His old battalion was on rest in the village billets when they hastily set off to battle positions. On their way, they were under artillery fire. The Company Sergeant Major, Jack's successor, was killed. Jack thanked his lucky stars that he'd left in time.

CHAPTER THIRTY-TWO
Spanish Flu

1918

Arriving in England safely, Jack found a new threat looming.

'Keep your bedroom windows open! Prevent influenza, pneumonia and tuberculosis.' On his way to Liverpool, he saw this on posters everywhere he looked. People wore mouth-masks on the streets, kept a distance from each other, and hurried about as if afraid to be outside. Other signs warned people to avoid congregations of large groups. Schools and cinemas were closed. The state of the country shocked Jack when he came back on leave that August. The epidemic of Spanish flu had seriously affected the troops, but the scale on the home-front surprised him.

In Liverpool, men sprayed the streets with disinfectant. In the News of the World he read more guidelines. 'It is advised to wash inside your nose with soap and water each night and morning. Force yourself to sneeze night and morning, then breathe deeply. Do not wear a muffler. Take sharp walks regularly and walk home from work. Eat plenty of porridge.' He passed some girls skipping rope and singing.

> "I had a little bird
> Its name was Enza.
> I opened the window,
> And in-flu-enza."

England seemed to have shrunk in his absence. It was noisier and busier. Smoke in the air filtered the light. Jack was used to smoke at the front, but the air cleared until the next night of fire. But here, it lingered day and night. People were scarred by the war, trying to smile but often frowning.

Arriving home he found his mother was anxious about her family catching the deadly disease. She tried to keep everyone indoors and didn't let anyone else enter the house: no visitors at all, not even relatives. Mabel, Mary, and Joe were all in the vulnerable age-group, yet they were expected to go to work as they were supporting the war effort. Father also continued working because otherwise there would be insufficient money coming in. Annie's school was closed, so she was home looking after little Reggie, now two years old.

Mother told Jack he would be susceptible. "The flu is vicious. It's unbelievably quick. People fine at breakfast are dead by tea-time. Within hours they cough, then turn blue, struggle for air and suffocate. They've converted the fire-station into an emergency hospital."

"What are the symptoms?" Jack asked.

Mother grabbed his shoulder and looked him in the eyes. "Tiredness, a temperature and a headache. You must be worn out after being at the front, so you need to watch out. Stay inside as much as you can, Jack. Lots of people have lost their lives because of this miserable flu."

"Don't worry, Mother, I'm happy to have a good rest at home for a few days. Where's Joe?" Jack asked, looking at his father.

Father pressed his lips tight into a grimace. "They've called him up for basic training and sent him to Kinmel Park in Rhyll. He didn't want to leave, but felt he had no choice. I told him that God forbids men to fight and that he can refuse, but he said he must do his part."

"Which regiment is he in?" Jack asked.

"Fourth Regiment Territorial Army, I think. It's all the same to me," Father scowled. "He wanted to follow in your footsteps."

"He'll be well trained," Jack said, knowing that was no longer true. They required so many troops at the front that training was now minimal. New recruits were expected to learn on the job, with all the risk of them making mistakes.

He could see the rationing had affected his family - they'd lost weight, looked tired, and were often hungry. No wonder with the shortage of sugar, milk, meat, and spuds. Whatever was available was not very nutritious. Mabel and Mother did their best to augment their diet by growing fruit and vegetables in the back garden. Jack gave them a hand by picking beans and digging up a patch where potatoes had been.

As Annie and Jack were both at home, they had time to talk. "Where's George now? Is he still at the front?" Jack asked.

Annie bowed her head. "No, he's on the SS Suffolk."

"As a wireless signaller?"

"They're taking troops to Durban. George is the Orderly Room Sergeant on board."

It baffled Jack. "I'm surprised they've sent him there!"

Annie's mouth fell open. "Didn't you know they gassed him? Didn't Mother write to you about it?"

"No. How is he? What happened?"

"He was close to the front when he smelled gas. He quickly dispatched a signal to warn others. The cloud of gas came his way, so he bolted, but couldn't completely avoid it. He said it was awful. He was gasping for breath, as if he was suffocating. Comrades behind him choked and fell to the ground. He was lucky, but it damaged his lungs permanently." Tears formed in Annie's eyes. "They declared he was of no more use at the front. They should have let him come home, but they put him on the ship."

Jack laid his hand on her back. "It's better than being in France."

Despite the Spanish Flu restrictions, Jack made his way to the art school to see whether there was anyone he knew. The door was open and, as he walked down a corridor, Miss Grime came out of a classroom. "Hello Mr Handley," she said, with a look of surprise.

Jack's heart skipped a tick when he saw her, and was grateful that she remembered his name straightaway. "Good afternoon, Miss Grime. I'm pleased to see you. How *are* you?"

Her eyes gleamed. "Very well, thank you. I've just finished giving the Preliminary Course lesson."

She was well groomed, he noticed, and so relaxed. "I'm surprised lessons are still taking place given the influenza."

She stepped closer. "We have wounded soldiers from the hospital every afternoon. Our classes are a distraction for them. The council has asked us to teach them skills to help them find work later. It's different, but I enjoy it. How are you?"

Jack liked the way she held his gaze. "I'm here on leave before going on officer's training."

Miss Grime tilted her head sideways. "Have you been promoted?"

"Yes, I'm an officer cadet now. After training, it'll be Second Lieutenant Handley," he said, with a satisfied grin.

"Congratulations. I need to move on to the next class now, but I hope I see you some other time."

"I'll look out for you," Jack said, sorry that their conversation had been so brief.

As she walked away, she gave him a slight tap on the shoulder.

After finishing his leave, he went to No.8 Officer Cadet Battalion, Whittington Barracks, Lichfield, on a six months officers' course. On 11th November, Jack and the other cadets were out in the fields on a map-reading exercise. He was sitting on a five-barred gate when the cathedral and all the church bells rang out at 11 a.m. They knew the war was over! There was a swell of excitement and cheers amongst the men, and they made their way back to the barracks. Parade was called and the highest in rank came forward to read from a document. He said the armistice was signed at 5am in the morning, in Compiègne, France, and was effective from 11am. The Allies had defeated the Germans.

The men's only interest then was to find something to drink to celebrate it but there was nothing to be had, not a bottle of wine or anything else. However, they soon put that right.

The 'Victory Christmas' was a grand celebration that year, with the surviving soldiers starting to arrive back home. But there was also sadness at the loss of so many young men. Nearly ten thousand Liverpudlians had lost their lives, the oldest aged seventy, and the youngest fourteen. Everyone knew someone close who had died, either in the war or of Spanish Flu. Jack had lost colleagues, friends, and comrades from the early days in the Territorial Force. Fortunately, none of his family had perished or been seriously injured. Joe returned safely.

Crowds filled the roads for Christmas shopping, as the population had been supplied with money. But no extra food, no turkey, was available. People celebrated at their firesides in restraint for those lost. Little went on in the streets of Liverpool, but the hospitals were busy with the seriously wounded and the Spanish Flu claiming lives.

Jack had his picture taken, wearing his officer cadet uniform. He looked smart, a cap with a white band perched on his head, a neat moustache and a white shirt and tie under his tunic. The image conveyed a true officer.

On 6th February 1919, they called him into the Major's quarters where he received his commission to the rank of officer. The Major presented him with four blue Chevrons and five medals: the British War Medal, the Star, the Meritorious Service Medal, the Victory Medal, and the Belgian Croix de Guerre.

After his seven years in the army, he was demobilised and posted to the Officer's Reserve. When he read his Discharge Certificate, he smiled. 'This Officer Cadet is exceptionally well educated, intelligent and capable.'

He returned to Liverpool with high hopes for a new phase in his life.

PART FOUR
Miss Grime

CHAPTER THIRTY-THREE
Art School

1913

Miss Grime had little interest in talk about Germany preparing for war. At art school classes, Jack Handley had spoken about what he saw coming and why he had joined the Territorial Force. At twenty-three, Miss Gladys Grime set her sights on becoming an artist and didn't want to think of her dream being ruined because of a war. She rather liked Jack — he was humorous, helpful and an independent thinker. She hadn't let him know she fancied him. Gladys enjoyed the company of other men too, but wasn't ready to have a close relationship with any of them.

Christina Lamont was her best friend at art school. Several years older, she had previously studied at Montrose Academy in Angus, and Edinburgh School of Art. Gladys's eagerness to learn, and Christina's pleasure in sharing her knowledge, made them a perfect match. Gladys was keen to know every aspect of the techniques she used because she settled for no less than perfection. Both students were ambitious. Christina wanted to be an art teacher and Gladys dreamt of being an independent artist, although the steps to achieve her goal eluded her.

As the summer holidays arrived, most classmates went travelling, including the young men with whom she was amicable. She could tell who liked her, because they sent postcards. Jim toured Scotland and dropped a card picturing Robert Burns. Gladys peered at the poet's portrait. She wondered what message Jim was implying when words from a Burns poem came to her mind.

> O my Luve's like a red, red rose,
> That's newly sprung in June:
> O my Luve's like the melody,

That's sweetly play'd in tune.

The next postcard Jim sent was from Aberystwyth, Wales. She'd been there and recognised the sweeping beach with the boats hauled up above the high-tide mark. She could make out the familiar Belle Vue Hotel on the sea-front and imagined herself walking along the promenade with him.

James Norton wrote a postcard from Paris.

Dear Gladys,
The Opera House here is the most beautiful in the world. The lowest
price is 7s 6d, so they make you pay.

The photograph showed Le Grand Foyer with its chandeliers, pillars and ornate ceiling. She day-dreamed about visiting Paris, the art-lovers' place-to-be.

It amazed her when a postcard arrived from Canada. Her heart ticked quicker because she rather fancied Frank, handsome with his dark hair and strong jawline.

Dear Gladys,
No doubt you will be surprised to receive this, but you see, I have not
forgotten you, and hope this card finds you quite well. I have a job as a
draughtsman in a large company here and am doing well. Remember me
to your father & mother. Hope you are doing big things with your
drawing.
Yours very sincerely, Frank Redmond.
PS. A postcard would be very acceptable.

Her heart sank and she let out a sigh, disappointed that he'd left Liverpool without bidding her farewell.

Her father's voice interrupted her thoughts. "Who's in Canada, love?"

She then turned the card over and looked at the picture of a street in Toronto with tall buildings. "It's from Frank. He's taken up a job there. I'd no idea he was leaving Liverpool. I'm surprised. He sends his regards."

Hoping he might return, Gladys wrote to him and soon received a reply.

Dear Gladys,

Hearty thanks for your kindness in sending me your two postcards. I was delighted to hear from you, and of your success at the school. Yes, I like Toronto, but I cannot say better than Liverpool, for I left all dear to me behind when I sailed out of the Mersey. I wish I could have seen you before leaving to wish you and your parents farewell, but it's too late to talk now.

Hoping this finds you quite well and kindest regards to Father & Mother, yours sincerely — Frank Redmond.

Gladys loved travelling, even if it wasn't far away — anything was better than being stuck in Liverpool all summer. Her parents had time and money to go on holiday. Father had a well-paid and stable job, and Mother supplemented their income with her tobacco and sweet shop. She kept the shop open seven days a week, throughout the year. That meant that Mother and Father took turns going away on holiday, so Gladys had a holiday with each parent.

She and her father sailed on the ferry from Liverpool to the Isle of Man, a popular holiday resort for Liverpudlians who could afford to make the journey. He hired a car, and they enjoyed the thrill of driving around the island, windows down, hair blowing in the sea breeze. They stopped in Peel to walk along the quay where fishermen were unloading their sailing-boats and tidying up for the day. In the warm afternoon sun, they walked to Peel Castle, which stood strong, commanding the bay. Gladys sat on a wall to sketch the view of the harbour while her father strolled around the castle.

He came back to sit next to her. Looking at her drawing, he said, "Enjoying art school, are you?"

"I truly am." Gladys stretched her arms. "I'm glad I've started day classes."

"I'm pleased to hear."

"Classes are more relaxing in the daytime — there isn't the hurry to get home before dark. There's time to chat."

"How do you see things progressing?"

Gladys put down her sketchbook. "I plan to do Industrial Design this autumn. It's creative but has a practical side, because what I design will be part of something."

"Something like what?"

"A wall, a glass panel, anything really. I'd like to design things that make peoples' everyday life more pleasing." She picked up her sketchbook again. "I hope to get a studentship again."

"That makes sense." Her father tilted his head slightly to the side. "I was wondering more about the longer term. What sort of life do you wish to lead?"

"Of course I'd like to have a family, a small family, just a couple of children. But I also want to be a recognised artist." Gladys looked towards a fishing boat entering the harbour. "Art isn't just a pastime for me. I aim to take it seriously, but I'm not sure how yet."

"Well, now's the time to concentrate on art, before starting a family," Father said, watching the boat approach the quay. Then he turned to face Gladys. "I noticed you had quite a few cards from men folk."

"There're one or two I'm really friendly with, but none have stolen my heart." She fidgeted, feeling slightly uncomfortable with the conversation. "I'm too preoccupied with my art studies."

Gladys knew her father would prefer her to marry a man with a steady income, but her ambition was to be more than a mother and housewife. She was relieved he didn't press her on the matter.

After arriving back home, Father took over managing the shop to allow Mother and Gladys to take the steam train to Bakewell for a few days' holiday in the Peak District.

In September, friends returned from their travels. They had taken their sketchpads, pencils, and pens with them. Some had done quick portraits or landscapes to earn a penny at the seaside resorts they visited. Holidaymakers willingly spent money after watching artists sketch or paint.

Back in Liverpool, Jim invited Gladys to accompany him to the newly opened Crane's Music Hall, where they saw an amateur drama group perform Shakespeare's Macbeth. James went for a more professional performance, taking Gladys to the Royal Liverpool Philharmonic to listen to Elgar's romantic music.

She enjoyed these evenings out and other contacts with her male friends, but avoided anything more regular or serious. She preferred to spend time with Christina and the Cubbin sisters, who were also art students. They discussed their homework, commented on each other's work, and went out together.

One such outing was to see King George V and Queen Mary arrive for a visit to Liverpool, accompanied by their son, Edward, the Prince of Wales. Gladys wondered at the Union Jacks, crowns and the letters G & M all over the centre. Thousands of people lined the streets as the royals inspected a parade and visited the docks. Even though she only caught a fleeting glimpse, Gladys had an uplifting day that made her proud of the city.

Pleased she had chosen Industrial Design, Gladys learned about art nouveau, about how it had a sense of movement, was asymmetric and full of curves and natural forms. The teacher took them to the Philharmonic Dining Rooms, where he pointed out the exuberant style of the architecture, a variety of gables, turrets and parapets. Above the entrance were sculptures of musicians. Inside, decorations adorned copper panels.

It surprised Gladys when the teacher drew them towards the gentlemen's water closet. He popped inside to check there was no one there, then he signalled his students to enter. The girls held back, giggling, but Gladys stepped forward, peering through the doorway and stepping inside.

She came out blushing and laughing. "Even if you've seen urinals before, you must come and see these."

The others followed and proclaimed their amazement when they saw the ornate urinals of rose-coloured marble.

The embroidery teacher gave his pupils a homework task, "Do an embroidery inspired by your visit to the Dining Rooms." Thinking of the natural curves she had seen in the architecture, Gladys sketched the design — three red irises with their green stems curling upwards.

CHAPTER THIRTY-FOUR
Suffragettes

1913

At school, the new Post Impressionism approach was highly debated. Gladys and her friends had seen the works of Gauguin, Van Gogh, Matisse, and Cézanne. The way they used colour and sought the essence in a painting appealed to Gladys, although she preferred to stick to her figurative style which was more suited to industrial design. The controversy led to several teachers leaving to work for a new art school set up by the progressive Sandon Studios Society. They wanted to change the perspective of art in Liverpool to stimulate creativity and innovation, rather than take the restrictive approach of the municipal schools.

At this time, all over England, women were demanding the right to vote in elections. Gladys and her mother followed these developments closely. Mother firmly believed women and men were equal, and that women should develop themselves and be self-reliant. That's why she had sent Gladys to the Rathbone Primary School, founded and named after a rich family. Mrs Rathbone led the Liverpool Women Suffrage Society and had a compelling influence on the school and the development of the girls.

Gladys and her mother regretted that the suffragette movement had become militant. They broke windows, set buildings on fire, let off bombs and did their best to harass men with political weight. Two local women were imprisoned in Walton Gaol and denied bail. They refused to accept prison discipline and food. Without being convicted, they were force-fed, thrown into a punishment cell, and locked in irons.

Eleanor Rathbone took a less militant approach, so Gladys attended several suffragette meetings. She believed women like herself should be free to develop their talents and earn an income.

Gladys tried to convince her friend, Christina, to join her in a suffragette march.

Christina frowned. "I think they're far too sensational and aggressive. I don't want to be arrested."

"They're not belligerent here in Liverpool. They dress up in colourful clothes, wave banners and ask people to sign petitions. All to attract public attention," Gladys explained.

Christina tossed her head from side to side. "I've never been to a march."

"At least we can watch," Gladys replied.

"Alright, but I'm not going to take part, only watch."

Gladys rushed her words. "They're marching all the way to London, starting from St George's Hall. We can wave them out from there. Our classmates have designed banners, so we'll see them there too."

On the day of the march, Gladys dressed to go into town. Similar to other art students, her dress was unconventional. She preferred a more colourful and natural look, less emphasis on the breasts and more on the waistline.

For this demonstration, she chose to stand out without looking aggressive. To match her soft complexion and auburn hair, she wore a simple light green jacket and a red beret, the colours of the movement. Her brown leather shoes peeked out from below the hem of her dress. In the centre of town, she met Christina, and the Cubbin sisters, Eileen and Ivy. Together, they made their way to the steps of St George's Hall, nodding to those they knew and greeting other students.

"Look at the size of the group," Gladys said, excitedly. "They're like an army - a battalion of women going off to battle."

"They're all wearing the same sashes," Christina remarked.

"Oh, I forgot about our sashes," Gladys said, opening her bag and taking out four green, white and red ribbons with the words 'Votes for Women'. Christina declined to wear one, saying it didn't suit her dress. But Gladys said, "It's only a sash", and popped it over Christina's head before she had a chance to stop her.

The army of women was preparing to march. Many had small banners, squares of dark red cloth, bearing the words 'Law-Abiding Suffragettes'. From their shoulders dangled canvas bags containing leaflets to hand out. The leaders, including Eleanor Rathbone, held enormous banners.

Gladys pointed to a group carrying sun-shades with the words, 'No Votes, No Taxes'. Christina remarked that quite a few men were present and wore 'Votes for Women' buttons. A banner even targeted men, quoting Tennyson, 'The woman's cause is man's: they rise together, dwarfed or godlike, bound or free'.

The crowd looked like a mix of women from all parts of society — rich, poor, plebeian, patrician. Gladys noticed a significant police presence around the square, but no sign of aggressive suffragettes. Ivy pointed to a woman wearing flowing gipsy-like garments and sandals, a little child at her side, carrying a standard 'Wives of England's Unemployed'.

Eleanor Rathbone's voice flowed out of a megaphone over the eager heads. She clearly explained the arguments the marchers should use to convert both women and men to the cause during the march. Loud applause and banner waving followed her proclamation.

Gladys and Ivy yelled out in support. Christina and Eileen watched excitedly. The march started. Gladys was bouncing from foot to foot, wanting to follow. "Come on, let's follow them."

She felt a sense of power emanate from the mass as they paraded through the streets. Gladys and her friends moved along with the crowd, their arms locked together. Gladys said, "The time for us women is coming. I can feel it. Our world is going to be much better than our mothers' and grandmothers'."

When they reached the outskirts of town, they left the march and went home.

In the paper the next day, Gladys read that the march to London had been a magnificent success, with thousands of women from all over the country arriving in Hyde Park for a grand, peaceful demonstration.

On another page, she was upset when she learned that a militant group of suffragettes had met at Trafalgar Square. Miss Sylvia Pankhurst had spoken, "We have come here to hold a council of war. The time for argument is past. Our motto is 'Deeds, not Words', and we will act." The crowd attempted to march to Downing Street to pass a petition to the Prime Minister, but a strong cordon of mounted police blocked their way. They arrested Miss Pankhurst amidst a scuffle, with women endeavouring to get their leader free with sticks and umbrellas.

When Gladys told her father about what she'd read in the paper, he snickered. "Your suffragettes are of little consequence to the Prime Minister. He's more concerned about the Balkan War and the positioning of France and Russia against Germany."

CHAPTER THIRTY-FIVE

A day at the beach

1914

August 3rd was a sunny bank holiday. Mother kept the shop closed so she could join Gladys and Father at the beach. She first did her normal early morning routine of saying her prayers and baking bread before breakfast. Gladys spread cold butter on a warm slice and let it soak in. Then Mother served her a cooked breakfast of bacon and sausages, scrambled eggs on toast, and fried tomatoes. After finishing, Gladys wiped her plate clean with another slice of bread.

With thousands of others, they crossed the Mersey to New Brighton. Holidaying men wore light trousers, blue jackets and boater-hats. Women wore long summer dresses, magnificent hats, and carried sun-shades. After disembarking, they sauntered along the promenade, passed the Battery, and stepped on to the sand. The fresh salty sea air filled Gladys' lungs. The repetitive sound of the waves had a calming effect. She saw an unbroken row of beach huts on wheels lined up on the high tide mark. They rented a hut and entered up the steps to change into their one-piece swimsuits. Father's was blue and white striped. The women had swimsuits that covered them to just above the knee.

Gladys couldn't wait. "Let's go in straight away."

Father shivered. "Let the water warm up a bit first."

"We can sit in the sun to dry and warm ourselves afterwards," Gladys said, already on her way to the water's edge.

She dipped her toe in the water and quickly withdrew it. Not wanting to put her parents off, she clenched her teeth, splashed water on her legs and arms, and slowly waded into the sea. Father still held back, insisting it was freezing.

"Come on in, you'll soon get used to it," Gladys shouted, and, eventually, both parents entered the sea. Gladys used powerful strokes to swim over the waves, but her parents, not knowing how to swim, remained paddling.

The expanse of sea gave Gladys a sense of freedom, but also a feeling of being unimportant when compared with the enormity of the world: just like a grain of sand on the beach. She felt the sun beating down on her head, the salt water getting into a scratch on her leg making it sting.

Looking back, she saw her father retreating to the hut and taking out the deck-chairs. She swam back to her mother, who said, "I can see you're enjoying it, but I'm going out soon too."

Gladys treaded water. "I'm going to stay in for a while." She swam back out to sea and thought how wonderful it would be if her future husband could swim too.

Her parents now sat in their deck-chairs, watching her. She guessed they worried about her going too far from the beach.

Gladys let the waves thrust her back until her knees touched the sand. She settled to dry in the sun. Mother had brought refreshments in a basket — sandwiches made of the freshly baked bread, fruit cake, apples and lemonade. By early afternoon it was scorching, so Gladys opened her parasol to avoid getting sun-burnt. It was the best day of the summer and everyone had a jolly good time. On the ferry back to Liverpool, Father bought the *Liverpool Echo*, which had a picture of a fleet of German warships setting out to sea.

The next day, they heard the Germans had occupied Belgium and that Britain had declared war on Germany. The papers were full of the news and a large announcement: 'Your King and Country need you. Will you answer your country's call? In this crisis, your country calls on all her young, unmarried men to rally round the Flag and enlist in the ranks of her Army.'

Gladys let out a deep sigh. "How terrible that those young men need to choose to risk their lives!"

"Many'll see the adventure and convince their mates to enlist," Father said. "Their parents will dread the consequences."

Gladys muttered. "What'll happen to my teachers?"

"Maybe one or two will volunteer, but it probably won't affect the school."

"But most male students are young and unmarried. We'll lose our classmates!"

"Don't worry. They'll be well-trained. It'll all be over by Christmas. Our troops will help the French push the Hun back to their own country in no time. Don't worry, we'll be safe. The war won't affect us here."

To avoid thinking about the war, Gladys immersed herself in her art. On a dry day, she packed her drawing gear and walked into Newsham Park, just across the road from the shop on Rocky Lane. She looked for a suitable spot to practise landscape studies. She carefully chose the composition — something in the foreground and an interesting view with perspectives. Light was an important factor, creating a sense of depth, with shadows of varying intensity.

Christina joined her to sketch and chat. They spoke about their exam results. Both had passed Perspectives and Industrial Design, but Gladys had failed Linen Weaving.

She shook her head. "I find it difficult to weave patterns. It's easy to make a mistake with the colours. I made a couple of minor mistakes, but by the time I'd noticed, it was too late to re-do it."

"That's why I didn't choose to weave," Christina said, and swung her arms up. "I've got good news to tell you."

"Well, come on, out with it!"

Christina smiled. "You remember I applied for that job at Ormskirk Grammar School?"

Gladys nodded.

"They've now appointed me as art teacher."

"Congratulations, well done," Gladys said, giving Christina a hug.

"I'm so excited to start."

"Will you be giving up your art classes?"

"Don't worry, I'll still be around; the post is only two days a week."

"I'm sure you'll enjoy teaching. Children are so keen to learn," Gladys said. "May I ask you something personal?"

"Of course."

"Being a teacher means you can't marry."

"If I ever meet the right prince, I'll give up teaching - at least, formal teaching at a school. We'll see."

"I think it's ridiculous that women teachers are prevented from marrying. It's something that needs to change when we're allowed to vote."

They continued sketching until Gladys asked, "Have you read the latest students' magazine?"

"I never really bother. Why are you asking?"

Gladys took the magazine out of her satchel. "Look here. There's a funny article about the Men's Common Room, obviously written by a man. He writes, 'One lunchtime we were short of cups and ventured into the Women's Common Room to borrow some, and were appalled at the sight which greeted us'."

"What! Appalled by what?"

"Listen. 'Row upon row of orderly girls were seated at orderly tables. The room itself was a perfect picture of orderliness. Everywhere beauty, cleanliness, orderliness rebuked us. Terrible, desolating, soul tormenting orderliness!',," Gladys quoted.

"They've been taking the mickey out of us," Christina declared. "I'd like to see the state of their Common Room."

"There's more." Gladys read on. "'We fled back to our own room and hysterically commented upon the contrast. At a large shiny table devoid of cloth or ornament were seated half a dozen of the men students. No sign of plate or saucer, and glorious disorder reigned. Two of them were drinking out of jam jars and one other from a sugar basin. At the fire, one man was toasting a large slab of bread on a long wobbly wire, and another was manipulating a savoury kipper suspended upon two pokers. Having finished our kipper, toast and tea with relish, we placed our feet upon that large shiny table, pulled deliciously at our pipes sending up contented puffs of smoke — smoke that persistently wreathed itself into one word — FREEDOM!'"

Christina pulled up her nose. "It's absolutely disgusting. I've heard they even have boxing matches there. Typical. Their idea of freedom is to have a lack of good manners."

"They think that's freedom, but I'm sure any man in there attempting to place a cloth on the table would feel far from free when his companions snatch it away and raise their fists," Gladys concluded, glancing a smile.

CHAPTER THIRTY-SIX

Christmas

1914

Little changed in Gladys's life as war raged on the Continent. It seemed a long way from Liverpool, especially as none of her family or close friends were involved.

At tea-time one evening in late September, Mother said, "I spoke to Aunty Lucy today. She told me her Alfred has enlisted."

Gladys bit her lip. "Oh dear, I hope he'll look after himself. I get on well with him when we sketch together."

"Was she upset?" Father asked.

Mother cleared her throat. "Yes, very. She sent Uncle Fred to the barracks to cancel it, but they insisted documents were signed and approved."

Gladys frowned and squinted. "But he can't be eighteen?"

"Apparently he'd lied about his age, told them he was eighteen and two months, two more years than his proper age," Mother replied. "They never asked for any proof and gladly took him on. Uncle Fred is livid. He fears for Alfred's life."

Father said, "I'm sure he'll be alright after several months' training. The war will be over by then, so there's no need to worry."

Come December, Gladys and Christina made Christmas cards of their own design. Gladys's pictured a happy family seated around the Christmas Dinner, toasting to a 'Merry Christmas and a Happy New Year'. She wanted to convey the message that families and their young men would be reunited.

She thought ahead to the Christmas festivities, and looking at Christina, she asked, "We're going to the pantomime after Christmas. Would you like to join us?"

"Yes, of course, I'd love to. What are you going to see?"

"Red Riding Hood. In the Shakespeare Theatre. I'll ask my father to get an extra ticket."

The continuous news about the war dampened any feeling of festivity. Father quoted an article in the Liverpool Daily Post. "Liverpool folk are having it brought home to them that their gallant King's Regiment, in which some of their bravest and best sons are serving, is doing more than its share to uphold Right Against Might on the bloody fields of Flanders. Isn't that the regiment Alfred joined?"

"I don't think so. He's with the Territorials, but perhaps they've merged into the King's, I'm not sure." Mother replied. "Aunty Lucy said he'll be home for Christmas because he hasn't gone to the front yet."

"A friend of mine from art school, Jack Handley, is also in the Territorials. They may have trained together," Gladys remarked.

Father continued reading. "It doesn't sound like the war will finish soon. The article says they're recruiting another thousand men for the King's."

Gladys's grandparents had long passed away, so the Grime family spent Christmas on their own. Gladys helped her mother decorate with festoons, holly, and other evergreens. Cards from a wide range of friends, customers and suppliers stood on the mantelpiece and side-cupboard. On Christmas Day, they sang their favourite carols, opened their presents, and enjoyed a dinner of roast beef, plum pudding and red wine.

A few days later, Father read from the newspaper again. "In a letter to the paper, a soldier in the trenches wrote there was an unofficial truce on Christmas Day. British and Germans troops stood between the trenches, discussed the war and exchanged cigarettes. He goes on to write that he admires the Germans. They are outstanding soldiers and a well-equipped army. Thanks to a hamper that his friends had sent, he had a scrumptious Christmas meal. He hadn't washed, shaved or taken his boots off for a fortnight. On Boxing Day, the bullets flew again. It's clear the war's not over, despite the truce in the trenches."

CHAPTER THIRTY-SEVEN
Riots

1915

As winter turned to spring, Gladys noticed the streets of Liverpool had a different bustle. The previous unrest, because of the suffragettes and the strikes for fairer wages, had disappeared. The mood was now businesslike. People hurried along — many working long hours to support the war effort in the harbour, or in the factories producing military supplies.

When she served in Grime's Tobacconist Shop, customers talked more about the negative impact of the war, often commenting on the blaring headlines across the newspapers Gladys sold. Food supplies were a worry because imports had been affected by German attacks on commercial shipping.

"Isn't it a scandal that shops are putting up their prices?" a customer complained. "Sugar has doubled in price."

"Yes, I know," Gladys said. "But you can't expect shopkeepers to sell at a loss. What else can they do?"

"Look! It says here, bacon, cheese, butter, cereals and tinned goods all see a steep increase," the customer read. "People are stockpiling food. Those with the money can beat the increases, but those without will be short. It's not fair."

Gladys gave a hesitant nod. "I hope we don't have to raise the price of cigarettes."

Other customers insinuated she should stop her art classes. "Why don't you join the other women supporting the country?"

"My mother can't run the shop on her own, so I need to be here," Gladys would reply, while turning her attention to the till and doing her best to smile.

Father and Mother supported her in her choice to continue at school. "There are enough women in the factories, and when this is all over, people will be glad of art to cheer them up," Father said.

Mother nodded. "We need the arts to take our minds off the horrors of war."

"And off the monotonous work in the factories," Father added.

"I'm pleased you feel that way. I'd like to think my art will have a positive effect."

"Aunty Lucy was in the shop today," Mother said. "She told us Alfred is now in the King's. They've crossed over to France."

Gladys sighed. "Let's hope they won't send him straight to the front."

In May, a German U-boat attacked the British ocean liner Lusitania as it returned to Liverpool from New York. The ship sank with twelve hundred souls aboard. The news had devastated customers coming to the Grimes' shop — some had family members who crewed on the Lusitania, and they were mourning their loss. Others had helped build the liner at Cunard's, remembering the proud day when it launched as one of the most luxurious and fastest transatlantic liners.

Touched by this occurrence, Gladys felt the need to express her feelings of fear and sadness in her artwork. She chose to make an etching. It was a technique she loathed because it was dark and colourless, but it felt suitable in this case. As she scratched the needle across the copper plate, the noise relieved her tension; the sound was aggressive and somewhat satisfying, as if she could erase that U-boat. She scored the sinking vessel with its four tall funnels tipping towards the waves. Nearby she etched a rock with a liver bird watching the catastrophe. The resulting print would be bleak and horrifying.

Mother entered the room. Seeing Gladys, she said, "There are anti-German riots on the streets. People are ransacking German shops!"

Gladys looked up from her work. "I'm not surprised. Everyone is so angry."

Mother wrung her hands. "A group of rioting women went into Kaufman's furniture shop in Ellenborough Street, took items out and burned them in the middle of the road."

Gladys raised her eyebrows. "It's not right. Those Germans aren't fighting against us, just doing the business they've done here for ages."

Starting back to the shop, Mother was impatient. "I'll check we've nothing obviously German in the shop. If we have, I'll conceal it."

When Father came home, Gladys saw how tense he was.

"I can't believe what I've seen." His voice was shaky. "People rioting in the streets - uselessly smashing things and harassing others. It's as if they've gone berserk. They shouted at me while I delivered the post. Saying I brought messages of death, death caused by the capitalists and the Germans."

"But you're just doing your job!" Mother said.

"With fewer men at the post office, it's hard work as it is, without being badgered on the street."

"People just don't think, dear. I'm having a problem purchasing cigarettes. Our wholesaler says imports are erratic and the forces are buying vast quantities. Our stocks are getting low."

"I disappointed a customer today," Gladys said. "He wanted to buy a dozen tins of tobacco. I told him I only had half a dozen because I didn't want him hoarding."

"What's all this mess?" Father griped, pointing to dirty rags and other odds and ends on the table.

"I've been etching."

"But why have you left everything lying around the house?"

Gladys shook her head. "Because I haven't finished yet."

Father sighed. "Can't you keep it all neat and tidy, in one place?"

Gladys glanced at her mother, then back to her father. "When I'm engrossed in my work, I'm not thinking about tidying up!"

Mother calmed them both down and helped Gladys clear up her stuff. In the midst of cleaning up, they were disturbed by shouting outside. When Gladys peeked through the front window, she saw a chase going on. They later learned someone had stolen two loaves of bread from the bakery down the road.

Father read the papers before tea, but Gladys skipped them, not wanting to know all about the war. She'd hear all she needed from her parents.

One evening, she and her mother were sitting around the fire when Mother mentioned that her own father had been a soldier. Gladys had never known her grandfather, because he died before she was born, so she was curious to know more about him.

"I didn't know Grandfather had been in the army. Which war was he in?"

Mother looked up from her knitting. "He didn't enlist for a war like the young men these days. He joined to make a living, to escape the poverty of Edinburgh." She paused. "I was only five when he died, so I can only recollect what I heard from my mother. She said they sent him to Ireland to help with the unrest there. After that, he was a guard at the Tower of London. Later, he was dispatched to South Africa and Ceylon, serving under the Duke of Wellington."

"I still don't understand why he joined the army if there wasn't a war."

"My father was very young when he started work as a labourer, perhaps only eight. He never went to a proper school and didn't learn to read and write. He wasn't as lucky as we are," Mother said, resuming her knitting. "When he was a young man he'd had enough of hard work and low pay, and heard how good life was in the army."

Gladys noticed her mother was absorbed in memories. "He was a real army man, disciplined and loyal. He never properly married my mother, they 'lived over the brush'."

"What does that mean?"

"They couldn't afford a church wedding, so they had an alternative marriage. Amongst family and friends, holding hands, they jumped over a broom handle, and were then considered wed."

Gladys laughed. "I've never heard of that before."

"It used to be quite common."

"Last week our linen weaving teacher spoke about tartans. By the way, I've passed my Linen Weaving exam, at last."

"Oh, well done!'

"Fortunately we didn't have to weave a tartan! Did your father's Jardine family have one?"

"My mother had a Jardine tartan kilt. It wasn't the usual red, green and blue, but black and white."

"That sounds unusual. Where did the name Jardine come from?"

"From the French word 'jardin'. The story is that the Du Jardin family came across with William the Conqueror. They built a castle in Dumfries. I'm trying to think of its name." She stopped knitting and stared at the floor. "Oh yes, Spedlins Tower. It had a dungeon where people were locked up by the laird if they'd done something wrong. One day the miller was thrown into the dungeons. The laird forgot about him, and no one gave him food and drink. He was later found dead. From then on, the miller's ghost haunted the place. The eerie noises were so bad that the Jardines left the tower for a mansion on the other side of the river — Jardine Hall."

"What a story! It's intriguing to think our ancestors lived in a castle," Gladys said, with a dreamy look in her eyes.

CHAPTER THIRTY-EIGHT
Alfred

1915

Art school closed for the summer, so Gladys spent more time sketching and painting outside — pen and ink drawings of countryside settings or watercolour studies of flowers. She relieved her mother in their tobacco shop more often, so that she could tend to the garden and visit friends.

It was a day at the end of August, Gladys was in the shop on her own, busy tidying the shelves, when the doorbell rang. She turned to welcome the customer, but her heart sank when she saw it was Aunty Lucy, with tears running down her cheeks.

Clutching the telegram to her breast, she blurted, "We've lost Alfred!"

Gladys clasped her hand over her mouth. "Oh god, how horrible!" She yelled for Mother, who came racing down the stairs, ran straight to Aunty Lucy and embraced her.

"We couldn't stop him! What could I have done? ...Our only son, and only seventeen."

Gladys broke into tears as she thought about Alfred, and his drawings.

"He was killed in action in France, the telegram said."

Mother took Aunty Lucy through to the kitchen and sat her down at the table.

"I knew this would happen," Aunty blubbered. "How can they send such young boys? It's shocking."

Mother reached across and squeezed her hand. "They'll say he died for God, King and Country. You can be proud of him for wanting to defend his country, but that's poor consolation."

"How am I going to tell the girls?"

"Don't worry about telling the girls at the moment. You need time to digest this awful news," Mother said.

"The worst thing is they'll bury him over there. We won't even have the chance to put his soul to rest. Only yesterday we had a letter from him. With it was this poem." With trembling hands, she pulled a piece of army paper from her handbag and passed it to Gladys, who read it out loud, stammering and crying.

"Mother, can you hear me?
I'm lying here all alone
In this foreign country,
So many miles from home.

I can see your gentle face
Tears shining in your eyes
When you left me at the station
And we said our last goodbyes.

My life is flashing here before me
I know my end is near
And running down my cheek,
I can taste a salty tear.

I can see our little house
On our little road
And all my friends I played with
Unlike them, I won't grow old.

And I can see my Father
A gentle man was he
When he came home from the docks,
He would rock me on his knee.

Forgive me Mum for leaving you
I know I've broken your heart
But I'm fighting for my country
I had to do my part.

Mother, I'll be waiting
At Heaven's open door
And when the good Lord calls you,
We shall never part no more.

Mum, I have to go now
I'm in a lot of pain
I'm waiting on my Saviour
Calling out my name.

I hope they take my body home
To that grand place of my birth
Then I can rest forever
In my good old Liverpool earth."

"My God, it's a farewell poem," Mother sputtered. Tears ran down her cheeks and she pulled a hankie out of her apron pocket. "He knew he was near his end, and must have gone through an agonising time with no one there to console him. How awful." She reached out to Aunty's hands again. "He was thinking of you all .... convinced you'll meet in Heaven."

Gladys then embraced Aunty and noticed at the bottom the words 'Written by Tommie Grimes'. As far as she knew, Alfred never wrote poems, so Tommie either wrote it himself or perhaps copied the original because Alfred no longer could write. She found it curious that Tommie was a Grimes.

The doorbell rang, and Mother signalled Gladys to attend to the customer. Her legs trembled as she walked to the counter.

Alfred's death was an enormous shock. He was their first relative to die in the war. Gladys thought about how harrowing it must have been for him, knowing he would never see his family and friends again, would never fulfil his artistic talent, or live his life fully. She couldn't imagine what that must have felt like.

Art school had been a safe harbour for Gladys, a place where she could avoid the horrific thoughts of the war. But by November, the number of students had dropped to three hundred and thirty, a quarter less than a year earlier. Each week there was another empty space in class, a familiar face missing. The Head of the Still Life Department had enlisted. His job was split between the Principal and two other teachers. Three students had lost their lives in action, and, in their memory, the school affixed a tablet to the wall in the entrance hall.

In the run up to Christmas, the students held their annual social evening, which was a grateful distraction from the gruesomeness in the world. The editorial in their magazine, The Comet, described it as 'an unqualified success, in spite of the fact that there were more difficulties to contend with than hitherto. On the other hand, the genus grumbler has greatly diminished in numbers and only exists as an interesting relic'.

Ten days before Christmas, the local newspaper reported, 'Dearer Christmas Birds: The French and Normandy turkeys will be off the festive English board, and so will the Italian and Russian birds. We shall rely chiefly upon Ireland, whose turkeys will be in a position to wipe the field clean.'

Thoughts of those not returning dampened the seasonal festivities. Each day saw another vacant workplace or a familiar face missing. On Christmas Day, the Grime family went to Aunty Lucy and Uncle Fred for the traditional dinner: rabbit this time, turkey was too expensive.

"We haven't got crackers this year. I don't want the bangs to remind me of the guns that killed my son," Aunty said.

Uncle Fred said a prayer in remembrance of Alfred.

"Ever-loving God, we remember those whom you have gathered from the storm of war into the tranquillity of your presence. In particular, we remember our son Alfred and feel assured his soul is at peace with you. May that same serenity calm our fears, bring justice to all peoples and establish harmony among the nations, through Jesus Christ our Lord. Amen."

CHAPTER THIRTY-NINE

Dreams

1916

At tea-time on a day in March, Gladys's father mentioned that the Government had introduced conscription.

"Will they call you up?" Gladys asked.

"No, no, no, I'm too old. They only want young men. Postmen like me help by delivering the letters from the lads at the front."

"How do people react when you bring sad news?"

"When they open the door, they turn pale on seeing me holding a telegram. Most grab it quickly and close the door. Others, standing in the doorway, read right there. I then feel awkward but wait patiently out of respect. It's always the same wording, 'Deeply regret to inform you that your son was killed in action', and the date and place. People are horrified. I give my condolences before leaving."

"I can't imagine receiving a telegram like that," Gladys sighed. "It's so impersonal."

Her father winced. "Telegrams are the worst."

At the post office, they nicknamed Father 'Dandy' because he was always so immaculately well-dressed. Preparing to leave home for his rounds, he looked at his reflection in the mirror, rectified anything out of order, and made sure his cap sat straight. With his satchel over his shoulder, he rode off with bags of mail on his bike.

Mother kept the tobacco and sweet shop going despite the war. There were fewer men to buy cigarettes, but stress meant that those remaining smoked more often. Supplies for Grime's Tobacco Stores were irregular and even stopped completely for a while. Gladys and her mother had to contend with unhappy customers who couldn't get their favourite brands, but on the other hand, it gave them the advantage of selling old stock.

Sweets were in normal demand, although supply was slow because of the shortage of sugar.

Gladys and her best friends, Christina and the Cubbin sisters, rounded off the school year with an afternoon tea in Coopers, the luxury store in Liverpool. They took their seats at a round table with a lace tablecloth.

"It's wonderful to be here together," Gladys said, taking off her scarf. "Since this nasty war started, we've had so little fun."

"My cousin has gone to work in the ammunition factory," Ivy Cubbin said. "They've been asking women to replace the men conscripted."

"What's it like?"

"She told me it's arduous and dangerous. The chemicals are extremely poisonous — a woman died after being contaminated."

Christina frowned. "Women shouldn't be doing that sort of work."

Gladys didn't agree. "But women are showing they can carry out men's work. If we can do their jobs, it'll show we're worthy of the same rights."

A waitress appeared at the table, asking for their choice of tea. They all opted for Earl Grey. She returned with two Wedgewood tiered cake stands, one with dainty sandwiches, the other with petite cakes.

Ivy chipped in, "When the war's over, I hope women remain in those jobs. It's sad men are getting killed, but I suppose after the war, they'll still need women in the factories."

"A sandwich?" Eileen Cubbin said, looking at Gladys, who then took a triangular-shaped cucumber sandwich. "I've heard you're spending more time in your mother's shop these days."

"Yes, I'm giving her time to visit people who've lost husbands or sons. She goes to console them, and to offer help. I also want to give her a break because we're having a problem getting supplies. Today I had a disgruntled customer shouting away because we'd run out of his favourite cigarettes."

Christina groaned. "People should be grateful to get cigarettes at all. How can they complain when there's a war?"

The tea arrived.

"Let's stop talking about the war," Gladys said. "Life's boring, so let's talk about a party."

The others chirped, "What sort of party?"

"We'll have our own little party on my birthday, ... if you're all still in Liverpool."

"Which handsome young men can we invite?" Eileen asked.

Gladys waved her hands as if encircling the group. "I thought we'd just have a picnic together. The four of us."

"There aren't any handsome young chaps to invite anyway," Christina said.

Eileen frowned. "How are we ever going to find husbands?"

Ivy turned to her sister. "We'll have to wait till they come back."

"I hope there'll be enough attractive men to go round," Gladys said. "The younger women will be competing with us."

"Let's have a big party when they come back," Eileen said.

"Who wants a picnic for my twenty-sixth?"

"When's that, exactly?" Ivy asked.

"The thirteenth of August."

They all concurred.

On Gladys's birthday, they came together in Newsham Park. She had prepared a hamper of food and drink. Sandwiches (made with her mother's freshly baked bread), hard-boiled eggs, plums, and a bottle of Pimm's. Christina and Eileen carried rugs, and Ivy Cubbin held a brightly coloured gift box.

Gladys took them to her favourite spot: a shady place under the elms, with a view over the lake. They looked attractive in their summer attire. Gladys wore a light dress with a flower pattern. Perched at an angle on her head was a straw hat with a broad rim and ribbon, with an added feather to mark her birthday. Christina had chosen a sporty blouse and skirt with a waist-band, pumps, no hat. Ivy and Eileen wore the latest cigar shaped dresses and smaller hats, and both carried a parasol. They laid out the rugs, sat down, and Gladys opened the hamper.

"That looks delicious," Ivy said, looking at the tidily filled basket, "but before we eat, we'd like to give you a birthday present."

"You shouldn't have brought a present," Gladys said, carefully undoing the yellow ribbon, her eyes wide with pleasure. She opened the box. "Oh, that's just what I need! Thank you all so much," she said, looking down at the water-colour brushes.

"You'd said you wanted to try your hand at water-colour, so we thought we'd encourage you to start," Christina said.

"How thoughtful of you," Gladys said, and gave her friends a kiss. "I see they're made of camel hair. That's the best there is. There's even a fan brush. Thanks a lot. I must try them later this week. How thoughtful of you. Let's get started. Christina, will you pour out the Pimm's?"

They enjoyed their picnic and were slightly giddy after more than enough Pimm's.

Gladys suggested playing a game. "Now, there aren't men around to flirt with us, so let's imagine some handsome young fellows. We're all suffragette supporters, so let's think which traits we'd like to see in men of our time. Shall we take turns to reveal what we've never expressed to each other before?"

Christina nodded. "Who's going to start?"

"I think Gladys should go first. It's her idea," Ivy said.

"Alright, I'll start. Let's begin with the traits we think are most important." She paused. "I think it's most important that my future husband should treat me as an equal."

"Equal in what way?" Eileen asked.

"I want an equal say in decisions affecting me and our household. Who's next?"

"Let me go next," Christina said. "I'm perhaps more conservative. I still want a handsome man." Her eyes sparkled as they laughed together.

"Of *course*, we want that. Good-looking is a prerequisite," Gladys said, pulling her shoulders back and raising her head.

"Well, let me conjure up a picture in your mind's eye," Christina continued. "The man in my dreams is tall, has broad shoulders, a clean-shaven face, no moustache or beard. His dark hair is short, combed to one side with a parting on the left, and, ... he's well-proportioned."

They giggled.

"Ivy, what are you thinking?" Gladys asked.

"I'm envisaging Christina's well-proportioned man," Ivy said, and they fell into a fit. When the laughter stopped, she continued, "I want a man who'll respect my opinions and let me be an independent thinker. I'd hate a husband who keeps telling me what to believe. I demand to have my own political view and to feel free to choose my own clothes, a one-piece bathing-suit!" More giggles. "Why can men just wear bathing trunks while we have to swim nearly fully clothed?"

Eileen finally brought her thoughts out on a serious note. "I want my husband to be a father who attends to his children's upbringing. Not a father who is only there to punish, but who will take an interest in them and treat daughters and boys equally."

"That's a good point, Eileen," Gladys said. "I hadn't thought of a husband as a father. I want a major say in the number of children we have. Have you any more thoughts, Christina?"

"In the end, it's important he has a stable job and a secure income. And, not unimportant, I want him to let me have time for art!"

Gladys looked up at the waving trees. "There's a breeze," she said, "and it's getting late. Let's make our way back." So, they gathered their things and walked to the shop.

In autumn, Gladys and Christina found it difficult to concentrate on their art studies. The continuous dreadful news about the war was a constant distraction and worry, and the dark, wet days were not inspirational. Gladys complained of it being cold everywhere. Coal rationing meant at both school and home fires were only lit when absolutely necessary.

They finished their exams in December, but Gladys failed Industrial Design and Linen Weaving; Christina fell short in Lithography.

They went to the annual students' social evening in December to buck their mood. Gladys was less depressed when she heard others had disappointing results, too. She laughed her head off when a group of students performed a hilarious play written by themselves.

CHAPTER FORTY
Art exhibition

1917

In March, the annual art exhibition took place despite the war. This time, it was for women only. Gladys entered her design work for the municipal scholarship competition. It was a wallpaper design in water-colour, based on a study of chrysanthemums: a botanical illustration showing buds, flowers, leaves and stems; art nouveau style, with petals curling in various directions.

On the last day of the exhibition, all the contributors gathered for the jury's verdict. They asked Gladys to come forward. She beamed when told they admired her work and judged it high quality. They awarded her the scholarship. Christina gave her a big hug.

In April, the US entered the war. Two months later, Father read in the paper that General Pershing and his staff had entered the Mersey on an ocean liner escorted by cruisers.

"They were welcomed by the Lord Mayor," he read out loud, to Gladys and Mother. "'The vessel arrived overnight. In the morning sunlight, the small crowd at Pierhead saw the black mass of a hull with a flag of the White Star flying at the masthead. The Americans travelled to London by train. After alighting, the party was driven to the Savoy in motor-cars.' Our lot has certainly put them in a posh hotel! The best is still to come. 'Within an hour of his arrival in London, General Pershing was out shopping in the West End.' It sounds more like a holiday outing than a war!"

"Well, let's hope the Americans will help us finish the war, even if we have to pamper them a little," Mother remarked.

"They've drafted an enormous number of men. I expect we'll see them passing through Liverpool on their way to the front," Father added.

Gladys felt a floating sensation, hopeful that the war would soon end. "Does it say when the American troops will arrive?"

"No. General Pershing has come to prepare."

At art school, Gladys saw young men again, although it wasn't a pretty sight. Some walked with crutches, missing a leg or foot. Others had lost an arm or hand, or were disfigured. She felt sorry for them and tried to cheer them up. Some liked to chat, others just looked dazed. The city council had asked the school to take them in — better than having them loafing about the streets, they said. The school board agreed lessons would help the ex-servicemen recuperate by giving them something useful to do. They could learn new skills, enabling them to work despite having lost a limb, or worse. The most popular classes were Furniture Making, Metal Work, and Lettering.

The reality of war struck the Grimes just after Christmas. A German submarine had laid mines in the entrance to the River Mersey to hamper shipping. A pilot boat ran into the mines and the Liverpudlian crew had 'no grave but the sea'.

CHAPTER FORTY-ONE
Church bells

1918

In January, Father read in the paper that rationing would soon start in Liverpool.

"What'll that mean for us?" Gladys asked.

"Luckily, postmen will have supplementary rations. I suppose that's because we walk and cycle all day."

"I'm sure people will flock to the shops to stock up," Mother remarked. "Which items are going on ration?"

"Sugar, meat, cheese, butter, and margarine. The Food Control Committee has appealed to retailers to ensure fair distribution, it says."

Gladys rubbed her cheek. "How can they do that? There'll be queues outside the shops."

Father consulted the paper. "They've already fined a lawyer in London for hoarding three hundred pounds of quaker oats, five hundred pounds of rice and a hundred and thirty pounds of sugar. They've also commandeered rabbits. The government has put eight hundred thousand rabbits in cold storage, probably to feed the forces. I thought there was a shortage of rabbits because of the bleak winter. I can't imagine where they found them."

"Well, fortunately, Gladys isn't a big eater. In summer, we'll have fresh produce from the garden," Mother said confidently. "We'll manage, I'm sure."

"Let's hope the war will be over by then," Gladys said. "When I was on Queens Drive, I saw the American troops on their way from the docks to the camp at Knotty Ash. Thousands of them marching and in motorised vehicles of all sorts and sizes. It was very impressive."

The school board awarded Gladys a free evening studentship for Embroidery for the 1918-19 school year. In addition, she took day classes for Jewellery and Enamelling, cloisonné work in particular. Learning new techniques appealed to her because they brought different angles to her artwork. Making decorative art from enamel meant learning to use copper and glass powder. In the oven, the coloured powder melted to form a vibrant surface between the copper contours.

Gladys's teacher praised her for a cloisonné panel depicting the five Greek goddesses Aglaia, Thalia, Euphrosyne, Cleta and Pasithea, singing and playing music, dressed in various shades of blue.

Like most artists, Gladys was never fully satisfied with the ultimate results. The design had to be perfect and the colours exactly as she expected. Her persistence to achieve excellence prompted the school management to appoint her as Assistant Teacher in the Preliminary Department for three evenings a week, to help with the extra work because of the influx of ex-servicemen. They paid her ten shillings per evening.

"There's now a second wave of Spanish flu," Father stated, while reading the paper on a day in October. "This wave is more serious because it gives people high temperatures for ten days. Doctors can hardly cope. It says rooms must be well ventilated and vitality maintained by exercising in the open air."

"They're thinking of closing elementary schools," Mother said, pulling back her chair to sit down. "Shall we start lunch?"

Gladys followed suit. "Oh, I hope the art school can stay open. I'd hate to miss lessons and seeing my friends."

"People are being told to avoid meetings and crowded spaces. Do I need to take measures in the shop?" Mother wondered, picking up a knife. "Will you have a piece of chicken pie?"

Father passed his plate. "Perhaps keep the door open to ensure enough ventilation. But wear a thick woolly."

"I don't want to wear a mask because that'll frighten customers away."

"Behind the counter, you won't be in close contact," Gladys said. "Shall we put a sign up saying 'only two customers inside'?"

"That's a good idea," Mother said.

Father tucked into the chicken pie. "Hmm, this is delicious. This is just the food the paper says we should eat — ample and nourishing."

Mother reached for the salt. "That'll be difficult for many people given their war-time larder."

On the morning of Monday 11th November, Gladys went to her jewellery class to continue work on a brooch. It was to be a forget-me-not brooch; the stems made of copper, the blue flowers made of cloisonné.

She was about to finish for the mid-day meal when she heard church bells pealing joyously. At first she thought it was for a wedding, but then she heard bells from all sides. The students looked at one another, their teacher, and then the principal popped his head through the doorway and called out triumphantly, "The war's over! Germany has capitulated. It's wonderful. School is closed for the rest of the day."

The scholars stood, grasped and embraced each other, and the classroom filled with an exuberant hubbub of congratulatory talk. Gladys looked for Christina; finding her in the hall, they fell into each other's arms. "I'm so glad it's all over," said Gladys.

"There'll be celebrations at the town hall. Let's go," Christina proposed.

"Yes, but first I want to go home to see my parents. Come with me, otherwise we'll never find each other."

Gladys found Mother and Father peering over the newspapers that had just been delivered. Her father looked up. "I can't tell you how relieved I am — we've lost too many lives already."

They all hugged.

Gladys took a deep breath. "I can hardly believe it! Christina and I are going to the town hall. Will you join us?" she asked, looking from one parent to the other.

"I can't leave the shop," Mother said. "Customers will be coming for newspapers."

"I'm expected back at the post office, but you go and enjoy yourselves. Watch out for the crowds and pick-pockets. And be aware of the flu - don't get too close to anyone and wear your face masks."

Gladys and Christina took the electric omnibus to the city centre where they met crowds waving allied flags — the Union Jack, the Stars & Stripes, the Tricolour, and others. Flags flew on every masthead and from many a window. Bells pealed, steam locomotives and river craft blew their whistles, cars honked their horns.

At the Town Hall, the number of people amazed Gladys. She spoke to workers who told her they had 'downed tools' at the docks and munition factories. Schools were closed, allowing whole families out on the streets.

Gladys gave Christina a jolt and pointed to the Lord Mayor on the front balcony. "We are at peace," he announced. Jubilant shouting, clapping, and merriment followed. The crowds paraded in high-spirits — noisy, singing and waving flags. Gladys found herself next to a wounded soldier. He had difficulty finding his balance in the crowd, so she supported him and gave him a hug. There were impromptu processions and musical accompaniments. American soldiers from the Knotty Ash Camp joined in and were as jolly as all. Wine and beer flowed freely.

The next morning, Gladys served in the shop and had time to glance at the Liverpool Daily Post which reported: 'There was no excess of drunkenness. It was a day of gladness, but also a day of sadness. Sorrow and sympathy made for quietness, and the joyfulness was balanced by self-respect and self-restraint. Lighting in the streets remained on, allowing crowds to stay out till midnight. Lamps illuminated the Town Hall, and the brilliance was a symbol of the passage from the darkness of war to the light of peace.'

By Christmas, those who had survived the war were returning to Liverpool — some injured, some suffering from shell-shock and trauma. They sought the comfort of their families and friends. Gladys looked forward to seeing men return to the art classes, remembering her pleasant discussions with Jack Handley and others.

PART FIVE
Jack and Miss Grime

CHAPTER FORTY-TWO

Annie and George

1919

In January, Jack left the army. For seven years, he'd appreciated the discipline and the no-nonsense mentality — you did as you were told, assumed it was for the best, were accountable for your own actions, and responsible for your men. Most of all, he missed the comradeship.

At twenty-seven, he was without a job and a home of his own. He had little choice but to return to his parents in Liverpool and looked forward to seeing his family again, even his father. Unsure whether his father would let him in, he sent a postcard: "Dear family, Leaving Lichfield day after tomorrow. Coming home till I have my own place. Will arrive at Lime St station on 17.24 train. Love, Jack."

Jack felt strange as he departed from Lichfield on a winter's day. A new phase in his life was beginning, but it seemed hollow and meaningless. He wondered whether his brother, Joe, would be at the station to meet him. When they were younger, they explored the secrets of nature together - in the woods and along the river. Having three sisters had strengthened their bond.

Nineteen-year-old Joe stood waiting under the clock. He helped carry the bags to the tram. On arrival at Langdale Road, Mother opened her arms wide. "Oh Jack, I'm so glad you've come home."

Jack hugged her. "It's lovely to see you, Mother."

"You look tired, but we'll soon beef you up. Let's get you some tea."

Father came in. "Good to see you back, Jack." He gripped Jack's shoulder. "Well, that damn war did no good. We're in a worse state than before all the madness started. You're lucky to be in one piece - what will you do with yourself?"

Jack took his cigarette tin out of his pocket. "Go back to work and find a place of my own, I hope. Can I stay for the time being?"

Father smiled. "It's cramped here, with no sign of Annie having her own dwelling any time soon. Ask Joe if you can share his room. You'll have to pay Mother for expenses."

Jack spent time re-connecting with his brother and sisters. Annie had grown to be a strong and determined woman who loved being with children and wanted a large family. She now expected her second child. Music was Mabel's passion, and she spent all her spare time at piano practice. Mary had a book-keeping job at the post office and dreamt of starting a family someday. Joe had nearly finished his motor-mechanic apprenticeship.

When the others were out at work, Jack and his mother sat in the front room. He was glad of the opportunity to talk about the war, to get things off his chest.

"How will you go about finding a job?" Mother asked.

"Hutchinson & Weston will be pleased to have me back. I'd rather find something more interesting, but it'll do for now."

"Work will take your mind off what you've been through."

"I hope so. I have terrible nightmares, wake up shuddering, and can't fall asleep again. During the day, memories flash back, both good and bad."

"How could you possibly have remained sane, seeing what you saw?" Mother asked.

"We could only keep our wits by being with our mates, telling each other stories and jokes, singing and sharing our news from home. A dousing of rum and a smoke helped escape from the horrors."

"Were you with the same mates all those years?"

"No. As we lost men, Companies were regularly merged. But whoever joined my unit, we got along well because we were all in the same boat."

Jack took his cigarette tin out of his pocket. Rolling a fag was such a routine that he barely needed to look at what he was doing. "Being a soldier on the front is a way of life. To survive, everyone has to work together and trust we'd help each other, even risking our own life to save another."

"Did you always feel you could trust others?"

"I trusted my mates, but the officers didn't keep their word, like the one who said we'd stick together, but then he took six months leave." He lit his cigarette and blew out the match. "The officers never fully had faith their men. They assumed we'd try to avoid doing things, steal stuff or lie to them. They weren't all that way, thank God."

"I can't imagine life in those trenches."

"In Belgium, the trenches were terrible, full of water and mud. We had to stand for hours in what was like a bath of icy cold water. If a major battle was going on, we'd be constantly fighting every night. In between battles, we worked on repairing the trenches and dugouts, and replenished our stores of food and ammunition." He reached out to tap cigarette ash in the ashtray. "When we were back at base for a rest, life was boring. If we could, we'd make our way to a bar for beer."

"You said you had rum."

"The army handed it out to soothe our nerves and wash away our fear. We drank together to cheer ourselves up. It helped us survive the cold and wet, and we handed it to injured mates to give them pain relief."

Mother exhaled. "I'm so relieved you've left the army for good, Jack."

"So am I, Mother."

Jack stood up. "I'm going to have a drink in the pub and see if there are any friends there."

But when he arrived at the pub, he realised to his dismay, there was nobody he recognised. Many of the young men he knew before the war had lost their lives, either in action or dying afterwards from fatal wounds. Others were back in Liverpool, but seriously injured and still in hospital.

Evenings passed, exchanging stories with George. Prior to the war, George served in the Royal Horse Artillery; he'd joined as a boy-soldier to escape his step-mother. He told Jack about his time in India and his telegraphist training, a skill which now enabled him to work in that position at the post office.

While they spoke, George coughed frequently. "Excuse me … I've been barking like this since we were gassed by the Germans."

Neither of them could share the terrifying details of their stories with others at home; it was too emotional. Only Mother showed an interest, but both Jack and George didn't want to upset her. People had little appetite for war tales.

Jack's father certainly didn't wish to hear about the war. "It's better to spend your time praying to God that it won't happen again," is what he said on the matter. On one occasion he turned to Jack's brother, Joe, telling him, "Remember, in Matthew, Jesus said, 'Put your sword back into its place. For all who take the sword will perish by the sword'. Jack survived, but the evil horrors of the war will be with him forever. Make sure you keep out of the army, Joe."

On an icy day in February, Jack heard Annie and George stumble into the house, sighing and panicking.

George was panting. "Annie fell down."

Jack helped her to a chair. "Sit down and get your breath back." He knew Annie was pregnant and that a nasty fall could lead to a miscarriage.

Mother rushed in with a glass of water. "What happened, love?"

Annie wanted to explain, but George had regained his breath. "A carriage careered towards us. It was going to hit us, so I pulled Annie away. She ... she lost her balance and fell. I couldn't ... hold her."

Grimacing, Annie put her hand on her left side. "Pain shot through to my leg. I thought I'd broken it."

"I helped her up, and we ... we managed to walk back."

Annie wrinkled her brow. "We heard shouting. Mounted police trotted along the road towards us. Mobs roamed the streets. Then this carriage came at high speed."

Jack saw Annie hold her side, obviously still hurting. She looked at her mother. "I'm worried about the baby."

"Where exactly is the pain?" Mother asked.

Annie felt her upper left-hand side. "It's here."

"What about your tummy and back? Any pains there?"

"No, it's my side. It's painful when I move."

"I think you've broken a rib," Mother said.

"Does she need to visit a doctor?" George asked.

"She needs some rest now. As long as there are no pains elsewhere, and no bleeding, there's no need to see the doctor."

Looking at George, Jack said. "I think I'd take her to the doctor, just to be sure."

George thumbed his ear, looked at Annie, and then responded, "It's painful for her to walk. Let's see how she is tomorrow."

Jack didn't agree, but left it at that, not wanting to interfere.

A month later, Jack woke up to loud voices. George sounded agitated, and Annie was moaning. To Jack, it was as if she was going in to labour, but that wasn't expected for weeks. He got out of bed and saw that Mother was trying to calm George down. She asked him to get the midwife.

Jack offered his help.

Mother spoke purposefully. "Wake up Father and Mabel. Ask her to bring towels and a bowl of warm water."

Jack woke them and went to the kitchen to make tea. The kerfuffle had woken Mary and Joe, who were already in the kitchen.

George returned with the midwife and took her to Annie. Soon after, he entered the kitchen. Jack saw a pallid face. In a matter-of-fact way, George said it was a girl, but small and weak. The placenta still had to come, but it didn't want to move. He was clearly worried and went back upstairs with tea for the midwife.

Half an hour later, George came down again, looking bereft. "She's had a second baby, but it was stillborn!" He sat down, his head in his hands.

Jack's mouth fell open. "Annie's had twins then?"

"Yes." George was at a loss for words. "Only one has survived and is very weak."

"How is Annie doing?" Father asked.

"The placenta still has to come out," George said, hands trembling. Then Mother called out to George, so he rushed back upstairs.

Jack heard George shout, "It'll be alright. We need to get her to better help. She needs to go to the maternity hospital as quickly as possible."

"The poor thing is too weak to be taken outside," the midwife said. "You must look after her here. Keep her well-wrapped at all times. Put her in a basket on top of the cupboard where the air is warmer."

"What about feeding her?" Mother asked.

"She's too feeble to suck for milk, so, for the time-being, give her a solution of salt and water. Only use cooled boiled water. Drip it into her mouth at regular intervals."

Mabel came into the kitchen. "Annie's fine. She's struggling to grasp what's happened. Her attention is now going to the living baby. I'm taking up warm water to wash her."

Annie was dead tired and needed to sleep. Mabel and Mary took turns to look after the baby, putting drops of salt solution in her mouth and making sure she was warm enough. Annie couldn't sleep well and kept asking how the baby was. And early the next morning, as they all feared, the baby died.

It devastated Annie and George that they'd lost both babies. George put it down to the accident when Annie had fallen on the icy street, remembering that she'd complained of a pain in her side.

Father had his own perspective on the loss of the twins. "It's all because of that stupid war. There was no nourishment in the food and too much anxiousness. Evilness will keep following us until the Lord grants us forgiveness."

As the baby had lived a day, they gave her a name - Beryl Louise. Jack accompanied George to the registry office for the dreadful task of recording both Beryl's birth and death. The registrar didn't record the stillbirth.

CHAPTER FORTY-THREE
Freemasons

1919

"You've been drinking!" Father pronounced, one morning. "Your wickedness will punish you. Your backsliding will rebuke you. Realise how evil and bitter it is when you forsake the Lord."

Jack felt watched all the time, as if his father was waiting to catch him out with devilish behaviour. Father believed the war caused soldiers to do everything forbidden in the Bible: killing fellow men, drinking, visiting prostitutes, gambling and worse. Jack was little impressed by his father's words but, in his heart, he knew alcohol dragged him down and that he must drop the habit.

He smuggled a bottle of rum up to his room where he could drink after retiring to bed. Waking up and feeling befuddled, he needed rum to get him going. Not wanting family members to notice alcohol on his breath, he woke early, dressed quickly and had a bite to eat before rushing off each morning. On his way to work, he put the flask to his mouth and let the strong liquid flow down his throat so the warm feeling could soothe him.

In the office, he sat down at his desk and started sorting documents. An hour passed and the effects of the rum wore off. With the flask in his pocket, he went to the gents. On coming out, he bumped into his boss who asked him to come to his office. "Jack, I need to talk to you about changes I want to make to our sales districts. Take a seat."

Jack took hold of the back of the chair and moved it further away from his boss's desk.

Mr Hutchinson explained he would make the districts smaller to reduce travel. Jack noticed a frown cross his boss's face and, from the look in his eye, Jack knew what to expect.

"Have you been drinking?" Mr Hutchinson asked.

"I just had a sip because I wasn't feeling well this morning," Jack replied, keeping a neutral face.

"I can't have that here. If you don't stop right now, don't bother to come again."

The comment struck home. Jack couldn't afford to lose his job and forfeit money that was going towards a place of his own. He vowed to limit drinking to evenings.

In the *Liverpool Echo*, Jack read that the School of Art had courses for ex-servicemen, free-of-charge. The men would have a welcome distraction, make friends, and learn skills for a new trade. The paper gave carpentry lessons as an example, leading to furniture-making jobs. Jack chose the evening drawing classes. He hoped the diversion might help him drink less, and that he'd meet students from years earlier. Perhaps even Miss Grime.

On his way to the art school on Hope Street, he passed a grand building with men standing outside. He greeted them and they asked him if he had a moment. Had he heard of the Freemasons?

Jack knew of them but had paid little attention, not wanting to be part of a confining religious group like his father. "I've heard of the Freemasons, but that's about all."

"We'd like to tell you about what we do."

"I'm on my way to school, but I'll come back another time."

"Come on Friday evening because we're holding a meeting for those interested in knowing more," one chap said.

"I will, thanks. Have a good evening."

At the art school, Jack was assigned to a class of ex-servicemen beginning a Preliminary Course. He felt at ease amongst the men and looked forward to exchanging war stories later.

As he entered the classroom, he saw the slim, well-endowed figure of their teacher, and realised it was none other than Miss Grime. She turned towards him, arched an eyebrow and her green-blue eyes twinkled. "Good evening Mr Handley, how wonderful to see you back. Take a seat. It's time to start the lesson."

His heart leapt and he cleared his throat. "Good evening Miss Grime. I'm very glad to be back."

Jack noticed she had matured, and thought to himself that she was now even more attractive. He wondered idly what it was that made her so appealing. When she looked at him, her eyes met his and gave the impression that she was both unreserved and inquisitive. When she smiled, she was at ease, inviting and caring. He couldn't help but wonder whether he was in love.

That Friday, Jack went to the Freemasons at St Michaels Temperance Lodge, where young men, mostly ex-servicemen, were showing interest in joining.

A leader explained their principles, "We believe all men are equal, irrespective of colour or race. Every true Freemason shows tolerance and respect for the opinions of others, and behaves with kindness and understanding. We trust in a Supreme Being regardless of religion, and welcome members of any religious background. We practise charity and care, not only for our own, but for the community as a whole. Freemasons strive for truth and high moral standards."

The principles appealed to Jack. He believed in honesty and truth, and serving society. The rituals and symbols reminded him of being in the army. He accepted the spiritual element because they did not confine it to one religious belief. Expecting to be with like-thinking men, he enrolled.

Soon after joining, he discovered the Lodge had a programme for ex-servicemen who wanted to stop their drinking habit. That was just the support he needed.

CHAPTER FORTY-FOUR
Dating

1919

It was spring, and Jack's world looked brighter. He'd weaned himself off the alcohol and felt much better. Not only had he physically improved, he felt revitalised. Hutchinson & Weston was still his employer because they provided a decent income, which compensated for his lack of pleasure in the building trade.

Once a week he attended art school, not in the least to see Miss Grime. When they met, she spoke about the lessons she took — jewellery, enamelling, and embroidery. "I love learning new techniques which stimulate my creativity. Making cloisonné is particularly intriguing."

"In what way?" Jack asked.

"I use copper wire to form the design. Then melt coloured glass powder in the oven, and carefully pour each hue in the right spot. It's amazing to see the vibrant result."

Jack maintained eye contact. "It sounds like a complicated process!"

"It is. I can never be sure of the outcome because colours change as the glass hardens." She showed him her latest cloisonné piece. which depicted a goddess and a lion.

"It's beautiful. I like the composition of her taming the lion, and his look with a pink tongue hanging from his mouth. Are you content with it?"

"I'm never completely satisfied. The background should have been a less brilliant blue."

"If I may say so, Miss Grime, I'd say you are a perfectionist."

"You're right, Mr Handley. I'm meticulous. I want my work to be top-notch in every aspect."

"Please call me Jack."

She smiled. "I will, if you call me Gladys, Jack."

He grinned, feeling elated they were bonding. "I'd be delighted, Gladys." In his heart, he wasn't fond of the name.

In early summer, they spent time together most Sundays. They loved walking and visiting art exhibitions. Jack's travels had taken him to many places in the Liverpool area, and he wanted to share the best with Gladys. They enjoyed trips on the train; to Manchester to see an exhibition, and to Southport for a walk on the beach.

On the sandy beach, they strolled as far as the Ribble Estuary, with the warmth of the sun on their backs. Jack found a sheltered spot. He opened his arms wide. "Isn't it lovely? Let's stop here and watch the waves roll in." They sat down close to one another.

Gladys beamed. "It's a beautiful day. I'm so pleased to be here."

Jack moved even closer to her and put his arm around her shoulders. They stared out to sea, but Jack wasn't really looking. His heart was racing; it was as if energy flowed between them, tingling him; he was euphoric.

When her head turned, he looked straight into her blue-green sparkling eyes, right through to her soul. They drew closer until they kissed.

He felt a wonderful sensation throughout his body and turned to embrace her fully, kissing her gently. Easing backwards, they lay down on the sand, kissing and cuddling. Eventually, they pulled apart, looking into one another's eyes, smiling.

Jack broke the silence. "I'm glad we're together. It's honestly the happiest day of my life." He put his finger-tip in the sand between them and drew a heart. With a prankish look in her eyes, she traced an arrow through it; he drew a G at the arrowhead, she added a J.

After a brief pause, he asked, "Would you mind if I call you Glad?"

She smiled. "If you like."

When it was time to introduce Glad to his family, he took her home for Sunday lunch. The complete family enjoyed her company, and Father behaved himself. After the meal, Glad chatted with sisters Annie, Mary and Mabel. Jack heard Mabel asked Glad about her design work and noticed how she bubbled with enthusiasm. Reggie was now three and ran around, enjoying the attention. The young ladies all loved him. He climbed on Glad's lap and she said how she'd love to have such a lively boy.

Glad reciprocated by asking Jack to come to her place to meet her parents. It was an hour's walk to Rocky Lane, the last part across Newsham Park. He saw a row of shops. One had a sign advertising the

Golden Clipper brand. A newspaper stand stood outside, and he saw Grime's Tobacco Shop above the window.

Glad was in the shop when Jack entered. "How can I help you, sir?" she asked.

"Your help is like nothing I've ever been offered," he joked, leaning across the counter to give her a kiss.

"Let me help you to the back room, sir."

She introduced her parents, and they all sat at the table. To celebrate Jack's presence, Mother brought out cigars, and Jack gladly accepted one. Mother then moved into the shop as a customer arrived.

Pa asked Jack about his past, and was impressed when Jack told him he'd left home at a young age to join the army.

"I had to leave home when I was young too," Mr Grime said.

"Did you enlist?"

"No, I was only twelve. I couldn't stand it at home any longer. They spoilt my younger brother, and I felt left out, ... ignored." He lit his pipe and exhaled bluish smoke. "I went to the docks and lived amongst men there for a while, and then at various other addresses. It was a hard time, but I've never regretted it."

"That must have been pretty grim."

"The dockworkers looked after me quite well. I worked alongside them and they helped me find a foster family. I really felt at home with them."

Glad drew Jack's attention when she stood up to come towards him. He turned back to Pa. "How fortunate."

She pulled at Jack's arm. "Let me show you the garden."

"Are you going to lead me down the garden path? To the enchanted garden?"

Glad laughed. "You don't know jack about my garden yet."

Out between the vegetable patches, Glad asked Jack whether he would like to accompany her on a school outing to Oxford in July.

At the university, a guide gave the art students a tour and pointed out the different architectural styles. Glad particularly loved the Christ Church Picture Gallery and its Italian panel paintings. She bought a postcard of the gallery and sent it to her mother, "This is a charming place. We are just having a walk round, then having tea."

In August, Jack went to London for commercial training and Glad joined him. They spent a Sunday at High Wycombe, both sketching and relaxing. Another day, they walked round the National Gallery in Trafalgar Square, where they marvelled at the works of famous artists like Vermeer and Da Vinci.

On Glad's twenty-ninth birthday, her cousin Sidie's brother took them boating on the Thames, right up to Hurley Lock. On her postcard home she wrote, "This stretch is one of the prettiest parts of the river."

Their days in London gave them ample time to exchange views on what they wanted in life. Glad said her aim was to combine teaching with developing her style of industrial design.

"Do you wish to have a family, Glad?" Jack asked. "To have children?"

"Yes, of course. I'll be a mother, a teacher and an artist at the same time. My mother had her own shop and me as a child, so I'll find a way," Glad replied, looking him directly in the eye, tilting her head sideways, her eyes twinkling. "It'll depend on my future husband. Will he be home every evening so I can go to art school?"

Jack tilted his head in her direction. "Well, if I was to be your husband, I'd want you to continue with your art. I'd have to find a different job though."

"Have you ever thought about what sort of wife you'd prefer?"

"One as beautiful as you are!"

"Ha, ha. Anything more?"

Jack grinned. "I wish my spouse to be intelligent, artistic, optimistic, compassionate and a suffragette."

"Are you trying to describe me?"

"What a coincidence, you match my criteria!"

"But are you likely to meet mine?"

"Well, not on the travelling score."

"I've been thinking. You said you're not thrilled about working for Hutchinson. Have you thought of being an agent for one of my mother's confectionery suppliers? Perhaps you'd travel less far."

"A change is appealing and I'm interested to know what they would offer."

"Mother is on good terms with Buchanan; they're in Glasgow. I'll ask her to contact them and see if there's a vacancy."

"Well, we'll have no shortage of chocolate."

John Buchanan & Brothers offered Jack the opportunity to be a commercial traveller throughout the northwest. When interviewed, he was asked about his military service, and they were impressed by his rise to the rank of officer and his account of caring for his men. He explained that his mates frequently changed, and he was never at a loss to find something to chat about in order to strike up a rapport. Mutual trust was crucial, he said.

The Buchanan district manager responded by saying he could tell Jack would easily get along with people. As that was essential for the job, he offered to take Jack on.

Jack accepted, even though it meant just as much travelling, if not more. A while in the confectionery trade would be a useful experience. He could always find something else later.

In September, Glad's friends were all back in Liverpool after their holidays.

"I'm thinking of doing a tea party," she said to Jack. "Would you like to come?"

"Who else will be there?"

"Christina, Eileen and Ivy for sure. Perhaps some others. I'd invite their boyfriends, but they don't seem to have any. As it's still pleasant weather, I thought we'd have a picnic in the park. We did that three years ago and enjoyed it."

"Sounds lovely to me."

When the day came, Jack helped carry things to the park opposite the shop. They all sat on blankets on the grass, happy to be together.

"Is there a special reason for this get-together?" Christina asked.

"First and foremost, I wanted to see all of you again," Glad said, picking up her glass of Pimm's. "Here's to us!"

"Here's to us!" they all chimed.

"Secondly, I want to tell you that school now has over six hundred and sixty students, so the board has extended my post as Assistant Teacher to the Preliminary Department for another year."

"Here's to the art teacher!" Eileen said. "What are they paying you?"

"Ten shillings an evening, three evenings a week."

"Wow, you'll be inviting us to Cooper's for tea again!" Ivy said.

"Wait, I haven't finished yet. Thirdly, I'm now calling myself an Artist Designer."

"Here's to the artist designer!" Jack cheered, and they all raised their glasses.

"Good for you," Ivy said.

"You're really preparing yourself for a professional career then, Glad?" Christina asked.

"Yes, I want to earn a living, not by working in the shop, but as an art teacher and designer. Design is becoming important in business, so I hope to do some paid work."

Christina picked up a package wrapped in brown paper. "Well, fortunately, we've brought something to honour your announcements."

The parcel was the shape and size of a painting, Jack thought.

Glad opened it carefully, and her mouth fell open. She turned it round for all to see.

The wonderful portrait of his love stunned Jack. Christina had portrayed Glad as beautiful as in his mind's eye. It was a crayon drawing with a light touch of water-colour on rosy cheeks and brunette hair. Her oval face had a fair complexion and dreamy eyes looked towards the future.

He noticed Glad's eyes filling with tears of happiness.

"It's magnificent Christina! How can I thank you enough!" Glad gave Christina a big hug and wiped her eyes.

Looking at the portrait again, it struck him that she wore no jewellery, no earrings, no necklace. It showed her purity and modesty. Jack moved to her and put his arm around her shoulder. "It's truly you, not only in likeness but in character."

On Armistice Day, 11th November, Jack was away on a business trip. It was a trying day which brought back war memories and sadness at the loss of so many lives. He kept thinking of Glad, and so he wrote her a postcard to help himself feel better.

Carlisle
Armistice Day
My Dearest,
Still stressed by the thoughts of the war. This card will be another little stepping stone over the four-day stream of a loveless week. Oh! I just wish you were here. We could have a very nice stroll this cold bright evening along the banks of the Eden.
Love to Ma, regards to Pa and heaps of everything to my love, xxxxxxxx.

Later that week, from Whitehaven, he wrote about arriving home a day earlier on an afternoon train, concluding:

Hope my darling is well and not criticising students too harshly, nor making too much jewellery. I have recovered from being stressed and am quite cheerfully philosophical today.
Love to Ma, and all I possess (which is all) to you, your Jack xxxxx.

CHAPTER FORTY-FIVE
Wedding

1920

Jack and Glad married on Saturday 21st August in St Bridget's Church, Wavertree, where his father had carved the pulpit. It was a dry day, dull and cool for the time of year, but the atmosphere in church was cheerful and warm. Their families and friends attended the service, even blind Aunty Elizabeth, who travelled from Manchester. Witnesses were Jack's brother, Joe, and Glad's cousin, Ivy Cubbin.

The honeymoon took them to Dartmouth, where they stayed two weeks in a house overlooking the estuary, towards Kingswear. Glad sent a picture postcard to her Ma, whom they now called Marsie.

Dear Marsie,

Am writing this on Prom. The weather is glorious. The picture is the view from our house, High Bank, which is like a little palace. We've got the dining room and front bedroom and they are swanky. The windows are like Mrs Brady's, with caressant curtains, and both rooms are furnished beautifully. In the dining room we have a big sideboard loaded with silver, two bookcases and a writing table, and in the bedroom there is everything for our comfort. The food is just tip top. We've just had a delightful dinner, consisting of lamb like chicken, beans like cream, potatoes like balls of flour, and delicious stewed fruit and cream. It's strange to be married, wear a ring, and be called Mrs Handley. The maid knocked on the bedroom door and said, "Dinner is ready, Mrs Handley." It's just like being in paradise, Marsie. I feel almost afraid to speak for fear I'll wake up and find it's all a dream. Jack is a gem and always will be. Can you send us some wedding cake as we only had a small bite? Much love, from Jack and self

With packed lunches in their knapsacks, they set off for walks along the coastal path. A trek west took them to Compass Cove Beach, a secluded spot where they could relax and have a swim. The next day, they boarded the ferry to cross the River Dart, and then walked east along the cliff path. Nowhere could they descend to the sea, so they perched themselves on an outcrop behind gorse bushes where they couldn't be spotted. The view out to sea was glorious, but they spent most of their time viewing and exploring each other. Another day, Jack saw rowing boats for hire, so they rowed up the Dart, exploring its inlets, especially those more remote.

At the weekend, the Royal Dart Yacht Club held its annual regatta. Yachts of all shapes and sizes arrived - some just sailing dinghies, others two-masters. Jack and Glad enjoyed watching the racing and walked around town to enjoy the hustle and bustle of crews and visitors.

Dartmouth
Dear Pa,
I wish you had been here last weekend for the Regatta. Dartmouth was quite gay, and I know you'd have enjoyed the boat racing. Have had two jolly days boating.
Love, Jack & Glad

On their return to Liverpool, they sent pieces of bride's cake to her relatives and friends who couldn't attend the wedding, including Glad's dear friend Christina, who had been away in Paris and Florence.

Jack moved in with Glad above the shop, but he looked forward to the day when they would have a place of their own.

About eight weeks after their honeymoon, one evening Glad came to sit on Jack's lap, bubbling with energy. "I've got something to tell you!"

"Have you won another award?"

"It's more exciting than that!"

"You've been given a new job?"

"I'm expecting a baby!" Glad cried, jumping up and down, almost hurting his knees.

Jack hugged her tighter. "Wonderful, my darling! That is exciting!" He put his hand on her abdomen. "It's amazing to think there's a tiny boy or girl in there."

She jumped off his lap and did a little dance. "I'm so happy!" Twirling, "We're going to have a little one and then there'll be three of us."

"Have you told Marsie?"

"She was pleased and excited. She's always said she looked forward to having grandchildren." Glad kissed him again and twirled round a couple more times. "I'll stop going to school because I don't want people to know. Besides, I'll save my energy for the baby."

"Yes, you need to take care and stay healthy. Will you have extra rations?"

"Marsie says so. But I need a note from the doctor."

"How are you feeling?"

She twirled again. "Better than ever. Can't you see? I'm jumping for joy!"

Jack danced around with her, thinking conception must have taken place on honeymoon, perhaps out on the headland.

1921

From week to week, Jack saw Glad grow. It wasn't fashionable to show your 'condition'. She bought new clothes, which gave her more room without making her look conspicuous.

"Are you going to give birth in the Maternity Hospital?" Jack asked.

"I'd prefer to be here with the midwife. It's more personal and comfortable. Besides, I think hospitals are places full of disease and no safer than home for giving birth. Marsie has arranged for a live-in nurse."

Jack smiled. "That's a relief."

"I'm reading advice for mothers having their first child. What do you think of this? 'Pregnant mothers should avoid thinking of ugly people, or those marked by any deformity or disease'."

"Haha, you'll have to keep out of the shop when the ugliest customers come in!"

"There's more. 'Avoid injury, fright, and disease of any kind. Handle the baby as little as possible. Turn it occasionally from side to side, feed it, change it, keep it warm, and let it alone'. That's because we mustn't spoil the baby or be overprotective."

"Umm!"

"It says, 'a baby should cry vigorously several times each day; it's essential to the development of strong lungs. Breastfeeding mothers could run dry by engaging in worry, grief, or nagging."

"I was going to nag you more, but we don't want you to run dry, do we!"

Glad put her hands on the sides of her belly. "Put your hand here. Can you feel it moving and kicking?"

Jack felt the movement. "The little person inside is eager to come out and explore the world."

The doctor expected the baby towards the end of June. Glad's pregnancy went well. She had several friends who already had given birth, and they gave her advice and support. She knitted baby clothes, as did her mother. They bought a cot and made bedding from old sheets they had. All was well prepared. They thought about names, not a complicated task as it was the tradition to name children after parents and grandparents.

To keep up her skills, Glad sketched and painted. She helped Marsie in the shop when it was very busy, but standing behind the counter tired her quickly.

Mabel often came to tea and talked about fortune-telling. Glad relayed the stories to Jack when he came home. "She asked for my empty tea cup and then peered at the tea-leaves left at the bottom and around the sides. She said I'm going to have a healthy child. It's more likely to be a girl than a boy."

"How can she tell that?" Jack laughed, cynically.

"She also said I'd have only one child. I thought she was saying I won't be having twins, but she meant only one in my entire life!" Glad clutched his hand. "I've always imagined having two or three. I worry that something will go wrong and stop me from having more."

"Don't worry about that now. How can tea-leaves tell your future? If you'd given them another swirl in the cup, they'd be in a different position. We'll make sure you're well looked after and healthy, then you'll be fine."

CHAPTER FORTY-SIX
Motherhood

1921

It was Tuesday 21st June, and the weather in Liverpool was sunny and pleasant. Fortunately, not hot, as that would be uncomfortable for Glad at her stage in pregnancy. She was eating breakfast with Pa and Marsie when Jack came to say goodbye before he departed for a ten-day trip to Wales.

"Darling, I'm off to catch the train. I hate leaving you, but there's nothing much I can do here."

They looked each other in the eye, their lips touched. He put his hand on her belly, as if saying goodbye to the baby. "Bye, love. It's amazing to think there might be a little one here when I return."

"Do take care, dear, and come back as soon as you can. I'm so excited about us being three," Glad said.

Jack's stomach hardened. He saw the tension in Glad's face; her smile was forced and her eyes reflected anxiety. Feeling terribly awkward about leaving, he placed his hands on her cheeks and gave her one long, last kiss.

Jack took the train to Newtown and walked to his lodgings. He asked the landlady to look out for any message from Liverpool about the birth of a baby.

On Wednesday, a week later, Jack returned to his lodgings after a protracted day's work. The landlady met him at the door. "Jack, there's a letter from Liverpool. Here it is. I hope it's the news you're waiting for."

Jack dumped his bag on the floor and quickly yanked the envelope open, his hands shaking in expectation. After glancing at the words, he exclaimed, "It's a girl! My wife's had a girl!" He instantly relaxed, his shoulders dropping. "She particularly wanted a girl, so she'll be delighted. Mother and baby are well." He beamed and felt warmth flow through his limbs. "The baby was born on the twenty-third, so she's already a week old!"

He wondered why they hadn't sent a telegram - it seemed strange, and he felt an urgency to leave immediately.

"I'm so happy for you, Mr Handley."

"I need to get home as soon as possible."

"It's too late to catch a train to Liverpool this evening," the landlady said.

"I'll go first thing in the morning."

"The first bus to Shrewsbury leaves at a quarter to eight. I'll have your breakfast ready by seven."

He arrived home just after midday and saw his mother-in-law at the counter. Straight away, he asked her, "How is everything?" His heart skipped a beat when he noticed how pallid she was. She showed only a trace of a smile. "You'd better go upstairs quickly. Glad's in bed." Marsie only showed a trace of a smile. "You'd better go upstairs quickly. Glad's in bed."

When Jack went into the bedroom, he saw the nurse sitting on the bed, wiping Glad's forehead with a cloth. It shocked him to see his love grimace with pain. Just then, she noticed him. "Hello dear, I'm so relieved you're back, I don't feel well."

He bent down to kiss her pale cheek. Her body trembled, and she was hot. He felt her forehead - she had a high temperature. She took his hand, pressing it against her cheek and kissing it. "I have this awful pain in my body." Her hand went to her pelvis. "It doesn't seem right."

Jack steadied himself. "That's dreadful. When did it begin?"

"It started the day before yesterday and seems worse today. Anyway, first go and see our dear girl. She's in Pa and Marsie's bedroom."

He saw the little one fast asleep in her cot. She was perfect, her soft face so innocent and pure. He was deeply touched and proud, and looked forward to holding her later. He went back to Glad, desperate to help her in some way. But what could he do?

"Has a doctor been in?" he asked the nurse."He was here yesterday and said there was nothing to worry about. He said she'd soon get better." She held out her hand. "I'm Miss Roberts."

Jack shook hands. "How is she now, compared to yesterday?"

"She's in more pain. It's keeping her out of her sleep."

"Miss Roberts, what more can we do?"

"We can only wait. Women are often poorly for a few days after delivering a baby. She'll get better soon."

But Jack wasn't reassured. He bolted to the doctor's surgery, where he asked to speak to the doctor urgently. He told him his wife was getting worse and demanded the doctor come again - that same afternoon, to prescribe a remedy.

Dr Richardson arrived later, and Jack again explained his fear that his wife was seriously ill. He knew a few things after being in the war, and sensed that Glad's condition called for more care. Dr Richardson went upstairs, spoke to Miss Roberts, and then asked Glad how she was.

"There's a terrible pain in my pelvis and lower back, all the time, doctor," she said. "I feel tired."

"Have you got enough breastmilk, Mrs Handley?"

"No, I have less every day."

The doctor touched her forehead. "You haven't got a high temperature, so it's nothing serious. You'll soon be better. Rest is what you need. And eat well."

On leaving, Dr Richardson spoke to Jack. "She'll be alright, but you better find a wet nurse to feed the baby. Miss Roberts will know where to ask."

Jack's nostrils flared. "I cannot believe my wife will be alright without anything to strengthen her. She's in pain and cannot sleep. Please, can't you prescribe opium to relieve her pain? Wouldn't that help her sleep?"

"There's no need for that, Mr Handley," said the doctor, moving towards the door. "Now, I have other patients to see. Good day."

Jack went up to see Glad. She was pleased they were going to get a wet nurse, and hopefully one that could come straightaway. Miss Roberts told him where to go, and late in the afternoon he came back with a woman who looked capable.

Miss Roberts changed the bedclothes, and it was only then that Jack about heard Glad losing blood.

His heart pounded at the thought, and, feeling overwhelmed, he raised his voice to Miss Roberts. "Why on earth didn't you tell Dr Richardson about her bleeding?"

"A loss of blood is normal after giving birth, Mr Handley. Trust me, there was no need to mention it."

Jack raged. "Even a week after delivery?" Memories of the war flashed through his mind. Images of men in severe pain fighting for their lives. Of the damp, dark cellar at Bleauport Farm and the row of dead figures covered with blankets. Thoughts of death surged through his mind - the loss of those close to him, the pain of seeing them die. In the army, he'd seen enough to know doctors make mistakes, or say it will be alright when they know it won't. He'd heard of mothers dying after giving birth.

Was he now to lose his love, she who was closest to him - his very dearest?

All night he lay next to Glad, but got little sleep, constantly worrying and thinking about what to do. Glad slept fitfully. When she woke, she complained of chills and low abdominal pain. Now and again she sat up in bed and spoke as if people surrounded her. Jack knew she was hallucinating, meaning her temperature was higher. There was an odour, too, that was difficult to ignore. And it brought back awful memories of drudging past dead horses with their putrid smell.

By Friday morning, Jack was in even more distress. His wife now had diarrhoea. Miss Roberts helped her out of bed, which was difficult because Glad was almost too weak to stand. Her voice was dull. She said little, and when she did, it was delirious. Pa and Marsie were extremely upset. Marsie did her best to help look after the baby so that Miss Roberts could give her undivided attention to Glad.

Glad was no longer aware of what was going on. When she spoke, she asked about her baby. "Where's my little one? I need to feed her. I don't want her going hungry."

Jack and Miss Roberts decided a physician needed to come again. He rushed to the surgery and demanded a second opinion. He told the doctor he'd seen enough men dying in the trenches, that he knew when death was near, and could tell his wife was in a terrible state.

"Who's the doctor here?" the physician said. "Who's experienced with deliveries? Stop worrying, Mr Handley."

"I insist on a second opinion. I want to be sure we've done all we can to save her."

"We'll send another doctor to look at your wife tomorrow."

Jack returned to Glad's bedside, gave her a kiss, and holding her hand, said the doctor had repeated his statement not to worry. "Another doctor will come tomorrow, to give us a second opinion."

A specialist from Rodney Green arrived on Saturday. He confirmed the pains were nothing to worry about. He said Glad was exhausted and needed to rest. "Make sure she has plenty of tea to drink. Apple juice is good. It's best for her to eat oatmeal and toast. She'll be better once she eats again."

Jack didn't believe it, but didn't know what else to do. He told himself that they just had to care for Glad as best they could, and hope for improvement. It was difficult to get Glad to eat and drink. She floated in and out of reality. Her clarity came back briefly, and with a feeble voice, she said, "Look after … my baby, Jack. Be a good … father for her." She then returned to her subconscious predicament.

On Sunday, Jack was completely in despair. His love was dying and no one could help. She lay there, eyes closed. She no longer spoke. Her body was shutting down. He knew the signs. His head and heart ached. Sitting by her side, he caressed her hand and whispered encouraging words, but there was no reaction. He tried to put on a brave face when Pa and Marsie came in. Marsie had the baby in her arms, hoping she would cheer Glad up. But she didn't react. Her breath was now shallow and erratic. She'd lost interest in her baby. Jack kept pleading with her to stay awake. He even shook her, hoping to resuscitate her. Pa prayed to the Lord to save his daughter that she may live to care for her child.

They were surrounding her when her breathing stopped.

Devastated and heart-broken, Jack blamed the doctors who hadn't grasped the seriousness of the situation. He was angry with himself, and a sense of guilt came over him. He believed he shouldn't have left her to go to Wales; if I'd been home he would have insisted Glad went to hospital.

Jack's sisters were beside themselves; Glad had been like a sister. They consoled Jack as best they could, telling him there was nothing he could have done, but he was too angry to listen.

He'd lost his appetite and wanted to be left alone, coping with his emotions by avoiding contact, dealing with his own thoughts. In no mind to arrange the funeral, he let Pa and Marsie sort everything out, but he couldn't avoid going to register the death of Glad - the cause: puerperal fever - and the birth of Gladys Lizette Augusta Handley.

The hearse arrived mid-morning on Thursday 7th July. After the coffin was loaded, they followed it down Score Lane to All Saints' Church, Childwall Abbey. It was only a mile, but it seemed an endless trudge to Jack. He still couldn't believe this was happening to him. His mind was not yet with the newborn, so Marsie carried her. Jack had suggested leaving the baby with the wet-nurse, but Marsie needed the comfort of her granddaughter at this sorrowful time. There was a massive turnout of people. Not only family and friends, but art students and teachers, shop customers, and some of Pa's colleagues from the post-office. They all felt the terrible loss of such a youthful woman, a budding artist, and a young mother.

Reverend Thomas began a prayer. "God, as we gather in this place to pay our last respects to our departed soul, Glad Handley, we ask you to come into our midst. Fill us with divine strength, that we may honour her life. Let your grace be upon us today that we may be able to support one another. Wrap your arms around us through this painful period and let your joy be our strength. In Jesus' name, we believe and pray. Amen."

The theme of his sermon was that the quality of life is paramount, not the length of life. "All present have seen how Glad lived her life. You have seen the purpose of her life — her belief that women should be equal to men, that women develop themselves independently through education and work. She put that into practise — in her artwork and in her teaching. Glad loved her husband, Jack, dearly. She believed in the importance of family and had given birth to their daughter before being stopped in her tracks."

Jack didn't want to weep, but he couldn't stop his chin trembling and tears forming in his eyes. He sat next to Marsie, who put her hand on his knee. His mother was behind him, and he felt her warm touch on his shoulder.

The reverend continued, "Many ask — why? Why would God take Glad at this point in her life? Isaiah fifty-five, says God's thoughts are higher than ours. We can't explain His purposes, and no explanation can or should remove our grief. We do know God's ways are best, and one day we will have a much clearer picture."

He paused.

And the baby's cry broke the silence.

PART SIX
Jack - A Single Father

CHAPTER FORTY-SEVEN

Dealing with grief

1921

Jack had seen death so often in his life, but it still plagued him. He felt hopeless. Not even during the war had he suffered hopelessness to the extent he did now. He no longer had a dear wife to be a mother for their daughter. A single father with a travelling job and no home of his own, how would he manage without his greatest love? He found consolation in his little daughter, who was full of liveliness and had her entire life before her. She would always remind him of Glad.

Seated in the kitchen with his mother-in-law, he looked at the floor. "Who will look after Gladys?" He turned to Marsie. "I don't want to burden you. I can't ask my mother. She's now sixty-two and lacks the energy to care for a baby. My sisters haven't offered, and I don't think I should ask them. They have their own lives and families."

"Perhaps we should find a nanny," Marsie replied.

"We'd need someone seven days a week, though!"

Marsie started doing the washing up. "There's a baby hostel on Beaumont Street, but I wouldn't want her to go there."

Jack stood up and paced back and forth. "I prefer to be sure she's well looked after, as if she had a mother. Glad would have wanted her to have a good upbringing and education."

"Beaumont Street is quite a way off."

Jack took the drying-cloth from its hook. "I think there's a bus service from the end of the road. I'll pay them a visit to see what it's like."

Jack's sister, Mabel, accompanied him to the Nursery Training College which housed the hostel. The cleanliness and orderliness of the place impressed them, and the staff were friendly. The head nurse explained they kept babies in small groups of five or six; each had a dedicated nurse with whom the babies could form an attachment. The hostel adhered to the latest scientific insights about how to bring up young children, like feeding at exact times, daily bathing, no kissing on the mouth, not even by the father.

Mabel and Jack believed it was a suitable place for baby Gladys, and shared their enthusiasm with Marsie.

She looked away from them as they told her. "I can't bear the thought of Gladys being in a place like that so soon. If only I could look after her — but I can't give up my shop."

"I'm sure it's best for all of us," Jack said, putting his arm around Marsie.

Mabel repeated that the high standards had impressed her; she was convinced Gladys would receive fine care there.

Jack asked Marsie to accompany him when he took baby Gladys to the hostel. He noticed she felt more at ease after seeing the accommodation and speaking to the staff. She met Mrs Jenkins, Gladys' primary nurse, who said she could visit as often as she liked. They liked each other straightaway, making Marsie feel confident about the baby's care.

Jack went back to work as soon as he could, needing the distraction to rid him of the thoughts plaguing him. He kept living with Pa and Marsie, but needed to get away on weekends because he found being with them difficult. Being out in the open air was what he preferred, so he took up golf. Another distraction was a rambling club and weekend walks in the Lake District.

He had never felt much support from his family. His father and sisters were always telling him what to do. Mother had a listening ear and understood him better, but she was long-winded and he didn't have the patience to listen.

On 31st July, he went to his parents for tea. Mabel, Mary, and Joe were home, too. They asked how little Gladys was faring in the hostel. Jack said she was healthy and growing fast. Mary insisted babies should be at home if there's family nearby. Her comment irritated Jack, and he told her, "No one offered to take her."

"You didn't ask us," Mary snapped.

"I'm not going begging. Everyone knew my situation. Besides, I don't want to be a burden on others. She's well looked after."

Mother and Father suggested going with Jack to see their granddaughter sometime soon.

"Isn't Reggie around?" Jack asked, wanting to play with him. They always had fun together.

Mother's brow wrinkled. "Annie and George took him to the seaside in Llandudno, for a holiday, but yesterday we had a telegram saying Reggie was ill and had to go to hospital."

"*How* ill?"

"We don't know. I hope we hear better news today."

Father cleared his throat. "It must be serious if they needed to take him in."

"That's terrible," Jack said. "It's horrible not knowing what's happening."

They were just finishing tea when someone knocked at the door. Mabel went to open it. She came back to the sitting-room holding a telegram and handed it to Father.

He opened it, read it in silence, his face creasing. "Reggie has passed away!"

"Oh God," Mother cried.

"What does it say?" Mary asked.

"It says, 'Reggie passed away today after a failed operation. Returning tomorrow, Annie'."

Mabel burst into tears.

"That's tragic!" Joe spluttered.

"It's the third child they've lost!" Mary shouted.

Jack couldn't find any words, as all the grief of the past weeks raced through his mind.

"I can't believe it," Mother wept. "How can God take such a lovely little boy from us? Only five years old!"

They were all devastated, unable to accept what had happened. Jack returned home feeling it was the end of the world. Death had come to him once again, ripping away someone close.

The next day, he went to console Annie and George. They had just arrived and were explaining what had taken place.

George had his arm around Annie's shoulder while she relived the episode. "Reggie was playing on the beach, building sand castles with George, when he complained of pains in his tummy. We returned to our lodgings, but he kept crying and screaming in pain. It was unbearable, ... insufferable to see him in that state." Tears streamed down her cheeks.

"We took him straight to hospital," George said, his chin trembling. "They did an emergency operation to remove his appendix."

"I wanted to stay the night with him," Annie stuttered. "But they didn't allow me. They said we had to leave and come back in the morning. I couldn't sleep all night."

George continued. "When we saw Reggie the next morning, he said he was still in pain. The doctor told us it was normal after an operation; said his body needed time to recover. But Reggie wouldn't eat and kept complaining of pain where the incision was made, and he was coughing a lot. We called the nurse, and she removed the bandage. The wound was red; puss oozing out. She fetched a doctor who said there was an infection, and that Reggie needed a second operation."

"They sent us away again," Annie said. "It was terrible not knowing how serious it was. When we went back yesterday morning, they didn't let us see Reggie. They said the infection had got into his abdomen. We sat in a waiting room for ages. We couldn't believe our ears when they said they'd lost him." She broke down in tears again.

Everyone was full of sorrow and found it difficult to find words. They gathered around Annie and George, embracing each other.

"Are we not to have children?" Annie asked. "What have we done wrong in God's eyes to lose three?"

"Is God punishing us for what I did in the war?" George questioned.

Father answered. "We cannot always understand God's ways. He has called Reggie to Him and we can only accept He has done it in His wisdom. Let us pray for Reggie."

After hearing the details of what had happened, Jack felt numb. His analytical brain concluded that doctors had failed again, but his heart only felt an emptiness. Reggie's death compounded his mournfulness because Glad had been very close to Reggie. Seeing them together had proved to Jack that she would have been a wonderful mother.

Marsie and Pa showed Jack compassion, more than he received from his own family who were now absorbed in mourning Reggie's death and consoling Annie and George. Regular visits to the Freemason Lodge helped him fill his evenings and share his losses with other men. It was a great temptation to resort to alcohol again, but he resisted by making sure he was not alone. When he could, he visited baby Gladys in the hostel, but soon realised he was not the type of father who took much pleasure from little ones. He looked forward to the time when she could play games, walk, and cycle.

In the dark days of November, he went out less and became depressed. On Saturdays and Sundays, he stayed in bed, not motivated to get up, sometimes wishing life was over. He became withdrawn, and although he knew it was happening, he couldn't seem to do anything about it. He also lost weight. At the Freemasons, a fellow took him aside for a chat. He asked Jack how he was doing, and Jack could no longer suppress his lack of motivation. The fellow reminded him he had a child to care for. That made Jack think of Glad's last words — that he was to look after their baby. He knew then he had to carry on for her sake.

By December, Jack was getting to grips with the loss of Glad and Reggie. He was not his old self — full of humour — but he gained confidence. He visited Gladys more often, sometimes taking another family member with him.

On a dark, rainy day, he went to pick up his mother to take her to Gladys. When he arrived, only Joe was home. He said their mother had gone out shopping. As she wasn't the most punctual person, they thought little of it and waited for her to arrive. An hour passed and Jack began to worry.

After a while, they heard a cab arrive, and Jack rushed out to help his mother — her dress was muddy and torn, and she had a bloody mark on her face.

"What's *happened*, Mother?"

"They knocked me down."

She hobbled into the house with Jack's support.

"Who knocked you down?" he asked.

"I was crossing the road … a car knocked me down … into the gutter." She sat down and Jack saw she was in pain. "I managed to stand up. The driver was kind and took me straight to First Aid. They said I've broken my ribs. I need to rest so they can heal."

"That's very painful."

"I daren't cough or laugh. It hurts too much," she said, unable to smile.

Christmas was not a celebration - 1921 had been a terrible year, and Mother's state compounded the feeling. She was weak, not herself, had bouts of heavy coughing, and only took shallow breaths. Jack noticed she forgot things and had difficulty concentrating. He heard Father had brought a doctor in who had told them to keep her warm and away from any draught. Mabel, the daughter most inclined to look after her mother, said Mother's lack of appetite distressed her. Jack paced around the house, again in despair and disillusioned by the lack of help from a doctor.

All they could do was replenish hot-water bottles and make her sip water. Father read poems to distract her from the pain.

CHAPTER FORTY-EIGHT

Better years

1922

In the new year, Jack spoke to his mother for the last time before she died of pneumonia and senility, aged sixty-two. Father said the Lord had taken his lamb to relieve her of the pain, and to comfort her in His presence; her hour had come and nothing more could have been done on this earth.

Mother's funeral at Holy Trinity left Jack heavy-hearted. Not that he'd been terribly close to his mother, who seemed fonder of younger Joe. It was the memory of Glad and her burial only six months earlier that hurt. He desperately wanted to move on — to get away from the sense of loss and the lingering distress he felt at all the deaths he had endured since being an adult. He had not yielded before, and would not yield now. He'd carry on, for Gladys' sake.

Jack was thankful for Mabel and her devotion to their parents, which lessened the burden on him and gave him the opportunity to get his own life on track. Words flowed from Mabel's mouth like a waterfall. "It keeps nagging at me that I should've done more to save Mother. If I'd kept her warmer, she may not have caught pneumonia. I should have asked the doctor to come again."

"I know how you feel," Jack said. "I blamed myself in the same way after we lost Glad. Later, I realised she would have wanted me to carry on with my life and not dwell on what's happened. You did your best given what you knew."

"Thank you, Jack," Mabel said. "I'll set my sights on looking after our father."

By spring, life had settled into an acceptable routine for Jack. For Buchanan, he travelled around northwest England and north Wales, visiting shops to promote the confectionery. In the stores already selling

Buchanan sweets, he asked for changes to the displays to bring their products more clearly into customers' view. In other shops, he investigated which competing brands were being sold, mostly either Rowntree's or Cadbury's, and offered Buchanan as an attractive alternative.

His parents-in-law were always happy to see him at weekends; his presence was no doubt a welcome distraction from the loss of their only child: their shared sorrow. He had nowhere else to live and felt more at ease with the Grimes than at home with his own father; living with *him* would only end in frustration for them both. Jack sometimes thought about finding a place of his own, but he wasn't ready to be on his own for fear of becoming depressed and reverting to alcohol.

As his mother-in-law had a shop, Jack helped her keep up with recent developments. He installed professional shop fittings to make the tobacco and confectionery products more visible. They affixed signs on the wall outside, advertising brand names. A cash register replaced the simple till. For customers low on cash, they introduced buying on 'tick' — on credit.

In his spare time, he kept fit by swimming in Newsham Park lake, or taking a brisk walk. Occasionally, Pa strolled with him and they spoke about the world at large. A recurring topic was the formation of Northern Ireland, the departure of British troops from Dublin Castle, and the uncertainty of what would happen. They worried that a wave of Irish families would emigrate to Liverpool.

The Freemason meetings in St Michael's Temperance Lodge were a mainstay in Jack's social life. He had long achieved full initialisation and enjoyed the ceremonial rituals which took place. He never missed a meeting when he was in Liverpool and wore a badge with the brotherhood's symbols - the compass and square, the architects' tools. For the Freemasons, the compass symbolised spiritual eternity and infinite boundaries. The square represented the realm of material, fairness, balance, and stability.

His sister Annie gave birth to a healthy daughter in May and named her Mary Josephine, after her parents Mary and Joseph, Josie for short. Jack was happy to find Annie and George elated to have started a new family. After losing three children, they were anxious about Josie's well-being and determined to keep her healthy.

Jack visited Gladys sufficiently to be an acceptable father, looking forward to when she would be old enough to play. Mrs Jenkins wrote regularly to Jack and Marsie to keep them informed of Gladys' progress. On her first birthday, neither could visit; Marsie was in her shop and Jack was in Boot, Eskdale. When he was back in Liverpool, he popped into the shop and Marsie showed him a letter.

23rd June
Dear Mrs Handley,
Gladys has really enjoyed her birthday and has been just lovely all day. She had a birthday party with ten babies and they all had a good time together. Gladys loved all the attention and felt awfully important!! It was sweet of you to send her a dolly. A box of chocolates arrived from her daddy.
Hope you are keeping well,
Mrs Jenkins

1923

Living with his parents-in-law, Jack had been able to save enough money for a week's break on Jersey, one of the Channel Islands near the French coast. Longing for a summer holiday, he booked a hotel in the main town, St Helier. The sunlight was brilliant as he strolled along the promenade in his shorts. Before breakfast each morning he made a point of continuing his routine of going for a swim or a brisk walk. Interested in exploring the rest of the island, he hired a bicycle, and headed off for the sweeping, sandy beaches at St Brelade's Bay. He stopped to relax in the sun, and, at a café ordered tea-in-the-basket, so he could sit on the beach. On the northern coast, he reconnoitered around the cliffs and tiny fishing villages. A day-trip to St Malo in France was on offer, so he bought a ticket. On board, he took deep breaths of the fresh sea air while he stood at the railing watching the seagulls fly past in the hope of some food.

In the French port, the language reminded him of his visits to the estaminet during the war. It also made him think of Glad and her desire to visit Paris; the city of art that her friends often spoke about. By coincidence, Pa was on a trip to Paris at the same time — he enjoyed travelling and wanted to see more of the world. Marsie was not keen on long trips abroad, so he'd undertaken the journey alone. Jack wondered whether Pa was doing the trip in memory of Glad.

CHAPTER FORTY-NINE
Gladys comes home

1924

Jack now spoke more easily about his time in the Great War and told Pa about the battles of Ypres. Pa wanted to see Ypres with his own eyes, so he travelled to Belgium. When he returned, he gave Jack and Marsie an account of what he'd seen. Ypres was being re-built, but most of the town was still rubble. The Cloth Hall and the Cathedral only had a few walls standing. He found the spot in the town wall where Jack had billeted seven years earlier. On Hill 60, the pillbox stood as if the war had only just finished — in a sea of bomb craters. The landscape was terribly scarred; dead trees stood amongst young green shoots. Trenches were plainly visible, as were remnants of military equipment. The recount of his trip brought all the gruesome details back to Jack.

Pa also spoke about his visit to the Hampton Court Exhibition on his return journey. The British Empire was in decline, so the exhibition in Wembley was intended to herald a revival, a bright future that would leave the gloom of war behind. The King had described it as, 'the whole Empire in little'. Pa said thousands of people passed through the entrance and spread out to the Palace of Engineering, the Palace of Industry, the Indian Pavilion or the other shows of the fifty-eight countries. He was impressed and proud. He'd always believed in the Empire, and the show reconfirmed his view. The Indian Pavilion was like the Taj Mahal. In the Ceylon Pavilion he saw a valuable collection of gems and jewellery. He had coffee in Jamaica and chocolate in Grenada.

When it was Marsie's turn for a holiday, she stayed on the Isle of Man with little Gladys, now nearly three, and sent a picture postcard.

Port St Mary
Dear Jack,

We arrived safely. I had a job keeping Gladys occupied on the ferry to prevent her from running off, fearing she'd fall through a gap in the railing. Mrs Collister (bookshop) welcomed us. With Glad, I've stayed here in the past. I felt proud showing off my granddaughter.
Marsie XX

After the summer holidays, Jack collected Gladys from the baby hostel so she could live at home. She attended kindergarten three days a week. Mrs Jenkins, who they now called Jenky, no longer worked at the hostel, so Jack asked her to be the nanny. Jack enjoyed seeing more of his daughter and playing with her. He took her to Newsham Park to play games of hide-and-seek, to feed the ducks and play with a ball. On those days, he allowed himself to be happy.

1926

On Gladys's fifth birthday, she was spoiled by presents from her father, grandparents, and Jenky. Jack knew he was spoiling her, compensating for the absence of a mother and a travelling father. He expected Pa and Marsie felt the same. It wasn't right to spoil her; he knew that. He decided he needed to put a stop to it happening in the future, and promised himself he would talk to Marsie about it.

In July, Marsie and Gladys stayed with Mrs Collister on the Isle of Man again. Gladys loved playing on the beach, but her grandmother didn't let her go anywhere near the water. After the school holidays, Jack walked her to her first day at primary school. From then on, Jenky walked her there and back every day.

1927

Jack's brother, Joe, was now the top mechanic at the motor car garage where he had been an apprentice. He told Jack about how he'd met the daughter of one of their customers.

"Mr Wickes' open-top Crossley came to our repair shop. I expected to see him at the wheel, but the young lady took my breath away. She said the oil needed refreshing, but I wasn't paying proper attention. I asked her to drive the car inside but then had to ask her again what required doing. It was embarrassing."

It was love at first sight. The family was happily surprised when they met Lily Wickes, a rich businessman's daughter. Jack was best man at their wedding, and little Gladys was a bridesmaid. The newlyweds moved into a semi-detached house along Childwall Priory Road.

When Jack took Gladys to see them in their new home, Joe told him about a plan to start his own garage.

In the same year, Jack's sister, Mary, married a man she'd met at her work in the harbour; he was a stevedore, and eighteen years her senior.

1928

Jack had used public transport for his trips, but as the business grew, he found it an inefficient use of his time. Joe had long suggested Jack would be better off with a motor car, so he bought one from him. It was a second-hand Wolseley Seven, a two-seater with an open top. Jack was thrilled and loved touring around. He took Marsie and Gladys to Formby beach and Knowlsey Park.

In the summer, he and Gladys, now seven years old, had a camping holiday, a new experience for her. He drove down to Stonehenge and the New Forest, where they set up tent amongst the trees. During the night, Gladys heard all sorts of noises outside and stirred her father several times. He said it was just animals roaming around in the dark, but they wouldn't trouble them. The next morning, Gladys woke up to find a wild pony peering into the tent. She soon got used to being in nature and enjoyed it.

1929

During the summer school holidays, Gladys was at home all day. Jenky went away for a break, leaving Marsie to mind Gladys. All went well for a few days, but one evening, Jack found Gladys whining. "Granny won't let me go out to play."

"She's been naughty," Marsie said. "She climbed up on the shop counter and danced around when a customer came in. I can't have that."

"It's not fair to keep me inside," Gladys whimpered.

"You did it before, and if you don't listen to me, I'll have to punish you."

Jack was unsure how to react. He couldn't blame Gladys for being bored, but he didn't want to undermine Marsie's authority. "Now Gladys, you must listen to Granny and do as she says."

After Gladys had gone to bed, Jack spoke to Marsie.

"She's a real handful," Marsie said. "I give her sweets from the shop to keep her quiet, but it doesn't help for long."

"I prefer she's not spoiled," Jack said. "We can't have her getting her way all the time. She needs to learn to obey."

Marsie sighed. "I feel so sorry for her not having a mother. I want her to be happy. What's the problem with spoiling her a little?"

Jack smiled, but bit his lip. "Glad wouldn't have wanted her daughter to be a spoiled child. We need to bring her up so that she realises she can't always have her way. We need to draw a line. She must learn to handle disappointments."

Tensions came to a head on Gladys's eighth birthday. She was disappointed about not having a proper party and became hysterical. It took all Marsie's energy and patience to calm her down.

Jack couldn't allow this to continue all summer, so he arranged for Gladys to spend time with a friend at Gartsang, north of Liverpool. While she was away, Jack and Marsie argued about what to do with Gladys. Jack said he believed she would be better off at a boarding school to learn to deal with other children and more discipline. Marsie insisted a child should be at home where she is loved and has friends outside school.

Given Marsie's strong reaction, Jack didn't push the subject. But he decided, nonetheless, to find an appropriate, affordable school.

On Wednesday 30th October, Jack grabbed a newspaper as soon as they were delivered to the shop. The stock markets had been bad for several weeks and had dived the previous week. He didn't have any shares himself, but the general market conditions affected his business. The uncertainties had affected sales in shops, making shopkeepers wary of any investment. It was the talk of the day when he visited clients. Some were worse off than others, but there was a overall feeling of pessimism.

The news from New York was appalling. The enormous losses on the stock exchange had wiped investors out. Selling was so fast that the tickers couldn't cope with the volume of transactions. A businessman with assets of over a million pounds had seen them drop to sixty-thousand overnight.

On Wall Street, there were scenes that had never been witnessed before. Brokers' offices were besieged by small investors wanting to know where their investments stood. Many had lost all their savings. People were screaming and cursing in the streets, women openly weeping. The US Government feared that the crash would force banks to go into bankruptcy. Canada was affected, but the London Exchange had been resilient. Jack knew it would hit England in due course, and braced himself for what was to come.

CHAPTER FIFTY
Being Daddy

1930

Jack continued to be irritated by the way his mother-in-law brought Gladys up. He was away most of the week, but when home, Gladys complained to him that Granny was strict, that Granny wouldn't allow her to play in the road, or do anything that could make a mess. But although she was strict with these things, he noticed Marsie gave Gladys some things she wanted in abundance, like sweets and cakes. In this regard she was spoiling Gladys more than Jack liked.

"She knows you'll give her what she wants, more than I will," Jack said to Marsie, his jaw muscles tightening. "If I deny her, she goes to you to get it."

Marsie took a deep breath. "I want her to be happy, that's all."

"I want her to be happy too, but she must learn she can't have everything she desires. She ..."

Marise cut him off. "Don't forget, *I* have to deal with her all week. You're only here at the weekend, and sometimes not even then."

"All the same, I'm her father and she has to listen to me."

"Well, I can't help that."

"I've decided it's best for her to go to a boarding school, an excellent school where she'll have a solid education."

"But how can you take her away from me? I'm a mother to her."

"She needs to be with other children, to be with those of her own age, to learn to consider others."

"Oh, am I too old now? Was I good enough to look after her when she was small, but now I'm not good enough?"

"That's not the point. It's what's best for Gladys that's most important."

"Glad would *never* have approved of it, *never!*"

"It's not fair to say that, and you know it!"

In Llandudno, North Wales, Jack found Hillside School in a large house on Abbey Road. The building looked tidy and was in a decent area of town overlooking the bay. The principal showed him round and explained she had forty girls. She spoke about the importance of outdoor activities, regular walks to the beach to play games and swim. That caught Jack's attention. He believed that outdoor team sports, discipline and manners were just as important as lessons in class. He'd learned the most from teaming up with other men in the army. Talking to people in the hotel that evening, he got the impression the school was well regarded.

Back home, he told Marsie he'd decided to send Gladys there. "She'll be better off going to boarding school and Hillside is a fine choice. It's a place I can afford. It has a reputable name, and I was impressed with what I saw. When I'm over there for business, I'll be able to pop in to see her, and it's not far from Liverpool for a Sunday day trip."

Marsie had tears in her eyes. "But she's only eight, Jack. Why don't you wait till she's older? It'll be such a big change for her. She's happy here at home with us."

"I want her to be more independent, to fend for herself, and to learn how to get along with other girls of her own age," Jack replied. "I've arranged for her to begin there after the February half-term, and I've ordered her uniform."

Marsie winced. "You know I don't agree. I won't be surprised if she's unhappy."

"As Gladys will be away, I've decided it's better for me to leave, too. Better to allow the air to clear and give you and Pa a rest."

"There's no need for you to leave us," Marsie said, but Jack could tell she wasn't asking him to stay.

"Mabel has said I can live with her until I've found a place of my own. I'll pop in to see you from time to time."

On the day of Gladys' departure, Jack and Marsie packed her belongings in a new trunk.

"Let me sort out the clothes," Marsie said, looking downcast. "Gladys, you won't need summer clothes yet, so I'll send them on later."

Gladys stood by, her head drooping. "Do I really need to go away? Why can't I stay here with you, Granny?"

Jack ignored the question. "Come over here and tell me which books you want to take."

"I'm not taking any books," Gladys replied.

"Listen, you're going to like it at your new school. You'll make friends with other girls, do sports, go to the beach. You'll love it," Jack said. "In the evenings you'll have time on your own so you better have a few books."

Marsie remained silent.

"Granny, why can't I do sports *here* and meet other girls that way?"

"Now, stop asking questions and help us pack," Jack said, raising his voice.

"I don't want books."

"Well, I'll put these in, then at least you have some in case you need them," Jack said. "Granny, she needs to wear her uniform for the journey, so don't pack that. She needs to arrive looking neat and tidy."

Gladys picked up the navy blue and black skirt, and the light blue polo shirt. "I don't like that uniform," she whined.

"It's a fine uniform and you'll soon get used to it," Jack said. "You're going to one of the best schools where they'll teach you manners. You'll be wearing a uniform every day."

"All the time?"

"Yes, for summer, winter, sports — everything."

"Even a nightgown?" Gladys asked.

"Look, I'm packing three of your own nightgowns," Marsie said. "One for wearing, one for in the wash, and one for in your cupboard."

"Will I have my own cupboard?"

"Yes, you will. And it'll have a key so you can lock it," Jack said.

Time came for Gladys to leave.

"We need to get moving," Jack said. "Say bye-bye to Granny."

Gladys and Granny hugged.

"I don't want to go!" Gladys wept, her face lost in Marsie's dress.

Marsie looked at Jack and he read her thoughts: *look what you're doing!*

He grabbed Gladys's arm, but she pulled it free and held on to Granny even more tightly.

"It's time, now. Time to go, dear," Jack coaxed. "Come on Gladys, I can't wait any longer."

Eventually, Granny said, "Run along now, dear, otherwise you and Daddy will be late. I'll write to you each week and come to see you sometime. Will you write back to me?"

"Yes, Granny, I'll send you letters and tell you all about school." Gladys gave Granny a big kiss and off they went.

It was a two-hour drive. The matron welcomed them in. Jack thought it best to leave quickly so that Gladys wouldn't have a chance to make a scene. He said goodbye, and that he'd come back very soon.

Matron took Gladys' hand, and turning to Jack, said, "The new girls may have their first visitor in a month."

He drove back to Liverpool, to Mabel's.

A month later, Jack went to visit. Gladys ran towards him, a big smile on her face. They hugged. He was glad she seemed happy. They sat on a bench in front of the school and she spoke about the girls in her dorm, their outings to the beach, and more. She was full of stories to tell.

"Let's walk up to the top of the Great Orme and have an ice cream there," Jack said.

"I'd like to take Joan Haines with me. She's my best friend."

"Yes, of course, go and fetch her."

They drove to the other side of Llandudno and walked up the rocky promontory that stuck out into the Irish Sea. From there, they had a good view back to town. The girls saw a playground and made a bee-line for the swings.

A few days later, Jack popped in to see Marsie and Pa. She passed him a letter.

Dear Granny,
Thank you for sending me the soap I wanted. I got it all right, and it is lovely. I'm quite happy at school. I would love you to come and take me out. Aunty Sidie has a car, so perhaps she can bring you. I will try to write you some nice letters as often as I can.
Love and kisses, Gladys xxxx

"Why don't you ask Sidie to take you," Jack said, thinking it would remove the pressure on him to go again so soon.

"It's such a long way to go."

"Make a day of it. Stop at a few places on the way. I'm sure Sidie will enjoy it too."

Eventually, Marsie and Sidie went to Llandudno. After they returned, Jack went to see Marsie.

"It was wonderful to see dear Gladys," Marsie said, smiling. "She really likes school and being with the other girls. We took her out for afternoon tea and she was very talkative — told us all about her friend Joan and the pranks they have together."

Finally, Jack breathed a sigh of relief.

1931

Dear Daddy,
Thank you for your letter. Sorry I could not write to you before. I have
been too busy writing Granny's letters and it takes me all my time. I had
a parcel from Granny and this time it included a picture of Grandan with
his spaniel, Marco. Grandan looks so smart with a white handkerchief in
his breast pocket and a pipe in his mouth. They are a grand pair. When
will you come to take me out?
Love, Gladys xx

Whenever Jack visited Marsie, she showed him the latest letters she'd
had from Gladys. He noticed that Marsie and Gladys enjoyed keeping
their special bond alive. He also couldn't help notice that, more often
than not, Gladys wrote asking for something to be sent. Marsie was
obviously still spoiling her, but Jack turned a blind eye.

Dear Granny and Grandan,
I hope you are both well. We are having quite nice weather here in
Llandudno. Please, will you send me some more Rupert books!! Will you
let me know when it is your birthday, and Grandan's? It was May Day on
Wednesday.
Good bye, Gladys xxxxxx

In the school summer holidays, Jack took time off work to be with
Gladys. He hadn't seen her for a while, and he realised she'd lost her
Liverpool accent. He was pleased the school had taught her to speak
proper English, which he thought more fitting for her future.

They travelled to London, visited Westminster Abbey, St Paul's Church
and bathed in the Thames. Although it was a holiday, Jack had another
reason to be in the city. The stock market crash two years earlier was now
taking its toll on England, affecting his work for Buchanan. He felt it was
time to change jobs and move to a different trade and was thinking that
London might have more to offer than Liverpool. He longed to see what
business was like in the capital, to look around the shops and investigate
the latest trends. He was contemplating getting into the shop window-
dressing trade.

On their way back to Liverpool, they went to Ann Hathaway's Cottage
in Stratford-on-Avon, because Jack wanted to acquaint Gladys with

literature. She saw a romantic picture postcard of the cottage and sent it to Granny.

CHAPTER FIFTY-ONE
The Great Depression

1933

England felt the effects of The Great Depression but Jack and his family were lucky to have enough income to survive. He did the weekly Football Pools in the hope of a good win to put towards buying his own property. He usually did Treble Chance, picking games to finish as a draw, in which each team scores at least one goal.

His brother, Joe, had plenty of work because rich men could afford to buy motor cars which increased the amount of maintenance for him to do. By now, Joe had enough experience to want to start his own business. His father-in-law, Mr Wickes, had come out of the stock market crash relatively unscathed and helped Joe launch a garage. Mr Wickes purchased the plot and had a workshop constructed. Joe secured a loan to invest in the equipment.

In February, excavation work started for 'Messrs J. D. Handley & Co.' on Hilbre Street, at Copperas Hill. While digging for the foundations for a hydraulic lift, workmen uncovered a shaft and construction paused. It was so deep they couldn't see the bottom. It turned out to be eighty feet in depth; an old well from copperas works a century earlier.

While Joe was in high spirits, Jack was less happy. People were buying less confectionery, so he found it increasingly difficult to sell Buchanan products to shopkeepers. There was a lack of work in the docks, leaving many men unemployed. The government introduced a social benefit system, but for most, it was insufficient, leaving families destitute.

At this same time, Gladys finished primary education and needed to move to another boarding school. Jack searched for a suitable school in Liverpool, but had to look further afield to find an inexpensive one.

He went to see Gladys for her twelfth birthday.

"As it's a special day today, shall we drive somewhere outside Llandudno?" he asked.

"Can Alice come too? She's my best friend now."

"Of course. Say we're going to Gwrych Castle. Before you fetch her, let me tell you about your new school. You'll love it because they do loads of art and drama. It's an enormous hall in its own grounds with lots of outside space and plenty of sports."

Gladys squinted. "Is it in Liverpool?"

"It's not far away. Easier to get to than Llandudno."

"I want to be near Granny, so I can visit her for weekends."

"There's nothing suitable in Liverpool. I'm sure you'll like the school when you see it."

Gladys ran off to find Alice Eaves. During the day, they spoke about the new school again. Alice said she'd like to go there too.

Gladys' eyes sparkled at that. "It would be *wonderful* if we could be together."

Jack turned to Alice, smiling. "You'll enjoy it there too. Let your mother know it's called Great Moreton Hall School. It's in Cheshire."

After the summer holidays, Gladys and Alice started at their new school. Jack visited a month later, and was unsettled when he saw his daughter's worried face and slumped shoulders; she wasn't her lovely self at all.

"What's the matter, dear?"

"I don't like it here," she said, staring at the ground.

"Why on earth not?"

"It's cold and draughty."

"It's been chilly weather. Wasn't there any heating on?"

"No."

"I'll talk to Matron," Jack said.

Gladys turned away. "They're very strict and the girls are so different — it's difficult to make friends."

Jack pinched the skin of his throat. "But you've got Alice here."

"I know, but we both feel looked down upon."

"Look at me," Jack said. "You're juniors now. At Hillside you were the oldest and now you need to get used to being the youngest again."

"We played Shakespeare's Twelfth Night last week. I had a small part and dressed up. We acted outside on the lawn. It was fun."

"There you go. So there are *some* things you like."

Jack wasn't too worried about Gladys being unhappy — she just needed to adapt, he thought. But in October, Marsie showed him a letter.

Dear Granny,

I hope you, Grandan and Marco are all well. I don't like my new school very much. They're so strict, it's like being in prison. Besides my friend Alice, I don't like the other girls much. At end of term there'll be a fancy-dress ball. Please, will you send me those blue, gossamer wings you made for me years ago. Alice would like to borrow them. She wants to dress up as a 'Good Gibbs Fairy' and I'm going to be the 'Gibbs Archer'. Love, Gladys xxx

"I sent her the wings and included some tuck. She doesn't seem happy there," Marsie said.

"She told me the same, but I think she'll get used to it. She loves drama lessons. Perhaps Sidie can take you to visit her. Then you'll see it's not that bad."

Pa showed Jack a book. "Have you read this?"

Jack saw the title: *The Greater Britain* by Oswald Mosley.

"No. I haven't," he said. "But I know Mosley is a fascist leader."

"Yes, he is. I don't agree with a lot he writes, but it's worth reading," Pa said.

"May I borrow it?"

As he read it, he could see that the idea of Britain regaining its strength as the most powerful country on earth had an appeal. It was about protecting British industries and farmers from damaging foreign imports. City financiers should stop making loans to foreign countries and invest in Britain. Mosley advocated an authoritarian state which would be above party interests. Jack could see through the convincing words — it was this approach that had brought Hitler and Mussolini to power.

He was further appalled when, in November, he read in the newspaper that Mosley had a defence force of three hundred Blackshirts trained to quell disorder, and that Mosley would hold a speech in Liverpool. They planned it in the stadium to accommodate a large number of people. The mayor expected violence and forbade the event, but Mosley turned up with his Blackshirts. To their surprise, the population drove them out of Liverpool, and Jack was glad such a clear statement had been made.

1934

Jack was prepared to leave Buchanan because sales were awful and he wanted a change of trade. In London, he'd seen wonderful shop window displays, especially at Selfridges in Oxford Street. They drew more attention with their moving mechanical figures. He saw an opportunity to introduce animation, on a smaller scale, to any shop window throughout Britain. With design and innovation coming from London, he knew he had to move there. As Gladys needed a better boarding school, he planned to take her with him. That would surely appeal to her growing interest in drama and music.

He took the train to London to look for digs. A newspaper advert caught his eye: a girls' school in Margate promoting manners, sport and art. He went there, and immediately knew that Gladys would love the view out over the cliffs to the sea, and would appreciate the fresh sea air.

Back in Liverpool, he visited Marsie and Pa.

"I was down in London last week," he said, "and I've decided to move there and change jobs. Gladys can come with me."

Pa and Marsie looked sad, but Jack continued. "I've found an excellent school for Gladys - Godwin Girls College in Margate. It's close enough for her to come home to me in London some weekends. She'll love the spot on the sea, the sports, hockey and tennis, and music."

There was little reaction from his parents-in-law, and he presumed they were down in the dumps about the prospect. But then Marsie explained that Pa's dog, Marco, had died. "You're so upset aren't you, love?" she said, patting Pa's knee. "You were best friends, always together."

Jack moved to a large semi-detached house: 46 Ferry Road, Barnes. It had enough space for himself and Gladys when she came to stay. It was close to the river, so he hoped to get back to his early morning swimming routine. Richmond Park was within walking distance and offered plenty of opportunity for brisk walks.

On Rochester Row, in Westminster, he rented an office, conveniently near Victoria station, from where there was a direct train to Margate. It was large enough for a showroom and service depot.

He took out a loan, set up the Handley Betterway Company, and had business paper printed with the slogan, 'Your advertising comes to life!'. The aim was to sell British and Viennese shop window animation, including turntables, moving signs, and novel neon lights. He purchased German and Austrian products because they were high quality, and suitable for continuous operation. Jack also approached the Czech firm of Emanuel Beranek and became their agent in England, selling their glass

Viennese display figures, advertising models and relief novelties. He looked forward to this new life - an exciting different business, and a fine change for Gladys.

At the end of school term, Jack drove to Great Moreton to pick up Gladys. The drive through the countryside was invigorating, the sun shining and his hair blowing in the wind. Gladys said farewell to the teachers and other girls. She was not sorry to depart as she had never really felt at home there; she was only sorry to leave Alice behind. She bade her goodbye with a tear and a hug, saying she hoped they would see each other again.

PART SEVEN

Gladys 'Bunty'
Handley

CHAPTER FIFTY-TWO
Letters from Margate

1934

Gladys was excited to be with her father in London for the summer holiday. It was her first time in the city, and, being thirteen, she found it overwhelming, although there was a lot for her to explore. Most of all, she loved the open-air concerts in Hyde Park.

At the end of August, they drove to Margate, and Gladys marvelled at the view from the top of the cliff in front of her new school. As she left the car to enter the building, she smoothed her clothes, apprehensive about meeting the matron and other girls.

She knew she would miss her grandmother, who was now a long way off; no longer able to come for the day to take her out, and no longer there to confide in. On leaving Liverpool, she had promised to write regularly, to tell her about school life.

Godwin College,
Margate
September
Dear Granny,
Our school is on top of the cliff above Palm Bay. It's the only building here, in bare surroundings. There is open ground all the way to Kingsgate Castle. I have heard that famous and rich people stay there. From the castle, they go down to the beach by a secret staircase through the chalk cliff. Our front windows are sea-facing, so we have a marvellous view out across the North Sea and see ships coming and going from London. I love walking along the sandy beach with the other girls. They are amicable; the mistresses, too.
Daddy chose this school for me because they advertise modern education and plenty of sports. I can't vouch for the quality of the education, but I

can confirm we have a good deal of sports. I play hockey, lawn tennis and cricket (to my surprise). We do gym on the beach and in summer we swim early every morning. I love the fresh air and the sea breeze; it's good for my complexion.

Margate is certainly not short of diversions and distractions. We can skip off to ride the scenic railway at Dreamland, to a concert at the Winter Gardens or a play at the Theatre Royal. But when out of school, we have to be careful to wear our uniforms with pride and watch our manners because there are prefects watching and ready to give punishment. Daddy came to see me today. We walked along the beach and found a spot to sit. I had my period and was quite anxious about leaving school, but it was all right. I'm happy about you calling me Bunty. I like it. At school, they shortened Gladys to Glad, which made me rather sad because I think of my mother. I feel so sorry that she left her life to give birth to me. I asked them to use my second name, Lizette, so they now call me Lizzie.

I hope you and Grandan are well.

Love and kisses, Bunty xxxx

1935

August

Dear Granny and Grandan,

Thanks for your letter. Daddy has taken me to Dartmouth for our holidays. I wish you were here too. It's glorious. Daddy told me he had his honeymoon here. He said my mom was beautiful and would have been a loving mother. I was happy to hear him talk admirably about her, but it made me feel even sadder I never knew her. While writing, I'm watching seagulls dive for fish. I remember you telling me you believe my mother came back as a seagull after her death. So she's here with us, after all. Tomorrow we're going boating.

Lots of love, Bunty xx

Bunty enjoyed camping in their little tent. She loved being in nature, living outside, and the chirping of birds. Her father looked for secluded spots with good drainage and a level area to pitch. He cooked their meals on a Primus stove, which worked on kerosene.

At times, Bunty felt uncomfortable being in the same tent. Her father went outside while she undressed, but in inclement weather, he remained inside. She turned away from him, but still had the feeling of being watched.

1936

March
Dearest Granny,
I didn't bring any tuck back to school but have ordered some from the grocers here, and they sent the bill to Daddy. I have enough to last till end of term but I did not get any cake. Please don't forget I've given up sweets for Lent. A cake would be wonderful, though. You must be moving to your new home on Swanside Road soon. I'd love to help you during the Easter holidays.
It was Aunty Annie's birthday last Thursday. I sent her the 'hankie' sachet, which I embroidered. We didn't go to church this morning as it was raining. We're having a lantern lecture tonight about domestic science as a career. I hope to play at next week's hockey match.
Love, Bunty xx

April
Dear Granny and Grandan,
During our singing lesson, the headmistress came in at 11.30 a.m. and told me there was a telegram from Daddy saying I could go up to London on the 2.08 p.m. train. I rushed to get ready, hurried through dinner and our elocution mistress met me at the station and took charge of me going down. Daddy was waiting at Victoria Station and took me to the Quebec Café for a gorgeous tea while listening to 'The Music Goes Round and Round', played at our request. It's great to be close enough to London to see Daddy on some weekends.
In the morning, we walked through Richmond Park to a Viennese café. After dinner, we listened to the King's speech. It was very interesting and not a falter in it. We went to church in the evening.
On Monday, we had a hectic time on the tube and escalators when shopping around Kingsway and Afrika House. After tea in Aldwych, we went to Tivoli to see Charlie Chaplin in 'Modern Times'. It was excellent and most funny. We did so much walking because the car was in dock, having something wrong with it. The next day, I went to shop in Kingston by myself. I bought some new skirts and a blouse with lifeboats and anchors on it.

I was sorry to hear from Daddy that his father was ill and fear for his passing away. I hope Aunty Mabel looks after him well.
Tons of love, Bunty xxx

Dearest Bunty,
I am sorry not to have written to you recently. We've moved to a new house in Swanside Road and were very busy decorating. We still haven't finished, but it is not far from done. Then we have the garden to organise, so never a dull moment. This is the first time we have moved into a newly built house. It is wonderfully light and spacious.
What a marvellous time you've had in London. We haven't been out for a long time. Perhaps we can go together when you come in your summer holidays.
I walked to Aunty Mabel's yesterday. Grandad Handley has bronchitis but is getting better, so don't worry about him.
Lots of love, Granny & Grandan XX

24th June
Dear Granny,
Thank you ever so, ever so, much for the exciting parcel you sent for my fifteenth. All the girls love to watch me unpack your parcels because you pack them in such a fascinating way. The gorgeous birthday cake was delicious. At night, I treated the dormitory to a feast. I've not heard from Daddy for my birthday.
We are still in quarantine for measles, and will be for another fortnight if no one else gets it. Consequently, we have not been to church today. Instead, we were on the sands all the morning. It was simply glorious! A boy that I like very much, from Cliftonville School, called Armstrong, was down on the beach with the other three prefects. You remember, I told you about him and my cousins tried to guess his name.
I have a horrible rash on both my arms from having strawberries last night, and being in the scorching sun this morning. Matron will put some camomile lotion on.
After term ends, I'm going straight down to Havant with my schoolfriend Joan for a fortnight. After that I'll come to see you in your new home. I can't wait!
Love, Bunty xx

1st July
Dear Bunty,
Your Daddy has been up here to see us. It was an unexpected visit, as he had to come on business. He stayed for the weekend as it was lovely weather. He took your cousins Roger, Audrey, Josie and Hazel for a spin up to Southport. They returned singing in the back of his open-top car. Aunty Mabel and Aunty Mary played golf with him.
I hope the camomile has done your rash well, and that it has now disappeared. Take care not to catch the measles, it's a horrible illness. I suppose you couldn't talk to the Armstrong lad, given the quarantine.

Last week, I went to Cooper's food store with a friend. We couldn't withstand the exquisite aroma of ground coffee and the look of the cakes! Let me know more about Armstrong.
Lots of love, Granny and Grandan xxxx

July
My Dearest Granny,
Last Saturday we went to Cliftonville Boys' sports day and had a marvellous time. I saw Armstrong, of course. He won the Victor Ludorum Cup, which is given to the boy who has gained the most points during the day. I was ever so pleased. He had six other prizes as well. We nearly didn't go because of the awful rain. Then, at the last moment, Miss Treestone told us to get ready. I was ever so bucked, and she knew everything about me liking Armstrong. She teased me, asking me if I knew the way! I led the crock there, racing as quickly as I could. We had to wait at the entrance for her to catch up. She said, "This is not a marathon race, Lizzie."
A gentleman gave us a lecture about the Isle of Dogs Society, which is in south-east London. The Isle of Dogs is a place where 20,000 people live in a swamp, and the society is building better houses for them.
Daddy has a bargain with me that if I write twelve letters, each of twelve pages and each page twenty lines, he will buy me a new small camera. I'm really going to do my best.
Tons of love and kisses to Grandan, Black Cat and self,
Bunty xxx

CHAPTER FIFTY-THREE
Coronation

1937

January
My Dearest Granny,
Back in London again and I wore my new hat four times. It has not been frosty down here. I hope you do not have any bursting pipes this winter. It's well worthwhile covering them all. Try to go outside for fresh air regularly and not stay in too much.
Last night, they promoted me to the position of sub-prefect, so I'll have several duties and a few privileges. I've moved to another dormitory, on a higher landing, and I like it there much better. I wish I had a bottle of wine to celebrate.
Daddy bought me a nice navy dress and a smart pair of handmade Austrian gloves. Can you possibly get stuff called 'honeycomb' for me? It is a sugary sort of sweet, yellow in colour. I would be delighted to have some. Thank Grandan for obtaining the book, and for not getting an old one. It was very thoughtful of him. Remind him to buy me those film books.
I have just had a dinner of cold pork, crackling, roast potatoes and pickles. We had trifle for our seconds. This evening we are having a lecture on the coming coronation.
Yesterday, the prefects and I went to serve an American tea at a house where guests had to buy something in aid of the Barnardo's Homes. It was good fun, and we had tons to eat. They simply stuffed their gorgeous little home-made cakes into us.
No half-term because this term is so short, but we are having a social evening. We are doing a comedy called 'House Full' and I am the British Matron.

I have new music of Ten Popular Songs. Maybe I will play them for you during the next holidays.

Thanks for the splendid parcel. I ate the jam roll at first sight, sharing among the rest of the dorm. The marzipan cake is lovely, and the Bakewell tart. I'm just about to finish the figs.

On Saturday we are going to Cliftonville Boys' prize-giving. Isn't it marvellous? I'll see Armstrong there. It will be rather fun.

Looking forward to seeing you, your loving Bunty xxx

March

Dearest Granny,

Cliftonville boys passed outside our school, all in 'crock'. I was elsewhere, but I heard girls shrieking for me. I rushed to my dorm and was greeted with yells. They were all by the window, gazing out. It then struck me what was the matter, and I dashed over, but I quickly receded when I looked down into a host of upturned, laughing faces. I saw Armstrong, he was walking with the master, and was the only one who didn't look up.

Last night, the girls in number eleven dorm had a midnight feast. They tucked in to sausages, half a chicken each, liver and bacon, potato salad, Russian salad, sandwiches, rolls and butter, fruit salad and cream, and cider. We want to get up a really splendid feast in our dorm next term.

On Friday, deportment badges, girdles and badges for the hockey team were distributed. I already have a deportment badge but received my hockey girdle and colours for the First Eleven team.

I am sorry to say that Daddy has decided not to come for Easter but I expect to arrive, most probably by train, next Tuesday or earliest excursion fare.

My trunk is all packed now, but those shoes have not been delivered. Please go to the shop or send Grandan. They have our money. You will remember the girl in the shop who served us. We must get the shoes or the money back. It is disgraceful. The Cable Shoe Shop on London Road, don't forget please!

Love and affection, Bunty xx

London

April

Dear Granny,

I'm writing from Daddy's office. Sorry I didn't write earlier.

Thank you again for everything. I know you always do your best for me, and I appreciate that very much.

Excuse the pencil, but this paper is rather thin for ink.

I had a postcard from Miss Bennet saying that I'd passed my Music Rudiments exam with ninety-five marks out of ninety-nine.

Tuesday night, we saw Shakespeare's 'Henry V' at the Old Vic Theatre. Last night, we went to the New Theatre for 'The Taming of the Shrew'. It was topping, better than Henry V. We both enjoyed it immensely.

I'm very busy. I have been getting up early and have been having extra lessons after supper. Time does fly, and I'm ever so eager to pass Senior School Certificate. The drawing exams are on Tuesday. We have to do designs, instead of anything we like. Those were the sort of things my mother used to do a lot, aren't they? I wish some of her gift would come to me for the exam.

Cheerio, love and kisses, as always, Bunty xxxxxx

At school, the girls looked forward to the coronation of George VI and Elizabeth on May 12th. They put up decorations, including three shields Bunty's father had sent. Margate was full of flags and glitter.

Bunty went to stay with Daddy for the occasion. They got up at four in the morning to watch the rehearsal outside Westminster Abbey. After some pushing and scrambling, they secured seats in the stand, free-of-charge as it was a practice parade. Despite the rain, they had a good view of each contingent that passed by.

On the day itself, they rose at three o'clock and went to Palm Square. Bunty thought it was eerie with thousands of people about in the darkness — soldiers, boy scouts, policemen, and first aid staff. As the public arrived, men were selling periscopes and chocolate.

Using her father's cases, Bunty erected a platform for herself, making her as tall as a six-foot-four man next to her. He lifted her up several times during the cortege. It was hours before anything passed, and then it all happened quickly.

Crowds filled stands, leaned out of windows, stood on roofs and occupied the pavements. The Eton boys were opposite them. All around, soldiers and naval cadets guarded the masses. The procession was a wonderful sight of various flags — the Australians, the Canadian Mounties, the Lancers, the Scots, and the Indians with their different coloured turbans. Bunty delighted at seeing Princess Marina, Duchess of Gloucester, Earl of Athlone, Princess Royal, the Lascelles Boys, Queen Mary, and the King and Queen. It was a magnificent show, and lasted till 2.30 p.m.

July
Dear Granny,
I need strength because my period is due on Wednesday, right in the midst of the exams. It is a nuisance. My first subjects, from 9 a.m. till 6 p.m., are English Composition, Geography, and Flat Drawing. The exams are not at school but in a hall in Margate, together with the boys. I hope Armstrong is there. It would inspire me if he were.
Can you send me a tin of crab and enclose three hard-boiled eggs, too? It is for our dormitory feast at the end of term. We've got everything except for the things we must get via a day-girl at the last minute because they cannot keep — lettuces, tomatoes, butter and rolls.
Daddy's business is not doing too well. He has fewer orders because of the situation in Germany. He says war noises keep coming out of Germany and the Austrian Nazis wish to join up. Shopkeepers no longer choose to buy his German products. Please don't spread the news, but Daddy has left his digs in Barnes and moved into the office on Rochester Row to save dough. He's also stopped eating meat to cut costs and says a vegetarian diet is healthier too.
Your loving Bunty, xxx

August
Dear Granny,
Hope you received my letter. I'm on holiday with my friend Joan. We have cycled to Goodwood Race Course through Chichester and back to Havant.
We've had a game of tennis and are going to have some miniature golf, tea, and visit Eastbourne. I can dive under the sea now and am trying the 'porpoise dive' and the 'rolling log'. I can show them to you if we visit the baths again and you sit up in the gallery, holding your breath.
Hopefully, I will return to Godwin for the next term, but I'm not sure. Depends on Daddy's 'dough' I expect.
It's hot and sticky, so I'm going for an ice cream from the dairy across the road.
Tons of love both, Bunty xxXxx

September
My dear Granny,
I'm ever so busy, working hard for my senior exams, taking extra French with Monsieur Briët, and French conversation lessons from Miss Bennett. They have promoted me to prefect and now I sleep in the prefects' dorm. We have our own sitting-room, which we go to when we want peace. It's cosy, but I wish we had some cushions. I enjoy being a prefect and the company of the other prefects; we have lots of fun and laughs. Last night, I treated them to a cream éclair each and a bottle of cider.
I only have two free nights a week, and then I have to study because we are having so many extra lessons now. They asked me to take the first and second forms, both for an hour and a half each week. I'm on duty for breaks, before dinner, and in the corridors after dinner to prevent girls from talking. I practise piano an hour a day.
The other night two boys, a Greek and an Englishman, climbed up scaffolding outside the school and reached our bedroom windows. They spoke to some of the girls. We had to intervene, asking the girls to stand back from the window. We tried to catch the lads, but they quickly scurried off. The next night Miss Bennett had the police round, but they did not spot the boys.
Last Saturday we had a marvellous hockey match against Queen's School and we won 8-1. I played wing and scored one goal, but had a nasty bash on my finger, too.
Love to both with lots of kisses, xxx Bunty xxx

October
Dear Granny,
I did a lot in London. I bought the sweetest dress of green taffeta covered with pink net. There are big roses round the skirt and huge puffed sleeves with a rose in the same style. There is no low neck, just a slight 'v' in the front. All round the neck there is a sort of ruffle affair. It is ever so sweet. It sticks out very well, and I had little flairs in it.
Next Friday we have a lecture where I will see Armstrong. I haven't seen him yet this term except every Sunday when the boys pass our window and wave. They stop and pretend to do up their shoelaces but they are really taking time to look at us and make signs! It is fun!

No more news, but one more thank you for your letter. I would love some
tomatoes and am pleased to hear the garden is coming on well.
Cheerio, much love and kisses to both of you, Bunty xxxXxxx

November
Dear Granny,
Daddy took me to the cenotaph at Whitehall in London for the two-
minute silence on Armistice Day. Everything was noise and bustle, people
trying to find spaces and pushing themselves to the front. Trumpets blew
and Big Ben struck eleven. Immediately, all was in perfect silence, except
for a barking dog and a crying child. Hymns were sung and men who had
served in the Great War marched past, arrayed in their medals.
This afternoon we go to the distribution of Royal Academy of Music
certificates. I have two to get, for Higher Music Exam and for Rudiments
of Theory.
On 6th December, I'm going to be confirmed.
I'm sorry to say I will not be coming to Liverpool for Christmas. I want
to spend some time with Daddy in London and a girl in the flat above has
asked me to spend Christmas with her and attend her New Year's Eve
party. So I will not see you till January 2nd. Daddy has just won a nice
sum with Littlewood's Pools, so that's a useful Christmas box.
Love to you both, Bunty xxx

CHAPTER FIFTY-FOUR
Exams

1938

February
Dear Granny,
All Daddy's hopeful orders have fallen through, isn't it awful? Some of his orders have dwindled down into miserable commissions. So he is low on 'dough'.
I've passed all my exams, except History and Botany. I intend to take the Civil Service exam. I talked it over with Daddy and he agreed.
When I was in London, Kenneth Tyce was disappointed that I didn't go to the pictures with him and his friends. He wanted me to promise that I'd go with them next time, but he added I would get out of it somehow. I can't shake him off. Please don't tell anyone because I don't want my affairs spread around Liverpool. I didn't tell anyone about such things, but Aunty Annie tried to make me confess I liked someone.
We have several people in bed with colds and high temperatures. Matron is laid up so the Junior Mistress has taken her place. I have taken her place in teaching 1st and 2nd forms. I bathed nine juniors last Friday night. It was fun. I am going in for the Thanet Music Festival, the solo playing for girls of 15 and 16. We're also entering the choir competition and I may have to conduct the singing.
I had a most mysterious parcel yesterday morning. It was a box of chocolates, and that was all, nothing to show who it was from. It had a Dulwich postmark. Most mysterious! Valentine's Day tomorrow.
I've just finished scoring for a ping pong tournament and have had a supper of bread, butter, cheese and Ovaltine. We didn't go to church today because we're in quarantine with a few cases of German Measles,

which I've already had. This evening we are having a lantern lecture on
'Weather and Science'.

It is half-term this weekend, so we have been going wild on paper-chases,
etc. I write with an urgent touch for 'dough' and stamps. One always
needs money at half-term. Our lecture night is on the 'British Empire' —
Grandan will be interested to hear that. It's a lantern lecture and I'll
work the slides. Tomorrow we go shopping and hope to go to Bobby's for
crumpets and cakes. This morning we were out for a long, breezy tramp
so we all feel very hungry. By Jove, one does get an appetite here.

Tons of love and kisses, Bunty xxxxx

March

My Dearest Granny,

The sun is simply glorious, warm enough to sit in the garden, and that
has been my occupation for the last few days. I was rushing down the
hockey field when I suddenly collapsed on my ankle and sprained it. It
hurt, but I continued to the end of the game, but then had to be helped
home by two girls. When nurse saw my ankle it had swollen terribly,
since then I can't go out, which is simply horrible.

We have a School Social at term end so we are busy rehearsing a singing
act, with the latest jazz songs in a cabaret scene. We are also doing a
play which is terrible because I have the most words to learn. I am also
performing a piano duet with a friend. It is the first one we have played
together and it is a jolly hard one. It's great fun duetting. I'm also in the
percussion band, not performing but I have to teach it to the juniors.

I feel I am coming back next term, and there is one thing which I must
wangle from Daddy somehow — a new tennis racket. I'll be in the tennis
six and need a really good one. I hope Daddy has just had a big order
when I ask him to promise me that.

Don't forget to have the front room finished when next I come, with the
piano along the wall between fire-place and window.

Love and kisses, Bunty xxx

May

Dear Granny,

*Many thanks for your parcel with the nicely cleaned and packed clothes.
I would like you to send on my green dress when you have dyed it,
because Daddy could only afford me one new one. Can you possibly
make me some of your famous shampoo because one needs something to
keep one's hair fresh in the summer?
I have inquired about the birthday cakes and Bowketts can make a
sponge and cream, 60 slices, for 10 shillings. I should like Snowwhite
and the Seven Dwarfs decorated on it.
The weather has been dull and wet so I didn't play with my new racket
until yesterday when we had a good time on the hard courts. Olga and I
play together. We are the only two in the six who really play net, so we
may be separated to build up the other pairs — I hope not.
My affectionate love, Bunty xxxxx*

*September
Dear Granny,
By the way, I'm awfully bucked that I have passed my Intermediate Music
Exam. I wore that green frock that you sent me, and it was such a boiling-
hot day, that it has faded utterly, so I can't wear it again. London is filled
with crowds demonstrating and war hangs in the air. The French Prime
Minister is here now. People are continually going in the Abbey to pray
for peace. War will be tragic for Daddy's business. He doubts I can go
back to school because of his lack of dough.
Love and kisses, Bunty xxx*

*October
Dear Granny,
Everyone at school is very happy that the war scare has passed over. If
there had been war, we would have been evacuated to Norton Manor,
Taunton, Somerset, with acres of grounds. All the schools here were
packed ready. It was very exciting and we owe a lot to Mr Chamberlain
for steering us into peaceful waters. Daddy was feeling alarmed. He was
in the act of packing up his business and raking in from all his debtors to
know where he stood, but now he is starting afresh again. We all tried on
gas masks yesterday. They smell of rubber, just as if you were going
under gas in the dentists.*

*I bought Miss Lawrence a box of chocs. It is fine liking someone at
school, because it fills up your everyday routine, puts some excitement
into it, and gives you added happiness, and misery in turn.*

*Two of my friends here have just been praising up my mother from the
tiny photo I have, of when she was about eighteen. I love you Granny for
being a mother for me, but I do miss my real mother when I see other
girls with their families.*

Love and kisses, Bunty xxx

November

Dear Granny,

*I did not write earlier because I had a fit of the dumps. I need something
nice to happen to buck me up. I don't want to burden you with my
troubles, but Daddy let me take the First Aid course, which costs 10
shillings. I've had three lessons, books and bandages, and now Miss
Freestone is asking for the fee. Daddy has not got the money and says she
will have to wait for it. His business is quiet at the moment. I haven't
enough from my pocket-money either.*

*I feel a bit better since Joan has brought me an enormous piece of her
mother's home-made chocolate cake. I was hungry because I only had
Bovril and pudding for dinner. I had my tooth out with cocaine and didn't
feel a thing. I only have 24 teeth left now. I'm expecting to have 4 more
fillings at Xmas. Last Wednesday, we played hockey against St Hilary's
and won 7-2. I gained the honour of shooting five of the seven goals.*

Love and kisses, Bunty xxx

December

Dear Granny,

*I'm full of lots of conflicting and emotional thoughts at the time. I have
failed my Civil Service Exam, but I'm glad. I didn't want to pass it really
and honestly. Miss Bennet has asked me if I would stay at school as I'm
doing well. Daddy gave me the option of staying on or having a short
period of nursing. I'd much rather stay on.*

*I've met some people who are very good-class, well-educated, kind and
well off. They have given me a different outlook on life and I feel much
happier. A desire has come over me to take Higher School Certificate in
art and literature. I realise I can only live a life of music and literature if*

I have the time and money to be able to indulge in the arts and to mix with like-minded people.
Love and kisses, Bunty xxx

December
Dear Granny,
I went to see Daddy last weekend. He said business is not going well. The order book is as good as empty. Now the Huns are threatening to make war, no one wants to buy products from Germany, or Austria. They only want things made in England. Daddy has told me there's no more dough for school. I was so happy and looking forward to taking the Higher School Certificate. But after the hols he says I need to go to work, to earn my own keep. I'm so disappointed. I was hoping to stay on at Godwin's. I'll have to say goodbye to my friends halfway through the school year! I've no idea what work I can do. I'll see you soon for Christmas. Daddy won't be coming.

Love and kisses, Bunty xxx

December
My Dearest Bunty,
I'm so sorry to hear that you cannot stay on at school. Daddy's situation must be terrible because he has done everything to give you a decent education. Try to see the bright side of going to work. You'll meet other people, be more independent, and perhaps see other people who like art and music. Will you stay in London? If you do, you'll be in the right place for art and music. We'd like to see you in Liverpool, of course, and can help you find work here. Let's talk when you are here for Christmas.
Love and affection, Granny xx

CHAPTER FIFTY-FIVE
The Blitz

1939

After New Year's Day, Bunty returned to London with no idea what she was going to do. She felt strange not travelling on to Margate to see her friends at school, but after talking to Granny, she saw the advantages of being in the city of art and music. It would suit her better than Liverpool.

"Bunty, I spoke to my bank manager last week," Daddy said. "He told me I can't borrow more money, so we'll have to manage. I mentioned you're looking for a job and he knows of a vacancy at the bank and will put in a good word for you."

"What sort of work will they expect me to do?"

"I don't know. You'll have to wait and see."

Barclay's Bank invited Bunty for an interview. The office impressed her, bustling with staff of all ages, and plenty of her own age. They offered her the position of book clerk, starting in February, for a six-month trial period. She went back to Rochester Row with a skip in her step, swinging her arms.

Her father was at his desk, staring at the window, hardly noticing her presence.

"Daddy, they've given me the job," she said, bouncing towards him and kissing him on the cheek. "I'm so excited about the prospect of a salary and meeting people."

"That's splendid news."

"Yes, I can now look for my own digs and be out of your way."

"There's no need; you may stay here!"

"I prefer my own place. Somewhere nearby so that we can see each other as often as we like."

Just around the corner from her father's office, Bunty found a room in a hostel on Vincent Square, Westminster. She was relieved to have her own space, but to also remain close to Daddy. It was thirty minutes by public transport to the bank's offices in Tottenham Court Road. When she had time, on decent days, she walked to work through St James's Park or passed Buckingham Palace and crossed Green Park.

Bunty surprised Daddy by treating him to dinner with her first salary. He was cutting his grocery costs by leaving out meat, so she took him to a modern vegetarian restaurant.

"Don't you miss meat?" she asked, while they looked at the menu.

"Not at all. I've been reading about vegetarianism. Meat-eating has brought about wars. Even Socrates said that there was insufficient land to grow crops and raise cattle at the same time. Communities had to expand their territories, cutting a slice off their neighbour's land, resulting in war."

"Is Germany threatening us because they need more farmland for food?" Bunty queried.

"Not directly. It's about controlling foodstuffs that come from overseas, from the colonies. Growing populations are no longer self-supporting and must import food," he explained. "In the old days, people grew all their own food, but industrialisation has made us dependent on others."

"Is it healthier not eating meat?"

"It's just as healthy, but it's more than that. It's a way of life. We must cease being beasts of prey to prevent war and losing nature. We should stop saying that animals have no feelings, and stop calling them 'livestock'. They're part of nature, like we are."

"I don't understand the war aspect of what you're saying," Bunty said.

"Going from slaughtering animals to killing humans is only a small step. The better we look after animals and nature, the better we'll treat others."

"I love nature, but I'd find it difficult to stop eating meat. I'm so used to it, and enjoy it."

"I feel fine without meat."

"I'm glad," Bunty said, wanting to move to another subject. "By the way, I joined the bank's Operatic Society and have been to their rehearsal. I hope to play the music but need to practise more. I only have half an hour before breakfast every morning and often have to work on Saturdays. Being on probation, I daren't refuse Saturdays."

"I knew you'd find a means to keep engaged in music; you loved that at school." His brow wrinkled. "I'm still worried about war. We've been able to maintain peace with Germany so far, but they've invaded Czechoslovakia, and we've said we'll support Poland if they invade there. I wouldn't be surprised if we get involved."

"Let's hope for the best. I suppose you won't be called up for service, luckily."

"No, but I'll join the Home Guard because I feel I have to help in some way."

"Shall we go? I've got tickets for Magyar Melody. It's a Hungarian musical in His Majesty's Theatre."

On Monday 4th September, Bunty picked up the Daily Herald and read the headlines, "WAR DECLARED BY BRITAIN AND FRANCE. Unthinkable, we should refuse the challenge. War Cabinet of nine. Churchill now First Lord of Admiralty." Just a few days later, Hitler started bombing London, particularly the docks in East London. The danger of bombs, and the consequences it would have for Daddy's business, appalled Bunty.

1940

The bombing continued and spread all over London, mostly targeted at military installations and factories, but many landed in residential areas. It always took place during the dark. The East End was so badly bombed that cockneys arrived in the streets of Westminster looking for shelter, their clothes in tatters, carrying babies, and dragging children with matted hair and filthy faces.

When Bunty heard the air-raid siren wail, she grabbed her gas mask, put it on, and hurried to Daddy's place, dodging people scurrying about. His building, with a cellar and door directly to the street, seemed safer than the hostel with its six storeys. If bombers were near, she saw them flying above in dark formation. Bombs whistled as they came down, ending with a sharp descending note and a bang, shaking everything. Streets looked strange because shop owners had taped the windows over to stop the glass from shattering.

"These bombs remind me of the shelling in the Great War," Daddy said, his hands jammed into his armpits. "The noise is different, but no less unnerving. We were out in open fields then. Being in the city is worse - all these buildings that can catch fire and collapse around us."

Bunty moved closer to her father as she heard a bomb whistle and explode not far away. "It's terribly frightening."

"Last night, I was on guard on the roof of Hobart House. Looking towards the East End, I saw a wall of flame in the sky. The scale was nothing like I'd seen in the trenches of Belgium."

As best they could, they continued with their daily lives, often tired after sleepless nights. For her twentieth birthday, Bunty walked in the Chilterns, with her friend, Kate. They enjoyed being out of the city in the fresh air and seeing Milton's Cottage in Chalfont St Giles. After arriving back in London, Bunty heard about an air battle above Kent. The Royal Air Force had their Spitfires fending off the Luftwaffe. She was glad she wasn't in Margate.

1941

On April 17th, whilst she was staying at Daddy's place, Bunty was woken in the middle of the night by Hitler banging on the window. Glass shattered across her bed and from somewhere in the distance came a muffled roar. Her first inclination was to turn on the light, but she remembered that lights weren't permitted. Carefully, she got out of bed, peering in the dark to try and avoid stepping on shards of glass. She found her father, and together they made their way to the cellar, hoping for safety in that room of cold and damp.

Before long, there was an enormous explosion and the building above them shuddered - dust trickling down through widening cracks. It was gritty in their mouths, and in their eyes. Daddy judged it unsafe to stay in the cellar, so they made their way up the steps, climbing over rubble, squinting through the clouds of dust, the pungent smell of smoke in their nostrils.

Out on the street, they looked back at the building — its shattered windows and the reeking gap in the upper floors. It was on fire and they daren't venture in to rescue any belongings.

Further up, people crawled out of cellar-holes and climbed over piles of rubble. Daddy went to help an elderly man. "Are there any others in there?" Daddy asked.

"Yes, the landlord, his wife, and daughter. Don't know how I got out," the chap replied. "Will you do me a favour, go down to get my coat?"

Daddy looked down the cellar-hole, through the darkness and smoke-filled air. It was a mass of rubble. Another man came out saying, "It's no use. One of them has broken his back, and he's blocking the way." Rescue men arrived and went inside. A guard appeared with a limp girl in his arms. He shouted "Door!" and someone found a detached door to lay her on, because there were no stretchers.

Bunty stared at the smashed windows in shop fronts further down Rochester Row. Their owners were running about to save their goods. Firemen arrived, but their water jets appeared useless against the roaring blaze. The front wall of Daddy's building collapsed, falling backwards into the flames. A German bomber crossed overhead, trying to add to the devastation. Bunty and Daddy flattened themselves against a safe-looking wall. Incendiary bombs and parachute mines fell around them, causing more blasts and fires. The blocked roads made it difficult for fire-engines and rescue teams.

By early morning, the flames were doused, but smoke still rose from the bomb crater. Bunty and her father were lucky to have survived unscathed. The noise abated, and she noticed the city had an uncanny quietness; she could hear birds singing.

Her father had lost all his belongings, including his business paper-work and everything Bunty had stored there. At least she had the hostel to go back to, but her father now needed, like so many Londoners, to find temporary digs.

CHAPTER FIFTY-SIX
Cheltenham

1941

The management of Barclay's Bank evacuated its employees from London because the Blitz was too dangerous and work had become almost impossible. They moved Bunty to the Cheltenham office. Her father realised it was the end of his own business, so he applied for employment in the Civil Service. Fortunately, they could offer him a position in Cheltenham.

November
Dear Granny,
We've found lodgings in Cheltenham. I'm in Westal Green, with a
landlady called Mrs Beckingsale. Daddy is just an eight-minute walk
away at Park Place. He went straight to the local War Office to report for
his Home Guard duty. They assigned him to patrol the fields at night. He
said it was terrible in the dark, rain and mud. Like in the trenches of
Ypres. Fortunately, there's no shelling here.
I'm sorry to say I won't be coming for Xmas because they asked me to
work on Boxing Day. I don't want to decline because jobs at the bank are
not guaranteed. In a notice, we've been told they're negotiating with the
Government to keep women under thirty in employment. Until that's
settled, it's unclear how long I can continue in my job.
It's lonely here. Besides Daddy, there's no one I know. The war has made
it difficult to start social contact with strangers and many sports have
stopped for winter. Cheltenham is not the same as London for music, so
on that score I'm also losing out. My letters to you are an important
outlet for my thoughts.
Love, Bunty xXXx

December
Dear Granny,
I'm all on my own here tonight. It's horrible. What a vast difference it must be for those who have a proper family with brothers and sisters, and friends. When you're alone, you can't help thinking a lot about yourself, and picking yourself to pieces, criticising yourself, and imagining things. Hoping and longing for wonderful events to happen.
I confess that every time I'm by myself I long to meet my fate in the shape of a really nice young man, who would empathise with me, and me with him, someone jolly yet understanding, clever but modest, well-dressed and smart but not vain. Someone to love and be loved by, to help and talk to. Wouldn't it be heavenly? But it seems as if I shall never meet him. I'm still young, but the trouble is there's no opportunity for me to chance upon the sort of people I like. When I speak to a truly pleasant man, I feel he is too far above me and would not look at me. I'm out of my sphere somehow. My ideals, hopes and ambitions seem to be too high for my standard of living.
Why do I worry you with all this? You too feel so lonely and sad, I know. But it's nice to write to each other about it because we only have each other to cry out to. I must still hope on, I know, and not be depressed and discouraged. I've been very fortunate in many ways, especially in having such a wonderful Granny who understands me so well.
Love and kisses, Bunty xxx
PS: Perhaps you would give me some tips one day on how to be attractive and get on successfully with young men. Please don't show this to anyone else because I'm shy about asking.
PPS: Daddy finds it difficult to adapt to an office job after having his own business. The bureaucracy makes him feel a tiny cog in a gigantic machine. He says he feels he's doing useless work, but at least he has a steady income. I want to cheer him up for his fiftieth birthday. Can you make one of your fabulous cakes?
Love and affection, Bunty XX

On 17th December, Bunty went to her father's room to prepare for his fiftieth birthday before he arrived home. She did her best to make it a memorable celebration and raise his spirits. The same evening, he showed her the letter he wrote to thank Granny.

My Dear Marsie and Pa,

Very many thanks for your kind present and happy thoughts. You and Bunty provided me with some really fine cheer and made my birthday one that I shall not forget as long as I live. It was one I never really thought possible. Bunty, with the aid of your parcel, provided such a delightful tea, gold and silver doilies, a lovely birthday cake with marzipan on top, silver balls and coloured jellies, and five sweet little candles. Then there was your marzipan sandwich, chocolate biscuits, currant cakes, nut-chocolate clusters, chocolate coconut pieces, date fingers and more. When I reached my room, I found her toasting buns and the kettle just about to boil. Your mantle of the hostess has surely fallen on her, for she delights in putting out a good spread and knows how to do it. The dear, dear girl made me a very happy man, chiefly in having such a loving and blessed daughter.

It's a sad thought to think one is fifty years old. But time cannot be stayed, and after all, I have gone much farther than in the last war I ever expected to go.

We would both give worlds to be with you all this Xmas, but it cannot be done. We have booked dinner at the Queen's Club at three shillings each. They have put up Christmas decorations and it ought to be quite a jolly affair, but not so good for us as being with you in Liverpool.

I'll be fire-watching tomorrow night. There's little likelihood of my being requested for a Home Guard commission. Unfortunately, there is more chance of Bunty being called up. I hope she will be able to stay in the bank.

No doubt you will spend Xmas at Mabel's, with my father and other sisters' families. Be happy together, making most of this short life that now only remains for most of us. We will be with you in spirit.

In closing, please accept our small present with great wishes and hopes for a peaceful time and a New Year that has good things in store and much hope to look forward to.

Keep smiling, love and many thanks,

Your loving Jack xxx

PS. I have enclosed a poem I've written.

The Xmas Truce

Our best love to you all,
Warm greetings and good cheer,
We lavish wishes kind on you,
To all we may this year.

This war defeats desire,
So must we tell you true
In wealth and time we can't afford
A gift for each of you.

The shop displays don't help
And coupons - are they spare?
Let's wait till 1942
And see then how we fare!

We'll hail our victory,
Perhaps let twelve months by,
Then we may yoke reunion gay,
With Peace and Yuletide high.

We wish to call a truce,
And make it really clear,
We think it wise, we all deny
Exchanging gifts this year.

In spirit we'll be one,
Our Trust will be in God.
He'll bring a Free and Peaceful Yule
He'll break the tyrant's rod.

Say you agree with us!
That Love alone will guide
Our thoughts to Hearts that yearn to be
With us this Christmastide.

CHAPTER FIFTY-SEVEN
Flower

1943

July, on Barclays Bank paper
My Dears Granny and Grandan,
Just back from my fortnight with you and I'm thinking back to how you
spoiled me on my twenty-second birthday. It's been a lovely break.
Now we are straight into our half-yearly balance week. We've been
working till 10 p.m. for several nights. It has taken the 'kick' out of me
and I need another two weeks with my Granny, but I'll have to wait
twelve months, except for a brief break for Xmas.
Thank you again and again for a thoroughly enjoyable time. All my life,
in days to come, when you are gone on, I shall look back and remember
the happy times I have spent with you, when you have spoiled me so
beautifully, and been my real Fairy Grandmother. It is lovely to have a
little spoiling when one's ordinary day is lonely, and, apart from loved
ones, in places strange where one has to fight one's own way and take
with thankful heart whatever is offered.
It was a pity that Daddy worked up a temper. It's funny how he always
gets like that with other relatives about. He doesn't realise that a little
conversation and outing with you, and a good few hours on your piano,
give me much more pleasure than racing about on a bicycle in old
clothes, fearful of missing half an hour of sunlight. We women prefer to
dress up a bit and strut around the town and chat, don't we?
Lots of love, Bunty xxxx

1944

Gladys was still lonely. Her father had less time for her, and was away most weekends with Miss Flower, a spinster aged forty-one, eleven years younger than himself. He'd met her at a First Aid training course, where they both instructed citizens in case Cheltenham was bombed. She'd been a children's nurse and came from Sheffield, where her father was a furnace bricklayer at a power station.

Gladys had set her sights on a higher class of woman for her father — someone who appreciated the arts, especially music and literature. She felt she had nothing in common with Miss Flower and found her blunt in her straightforwardness and honesty.

Her father wanted to settle down, find a partner and a place of his own. Gladys could understand that; he'd never really had his own home. But now she had to compete with Flower for his attention. Seeing him less frequently, she had to revert to writing him letters.

Dear Daddy,
I thoroughly enjoyed last weekend and now feel so much flatter and lonelier by comparison. I don't want to do anything but sit in the sun and read about ballet.
In your letter to me, you ask whether Flower and I had any rupture that weekend. No, I think we both felt awkward and were consequently unnatural and aloof in behaviour. Of course, it is hardly fair to ask me to give my opinion of Flower because I've seen so little of her and you yourself have told me next to nothing about her. I certainly have nothing against her but natural jealousy and prejudice, which I shall always do my best to conquer because I know it isn't right.
If you feel she would make you an agreeable companion for the rest of your days, and help you build a belated home, I shall be glad for your sake that you are settled with a kindred spirit. If I should marry, our ways may lie apart as they have so consistently up to now.
As long as she lives, Granny will be my first home really, as it is there, and only there, that I find my mother. So you mustn't be too harsh when I'm there on holiday because it is a convenient haven in these war days.
Perhaps after the war I shall be able to strike out and travel to unexplored regions and meet new people, young people, and have jolly times as I wish to.
When I'm with Granny, we like to have our quiet chats, as for each of us there is no other woman so understanding. I receive a mental uplift from

her naïve confidence and pride in me. The spiritual help of being with those who enjoy one's presence is very great. It warms my heart to find Grandan making his jokes and telling all the old tales because he is glad I'm there. I'm always overjoyed to have the opportunity to use their piano.

So if you bring Flower, don't expect me to be out and about all the time with you, as Granny and I will want to be on our own occasions. We may have many times together after they have passed on or when away from Liverpool.

So Bye Bye, tons of love and kisses, Your 'ever' loving daughter, Gladys xxxXxxx

Dear Daddy,
Remember that I repaid both fares back to you to compensate for you paying in Prestbury's? I paid you in the cafe at the time. That was 3 shillings and at the hostel 5 shillings, including the booking fee you made of 1 shilling. I might have mumbled something to Flower about you paying the shilling in advance, but I don't know. She watches the cash, doesn't she? I don't want to be unpleasant but I found that controversy over the expenses quite uncalled for.

Flower seems to brighten up just before I am leaving. Otherwise, she strikes me as being too quiet and uninterested for anyone possibly contemplating a partnership. I find her inconsistent and she is not a type that I would take seriously or be particularly interested in. I would only give her high marks as an easy companion to a restless and unusual nature. And high marks for neatness and pleasing form and colour, in a world of drabs and eccentrics with loose and slovenly ways.

Tons of love & kisses, your ever loving daughter, Glad xxxXxxx

Dear Granny,
Daddy seems exhausted lately, and he goes to bed so late. He really does grow more and more like Grandad Handley every day. At times, he looks older than his age. He's so thin, round-shouldered and pale now, and doesn't seem to have the heart for anything. His mind is always wandering. He can't remember little things very well, and is very nervy and jumpy, and irritable sometimes. He doesn't bother about manners or dignity, and yet he is quite pleasant suddenly again.

We do not have any serious differences now. I really do try to be more patient and understanding. I give way to anything and attempt never to argue as I used to at one time. I try to be cheerful and jolly with him, but it is difficult when he is constantly falling asleep. If only he had a pleasant home to be properly cared-for and helped.

Oh! Well, as you say, better days are ahead as long as we can live to see the end of this beastly, horrible war and that blackguard - Hitler! We must have faith in God, I know.

Did I tell you I had a 4/- a week rise? I earn £2/5/- a week now, so I'm still below the income tax, thank goodness.

Your own loving Bunty xxxxxxx

Gladys was worried about finding a man to suit her, so she went to see her Aunty Mabel the next time she was in Liverpool. She had heard that besides reading tea-leaves, Mabel had taken to studying the stars and making horoscopes. She also did numerology — telling people's characters by transforming their names into numbers, which signified types of personality.

She asked her aunt to tell her future and whether she would marry. Without replying, Mabel put the kettle on, took a teacup out of the side-cupboard and dropped some black tea in the cup. She poured on boiling water and told Gladys to wait for it to cool down.

When Gladys drank the tea, Mabel asked her to leave a little in the cup, "Now, swirl the cup round three times in one direction and then three times in the other direction."

Gladys did as instructed.

"Cover the cup with the saucer and turn it upside-down… That's right. Now leave it for a minute," Mabel said. "The tea-leaves need time to find their right place."

"It's so exciting, I can't wait," Gladys said.

"Now rotate it three times while asking your question. Turn it upright and take off the saucer."

"Like this?"

Mabel nodded.

Gladys articulated carefully, "I wish to know when I will meet the man of my life."

"That's right, put it down so that the handle points to the south, towards my front window... Remove the saucer."

Gladys peered into the cup. "The tea-leaves are now dispersed on the bottom and sides of the cup."

Mabel picked up the cup. "Those near the rim tell us about the present, those on the sides the near future, and those at the bottom the far future. You see, most of the tea-leaves are on the sides, so that means you'll meet your love soon."

Gladys' lips parted. "That would be wonderful. When will that be?"

"We can't know for certain, but probably this year, perhaps in the coming months. Now let's take a closer look. Can you see a pattern on the sides?"

"They're in a wavy pattern, reminding me of water."

"That's what I see too. Water symbolises emotions, the waves being the ups and downs in life. It means your life needs to be more stable before looking for love. You need to explore your inner self, and that discovery will invite new romance."

"What does that mean?"

"I can't say ... Think about how you come across to other people, and whether you need to be more inviting. Think about why you come across the way you do."

"How do you think I come across, Aunty?"

"Perhaps you need to be less judgmental and accept people as they are."

"That's difficult for me. I easily find fault in others."

"Try to see the good side and focus on what you like about them. When you've found the man you love, come back again and we'll look at his personality."

It surprised and upset Gladys when she had a letter from her father saying he was engaged to Beryl Flower, and going to Stratford-upon-Avon for a brief holiday. She was disappointed that he'd not spoken about his plans, not involved her, just announced it.

April
Dear Daddy,
I am thinking of you now at Stratford. The weather is perfect, so you should have a good time. Mr and Mrs B send their congrats and best wishes. I can't help telling everyone. It is such remarkable news after all these years, and I am filled with joyful anticipation of the happiness and contentment that awaits you. If anyone deserves it, none more than you. So many of your years were given to frightful frustration and loneliness, and you have done your duty throughout as a most loving and devoted father. It is time you had someone to fully understand and look after you. I am sure Flower will, and maybe she will bind us together all the more.

I am sorry I have criticised before, but I've been honest and have been at a disadvantage as I hardly know her, and have been kept in the dark. I have noted several good qualities and alone the fact that you are so confident of complete understanding means everything. Why has your engagement been so sudden?

Last week, I was on a ramble and met a nice young man. I hope to seen him again soon.

Love, Gladys xx

5th June

Daddy,

I am sorry to hear that Flower pushed the engagement, and that you had a difference. I am rather disappointed in her with one thing and another, but perhaps she is more attentive and thoughtful when you are on your own. I hope she is not doing all the taking, because you have taken on a big responsibility. I hope you won't be led on into marriage unless you are really happy and certain about it all. But you must know best, only don't forget that after all your years of being on your own, you are sure to need someone who will readily and easily acquiesce to your ideas after you're married. I sound like a grandmother, so forgive me for saying all this, but I do want your marriage to be a success.

Why is Flower so indifferent and uninterested, and quiet in manner? Is she only that way when I am about? She didn't once mention your engagement or talk about anything with me. I meant to ask you why you made up your mind so suddenly, too.

Love, Gladys xx

June

My Dearest Gladys,

Thank you for expressing your concern, but I have no need for your advice. Flower and I are happy together, and both of us are aware that we have been on our own for many years and have our set ways. I hope you can understand and accept Flower. She has her ways. She is a down-to-earth person and can be very straightforward, but she is caring and means the best.

I worry about you. I know you are lonely, and I can only wish that you find someone soon.

Your loving father, XXX

13th June

Dear Daddy,

I did not mean to give advice, but anyway, I did want to say something to express my thoughts and concern. I must add that it is not only the apparently strong, dominant types that can be unpleasant. The small, seemingly weak, can be very awkward and cunning, I know. Anyway, as long as you like Flower enough to persevere despite all the disadvantages you speak of, then it should be alright.

Don't worry yourself about my thoughts, because I can soon adjust myself to new ideas. It would have been so much better if you had told me about Flower from the beginning (you rather underestimated my understanding), and I should have followed it up with great interest and it wouldn't have been such a shock as it was at first. It would have helped you to talk it out too.

So now, I will practise what I'm preaching and tell you about Harold Pantlin. He's the young man I met on the ramble. I've seen him a couple of times and he asked me to a dance. It was last night, but was sold out, so we went for a walk instead. We like each other a lot and hope to go on holiday together in August.

Love, Gladys xx

CHAPTER FIFTY-EIGHT
Harold

1944

Gladys and Harold climbed on their bicycles and set off from Cheltenham for a summer holiday. It was a sunny ride up hill and down dale, in the delightful wooded countryside of the Cotswolds. They camped in the historic wool town of Painswick, with its houses built of mellow Cotswold stone. The next few days they travelled through Oxford, over the Chiltern Hills to Reading, then on to Guildford and Dorking. They marvelled at the view from Boxhill before cycling on to Harold's parents in Carshalton.

Carshalton
August
My Darling Daddy,
We've arrived in Carshalton after a wonderful trip across country.
Harold's mother made me feel welcome. His father is away, so I haven't met him yet. Yesterday she took us to church. The Rector gave a splendid sermon, especially advising young couples how to be sure to marry on a sound Christian basis and to bring their children up likewise. I thought it so nice of Harold to say afterwards that we should try to keep to it. He really has got fine principles. He is so understanding and sympathetic and seems all consumed with the ambition of giving me the joy I have missed in life, such as a home and things of my own, and the chance to do what I want to do. Harold loves me very much, and I am convinced it is the kind of love that will always last. He has never ceased to tell me he loves me.
I am sure we are right for each other as we enjoy such harmony. He may look young to you and perhaps not quite what you have imagined for me, but he has made my dreams really come true. It is so marvellous. I never

thought it possible that I should meet anyone who would so satisfy all my desires as Harold does. I grant you that because he has a London accent, his speech is not ideal, but that is a mere detail and never worries me when I am with him.

There is no question of me marrying him for money as his father had bad luck just as you have, and Harold has had little chance to save. I am sure he'll always be thrifty and sensible, and make a splendid husband. Mrs Pantlin looked very smart and nice on Sunday, so did Harold in his best suit and overcoat.

We are wizards at table tennis now, but Harold usually beats me.

Your loving Gladys, XXxx

After the holiday, Gladys met her father over the weekend. He inquired about the trip and she told him how much she had enjoyed it, and how fortunate she was to have found a soulmate in Harold.

She could sense her father was preoccupied, as he chewed on his lip and rolled a cigarette.

"While you were away," he said, "I had a terrible accident with the car."

"Oh dear, are you all right?"

"I'm all right, but I ran over a pedestrian."

Gladys covered her mouth with her hand. "Oh God, what happened?"

"I was driving along the road in the dark when a man suddenly stepped out in front of me. I slammed on the brakes and tried to avoid him, but couldn't help knocking him down."

"Oh, how horrible!"

Her father grimaced. "I jumped out and could see he was bleeding terribly. Someone came running over and called the ambulance. When it arrived, the ambulance man said it was too late."

Gladys touched her father's knee and then gave him a hug.

"I've decided to get rid of the car and never drive again."

"I can understand, but do you really need to? It wasn't your fault the man stepped out without looking."

"I can't stand the thought of that happening again," her father said, swallowing hard. "Anyway, we'll manage without. Flower and I are determined to move away from Cheltenham. We have no connections here."

"Where will you move to?" Gladys asked.

"We don't want to go to London, Liverpool or Sheffield. The Civil Service has offered us positions in Droitwich, and as we'd like to be in a small town, we've accepted. I'll find digs. Flower has her eye on a cottage."

"I'm surprised you've decided so quickly and even found a place for Flower."

"The office made the offer but wanted us to decide promptly."

"We'll be going our own ways even sooner than I expected," Gladys said, thinking it was probably for the best. It would relieve her of the pressure of looking after him and she'd be freer to choose her own path with Harold.

Cheltenham
September
My Darling Daddy,
Did you get my telegram to inform you that Harold and I couldn't come today? Perhaps we can the weekend after next. It disappointed me that you didn't mention Harold in your letter, but you don't know him yet, so there is little for you to say.
Anyway, we are still very much in love. I'm sure our meeting was arranged in heaven. He is going to Henley next week with the boss, to look at some American inventions. We hope that one day we will have a home that you can visit. Maybe you'll have one of your own too!
Did you hear me singing 'on air' this morning? They broadcast the parish church service as it was a special presentation of the USA flag, and Lt. Gen. Lee gave a fine address.
Bye Bye, tons of love & kisses, Glad xxxXxxx

Cheltenham
October
Dear Mr Handley,
It was with great pleasure that I read your letter indicating in such a warm manner that I meet with your approval. I am truly thankful that the impression of my character created on Sunday has led you to place confidence in me. My conception of Gladys is of a beautiful personality possessing those infinitely precious values which you so modestly tabulated. I shall endeavour therefore, to uphold your confidence by giving her all that love and hard work can procure.
I take this opportunity to thank you for the hospitality you extended to me, at the same time expressing the hope that the day is not too far distant, when I will be able to return the compliment.

Wishing Flower and yourself all the best in the way of happiness, I remain, yours very sincerely, Harold N. Pantlin

Cheltenham
My Dear Daughter,
Many thanks for your letter. I'm so glad to hear you're enjoying time with Harold. I must say that when I met him, I was disappointed he hasn't done his duty to fight for his country. He said he'd not passed the medical evaluation due to poor hearing, but I couldn't detect a hearing impediment at all. It is a well-known trick to pretend to be partially deaf when taking the test.
However, I was impressed when he explained he worked as an electrical engineer at Rotol in Cheltenham, and was studying for a higher level in the evenings. He said Rotol was with Rolls Royce and the Bristol Aeroplane Company to produce the fine propellers for the Spitfire.
Looking forward to hearing your stories when we meet again.
Love, Daddy xx

Liverpool
December
My Darling Dad,
I am very sorry but it doesn't look as if I shall be able to come to your wedding because I am still not well. I knew rushing round to relations here in Liverpool would crock me up. I wouldn't have gone to anyone if it hadn't been for introducing Harold. In spite of dragging myself around, I received no sympathy, but antipathy. We went to Aunty Annie's to meet all the family. Aunty Mary and co were there, and she was really rude to us both. I can now understand why my cousins Audrey and Roger never wanted to visit her every Sunday. I shall have to give up seeing relations, as they only upset me.
Last night I fainted, fell down the stairs, and turned hysterical. I made it to the doctor, but collapsed at the door. He doesn't think me fit to return home for a week or two, and if I'm not better I need to go for an x-ray. I went to the dentist yesterday, and he tried another tooth for the neuralgia trouble. It gives me such a stabbing, burning pain in my face.
Lots of love, Glad xxx

CHAPTER FIFTY-NINE
Love letters

1945

Jack and Flower married quietly in St Peter's Church, Droitwich, on 6th January, in the absence of Gladys and Harold. His brother, Joe, came down with Lily, but no other family attended from either side. They didn't want a fuss. Gladys was still ill in Liverpool, and Harold was in Cheltenham for work.

Cheltenham
My Darling Gladys,
Paddy called today and came up to my room. He was greatly taken by your photographs, which faced him as he entered the door. He has nearly as much admiration for you as I, be it from the point of view of your lovely face and character. Paddy said he wished he could model you and took my breath away with the artist's description of your character gained from his seeing you.
I went for a walk to Leckhampton Hill but felt very melancholy without you, dearest. Leckhampton holds such important memories for sitting there on that hot Saturday evening when we began to know each other. Walking up hill and down dale, I pondered on our previous excursions. I miss you so much it is really painful to pass over ground we have trod together on my own. I thanked God for the ability to appreciate the natural beauty, and I thanked Him for you, darling Gladys. You, the only one to fit so perfectly into my modes of thought. Over and above all the tangible reasons for loving you, there is a bond between us such that only God can explain. There is an unexplainable connection in our minds that wells up like water from a spring.

I didn't think it possible this time last year that another individual could, by her absence, make life seem so empty, but then I wasn't in love with the world's most wonderful girl. A year ago, I saw a lady possessing a strong will coupled with a generous and kindly nature, someone who had been through fire and water, and had withstood the test.

If you feel depressed, think of our future together as husband and wife. Think of the many and varied facets of life's diamond that we shall enjoy together. We are currently in one of those trial periods which we talked about in the early days. In my opinion, our love for each other has been fortified by the events of the past few weeks, especially Xmas.

God bless you dearest. Yours with love, xxx Harold xxx

Liverpool

Dear Harold,

You write such lovely letters; they cheer me up. Life's diamonds we shall enjoy together, exploring the many facets, in matrimony and with children, I hope. I long to be back with you, holding your hand as we climb the hills. I cherish the memory of when you picked me a bouquet of wildflowers.

I'm fed up being here with Granny. She's splendid and I enjoy her company, but it's you I want to be with. If only this illness would go away. Look after yourself.

My greatest love and lots of kisses, xxx Gladys xxx

Cheltenham

My Darling Gladys,

This evening I purchased your ring and am even more delighted with it. It scintillates as one twists it in one's fingers — so symbolic of the many facets of your beautiful mind. Its charm fascinates me as I am partial to a well-cut diamond set in eighteen carat gold.

At the concert the other night, I missed your interesting comments and the look that passes between us when we are thrilled by a certain passage of music. I missed your laughing smile, the sensitive touch of your fingers in my hand, the delicately pressed curves of your lips. More than ever, I am convinced we were meant for each other.

Yours with love, xxx Harold xxx

Cheltenham
Monday 12th February
My Darling Gladys,

Before I go any further, let me say I was so happy to see with my own eyes and hear with my own ears that you are better in health. Never again will I allow you to get into such a poor state as you were before Christmas. God has answered my prayers and is really strengthening you.

Of course, the main reason for my feeling of happiness is our betrothal on Saturday evening. Thank you, dearly beloved, for accepting my proposal so many months ago. As God is my witness and judge, for the rest of our lives together, I'll cherish and love you, dearest. Your days of infinite loneliness are over. No more camouflaging your true self to fight the world alone. No one shall hurt you without my knowing something about it.

I think I can promise you all the treasures that are priceless in this life. Together, you and I will walk hand in hand, not only through the beauties of the English countryside, but through the great, unchartered land where music, art and literature are the counties. Above all, the love we now bear with each other will grow in glory, ever expanding and engulfing us to swamp away all troubles.

How I enjoyed the weekend with you, to watch your every movement and come up to you and hold you close. To kiss those cheeks, that brow, that nose, those lips! Ah, those lips! Surely we were in heaven together last night while those two never-to-be-forgotten kisses united us as one! I have confidence in you being the ideal wife and it shall always be my greatest pleasure and foremost task to see that, at all times, you are happy in that position.

You will recall me talking about a promotion to Section Leader at Rotol. I spoke to my boss about it and he confided in me that it depended on the building of the new factory solely for electrical equipment. The sales department had orders for £1 million's worth of electrical equipment and the necessary plant would have been an investment of only £30,000. The proposal was turned down, could you believe it? By the chief engineer. He's a mechanical engineer and obviously hostile towards the electrical department.

I hope you get on all right at the dentist and don't have to go again. I'm sure you'll have most of your troubles cleared when your teeth are OK.

God bless you dearest of girls, yours with love, xxxx Harold xxxx

Back in Cheltenham, in May, Gladys went to her local shop and saw the headline on the newsstand: 'HITLER'S END.' She bought the *Gloucestershire Echo* and scurried home to read, 'Hitler is dead, and the world rejoices. Just how he died is a matter of doubt. German radio tells us he died in the struggle for Berlin, fighting to the last breath against Bolshevism.'

Gladys was relieved that the terrible Führer had gone, but when she read that Admiral Doenitz was his successor, she feared for what the equally reckless and ruthless man would do. He was the one who had promised to starve Britain into surrender by attacking merchant ships.

Harold was at work, so she shared her mixed feelings of hope and fear by writing to Granny.

Five days later, on 7ᵗʰ May, the headline was: 'END OF WAR IN EUROPE, Doenitz Orders the Unconditional Surrender of Germany.'

Gladys felt rejuvenated and wanted to share the wonderful news with someone, so she went straight to her landlady, Mrs Beckingsale, and they hugged.

Harold arrived home early, saying that everyone had been sent home to celebrate the good news. They embraced and kissed, knowing that their life together would now be even more rewarding than they had dared to hope.

Gladys and Harold strolled to the town hall and, on their way, saw people preparing for street parties. As evening came, there were parades and mass gatherings in the centre. It delighted them to see the street lighting back on for the first time since 1939. The mayor spoke and asked the gathering to join him in prayer and thanksgiving for the victory.

In Liverpool, the family had survived the war, although Grandad Handley and Aunty Mabel had a near miss when a bomb struck the neighbour's house and damaged theirs. Joe had not been in the forces, but did his stint as an Air Raid Precautions Ambulance Driver. Gladys rarely saw Joe and Lily, as they kept to themselves. When they did meet, she loved their two Yorkshire terriers and thought the dogs perhaps compensated for them not having children. Joe had kept his garage going during the war and still sold upmarket cars: Wolseleys and Rileys. He drove a Riley himself, always saying it was the best car there was.

For Gladys's birthday, on Saturday 23ʳᵈ June, a parcel from Granny arrived. It was full of cakes and a Rowntree Dairy Box of chocolates. As a glorious day was forecast, Harold surprised her by suggesting they would go out. He wouldn't say where they were going, but that they would take a picnic and wear walking gear. Gladys made some sandwiches and packed some of Granny's cake and chocolates. They caught the bus to Coberley, and then Harold found the footpath for a walk to Chatcombe Wood.

In a sunny, secluded spot, Harold spread out a picnic cloth. While eating lunch, Gladys spotted some wild strawberries and plucked some to send to Granny. They then laid back for a long kiss.

On Sunday they went to an outing of the Institute of Electrical Engineers. They had invited Harold as a candidate member, pending full membership when he had his certificate. They put on their finest clothes, wanting to make a good impression. The members, obviously well-to-do, congregated in a factory and were shown around. Gladys did her best to fit in with the occasion, and she loved it.

CHAPTER SIXTY
Torquay

1945

Cheltenham
August
My darling Granny & Grandan,
I'm fully underway preparing for our wedding on 29th December. Don't
worry about the journey to Cheltenham and how we manage things; it
will be alright. You must bring your little foot warmer and wrap up well.
I've decided it's best for you to stay with me at the Lansdown Hotel,
which is right at a bus stop and near the station. Your bedroom, with a
fire, is on the 1st floor. Our reception and going-away will be in the same
hotel.
I'm looking forward to seeing you at the beginning of December. By then
I hope to have all my clothes ready. I've bought the material for the
wedding dress, a lovely embossed satin with flowers all over it, and a
beautiful sheen; a long dress with long sleeves. Mrs Beckingsale has
offered me her veil. My going-away outfit will be a turquoise dress and a
red coat. Now I only have to buy white satin shoes, court style with a
medium heel. I have some silver ones I can always fall back on, but they
are flat-heel and I want higher heels to make me taller against Harold,
and to emphasise my dress. I'll have an orange blossom circlet and red
roses.
Tonight we speak to the Rector. We shall have the organ, but probably not
the choir. He was reverend at Sefton Park church for many years, so he
knows Liverpool.
Must close now, Tons of Love & Kisses, Bunty xxxXXXX

Carshalton
August
My Darling Granny & Grandan,
*Harold and I are enjoying our first holiday since the end of the war. We
are in Carshalton with his parents. Yesterday, we went for a bus ride to
Tunbridge Wells which was very pleasant, even though the weather was
dull and cool. We enjoyed a meal of fried plaice, the first the restaurant
had seen for months, and apple Charlotte, very good, but not as delicious
as yours. I always go off food after being with you.*
*What do you think of the atomic bomb? It's a horrible invention. We'll all
be blown off the face of the earth if we don't look out. What a world.*
*Tonight we're going to the theatre with Mr and Mrs Pantlin to see Emlyn
Williams in 'The Wind in Heaven'.*
Tons of Love & Kisses, Bunty xxxXXXX

Harold's landlady, Mrs Barter, offered them a little cottage in her garden
— renovated, fitted with an extra window, and re-painted throughout.
The large living room and bedroom delighted Gladys. There was electric
light and gas, but no tap water, no sink or bath, and no indoor
convenience. Mrs Barter said she would allow them to use her bathroom
one night a week. Living quarters were difficult to find since the war, so
they felt lucky to have such a place for a weekly rent of fifteen shillings.
It was a good start and Mrs Barter was a homely, sensible person.
Harold's parents worried he would be distracted from studying for his
exams at the Technical College if he lived with Gladys, but he convinced
them he could study better in her presence.

Gladys started collecting her trousseau. The cottage had a decent bed
and cupboards, but no table and chairs. She bought aluminium saucepans,
an electric fire, and linen with coupons. Her father promised a canteen of
cutlery, Mrs Barter half a dinner set, and Mrs Beckingsale a coffee
percolator. Granny sent some pots and pans.

Cheltenham
15th October
My Darling Granny & Grandan,
*I've included a packet of Will's Cut Golden Bar tobacco for Grandan's
birthday. I have a terrific lot to prepare for the wedding and I'm in a
rush. I'm still trying to get white satin shoes with medium size heels.
Flower will be my Matron of Honour. I'm finishing at the Bank and will
come to you on 3rd December to be with you for Christmas. After Boxing*

day we can travel down to Cheltenham together for the wedding. Daddy has suggested that we invite Uncle Joe and Aunty Lily so that they could drive you here and back by car, but it would be awkward not inviting the rest of the Handleys. We want to hold the wedding here as it's easier to make arrangements and to travel to the south coast for our honeymoon. I wish it was a better time of the year for you to travel, but we can't help it. I do hope you will be able to make up your minds to come, as I should be lost without you.

Mr & Mrs Barter are being very kind having everything spruced up. She went to get us a gas cooker today but they cost £20. Yesterday I painted from 10 a.m. to 6 p.m. while Harold put in the electric lights.

We are thinking of going to Torquay for a week's honeymoon and considering a gorgeous hotel, but it is very expensive.

They've awarded Daddy a certificate and medal in recognition of his time in the Home Guard.

Tons of love and kisses, look after yourselves and keep well, Bunty xxx

29th October
Dear Granny,

We heard our banns read out yesterday. They got a few details wrong, but never mind. We've painted the ceilings at our cottage. It looks bright, clean and pretty now. Half a ton of coal arrived today, and I bought 12lbs of flour in case it goes on points.

I've had a letter from Aunty Mary saying it doesn't matter about inviting them to the wedding on account of expense, but I haven't heard from the others yet. Harold thinks he can get a 22 carat wedding ring from a local shop. I found a shop that had satin shoes but not my size. I have enquired about your port and it will be alright if you can pour it all out into a decanter and then if there is any sediment, just strain it through butter muslin. Is it vintage or not?

Am tired tonight so will say bye-bye.

Tons of love and kisses, your own Bunty xxx

In the Parish Church, at 11a.m. on Saturday 29th December, Gladys was given away by her father. The organ played as they took their time walking up the aisle. Her favourite cousins were present; Josie was a bridesmaid, and Blanche Done stood next to Granny and Grandan, who had travelled from Liverpool. The Cubbin sisters, Ivy and Eveline, had smiles on their faces. On the other side of the aisle were Harold's parents, sister Dot, and her husband Pip, the best man.

Gladys revelled in all the attention as she made her way up the aisle, although her veil came loose at just the wrong moment. She kept a smile, but it turned to a grimace when there was no assistance from her father or Josie. She fixed it herself, as best she could, without stopping. When the service commenced, a broad smile of delight returned.

After the service, Pip ushered everyone to the reception in the hotel. Gladys and Harold arrived first to receive the guests. Gladys had planned the day so very carefully, but it fell behind schedule in the end, because her father was late for the reception. Granny presented the couple with a wedding present that amazed Gladys — a silver kettle.

Gladys and Harold cut a slice of the delicious wedding cake that Granny had made, and Gladys couldn't help mentioning that it wasn't quite cooked in the centre.

A four-course wedding breakfast followed: cream of tomato soup; a selection of cold dishes including salmon, chicken, salad Nicoise, Russian salad, and potato crisps; brandy snaps, lemon and orange jellies, and mince pies; banana ice cream with chocolate sauce.

Gladys' father gave a speech in between courses. Gladys felt that it was too long, and she felt herself stressing about being in time to catch the train for their honeymoon. In the end the newlyweds didn't have time to finish their meal, and rushed to the station for the four-hour journey to Torquay.

Palm Court Hotel, Torquay
31st December
Darling Granny & Grandan,
Do hope you arrived home safely and that Grandan's cold is better. Our hotel is fabulous with dinner dances every evening, an orchestra playing, and delicious food. Wondrous view out to sea from the bedroom. Torquay is a remarkable shopping centre. We have walked to Cockington which is a quaint old village full of thatched cottages. Another day, we climbed over the cliffs, enjoyed the view out to sea, and descended to Meadfoot Beach. There was no one there. We are going to the New Year's Eve ball tonight. Married life and being Mrs Pantlin is wonderful. We are so happy.
Tons of Love & Kisses, Bunty & Harold xxxxxx

CHAPTER SIXTY-ONE
Killarney

1946

Cheltenham
13th January
My Dearest Dad,
You must wonder when you're going to hear from us. Many thanks for your two letters. After a marvellous honeymoon, I'm settling in to our new home. Rotol sent Harold to Grantham last week, and he has gone back today for the entire week. So I'm feeling pretty sad being on my own again after a very happy, busy weekend, cooking in full form. The meals turned out well except for my pastry. I need to practise that. It's cosy and comfortable here. The bedroom is rather damp but we have the electric fire in there. Harold has made a wireless for me so that I can listen to music. It would be very quiet and too lonely without it. Mrs Barter is very good to me. She is always about for company during the day. Your cutlery canteen is superb, don't know what we'd do without it.
I will send photos of the wedding when we have more printed. Everyone thought how attractive and young Flower looked. It struck most people how wonderful Granny & Grandan were.
When can you come over here? Both of you, if possible. Harold hopes to be home next weekend but there's a possibility he may have to work.
Must get myself some supper and go to my lonely bed.
Lots of Love & Kisses, Gladys & Harold xxxx

When Gladys could no longer stand being on her own all week, they moved to Grantham. She was sorry to leave the cottage they had decorated together, but she enjoyed seeing Harold every lunchtime and evening, even though he had to study for his exams at the Technical

College. He worked and studied hard, sometimes only sleeping a few hours.

31 Avenue Road, Grantham
10th March
My dear Granny & Grandan,
Many thanks for the wonderful birthday present in the shape of your cake. It tastes jolly good, and we enjoyed ourselves eating some of it at teatime. It seemed a pity to cut into its pretty arrangement. I appreciate the fact that you gave up the whites of your precious eggs for the icing. Thank you for the telegram that came yesterday.
We enjoyed my birthday by walking onto the hills to the east of the town, and listening to the radio. The weather was excellent; so warm and sunny, with glorious expanses of pale blue skies.
Gladys is now preparing our Sunday lunch. She is indeed a wonderful wife and manages exceedingly well. In view of the fact that I come home to lunch every day, she has her work cut out. There's always a good meal ready.
Once again, all my deepest thanks for the present.
Your loving grandson, xxxx Harold xxxx

With no family, friends, or work in Grantham, Gladys lacked social contact. She missed Granny terribly, missed music, and missed art in general.

Although Harold liked his job, he took a job at English Electric's Napier Engines in Liverpool for £9 a week. There was no affordable housing available, but Granny offered them space in her house from July. She gave them the front bedroom and the front sitting room; Granny and Grandan used the back bedroom and dining room; they shared the bathroom and kitchen. A small bedroom above the front door was used for storage.

Gladys was tremendously glad to be back in Liverpool. In his new job, Harold still travelled, but at least she was in Granny's company and there was more to do in Liverpool.

She helped make jams, pickles and jellies from fruit in the garden — plums, raspberries, damsons, gooseberries, blackberries, redcurrants and blackcurrants. She filled the coal hobs and brought them to each room with a fire. Coals were delivered once a month in hundredweight sacks, which the coalman stacked behind the shed. Milk, bread, groceries, and fish were brought to the house by horse and cart. Yellow cream topped the milk, and the butter was salted. They had a cooked lunch every day, such as steak and kidney pudding, marrow stuffed with mincemeat, or cauliflower and macaroni cheese. Common sweets were egg custard, apple pie, rhubarb crumble, tarts, flans, treacle tart, or, Gladys' favourite: trifle.

1947

115 Swanside Road,
Liverpool
12th August
My darling Dad and Flower,
Here we are again. Had expected a letter from you waiting for us when
we arrived home from our holiday in Ireland. How have you been these
three weeks? Gathering all the fruit in the countryside to send us, I hope.
We had a fine time. The tent only got wet one morning in Killarney. Our
crossings were very calm but in a forty-four-year-old boat. Compared to
staying in a hotel, camping allowed us to do and see a lot more. It was
very interesting going in the farmhouses and sitting before turf fires,
watching the bread being baked, and all the children staring and
giggling. They are very shy. We found the country folk, although poor,
very generous and kind, and interested in our coming and going. Not so
in the town where they were out to make all the money possible on tours.
They didn't get much of ours.
The farms are tiny on poor, rocky land. I've never seen such small fields.
Sometimes there's merely one haycock in a field but they do make them in
fine bee-hive shapes. The farmhouses look spotlessly bright, painted
white, cream or yellow, pink and blue. Inside it's a different story. Only
one room below which you go straight into, with an enormous fireplace,
bare floors, chairs and tables, a crucifix and pictures of Mary and Jesus.
The catholic religion is a panacea or dope for the poor farming folk.
There are crowds of priests about the country and they mostly seem well-
dressed and enjoying themselves on a higher scale of living than the
ordinary folk. I didn't wear my shorts because the people are antiquated
in their ideas. Everyone stared at us as it was, thinking we were mad to
be walking. The countryside means nothing to them except as a
livelihood, and they have never seen walkers before.
Food was expensive and without variety. It was difficult to get bread,
butter, cheese etc. Fresh fruit and veg were scarce, fruit being only

tinned. Most of their things lack our quality. One soon sees the difference that industry makes to a country. Cork is a fine city with plenty of good shops. The food in the cafés was poor. Every course of the lunch we had to send back as inedible.

The Irish temperament comes home doubly in the towns where their vagueness, shortcoming of organisation, and timeless sense are more apparent. One can admire their lack of materialism, but that attribute is inclined to breed laziness. They don't say 'yes' or 'no', but 'it is' or 'it is not'. None seemed to have any ill feelings towards the British and their newspapers were full of our news.

What's the fruit position? Any greengages and damsons? Aunty Mabel called last night to bring us a few blackberries she had picked near her office. Last time I saw Josie, there was no hope of her marriage. Len has to find a job first.

England's situation looks bleak. I can't believe we're still on rationing more than a year after the war. It's even worse now bread is rationed because rain ruined the wheat crop.

Lots of Love & Kisses to you both, Gladys & Harold xxxXXX

PS. We're going to start philosophy evening classes together when we get back.

115 Swanside Road,
Liverpool
13th September
My Darling Dad & Flower,
Hope you're both well. I expect you are out with Aunty Lily and Uncle Joe tonight. Are they treating you both to a superb dinner at the Raven. Josie is engaged again! To a man in her office who bought her the gold watch, Terrence Halliwell. He wants to get married in November. Aunty Annie's breath is rather taken away as she can imagine them staying with her and bringing a baby on her, like Hazel did.

We went to town yesterday to celebrate the certain knowledge of a coming baby! The doctor confirmed it and reckons it should arrive on May 1st. He said, if it was a boy, I was to return for circumcision. He gave me a certificate for an extra ration book and a milk card. So now Flower, you can get busy knitting away. What a lot of things to think about. It's exciting.

I've told Gran and Grandan. Harold and I have decided to stay living here. We can't afford a place of our own yet. Gran and Grandan are eager to keep us and the baby. The smaller front bedroom will be the baby room.
Generally, I feel rather heavy, and have very slight nausea in the mornings.
Bye Bye for now, just going to have a stew supper with garden veg.
Love from us all, Gladys xxxXXX

During the Christmas break, Gladys and Harold went to see Grandad Handley, who had moved in with Mabel prior to the war. At eighty-six, his days were counted, especially since his bronchitis had worsened.

It was a short walk to Campbell Drive. "Tell me more about Aunty Mabel and Grandad," said Harold.

"Mabel is still a spinster. She plays golf and is a vegetarian, like my father. She loves to play the piano and sings in the Liverpool Philharmonic Choir. She's always been the one to care for her parents."

"So that's why Grandad is living with her."

"That's right. It's done him good to be here. He's a milder man now. He used to be with the Plymouth Brethren and was very strict about living by the bible. Aunty Mabel told me he's reflected on his life, and is ashamed now that he treated her mother unfairly, perhaps even cruelly, and caused so many rows. He feels guilty about not being a good father, and only supporting his children materially, but not emotionally. His mind has become too fuddled to read books and poems; he can't concentrate."

They opened the front gate and went to knock on the door. Harold pointed to copper letters fixed to the wall. "Why has Aunty Mabel called her house 'Coreley'?"

"That's where the Handleys came from. It's in Shropshire. Grandad grew up there. I think she put that name up to make him feel at home here."

Mabel let them in. Grandad Handley sat in the front room, just staring towards the window, not yet registering their arrival. They said hello, and he turned to greet them, but the look on his face conveyed he wasn't sure who they were. Gladys went through to the kitchen with Mabel.

"How is he?" she asked.

"He's slowly going senile. I've seen it coming for a long time," Mabel said. "I doubt whether he'll survive the winter. I read to him, play the piano, and sing old songs he remembers. He tries to sing along, but doesn't have the breath."

Gladys sighed. "How sad."

"We manage," Mabel said, forcing a smile. "Tell me about how you're getting on. When will the baby arrive?"

"It's expected early in May. He or she is already quite lively, kicking me at times."

Mabel's eyes lit up. "That's Taurus. You know what they're like? ... They're perseverers and know how to get things done. Also thinkers, wanting to understand before committing. Some people think they're slow, but they're pondering. They like eating, so your baby will enjoy breastmilk, I'm sure."

Gladys smiled. "We'll see. I certainly hope it drinks well."

"Be sure to record the exact time of birth. I'll need that to do a proper astrological character sketch. Will you be giving birth at home?"

"I've decided to have it in hospital. Daddy pressed me to go to hospital, not wanting the same to happen to me that happened to my mother."

"That's a safe choice. I'm sure you'll be well looked after."

Gladys pursed her lips. "It's safer, but they'll keep me there for ten days. Harold won't be allowed in for the first few days. I'll miss him and I'm sure he can't wait that long to see the baby."

CHAPTER SIXTY-TWO
A happy event

1948

Droitwich
1st May
My Darling Daughter,
We're thinking of you every day, wondering whether you are in labour and expecting a phone call at any moment. Is your preference a boy or a girl?
Our news is that we've moved to our new residence, which is much more comfortable. The location on Old Coach Road is ideal, on the edge of town. We have knocked the two cottages into one, making a spacious home. The plot is a grand size and I'm looking forward to reorganising it. I envisage a lawn, pond, and flowerbeds near the house. Further up there will be vegetable patches, berries, and fruit trees. The small clump of tall trees at the end of the plot will remain wild and form a lovely backdrop. It's further from the office, but that's fine. At last, I've achieved my goal of being independent of landlords and landladies.
We had a telephone installed so that you can give us a ring when the baby's born.
All my love, Daddy XXxx

Liverpool
6th May
My darling Dad & Flower,
Before I forget, I must tell you that Mrs Morrison next door has given me
her phone number in case you wish to ring any time: Stoneycroft 4148.
I'm very well and visited the clinic today. They say I have still a week to
go. Amazing, isn't it?
I've been doing gardening and am getting a good bit of knitting done and
am making myself a cardigan.
You can be sure that I will be in hospital for Whit, so don't come then. A
month after the baby arrives would be soon enough. That gives me a
chance to settle down at home and get into the new routine. I know you
will be impatient to see us all, but try to wait a bit.
I don't mind whether it's a boy or a girl. The good health and normality
of the child are my chief concern. Harold doesn't mind except he'd like a
boy to play trains with!
Love & Kisses, Harold & Gladys xxxXxxx
PS Send me your telephone number.

In the early morning of Sunday 9th May, Gladys felt the first contractions, and woke Harold.

"Harold! Wake up, now. I think the baby is coming. Will you wake Granny and ask her to go to Mrs Morrison to phone for the midwife?"

Harold frowned. "I thought you were going to the hospital!"

"Yes, but the midwife needs to come first. She'll check whether it's time to leave."

Harold woke Marsie and then sat on the bed with Gladys. "What do you need to take?"

Pointing to the corner of the bedroom, she said, "I've got that bag ready." She held her breath as another stab of pain went through her. "Will you help me change into those clothes on the chair?"

The midwife arrived and confirmed it was indeed time for Gladys to go to hospital. Granny rushed back to Mrs Morrison to order a taxicab. When it showed up, Harold helped Gladys downstairs and into the car, taking a seat next to her. "Mill Road Infirmary, please," he told to the driver.

On arrival at the infirmary, Harold helped Gladys into a wheelchair, and nurses wheeled her away. He was told he couldn't proceed inside, but could phone later in the day for news. The nurse added that he wasn't allowed to visit until Wednesday.

10th May

My dearest, darling Wife and Son,

Thank you, sweetheart, for making me so happy! It is wonderful to be a father, and of a son too!

How are you feeling after the long labour time? I hope you have been able to get some sleep during the night. I phoned 4 times yesterday, at 2-hourly periods, before I knew at 11 p.m. that Michael Biron had been born at 9 p.m. What a day you must have had!

Have phoned the hospital and learned that all is OK. Everything is bright with the world this morning. Sunshine, a superb wife, mother and SON! I feel strongly moved deep down inside, just like on our wedding day.

Am going to drop this letter at the hospital and register the birth at the registrar's office in West Derby Road. According to the staff on the phone, I can't see you until Wednesday evening, but am going to try tonight, if only for a minute or two. Perhaps you can put in a good word with the ward sister.

Well, must close as there's much to do, telegrams, etc. Several people in the road have enquired after you and they all say how fit you have looked.

Cheerio, my Beloved Darling, hurry up and come home,

With all the love in the world, Harold xxxx

TELEGRAM 10th May

To Handley, 48 Old Coach Road, Droitwich

Michael Biron arrived 9pm yesterday. Mill Road Hospital. Both well. Love Harold.

Mill Road Infirmary

13th May 1948

My Darling Harold,

I feel I must write to you about this happy event of my being up for the first time. I sat on a proper lavatory seat and had a stand-up wash. What a relief it was to swing my legs over the edge of the bed and enjoy the fresh air. I felt uncertain and light, was afraid to walk quickly, but I am more confident now and not as sick as I had expected. The best of being up is that I can peep at Michael more often.

It surprised me to find how slim I am. My breasts seem to have shrunk too. They had got very full and hard the last day and were burning in the night. I let my brassiere out to its complete extent. Now I had better sew it up again. The sister says they are well rounded and that they will go back to their normal size when the feeding is established. Michael is having his ten minutes on each side.

He is regaining his weight and they don't let you out of here until he has regained his birth weight, not an ounce less. He is very good, sleeps soundly between meals, and doesn't even cry when dirty.

It's amazing how seeing you put new life in me. I had felt bottled up with little zest, but now I'm my usual self. Please come on your own next time; it's not the same with other visitors.

If you want to take the chance of going away for a night, don't let me stop you. Perhaps you can get a fine couple of days in the country. Even go to the Lakes!

You are a naughty man; you forgot to give me my knitting pattern. Thank you for bringing the eggs and oranges. I hope you are opening the tins of sausage for your breakfast.

I have asked the ward sister about circumcision. She will examine Michael and advise if necessary. She says it's best left as nature made him and, if the foreskin is too tight, I can massage it myself. It's exciting. I now change his nappy myself.

Bye bye darling, may time go quickly.

Lots and lots of love, your adoring wife, Gladys xxxx

C2 Maternity Ward, Mill Road Hospital

15th May

My Darling Dad & Flower,

Many, many thanks for your telegrams and letters to us both. It's great to have it all over and to have a son. I am so happy. He is such a sweet babe with a well-formed face and lots of hair. Labour was eighteen hours in all.

I have quite a little show of cards by my bed and a lovely bowl of anemones. My other flowers are in the centre of the ward. Aunty Mary sent two pixie hoods and the Pantlins a cheque for £1 with which I shall buy a pram shade. One of Harold's sisters sent a carrying chair for when he can sit up.

They thoroughly look after us here. We wake at 5 a.m., feed the babies 6 times a day for about 45 minutes as it's rather a struggling affair till they get used to it. He is feeding well, and all is well with my breasts. The babies are in little cots swung on the end of the beds. We don't do exercises but crawl to the end of the bed to get the babies, which gives us some exercise on tummy muscles. We have an hour's sleep in the afternoon on our tummies, on a pillow, to help our figures, and they encourage us to sit up as much as possible to drain away everything.

I'm sure Flower will be interested in all the baby details and you must be longing to see Michael. Will you both be able to come to Liverpool? I need a few weeks to settle in first, but then you can stay and we will sleep on the floor.

I think Michael has Harold's pointed chin but my colour hair. Yes, you've got the names right, Michael Biron. The latter is Shakespearian.

Harold will be here soon. Isn't it cruel? He has only had a little peep at his sleeping son, as yet. How I long to be with them both.

It's so very exciting to think of the future and how we'll watch Michael's development as an ever-increasing source of pleasure and interest, no doubt mingled with anxiety.

Lots of Love & Kisses to you both, Michael & Gladys xxXxx

Addendum

Family tree of main characters

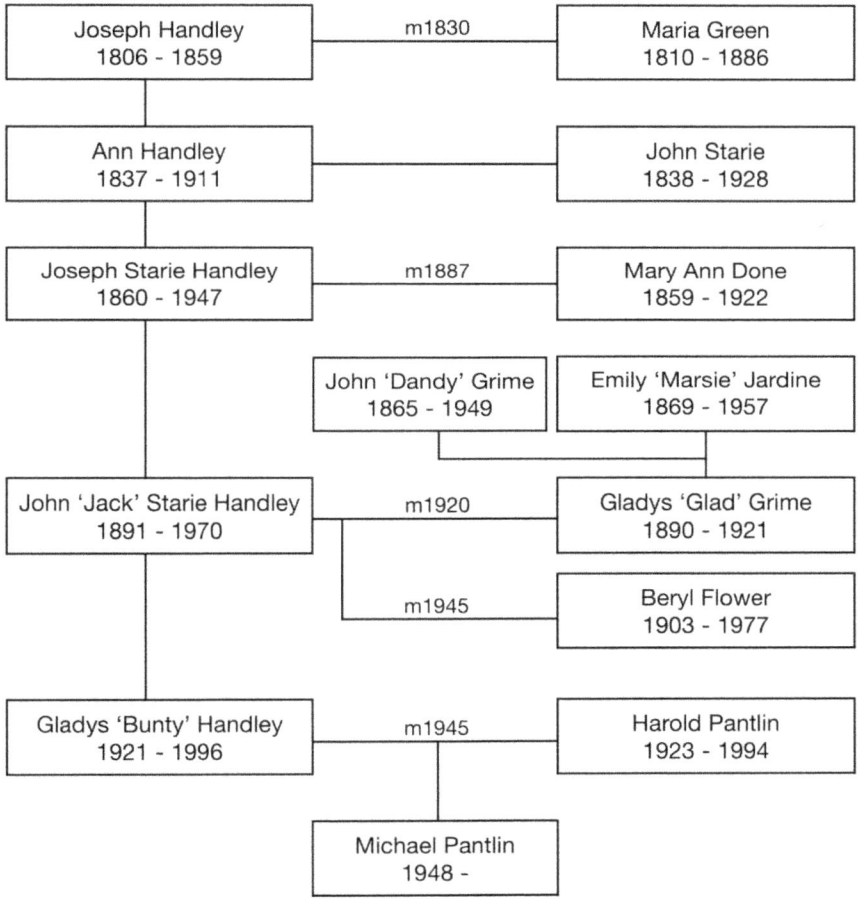

Map showing key places

Edinburgh

Lake District

Llandudno

Liverpool

Shrewsbury

Grantham

Coreley

Droitwich

Cheltenham

London

Margate

John Starie's farm, The Hemm, Coreley, Shropshire

Picture taken in 2009 by the author

Jack Handley, age 24, Machine Gun Sergeant, June 1916

Portrait of Glad Grime, by her friend Christina Lamont,
for Glad's twenty-ninth birthday, 1919

Windmill by Glad Grime, 1912

Jack Handley's sisters and cousin at Broadstairs.
From left to right: Mary, Annie,
cousin Blanche Gwilliam (nee Done), and Mabel

Gladys & Harold Pantlin's Wedding, December 1945

Left to right:

Mrs Pantlin, Mr Pantlin, Harold's brother-in-law Ernest Massey,

Mr John 'Dandy' Grime, Harold Pantlin, Gladys Pantlin,

Mrs Emily 'Marsie' Grime, Gladys' cousin Josie,

Jack Handley, Beryl 'Flower' Handley

Sources

Books

In the Days of Rain by Rebecca Stott, life in the Exclusive Brethren in the 1960s.

Father and Son by Edmund Gosse, life in the Brethren in the 1900s.

Oh, Beautiful by John Paul Godges

The Diary of a Shropshire Farmer by Peter Davis.

Talking with Past Hours by Jane Killick

The Historical Record of the 72nd Regiment by Richard Cannon 1886

The Records of the 90th Regiment Light Infantry by Alex M. Delavoye 1880

History of the King's Regiment (Liverpool) by Everard Wyrall 1928

Life in Army Barracks 1855 - 1871 by Hilary Greenwood 2011

Routledge's Manual of Etiquette

How I became a socialist by William Morris 1894

A Victorian's Inheritance by Helen Parker-Drabble

Websites

Because of the dynamic character of the internet, any web addresses may no longer be valid.

British Newspaper Archive, www.britishnewspaperarchive.co.uk

Plymouth Brethren Archive, www.brethrenarchive.org

Preach the Word, www.preachtheword.com

Museum of Freemasonry, http://museumfreemasonry.org.uk

Lane's Masonic Records, www.dhi.ac.uk/lane

World War II Today, www.ww2today.com

Ancient Pages, www.ancientpages.com

Worcester News, www.worcesternews.co.uk

Historic UK, www.historic-uk.com

Wikipedia, www.wikipedia.org

Google Maps, www.google.nl/maps

Old Maps of Britain, www.archiuk.com

Victorian History, http://vichist.blogspot.com
Daily Mail, www.dailymail.co.uk
Merchant's House Museum, https://merchantshouse.org
Social Life in Victorian England, https://sites.udel.edu/britlitwiki
All Things Victorian, www.avictorian.com
Lives of the First World War, https://livesofthefirstworldwar.iwm.org.uk
Liverpool Echo, www.liverpoolecho.co.uk
World War I, www.worldwar1.com
The Long, Long Trail, www.longlongtrail.co.uk
Great War 1914 - 1918, www.greatwar.co.uk
Ancestry, www.ancestry.co.uk
Scotlands People, www.scotlandspeople.gov.uk
Find My Past, www.findmypast.com
The Genealogist, www.thegenealogist.com
Society of Genealogists, www.sog.org.uk
British Parish Registers, https://www.freereg.org.uk

Physical archives
Liverpool Museum
Liverpool School of Art Archives, Liverpool John Moores University
Shropshire Archives, Shrewsbury
National Archives, London
London Metropolitan Archives

The Author

Letters from the Past is Michael Pantlin's first creative non-fiction book. Michael was born in Liverpool, but spent most of his life in Amsterdam working for KLM Royal Dutch Airlines, and as an executive coach. He has a master's degree in Industrial Engineering. His previous publication, *How I Survived the Great War*, was a collection of John 'Jack' Handley's war memories, which Michael edited.

Acknowledgements

This book would never have been possible without my mother's archiving work — keeping documents and pictures in an organised fashion. She'd have been gratified to know that her diligence had come together in this form.

My thanks to those who have helped with the research: my cousins Gerry Summers, Tony Davy, Hilary Cheetham, and Robin Halliwell. Barbara Handley and George Bancroft offered stories about their branches of the Handley and Jardine families.
Posthume praise is for my Grandad Jack for his writings, my great-grandmother Marsie for keeping letters and postcards safe through two world wars, and my cousins, Audrey and Roger, who allowed me to interview them.

During the writing process, I was grateful to those who helped me learn to write a proper book, in particular my writing coach, Joanne Burn, for her guidance in helping me make this book more like a novel. Lynn Palermo, and her endless video tutorials in the Family History Writing Studio, were a great help in the early stages of understanding how to write in this genre.
Kerry Hadley-Pryce's creative writing workshops helped me expand my creativity, while Anne Rainbow, the Scrivener Virgin, helped me master the writers' tool, Scrivener. I was helped along the way by other writers who shared their experience with me and made me persevere: Elizabeth DuBois, Ann Ward, Cynthia Young, Paula Allen, Eva Bachman, Jennifer January Asbill, Brenda Litolff Barber, Berend Warrink, and others.
I had encouragement from my brother, Richard, who gave his feedback on various drafts, and Niels Reinbergen, the first to critique my initial draft manuscript. I couldn't have missed the ongoing support from my wife, Henny, who read and corrected every page of every draft - picking out details I would never have seen.

In the publication process, I was thankful for the help of my son, Martijn, who designed the cover and built the website.

www.ingramcontent.com/pod-product-compliance
Lightning Source LLC
Chambersburg PA
CBHW071159020726
47502CB00002B/474